Four-Peace

Four-Peace

Kevin K. Casey

LAMAR UNIVERSITY *press*

ISBN: 978-1-942956-05-1
Library of Congress Control Number: 2015940808

Lamar University Press
Beaumont, Texas

For
The Old Tentmaker
Eddie Fitz
Vixen, Fink, Grand Inquisitor, Lornado
and 79007

Books from Lamar University Press

Jean Andrews, *High Tides, Low Tides: the Story of Leroy Colombo*
Charles Behlen, *Failing Heaven*
Alan Berecka, *With Our Baggage*
David Bowles, *Flower, Song, Dance: Aztec and Mayan Poetry*
Jerry Bradley, *Crownfeathers and Effigies*
Julie Chappell and Marilyn Robitaille, editors, *Writing Texas, 2013-14*
Terry Dalrymple, *Love Stories, Sort Of*
Chip Dameron, *Waiting for an Etcher*
Robert Murray Davis, *Levels of Incompetence: An Academic Life*
William Virgil Davis, *The Bones Poems*
Jeffrey Delotto, *Voices Writ in Sand*
Gerald Duff, *Memphis Mojo*
Ted L. Estess, *Fishing Spirit Lake*
Mimi Ferebee, *Wildfires and Atmospheric Memories*
Ken Hada, *Margaritas and Redfish*
Michelle Hartman, *Disenchanted and Disgruntled*
Michelle Hartman, *Irony and Irreverence*
Katherine Hoerth, *Goddess Wears Cowboy Boots*
Lynn Hoggard, *Motherland, Stories and Poems from Louisiana*
Dominique Inge, *A Garden on the Brazos*
Gretchen Johnson, *The Joy of Deception*
Gretchen Johnson, *A Trip Through Downer, Minnesota*
Laozi, *the daodejing*, tr. David Breeden, Steven Schroeder, Wally Swist
Christopher Linforth, *When You Find Us We Will Be Gone*
Tom Mack and Andrew Geyer, editors, *A Shared Voice*
Jim McJunkin, *Deep Sleep*
Dave Oliphant, *The Pilgrimage, Selected Poems: 1962-2012*
Janet McCann, *The Crone at the Casino*
Erin Murphy, *Ancilla*
Kornelijus Platelis, *Solitary Architectures*
Harold Raley, *Louisiana Rogue*
Carol Coffee Reposa, *Underground Musicians*
Jim Sanderson, *Trashy Behavior*
Jim Sanderson, *Sanderson's Fiction Writing Manual*
Jan Seale, *Appearances*
Jan Seale, *The Parkinson Poems*
Carol Smallwood, *Water, Earth, Air, Fire, and Picket Fences*
Glen Sorestad, *Hazards of Eden, Poems from the Southwest*
Melvin Sterne, *The Number You Have Reached*
John Wegner, *Love is Not a Dirty Word and Other Stories*
Robert Wexelblatt, *The Artist Wears Rough Clothing*
Jonas Zdanys, *Pushing the Envelope*

For more information about these and other books, go to
www.LamarUniversityPress.Org

CONTENTS

I. Paris of the West
    1 Champagne, Baby
    8 Fat Ones Like Us
    14 ⬟
    19 Jeremiah Corona

II. Barbary Coast
    27 Living History
    33 The Ides
    39 ⬟
    45 Beauty and Warmth

III. Peninsula to Peninsula
    53 El Camino Real
    58 HPE 625
    64 ⬟
    70 Equinox

IV. Sanguine
    79 Lazaretto
    85 Lone Blush
    91 ⬟
    96 Pronouncement

V. Golden Gate
    105 Gettin on Down the Road
    112 The Grand Ole Opry
    119 ⬟
    123 The Coughing Cowboy and the Reefer Man

VI. Big Green
    131 The Farm
    138 The Fruitcake
    145 ⬟
    149 Solstice

VII. Pearly Hiatus
    157 Bent Out of Shape
    162 Lost Moon in the Darkroom
    168 ⬦
    173 Tarantula Hawk

VIII. Flatland
    181 No Creek
    188 Delta Breeze
    194 ⬦
    198 Knucklehead

IX. Quicksand
    207 They Drive by Night
    212 The Man Who Cheated Himself
    217 ⬦
    222 Vertigo

X. Backtrack
    229 Stumble
    234 Smoke Stack Library
    239 ⬦
    243 1 in 649,740

XI. Blue Garden
    251 Erelong
    257 Golden Goat Rodeo
    263 ⬦
    268 Pell-Mell

XII. Depth of Field
    277 Circle of Confusion
    282 Focal Plane
    288 ⬦
    293 Miles Where Arroyos Crack

I. Paris of the West

Indeed, indeed, Repentance oft before
I swore—but was I sober when I swore?
    And then and then came Spring, and Rose-in-hand
My thread-bare Penitence apieces tore.

And, as the Cock crew, those who stood before
The Tavern shouted—"Open then the Door!
   "You know how little while we have to stay,
And, once departed, may return no more."

Champagne, Baby

Mere hours into the New Year, Jason Spearman offended. His cute quip about romance, attraction, and body weight had stung the bartender he tried to charm into serving him liquor at 7:30 that Saturday morning. The charm had not worked. In fact, he fled the cobalt fire emanating from those angry, possibly sad eyes. After a few macho guffaws on the safety of the sidewalk outside the tavern, Jason turned west and walked to the intersection of Geary and Van Ness. There he did not guffaw or even chuckle. There he felt a cold damp morning in flat static grey light. There he felt guilt at the pain his words had caused, and there he felt a faint stirring of attraction, perhaps desire, and perhaps there he began to form a plan.

The default rule, the universal absolute that all woman love chocolate and cut flowers, came to mind, and he sauntered down the hill toward Union Square. After returning with a gift and an apology, who could refuse his charms? Surely not the Rubenesque Celtic beauty with the corrupted, Americanized brogue. Then again, perhaps candies could draw too much attention to the tender feelings of the fat girl who was neither fat nor young enough to be still a girl. Flowers, not sugar would assuage, but in the city waking to a multitude of hangovers cut roses might be hard to find. Jason stopped, scratched his head, and took a generous pull from a metal flask before grimacing. Down the hill past Polk Gulch past the Tenderloin and into the new and clean Union Square he would find a hotel and a concierge. Twenty bucks and a good concierge can find a solution to any problem.

A Benjamin and several Jacksons lighter he returned to the vicinity of the tavern carrying a bouquet of carnations because roses had proved elusive. He muttered tentative greetings, practiced apologies, and rounded the corner of Geary and Taylor to see a half block to the west the entrance

1

to the tavern and the golden haired barkeep he had affronted. Over the tops of pink petals at the end of green stalks he clutched at his chest he watched as she stood outside the tavern door and drew on a cigarette. Some of the long flaxen tresses had come unbound from the elastic band at the back of her neck, and his eyes followed them over her shoulder. Had the apron with cords crossing in front and tied in a bow in the small of her back not pressed the oversized white bartender button-down shirt flush with her midsection, he might not have noticed her gorgeous endowment. But he did notice. And he cursed himself for the juvenile wit that insinuated she was anything other than lovely. After tossing her cigarette to the pavement, she looked ahead and to her right, and she saw a man in a suit holding flowers. She paused, and for an instant so did the man with the flowers.

He leapt backward to put a corner of a building between himself and her line of sight, and in doing so he collided with a group of young backpackers from a nearby hostel. One of the heads of the carnations came off its stalk and fell to the sidewalk. Petals, wispy pinkish-white slivers from other, still intact flower heads fluttered in the air, and a raven haired beauty clutching the arm of a young man laughed, and Jason too laughed and apologized.

Westward he carried the flowers unable to think what to do with them and unwilling to discard the most expensive yet dull looking bouquet he had ever purchased. Onward up toward the Lower Haight he decided to abandon the mission to appease and possibly woo. A beauty like that did not need him to inform her of her pleasing geometry, her delightful proportions and curves. He decided to abandon the quest before he hurt more feelings as he knew he certainly would. Instead he would revert to an earlier, not fully completed task: acquiring booze. The morning, the year had started that way.

He had made a conscious effort to avoid noticing the exact second the clock struck midnight. For the hours preceding and following midnight he had packed the last of the items still in the overpriced top-floor flat. Days earlier, the person he had shared the lease with called to bring Jason out of a stupor. She said Jason had missed the move out date by over two months. She had moved out, left Jason, in September. If she told Jason the truth, then he had been on a bender for a solid three months. And it had taken nearly three days for him to dry out. The first day consisted of much shaking and pain and paranoia while the second brought less noticeable shaking but plenty of paranoia. Halfway through the third day, he felt strong enough to acquire cardboard boxes, and after two more days of packing pillars of stacked and packed boxes stood in the various rooms of the flat. The same day he telephoned the movers, she called again. This time in painful sobriety he listened more and shouted less. In fact, he had not shouted at all. He felt for a moment genuinely contrite, and that is perhaps what made her cry. She cried, and she said she still loved him, but she also said, again, that she could not endure his drinking any longer, and she said she particularly feared that day, New Year's Eve.

And that made Jason angry. Because it is a lot less painful to be angry than to be honest. So he closed out that last conversation by telling her to worry about herself and not him or his drinking. He did not call her names that time, but he was plenty mad. Righteous indignation took hold and got him through many hours of packing that New Year's Eve. After the festive fireworks had stopped, and after drunken revelers ceased breaking glass and retching in the street, the quiet outside came inside, and in the stillness of the dark flat full of boxes he sat on the cold wood floor, looked ahead at a blank grey wall, and realized with clarity that she had gone. He had driven her away yet been surprised when she departed. That hollow feeling in his chest returned, but anger dangled a lifeline. He grasped the line, clung to it, and reminded himself that blame for all failure rested with her.

He snatched a dark suit, white shirt, and dark tie from the wardrobe. The suit had been tailored many pints ago, but he thought he could still pull it off. Jason made a pot of coffee at 3 a.m., and then he commenced shaving.

Away from the tavern and the Celtic barmaid, westward he carried the flowers while trying to think of someplace to go and something to do. The early hour complicated the task of finding a watering hole, but Jason knew his best bet, or at least his closest, lay along Haight Street, and so he continued west. Near Buena Vista Park he heard a calamity. Beyond the edge of pavement, a steep hill thick with bushes stretched up into the park, and from the bushes Jason heard snapping twigs and earnest pleas. "Oh Lordy. Oh Jesus. No . . . ."

A gift from the brambles, she tumbled down the steep incline and burst from the leafy wall. She wore torn orange stockings under a faux leather skirt, scuffed flats, and a fuzzy pink sweater. A branch tore one strap of her shoulder bag loose, and contents spilled across the sidewalk.

"Gladys! My princess," Jason exclaimed. He surveyed the items strewn, and he gathered them while she adjusted her wig. Hairbrushes and makeup and skimpy little garments tumbled over the curb and into Haight Street. Jason picked them up, and when he came to a plastic pink zippered pouch he said, "Damn, darlin, if this was any hotter pink it'd catch on fire." He handed her the pink case and looked at her pink sweater and orange leggings. "You sure do clash in the daytime. You all right?"

"I'm all right. And I don't clash, baby. You're still a little bit rude."

"Me? Oh not me, darlin. I'm still just a lonesome cowboy from Isom, Texas." Jason reached toward Gladys and picked at bits of twig and leaves in her wig and stuck to her fuzzy sweater. Gladys flinched at first, but then seemed genuinely pleased by the attention.

"Did you change your mind about dating, baby?"

"Dating? Oh hell, princess, you can do a damned sight better than me. I just want to have a drink with you. Just like before. Remember?"

Gladys looked at Jason and smiled. Unlike when he first met her hours earlier in the predawn dark, the mid-morning light revealed more of the ebony t-girl. Under the crooked wig, the neon green and considerably smeared eye shadow, the clown-like too-loud lipstick, and a considerable amount of razor stubble from a beard courser and denser than Jason's own, under all that Jason saw something he had not seen before. Somehow in those tired chocolate somewhat bewildered eyes Jason saw a kind of strength or prettiness or maybe even beauty. Hours earlier he had first encountered Gladys and invited her to drink.

Sometime between four and five he had stomped down the rickety stairs from the top-floor flat clean shaven and in his mirror-smooth shiny black wingtips. Having spared the landlord and other tenants the noise of nighttime revelry, he felt justified in making a morning-after stampeding sound on the wooden stairs. The last door before exiting to the porch belonged to the landlord. Jason stood before the landlord's door for a moment, and he felt a strange childish desire to deface it in some way, but instead he clasped a hand over his mouth in an effort to stifle laughter as he stepped out onto the porch. He remembered a morning with a painful hangover and a conversation about five hundred dollars with his previous flatmate. She had been distressed that the rental deposit returned had been reduced by five hundred dollars. Upon inquiry with the landlord, she discovered fury. Amid the landlord's red-faced vehemence and spittle she determined that the shortfall in the deposit came as a consequence of

Jason's creative modifications to the apartment. It seemed that on the day Jason learned that the flat would be shown, he felt the need to lash out at his previous roommate, but she had already left weeks ago. Instead he amused himself with removing the bolts from door hinges and shutting off the water to the apartment and tampering with the fuse box. The landlord had not been specific about whether the broken glass from the bedroom door or the inoperative toilet had fetched his ire, but he did specifically and in vitriolic detail recount both events. It seemed that a young couple had come to see the apartment. When the young man pulled to open the bedroom door, the entire door came loose from the hinges, fell to the wooden floor, and the top half of the door constructed of glass scattered to every corner of the dwelling. This unnerved the young woman, who immediately had to use the bathroom to relieve a disturbance in the lower gastronomic regions, a disturbance the landlord described in livid vivid detail. The woman did not know she used an inoperative toilet, and rather than tell the landlord after the assailed and beleaguered bowl failed to flush, she had grabbed her mate and fled the apartment without a word. The landlord did not make the sale.

Jason laughed as he descended the porch steps, and aloud he chuckled, "Five hunerd. Fuh-eyev hunerd! Was it worth it?"

Debris littered Haight Street. Jason stepped over broken glass and turned north on Fillmore. Just as he rounded the corner she saw him, and she issued a plea in a voice as deep as Jason's own. "Mister, can you please help me? My mother just went to the hospital. I just need a few dollars, or a couple, please."

"Just now?"

"What, mister?"

"Your mother went to the hospital?"

"Yeah. She's hurt. Oh please, can you help me?"

"What happened to your mother?"

"What?"

Jason paused, smiled, and asked again. "What happened to your mother? Why is she in the hospital?"

The creature with shoulders too wide for such a narrow waist tugged at her wig, stammered, and then said, "She was shot."

"Shot?! Oh my. Your mama done went and got in a gunfight. You must need a drink."

"No, no. I don't drink. My mother. Oh my poor mother."

5

"I just thought maybe you needed a drink. I need a drink. I guess there won't be any place to get any till six. That's too bad. Oh well. But hey, we can go to the hospital. Let's go."

"What?"

"We can go to the hospital to see your mom. What's your name, darlin? I'm Jason."

"Gladys."

"Gladys?! That's my favorite aunt's name. You wouldn't have any relatives down in the Cross Timbers region would you? No? Well, how about that drink, Gladys?"

Despite not being a drinker, she had a considerable amount of persuasive power over the young Hispanic or possibly Middle Eastern male that attended the late night corner convenience store. Well before the legal hour of day for alcohol sales, Gladys took Jason's twenty and returned with a four-dollar pint bottle of rot-gut vodka. And despite not being a drinker, Gladys shared what was left of the vodka after Jason filled his metal flask. After a few passes back and forth, Jason noticed a slug left, gave the bottle to Gladys, wished her mother well, and told her to keep the change. An hour or two later in the still weak new day's light, Jason had found the tavern with the blonde barmaid.

With the contents of Gladys's bag replaced and her wig more or less straight, Jason added to her burden by handing her the carnation bouquet. "There. Pretty flowers. Pretty girl. Now let's go get that drink."

Arms linked they proceeded west on Haight Street and soon encountered an Irish tavern with a sign advertising New Year's Day bloody marys. Inside at the bar, sitting atop a barstool and surveying his companion in her sartorial splendor, Jason asked, "What do you drink?"

"Champagne, baby."

Jason asked the bartender for a bloody mary and a mimosa. Halfway into their drinks, Jason and Gladys began communicating in a dialect composed mostly of laughter. Her laugh began in the baritone region but climbed in pitch as she grew more amused, and Jason liked the sound of a happy Gladys. He told more stories. After the one recounting his meeting with the Celtic Barmaid, Gladys's laughter stopped.

"Oh no, baby. You can't say that. You are so rude." She rubbed her hand back and forth across his crumpled shoulders. After a moment, he sat up straight, shook off the melancholy, and suggested they get something to eat. Across the street at the taqueria, Gladys had a burrito, and Jason

6

had three beers.

He left her in front of the taqueria. The busted up carnations looked better clasped against her fleecy pink sweater, and Jason began to walk away but not before being seized and hugged. He felt her scratchy beard on his ear.

Down in Lower Haight heading east, Jason saw the darkening late afternoon sky, and he thought about a tavern farther on with a shapely blonde.

Ah, make the most of what we yet may spend,
Before we too into the dust descend;
Dust into Dust, and under Dust to lie,
Sans Wine, sans Song, sans Singer, and—sans End!

Fat Ones Like Us

Jason downed the last of his tequila and set the shot glass next to his beer. Gwen still spoke to the other bar patron, a middle-aged rotund brunette. Occasionally while leaning in to better hear the patron over the noise of the jukebox, Gwen's shoulder wrap came loose. With each replacement she further disturbed her ample blonde mane. Away from her tavern of employment and in more leisurely attire, Gwen captivated Jason, and he watched her in conversation until her posture took on a more rigid stance moments before she returned to her seat next to him at the bar.

"Hey darlin, how about a drink?"

Gwen did not answer. She fixed a stern glare on the bottles of booze behind the counter. She did not look anywhere else nor speak.

"What gives, baby girl? You all right?"

"I'm fine. That woman said something. I don't want to talk about it."

"Well, where the hell is she? You say something to my friends, you gotta answer to Joe Buck. Where is she?"

"Oh, leave her alone, Joe Buck. Joe Buck?"

"Yep, I'm brand spankin new in this here town, and I'm hoping to get a look at that red bridge or maybe your Irish jugs."

Gwen laughed and slapped at Jason. "You cheeky bastard." For a moment she smiled, but then her serious mien returned.

"Hey, if you ain't having a good time here, lets git." Jason stepped away from his bar stool and reached for Gwen's hand.

Outside the bar on Divisadero Street amid the myriad light colors reflected from the wet pavement, Gwen pulled her shawl up around her neck. "You too cold, darlin? We can go by my place. Last chance to see it before the movers come."

Gwen did not answer. She looked ahead out into the street perhaps evaluating possible responses.

Jason too looked out into the street for a moment before clapping his hands and jumping in the air. "That's it. I can fix ya. We don't need to go to my place just yet. I got something else to show you. Don't worry, it's outdoors, and it's too cold to ravish you out here. But follow me, honey."

Jason held Gwen's hand and pulled her into a liquor store. She declined to offer preferences, so Jason purchased a pint of vodka, a pint of tequila, and a pint of whiskey. "Well, ya know, last call is coming pretty soon."

At the intersection of Divisadero and California Streets, Jason hailed a cab and first instructed the driver to go to Laurel Heights. A little later, Jason asked to be dropped off at Lyon and Jackson Street.

Gwen looked about at the residential neighborhood in slumber. Jason reached for her hand, and they walked north on Lyon. "Hear that?" Jason asked. Both listened, and again they heard the distant fog horn. In silence they proceeded north until they passed Broadway Street. Both stood and marveled at the endless number of steps that made the concrete staircase sloping down toward the bay. Descending down the wet steps, Jason removed his hand from Gwen's and wrapped his arm around her waist. "Tell me what that lady said to put you in such a sour mood."

Gwen stopped and began rummaging in her purse. She extracted a cigarette from a pack of Marlboros. With a jet of wet smoke, she said, "We were talking, and she saw you. Then she says . . ." Gwen's voice trailed off while the brogue of her native land became more noticeable.

"Got it. I got it. Say no more. She knows me and warned you. I've done some bad things. Sorry to have put you into that. I didn't mean to."

"What? No. That woman didn't know you. She saw you and she says to me, 'Ooh, he's a fine one. Fat ones like us usually don't get that kind.'"

A laugh started to rise, but Jason killed it at the base of his throat and let the remnants escape as a cough. "What the hell does that old bag know? She was drunk. She is a drunk. And you know all about those kind of folks. Hell, she was probably seeing double and thought you was twice as big . . . Nevermind that. Lemme tell you a story."

"No. Not another story. You drank a lot. You did something stupid. The end. I've heard those."

Jason smiled and moved closer to Gwen. "This is a different kind of story. It's about somebody else. But I need something first." Jason reached

9

and took Gwen's cigarette. "See, I have a nephew. Not a real nephew but good friend's kid. He's in college now with his big sister, my not real niece. Loved them both, just adored them, you know. When they were little, oh, like nine and eleven, we all lived in the same town, Monterey." Jason took a draw from the cigarette and expelled the smoke in a long thin stream. "When they were little, both their parents worked so the kids stayed with me during the day. We'd terrorize the playgrounds in town and the candy shops on Cannery Row. Good times. And then they became teenagers, and I needed to move away to hide the drinking." Jason took another drag from the Marlboro. "That wasn't where I meant the go with the story, the drinkin, that is. This ain't a story about drinkin. Anyway, right before my nephew was fixin to head back to Texas to go to college we were talking, and I gave him some advice. Like a lot of my advice, this bit got my nephew's mama mad at me." After another draw from the Marlboro, Jason leaned in close to Gwen's ear and lowered his voice to a whisper. "So I told my nephew about some of my trials after leaving home. Told him about some times and opportunities with young women, but them young women was tobacco worms, smelled and tasted like cigarettes. How do you kiss a girl like that? All that beauty matched with a mouth that tastes like an ashtray ain't no kind of good. The thing to do in that situation is to take a smoke yourself. Don't inhale, and you won't get the habit. And you won't be tasting that ashtray anymore cause you taste like it too. See?"

Perhaps no longer suspicious of his motives or perhaps with an agenda of her own, Gwen agreed to visit Jason's apartment because he claimed that he must stop there before going to breakfast. When they arrived at his apartment at 3 a.m., Jason led her up the rickety stairs to the top-floor flat, and he requested that she stomp as loud as possible or at least as loud as he did. Inside the apartment, Jason dodged between box pillars and made his way to the still unpacked stereo. He played Marvin Gaye at a volume inappropriate for the wee hours, and he told Gwen to make herself at home as he passed by on his way to the bathroom.

Once behind a latched door, Jason's smile changed and contorted in distress. He held his midsection with one hand and reached into a cabinet with another. While he drank the pink liquid, he leaned against the wall and sank to the floor. He held his midsection with both hands and rocked back and forth taking deep deliberate breaths. With difficulty he pulled himself up to the sink and washed his face.

Again smiling, Jason left the bathroom and moved toward the music.

In addition to Marvin, he heard another voice, a feminine one and not one of Marvin's famous duet partners but rather a live voice. With stealth, on tip-toes, Jason peeked around a stack of boxes, and he saw Gwen examining a large camera while she sang with Marvin. Jason listened until Gwen looked up and smiled. She said, "I like the soul music. What's this thing?"

"That thing is a camera. A Russian one. No, Ukrainian. Hey, you sing. You really sing."

"You think so?"

"I can't be the first to bring that up. You ever do any real singing?"

"Real singing?

"Like with a band or something?"

Gwen beamed. "You don't know? I thought you knew. Yes, I sing."

"I had no idea. You were tending bar when we met. Can I hear more of your music?"

"Tell me more about this camera. Why is it so big?"

Jason did not answer. He looked out the bay window and asked, "You got any of them Marlboros left?" After Gwen gave Jason a cigarette and lit it, Jason took a drag, seemed dissatisfied, tore the filter off, and took a deep filterless draw. "Yep, you was tending bar, and this old lonesome cowboy was lovesick right off the bat. Never in my life had I seen such gorgeousness. Why after one look at you and . . ."

"Knock it off. Tell me about this big camera."

"It's big because it uses big film, medium format, 120. It's a copy of a Hasselblad. They call it a Kiev. Just an old useless antique now. Damn, my stomach still hurts." Jason entered the kitchen and took a beer from the refrigerator.

"And why do you have such a big camera?"

"Fer takin big pictures, darlin."

"Are you a photographer?"

"Hell no. I'm not an artist, a bum. I have a job, usually. I don't want to talk about pictures. That thing is a useless antique. Nowadays folks make pictures with computers. Let's talk about music."

"Okay, from this collection I can tell that a black man of taste put it together. From where did you steal it?"

"You've known a bunch of tasty black fellers, have you?"

"Watch it, you cheeky bastard."

Jason chortled and said, "That's just a part of my records. The rest are already in storage, where all this is going when the movers come by this afternoon. Got all kinds of music. You're Irish. You probably like country music, right? Most of the Irish in the movies do anyway. I have tons of Bob Wills and Hank Williams and Willie Nelson and Buck Owens . . ."

Gwen interrupted, "Johnny Cash?"

"Sure, sure I got some of him too."

"What specifically do you have of Johnny's?"

"What? I don't know."

"Bollocks. What do you have?"

"I . . ."

"Have you seen The Johnny Cash Show?"

"Never even heard of it."

Gwen seemed incredulous at first, but then she came to accept that Jason had never seen a particular television series from the late 1960s. The prospect of introducing Jason to the series seemed to enliven Gwen, and she suggested that they go back to her place where she could prepare a breakfast while they watched the show. Jason agreed but took along six beers from his refrigerator.

In the predawn, Gwen's housemates readied for the workday, so Gwen and Jason waited outside. Gwen took Jason's beers inside the house and returned with a different brand in a colder bottle. She said, "We can let them finish getting ready and then go inside. Tell me more about your family."

"Family? Ain't got no family. All dead."

"But you told me about your niece and nephew earlier. Are they dead too?"

"Oh, hell no. They're good. The boy, call him Fink, is a natural born world shaker and smart. His sister, Vixen, is the most drop-dead gorgeous thing they ever saw down in San Marcos, and, oh my, is she smart. Damned fine artist too. But they're my friends' kids. No real blood relation. They started calling me uncle when they were little so I started calling them names too."

"What about your parents?"

"Told you, dead. My parents died when I was too little to know them, and I was raised by grandparents and great grandparents and stuff. Spoiled rotten. End of story. Got good friends, though. Family-friends or friend-families. Love em. None of them live in California anymore. What about you? You got parents?"

"Dad lives in Dublin. Mum lives in London."

"So you're half English?"

"No, you irreverent devil. I am not English. Mum moved to London after the divorce."

"And now you're here. Going back to Ireland ever?"

"I'm going back for a visit in a couple of weeks. But to live . . . I'm where I need to be for now. You? When are you going back to your farm in Texas?"

"Ain't got no farm, darlin. If I had any land down where I come from, it'd be a ranch, not a farm. But you can't expect a chippy from the bog to know the difference. Ain't been to Texas in a long spell, and I ain't fixin to go. This is home. Has been for a long time. Guess I need a new apartment, though."

"Where's that place you say you come from? Eyesore? 'I'm just a lonesome cowboy from Eyesore, Texas.'"

"Isom, damnit. Isom."

While they watched the first episode, their positions on the couch grew closer, and by the end of the show Jason reclined semi-sideways, and Gwen melted alongside. "Well, now I can see why I never saw it. It has that Bob Dylan subversive and some other hippies. There must have been something more wholesome on other channels, or maybe I just can't recall a show from when I might have still been in diapers. When were they showing this over in Ireland?"

Eyelids sealed and her head resting gently on Jason's shoulder, Gwen breathed softly. Jason turned his head a little and drew in the scent of her hair. After the second episode he slid slow and extricated himself from the couch, took a beer from the refrigerator, and went to the front door. He checked to ensure the door would lock behind him and stepped outside to a brisk mid-morning and set off to meet the movers who would remove the last of his items from the overpriced top-floor flat.

This hotel room might be the end of me. It ain't fit for people. Folks ought not stay here, and the slumlords at the front desk behind that half-door and metal grate ought to feel ashamed when they take money for one of these. Roaches go everywhere, and they're big. One of em on the wall got a knife flung at him yesterday, but the knife missed. A big chunk of drywall flew off the wall, and some of it stuck on the knife handle, and that's just as well cause bug guts on my blade ain't no kind of good, and I never could throw knives. If ever that sort of thing had been in my bag of tricks, I lost it. So much forgotten. Can't even remember the names of important stuff like the tack for the horses or even all the colors of the horses. So long ago.

In sleeping, though, some things come back just like they're happening right now. Just a little while ago Chico stepped his unshod hooves through bunches of buffalo grass and sideoats, and we both saw down the red dirt walls of the canyon past the juniper and mesquite and yucca, and running through the middle of all that, a band of gold sand holds a blue ribbon of water. Chico don't like crossing water, and grandparents never get tired of talking about quicksand, but that's where the tadpoles are, and so that's where we're fixin to go, down there into Dixon Creek, two miles from town, way beyond the range set by old folks afraid of quicksand.

Right here, right now in this bed, this awful filthy bed, I can let loose of this jug of hooch. Put the cap on. Let it rest against the headboard and try not to notice those old snipe burns. Close eyes. Keep these eyes closed long enough and reach down. Lean forward and reach past the saddle horn. Let arms go on either side of the pommel. Put those hands, both of em, on Chico's withers. One hand on a white patch and the other on a brown-red one because Chico is a paint. Move hands back and forth. Smooth, maybe a little oily one way but rough spikey the other way. I'll take a curry comb to him when we get back. Curry comb. There's one forgotten for a time. Haven't touched or seen a curry comb in ages. Move hands to my face and smell him though these decades. Makes me want to cry, but I can't afford to cry right now because crying always leads to being mad. And I'm gonna do my damnedest not to get mad today.

Pacing is a dumb thing to do, and when not in bed that's all I do. Windows, got two, face Van Ness and Bush. The window facing Van Ness shows the liquor store where big jugs of hooch can be got. Great location. Too bad about the roaches. Pacing is all there is to do cause it rains. Seems like it's been raining for days. Dreary.

The pretty blonde barmaid is gone. My reliability lacked, and her patience run out. Should have called. Could apologize and in time have another go, but I won't. She's better off. I'd just waste her time and disappoint her all over again, and that ain't no kind of good.

I ought to be doing something, moving on with life they call it. Moving on where, though? There ain't no place to go. This is it. Could go back in the direction I come from, north, but it's even wetter up that way. Could go where I lived before that, back in the direction of home, but all I'd get is better barbecue and no good Chinese food. Everything else stays the same. Get drunk, get in trouble, get outta trouble, and get drunk again. That's pretty much it, here or there.

Ah, nerts. This is just silly letting myself wallow in sadness. It's that damned dream that has me all bent out of shape this morning. One second having the dream and the next hearing and seeing cold rain on these grimy hotel windows. It's just the dream, that's all. That and drinking myself to perdition when I ought to be looking for honest, wholesome, gainful employment. But mostly it's the damned dream. I ought not call it damned cause it's the prettiest. Any one of the versions has the most beautiful country. But that beautiful country can't exist. I've been all over the land where the dream is supposed to happen, and it just can't be. It's an impossible picture, and it comes to me when I'm already all knotted up in my head. The more troublesome things are in the day, the more likely to have the dream at night. That's what it seems like anyway, and I've been having that dream or some part of it since I was little. How far back I can't say cause at some point the dream and the real mix. Some of the things in the dream was real at one time, like me being a little kid or me being a handsome almost-man or me having a horse. And of course there's the location, which is both real and impossible. The Texas Panhandle is a real place, and a person can go there easily enough.

Ain't no way, though, that the places in the dream can be in the Panhandle. I ought to know, and I do know. It's just flat impossible. The main colors in the dream are blue and green, but anybody that has ever been to the Panhandle won't be leaving with those colors in mind. That plain stretching in all directions from towns that aren't on the river breaks or down by Palo Duro is yellow except right after spring rains. Where that yellow plain gets busted up, there's usually rust red dirt. Blue and green just ain't real predominant colors in the Panhandle landscape that most folks see. But they are in the dream.

There's four versions of the dream. One even has a map, a glimpse of a map in the dream. The place itself is one of such beauty that it hurts just a little bit to picture it in my head, asleep or awake. Either way, afterwards it feels like there's a big hole in me like maybe I'm just a ghost. The map glimpse offers a real head scratcher cause I know that part of the Panhandle real well. It's a part that lives up to the vision of the Llano Estacado, a flat treeless plain. Ain't no way the dream can be real. This version shakes me up for some reason. Don't know why.

Other versions are easier to picture. There's the one where I'm driving on Highway 136. Just before the highway turns south away from being parallel to the river, there's another road going north. In real life, there is such a road. The closest real road is the one that goes up north and then branches to the east for Alibates and west for McBride Canyon. In the dream, the road don't branch. It just goes straight ahead to the river, but the river ain't itself in the dream. It ain't no trickle of brown water over a strip of sand. It's a line of swimming pools, one after another. The river runs through the swimming pools, filling up one and then emptying over waterfalls into the next. The pools ain't the turquoise things folks have in their backyards. They're more like that big one down in Austin called Barton Springs. And just like at Barton Springs, the water in the dream river that runs through pools is clean and clear in the shallows and a bold blue darker than the sky where it's deep.

It's for sure impossible.

Been having that version so long that the look of the water and the changes to the river I knew so well don't hardly bother me nearly as much as who is with me. In that version I'm always with two people, and the damnedest thing about it is that both them young women were real. In the dream we're all happy. Everybody is happy. We swim and laugh just like we did in real life. But in real life I knew each years apart and far away from the Texas Panhandle. In the dream, though, we're at the same place at the same time and happy.

There's one version where I'm always alone except for Chico. Starts out

16

with me and Chico heading out on what was once the Sanford Ranch. No fences like there are now block our way. We come to a stand of mesquites, not much other than a bunch of bushes. I'm still little in the dream, always a kid in this version, and when I jump out of the saddle Chico's thirteen and a half hands are nearly up to the top of my head. I hold the leather reins as we walk past the mesquites getting ever taller and thicker. Soon they're big like the mesquites down farther south where it's wetter. The more we go in the thicket the taller it gets until we get to a clearing that's shaded by trees so high we don't see the tops. There's these stone fountains and statues of the kind like in castles or movies, about a half dozen, that stand in the clearing. They're old. And nobody but me and Chico know about them cause no one else ever goes in the thicket. And that's where that version ends. Me and Chico looking at the fountains that we ain't never gonna tell about.

The one with the map glimpse causes me considerable vex. In real life, that part of the Panhandle is flatter than jokes about the Panhandle. Folks that think they've seen wide open spaces are still left feeling like it just ain't natural for land to be so empty. Of course it ain't empty. That's just what folks think. But right there where that version of the dream is supposed to take place is pretty damned empty even by me and Chico's standards. But Chico ain't ever with me in that version of the dream. In that version I'm always grown. The place itself looks like other places in the Panhandle, but there's too much of it. It's got a nice stream of clear water, which ain't that common in the region. There's lots of cottonwoods like in that grove where I once fell off Chico into that creek, Bear Creek maybe. I've never seen so many cottonwoods in one place, and they're huge, just like some of the pecan trees down in Austin. There's a sense of some canyon walls, tight sheltering ones like some of the tight canyons on the river breaks or down around Palo Duro. But I never see those walls. I just kind of figure they're there.

Maybe it's the impossibility, that the places can't be, that bugs me. That word dream can also mean a thing wanted, but these dreams are more than wishes. They must be needs cause they keep coming back. And the forth version, the one from a while ago, the one that came after me and Chico went after tadpoles, it's the worst or the best. It's beautiful, but it leaves me with that ghost feeling more than the others. I don't want to think about that one. I can think about and describe the other three, the one with the swimming pools, the one with the fountains, and the one with the cottonwoods, but that forth one . . . I need to leave that one alone.

This staying cooped up ain't no kind of good. Rain ain't no excuse. Need to get up and out and moving and shake off this grey dread that gets all over me. Dark and cold outside with visions of impossible places in my head gets me in a bad way, and there just ain't no reason to go along with it. Ain't no reason to get teary over a long-gone horse, places that ain't even real, and tricks of my memory. If I was fixin to get all wound up and frayed over something, maybe I ought to pick something closer to home, like this shambles I've become. Ah, nerts indeed. I'm not going to do this. I'm not going to get all broke up about nothing. I'm just not gonna do it. Soon, maybe this morning even, I'll get out of this dingy room and get away from the drinking. I'll enjoy this beautiful city, and I'll get some kind of life back. I'll do it.

For now, though, I'll stay with the hooch. Done right, there won't be no more dreams. No more dreams about impossible places, horses to miss, or places that can't never be found. Those dreams hurt, and they don't do me any good, not like the booze anyway.

And lately, by the Tavern Door agape,
Came shining through the Dusk an Angel Shape
Bearing a Vessel on his Shoulder; and
He bid me taste of it; and 'twas—the Grape!

Jeremiah Corona

Jason parted the curtains, and blue exploded upon him. Eyes closed, he released the curtains, waited a moment, and then parted them again. Peeking through one eye he saw but doubted the reality of a clear cloudless sky. Twisting in contorted shapes to get a better view through the glass, he still felt disbelief. Buildings ahead and to the left and right jutted into uniform azure. Jason pulled the blanket from the bed and wrapped it around his shoulders. The wood framed window refused to budge, but Jason refused to quit tugging and prying, and in a flash the window shot upward with force and a loud bang to deliver Jason's second unbelievable sensation of the morning. After recovering from the momentary shock in thinking he had broken the window, Jason let the blanket fall from his shoulders, and he stood before the open morning stunned.

What little breeze passed through the window conveyed warmth, not an intensification of winter chill. When surprise passed and turned to eager joy, Jason looked first at the clothes hanging in the wardrobe and then at his face in the mirror. Again he looked back at the wardrobe and studied his options. And then in a flurry of energy Jason moved about the room.

Outside the main door and security gate, Jason passed on the sidewalk below his still open window, and once beyond the shade of the building, he felt the morning sun's full warmth. Unable to control a wide grin, he turned the corner and entered a convenience store. When he reached the counter with his items, a banana and two hard-boiled eggs, the Middle Eastern man looked at him with amusement and asked, "Big hurry today?" Perplexed by his amusement, Jason paused a moment and then removed the toothbrush from his mouth and placed it in his jacket pocket.

"Yes, I'm in a hurry to enjoy this beautiful weather."

When he reached Market Street, out of habit he headed for the stairs leading down to the light rail station, but then he stopped. Even on Market Street, mostly shaded from the early morning sun, the warmth held. Jason looked up the street toward the Civic Center and in the direction of the Embarcadero and then down the street in the direction of The Castro. He took the route to the southwest.

He had planned to take a detour through Buena Vista Park, partly for the exercise in climbing little hills but mostly for the scenery. Someplace east of the park, though, he caught sight of the fist. Atop Corona Heights bent ochre stone digits brandished the might of the hill under the unbroken cerulean. As he looked up at the summit and the rusty Franciscan chert, he thought of Tule Canyon breaking the Caprock hundreds of miles to the east and south.

The flat grassy park gave way to a walking path that circled the fenced dog park. On one end of the fenced park a man flung a frisbee for a long-haired black retriever, and in the other end of the park a woman tossed a tennis ball for a little terrier. The retriever pursued the whirling disk in long rhythmical strides sometimes capped with a jump for a midair catch while the terrier went after the ball in loud growling ferocity. Neither missed their prey, and while the retriever returned the disk with poise and patience, the terrier dropped the ball at the woman's feet and barked sharp and constant until the ball returned to flight.

Past the dog park the path steepened, and Jason coughed as he climbed. Pausing to catch his breath, Jason first had to endure another long bout of coughing. He wondered for a moment if he had become ill, but the splendor of the morning kept his attention, and he pressed on up the path still coughing intermittently and chuckling a bit at the prospect of climbing the remainder in dress shoes. As the dirt path gave way to a smooth stone passage, Jason knew he neared the top, and he looked up to see sorrel boulders. After a moment to let the coughing pass, he entered the path that led between boulders and snaked the way to the top. Inside the tight chasm at the summit, Jason saw another figure and gasped.

"Whoa . . . Jeremiah Johnson. Uh, howdy."

"Hello, yourself," came from the mass of white fur. A man of more than a foot shorter than Jason seemed half hair. A thick snowy mop sprouted from the top of the man's head and flowed down over his shoulders to be joined by more hoary fur coming from his face and chin. The fleecy mass from both sources ended at the man's waist and revealed old and well-worn oilcloth trousers. Beside the man at his feet stood a leather satchel or backpack also with signs of advanced age.

"Did you leave the pack mules down below?" Jason asked.

"Come again?"

Jason laughed and coughed a bit. "Just kidding. Didn't expect to see . . . uh, somebody that, uh, didn't look like part of the city. For a second this hill seemed like way out in West Texas or maybe the Ozarks. Nevermind that. Beautiful morning, ain't it? My name is Jason."

"Bob."

"Well, Bob . . ." Jason paused to cough and then continued, "I need to rest a minute before leaving you to the mountain. You don't mind if I stay a minute?"

"It's a free country, mostly."

Bob sat silent and motionless looking out across the sweeping vista that encompassed the entire northeastern part of the city, the bay, and framed at the top by the hills of the East Bay. Though bright and climbing, the sun remained closer to its starting point on the southeastern horizon. Jason breathed heavy and coughed. He sat on the smooth reddish rock and mopped his brow with a handkerchief. As his breathing slowed and time between coughs increased, Jason noticed the lack of motion and sound coming from his new acquaintance.

"Hey, Bob sorry about the Jeremiah Johnson comment."

Bob shrugged his shoulders but did not speak. He continued to gaze. Jason also saw the grandeur of the scene, but a growing sense of discomfort or guilt grew. "It sure is a beautiful morning, ain't it?"

Bob did not answer, and Jason folded his handkerchief before returning it to a pocket. Jason stood, looked at the view of downtown, turned and looked north at the hill that made Buena Vista Park, then turned some more to where Bob sat. "You look like a fellow that's deep in thought. I get that way sometimes. If you're gonna be here a while, you might want some breakfast." Jason removed the banana and two eggs from his jacket and placed them on the smooth rock. Beside those he placed a bottle of water. "Better be getting on, but help yourself and enjoy the day."

Bob looked at the food then watched as Jason walked back in the direction from which he had come. Bob picked up one of the eggs and gently tapped it on the rock. "Hey, there. Jason is it? I sure appreciate the food. Do you have to go? I could use some company if you have any time to spare."

Jason stopped and turned. "Time is something I got a lot of these days." He returned to the spot where he had sat before. "And I'm not in any big hurry to climb down that path again."

Bob finished the second egg and reached for the banana. "I appreciate the food. I missed breakfast." After tossing the banana peel, Bob stood and walked over to his pack. He moved it from where it leaned and from behind it he produced a large bottle of red wine. Jason saw the shape, big jug-like on the bottom rising to a stem with a round hole of a handle, and Jason estimated that the nearly full bottle held over a gallon. He saw the dark liquid tilt one way and then another as Bob extended the bottle. Jason reached for the jug, unscrewed the cap, and took a drink. After swallowing, he closed his eyes and exhaled slowly. He felt the warm scent of the grape rise up through his chest and out his nose, and he savored the sharp feelings on the sides of his tongue.

"I'm not supposed to do this," Jason said. And he took a second drink before capping the jug and returning it to Bob.

"You're not supposed to drink wine?"

"I'm not supposed to drink anything with alcohol," Jason answered. "Been spending too much time down deep in a bottle, and now I'm supposed to be figuring out how to get by without drinking all the time."

"I got just the thing for that," Bob exclaimed. He returned to his pack reached inside and removed a clear plastic bag with green nuggets inside. "This stuff will help with anything. I grew it myself."

Jason smiled. "I appreciate the thought. But I've never been one for the reefer. Bob, you gotta admit that green sure does compliment your outfit. You get a bandana tied as a headband and a peace symbol and you could be a tourist attraction over there on Haight Street. Still though, I do thank you. Maybe just one more drink wouldn't hurt, right Bob?"

Bob passed jug and said, "My name isn't Bob. It's Patrick. I didn't know what to think of your mountain man comment, and I've had a rough last couple of days."

"I'm sorry to hear that, Bobrick. How rough have the last days been?"

"I got released from jail this morning."

"Oh, no, not the jailhouse. I'm sorry to hear that, pardner. I haven't been in a spell, but they know me down there on Bryant Street. You got out just this morning and toted that big bag all the way up here?"

"Yeah. The jail cell had a little window, and up a hill I saw a big pink building. At different times of day it was more or less noticeable, always pretty. Without a place to go after jail—they impounded the car—I searched for the pink building. I never found the building, but I found this place."

Jason looked puzzled for a moment. "Big pink building . . . Big pink building up a hill. If that window at the jailhouse was facing this way, there's only one building that could be. Matter of fact, you can see it from here." Jason pointed to the north. "It's just right over there next to Buena Vista Park. Say, that's funny. I was heading to Buena Vista, but I ended up here. Glad I didn't have to tote a heavy pack."

"Oh it's not heavy." Bobrick hoisted the pack with one hand. "All it has in it is kind bud."

"Wow. So you got turned loose from the jailhouse and scored a big bag of dope all in the same morning?"

"No, it's my bud. I grew it. The cops gave it back to me this morning. They did break the bags in a few places, and that's why it smells so strong."

"Wait a minute, pardner. Are you telling me that the law locked you up but then gave back your dope? Man, only in San Francisco. Is it all right to ask what they locked you up for?"

"A traffic ticket from way back, over fifteen years ago. Somehow the fine didn't get paid, and somehow that never came up until now. Day before yesterday while coming down from Sonoma to work out a deal for business with a dispensary the cops stopped me for speeding, and now the dispensary deal is gone, and my friend's car is impounded. Now I'm stuck hiding in these rocks."

"If the cops didn't take your dope when they had you locked up, why do you have to hide out now?"

For the first time Jason noticed Bobrick smile. "Friend, it's not the police to fear. I don't want to get jacked, ripped off. This pack smells."

"Only in San Francisco . . . Man, this place is the wild, wild west. The cops give you back your dope, and now you gotta hide out from the bandits. Maybe you'll be all right if you stay out of certain parts of town."

"Getting jacked isn't my only problem," Bobrick said. "My friend's car is impounded, and that's going to hit him hard. He needs it for work."

"That won't be no kind of fun to tell him the car got locked up."

"Oh, he already knows. I called him from jail, and he offered to send me a bus ticket."

"Now that's a good friend," Jason said as he took another long drink from the big jug of wine. "A friend you can be honest with is a good friend indeed. I got some friends, but I keep em by hiding. I go years between seeing them and sometimes even talking to them. You got good friends, Bobrick."

"Yeah, and it makes me feel terrible that my buddy's car is impounded. He's mostly disabled."

Jason drank from the big jug of wine and looked ahead at the hill of Buena Vista Park. "You have friends, good ones. I got good friends too, but I don't treat em so good. Been putting off letting them know I'm still alive after my last screw-up." After another drink, Jason looked up at the sky. "There's still plenty of daylight left. How much you figure it'll cost to get your pal's car out of lockup?"

"No idea. More than I have. I'm sure of that."

Jason held the jug of wine, now only a third full, and he tilted it back and forth watching the dark liquid lean in opposition to the direction of the mouth. Through the green glass he saw the tree covered hill that composed Buena Vista Park. "You know, Bobrick, it's a shame that we have to disappoint good friends. There ain't nothing I can do for mine today . . . Well, actually there is, but I don't have the guts to make that call and those apologies. But, Bobrick, there might be something we can do for your buddy right now. It just might be that you can drive your pal's car back to him. I think we might be able to do something. I'll need your help, and we'll need some more hooch. That's for sure. Whadaya think?"

II. Barbary Coast

Come, fill the Cup, and in the fire of Spring
Your Winter garment of Repentance fling:
      The Bird of Time has but a little way
To flutter—and the Bird is on the Wing.

And much as Wine has play'd the Infidel,
And robb'd me of my Robe of Honor—Well,
I wonder often what the Vintners buy
One half so precious as the stuff they sell.

Living History

"Just up here on Waller we're gonna take a left and head west toward the park, but we gotta stay off Haight as much as possible for now. I don't remember exactly which street the surplus store is on, but I'll recognize it when I see it."

Bobrick struggled to keep up with Jason's enthusiastic gait, and the well-worn and fragrant backpack bounced when Bobrick had to trot now and again to match Jason's invigorated long strides. To share the load, Jason had volunteered to carry the jug of wine, and periodically he took long swigs. One such draw while crossing the street did not go down as intended, and while Jason sputtered he bent forward as far as balance allowed to prevent a trickle from snaking down his chin. "That's all we need. Red wine on this white shirt won't be no kind of good."

"Tell me again how we're going to sell this kind bud," Bobrick said.

"We're not going to sell anything except the privilege of taking pictures with a bona fide summer-of-love hippie. Trust me. Don't know why I didn't think of this sooner. Well, guess I did think of it sooner but didn't take it seriously maybe. This is going to work. You'll have your pal's car out of impound before sunset. Guaranteed. Oh, hey, this is our street."

Bobrick followed Jason in his abrupt right turn, and he watched as Jason set the empty wine jug on the sidewalk outside a liquor store. "I'll be just a second. Don't go nowhere." When Jason emerged from the liquor store carrying a quart bottle of beer, he said, "Surplus store is a couple doors down. Hold this beer for me. Have some if you like. I'm gonna need it to get me through our project."

A black canvas duffle bag and two plastic bags full of wares caught in the door of the surplus store as Jason tried to leave. After opening the door once again to extricate himself, Jason hurried over to Bobrick. "We gotta head back up Waller to Buena Vista Park, and then we'll be set."

Jason huffed and coughed climbing the narrow paved path to a picnic table. First he placed the duffle bag and plastic bags on the table, and then he motioned for Bobrick to drop the backpack alongside. After a long gulp from the quart bottle, Jason reached inside a plastic bag and handed Bobrick a red bandana and a fist-sized peace sign medallion on a hemp necklace. "Do that bandana as a headband and wear this peace sign around your neck. Then we got to get to portioning your dope."

"You sure aren't going to sell any all dressed up like a lawyer or detective. I thought you said we weren't going to sell any bud."

"I did. I did say that. We're not going to sell it exactly, but it'll get sold. Trust me. We gotta get moving to get this done soon. You face this way, and I'll face your way, and we can stop with the dope if anyone happens to mosey on by."

The two men, opposites in appearance, took green nuggets from the backpack and filled sandwich-sized plastic bags then placed them in the canvass duffle bag. Once the soiled backpack had been emptied and the overstuffed duffle bag zipped shut, Jason added a new item to the inventory on the table. He opened a bag of fake grass the kind used in Easter baskets, and he said, "Roll up a few joints with this stuff and have em stickin out of your shirt pocket. I'll get to work on the pack." Jason stuffed the fake grass in the opening of the pack so that it gave the appearance of overflowing with bright green hay. After another gulp from the quart, Jason lifted the dirty backpack to this face. "It still has that authentic smell," he said while slinging the pack over one shoulder. "You carry the dope bag, and I'll take the photo prop and this here soon-to-be dead soldier." After guzzling a good portion of the bottle, Jason belched and said, "Scuse me. Better follow me. We gotta head down by Golden Gate Park before heading over to Ashbury."

At the intersection of Stanyan, Jason surveyed both sides of Haight Street. "You have any cash?" Jason asked. "One-dollar bills are best, and you'll get em back real soon. Oh, and I'm going to need a few bags of that dope. Let's start with the smallest ones." Bobrick watched as Jason approached a group of youths sitting outside a music store. Jason smiled and visited. He handed over one of the small sandwich bags, and then he moved across the street to another figure disheveled and too tired looking for his few years. "Yeah, man, really just want to give you a dollar and some free weed. All I ask is that you share it if you can. And if you or anyone you share with likes it, and I know you will, I'll be over at Haight and Ashbury later." At another group of street kids, Jason gave sandwich bags, and he said, "No, no I don't want to step on anybody's toes. I'll just be here today, and all I want is to get enough to get home. Yall can understand that, right? I don't want any trouble at all. But if trouble comes . . ." Jason patted the underarm portion of his jacket with his right hand. "If trouble comes, the fat man still has a few tricks." Jason continued zigzagging giving money and sandwich bags of marijuana to the youths who maintained a constant presence on Haight Street.

At the intersection of Haight and Ashbury, Jason turned to Bobrick. "It's almost show time, but we need one more thing, and it's gonna cost. Wait here just a second."

Jason stood near the crosswalk, and he watched the pedestrian traffic moving up and down Haight and sometimes lingering at the intersection of Ashbury. A group of young Asians stopped to take photos with the street signs in the background, and Jason approached them. After pleasant greetings, Jason snapped photos for the group with one of its member's cameras. After handing the camera back to the owner, Jason had a short conversation and then accepted cash before reaching into his jacket pockets for multiple sandwich bags. He then hurried back across the street to Bobrick, and grinning he said, "Hey pardner, they bought all I had. We're in business. Let's git over to that store."

Bobrick followed Jason into a store and passed through a wall of incense smoke. Jason stopped in front of a rack of serapes, and he selected the largest one. "This one ought to do all right." Jason placed the serape over Bobrick and saw that it hung down low, revealing only Bobrick's boots. "Perfect. Just one more thing." Jason grabbed a pair of leather sandals, put them on the counter near the register and told the clerk, "We'll take these and that blanket he's wearin."

Back outside the store, Jason instructed Bobrick to trade his boots for the sandals, and then Jason crossed the street to a liquor store and emerged with small bottles of clear liquor. He drank one and placed the rest in pockets before taking the soiled backpack from Bobrick and placing it against a building at the corner of Haight and Ashbury. On the ground near the pack he placed a couple of dollars and weighted them with coins. "Now for the bag with the goods." Jason helped Bobrick remove the serape and hoist the black canvass bag onto his back. Replacing the serape concealed the bag but left Bobrick with a predominant hump. "Just stand with your back to a wall as much as you can. You ready? Remember, you don't have to say anything. Just let the folks take their pictures. All right then. Here goes." Jason drank another little liquor bottle, coughed, and smoothed his hair with his hands.

"Visitors! Friends! You have come here to this magical place, this Paris of the Pacific, where it all began back in '67. I know since I was a product of '67, though if you do the math you can see that my parents got a jump on the Summer of Love by a few months, and though I was born right here in this City by the Bay, I was conceived in a VW van enroute to the summer that changed the world. Most of those that started the magic, the real McCoys among the so-called hippies are sadly all gone. But one of their hairy tribe remains. Yes, ladies and gentleman, my friend and mentor, Jeremiah Corona, was here in the Summer of Love, and he's been here ever since. While most of the other hippies left to sell out and become stock brokers, my friend, the original Harry the Hippie stayed right here and kept the spirit of peace and freedom alive. Mostly he lives in a bedroll over at Golden Gate Park, so any donation is greatly appreciated. We're here today just like you are, to pay respect to the ideas of peace, love, and super trippy weed."

Jason stopped his oratory and coughed into a handkerchief as he walked back to Bobrick. "We got em lookin, but they ain't stoppin. We need a little more of a crowd." Jason took another of the small bottles of liquor from a pocket and drained it in one gulp. After much coughing, Jason caught his breath and watched for the pedestrian light to change before skipping and dancing into the middle of Haight Street. Perhaps to some beat heard only by Jason he hopped about flinging his arms up and to the sides. In some ways he appeared to mimic Cab Calloway with his hair flying at the gyrations of his neck and head, and in other ways he looked like a lunatic hopping about on one foot. As abruptly as he began the calamity devoid of rhythm or flow, he stopped and calmly strode back to the sidewalk where he fixed his hair with a pocket comb and shouted, "Sorry about that, folks. I do get a bit of fever with them spells. My mama denies it, but I suspect that we got some of the brown acid at Woodstock."

While a middle-aged couple took turns taking photographs with Bobrick, Jason continued his grandiloquence. "Yes sir and yes ma'am, this here is the last of the authentic Haight Street Hippies. Jeremiah Corona was here for the beginning, middle, and he'll be here until his end. It is a fact that he has not left his post except for one time. In June of '67, he went down to Monterey to help put together a concert some of you might have heard of. While the concert went on to legend, Jeremiah suffered the first of tragedies that stole his own music. A crushed hand stopped his guitar playing, and two years later a house fire right over there on Masonic Avenue ruined his vocal chords for good. He used to sing like an angel, but now he can't hardly talk. So friends, step up and say hello to the last of his kind. Suggested donation is just five bucks, but stopping to tell Jeremiah Corona where you're from and why you've come means a whole lot to a fellow that sleeps in a bedroll night in night out."

Amid his raucous speechifying, Jason noticed that some of the street kids he had spoken to earlier had gathered. After speaking to a couple of them, he approached Bobrick and began to open one of the small bottles of clear liquor. Jason stopped, recapped the bottle, and chucked it sidearm into a street drain gutter. He removed the remaining bottles from his pockets and did the same. While standing behind Bobrick and reaching inside the serape, he said, "Now we're rollin. Good thing too. I'm feelin a little woozy from the hooch." After exchanging bags for cash, Jason resumed his ballyhoo. Alternating between alerting tourists to the presence of living history and catering to the needs of the street kid customers, Jason took time to remind Bobrick to keep watch on the growing pile of donations near the soiled backpack. Time after time, Jason picked up bills and handed them to Bobrick.

During one of his trips to the canvass bag hidden under the serape, Jason appeared surprised. "Hey pardner, we're done. Just these last two bags, and those fellas over there want em. Let's pack up and head over to that coffee shop. I got a fearsome headache." While Jason presented the last of the sandwich bags for cash, Bobrick removed the serape and sandals and placed them in the canvass bag. Jason coughed into his handkerchief and leaned against a wall before entering the coffee shop. At a table seated across from Bobrick, Jason rubbed his temples.

"You all right?" Bobrick asked.

"Will be. Wish I hadn't drank. Had a little while without and thought I wasn't gonna do it no more." Jason fixed his hair with a pocket comb. "I'll be all right. I'll just have to make sure to get something to eat before going to drink again, and then I'll be back to yesterday. What about you? You doing good?"

"Are you kidding me? You got more than enough to get the car back and then some. You should take some of this. It's way more than I could get selling to the dispensary."

"No, no I'm fine. You take that dough back up to Sonoma."

"I insist. You have to." Bobrick slid a mound of cash across the table. "I'd still be up on that hill if you hadn't come along. Take this too. A souvenir." Bobrick removed the peace sign medallion.

"All right then, friend, Bob-Patrick. It's been fun. I recommend that with all the cash you're carrying that you take a cab down to the impound yard."

As he waved goodbye to Bobrick in the taxi, Jason saw the long shadows cast by the late afternoon sun, and he felt a little bit of breeze though the temperature remained warm. More than anything he felt the craving for drink at odds with his sense of guilt. Passing the edge of Buena Vista Park, he thought about taking a route through the park, but fatigue kept him on the sidewalk moving into Lower Haight. He thought about the need to eat before he succumbed to the booze craving, and he dreaded going to the dingy hotel room and solitude after being surrounded by so much good will and excitement.

On Market Street moving toward downtown, Jason saw various eating establishments, but nothing seemed appealing. Somewhere past Castro, maybe close to Church Street, he saw a diner with an old marquee style sign jutting from the building. As he neared, the warm smell of grease seemed inviting and made him more aware of his fatigue. Jason leaned against a wall and turned red under the glow of the marquee in the early evening twilight. Another handwritten sign inside the window of the diner caught his attention. It read, "Best hamburgers in the world." Jason smiled and thought about the best hamburger he ever had. He closed his eyes and the red glow of the marquee changed to silver light surrounding silver metal bleachers where a skinny buck-toothed ten-year-old sat at the tip top row and buried his face into a burger wrapped in paper.

"Yeah . . . was that '76 or '77? Top of Texas Rodeo. Pampa, Texas. That was the best burger."

Jason smiled, smoothed his hair, and entered the diner.

YESTERDAY This Day's Madness did prepare;
TO-MORROW's Silence, Triumph, or Despair:
 Drink! for you not know whence you came, nor why:
Drink! for you know not why you go, nor where.

The Ides

Nearing the donut and coffee shop he tried to induce coughing in the hope that he could then enter and exit the shop without a coughing fit. A steady stream of customers entered and exited, but most of the tables remained empty. The early morning customers wanted their pastries and coffee, and they had places to be, like work and school. Jason had no place to be, no appointments or even any plans. Near the door, an occupied table looked more like a campsite. A man sat at a table piled with dirty coats and scarfs and gloves. Outside on the other side of the window opposite the table, a wheeled shopping cart held a dirty old canvass tarpaulin, newspapers, and assorted bottles and cans. As soon as Jason opened the door, he heard the shout, "The Ides!"

Once inside, the shouting continued. "The Ides. The Ides." Jason looked at the man at the table piled with winter garments, and the man said, "Today is the Ides. Today is the Ides of February!"

Jason first responded with a blank even pain look then managed a slight smile and said, "If you say so, Barry, then it is. Good morning."

Taking his place in the short line, Jason wondered if it felt odd to speak because of the lingering cough or because he had not spoken to anyone in nearly two weeks. Perhaps after a time it just felt odd to speak. Once at the counter, Jason managed to complete the transaction without words. He pointed at the self-serve coffee station and presented the money. Before moving to the coffee, Jason paused, gave the woman at the counter five dollars more and pointed to Barry siting at his campsite table and muttering. The woman smiled and nodded, and Jason poured his coffee. On his way out, Jason said, "Have a good day, Barry."

Back outside in the early morning sun, Jason felt the urge to cough, and he looked about for a place to set his coffee. While he placed his coffee on top of a newspaper stand, he glanced at headlines and waited for the discomfort to come. He held the metal box full of newspapers to steady himself, and he coughed until his eyes watered. Recovered, he crossed the street, walked a block, and dug in his pocket for keys.

Inside the grimy hotel room, he poured coffee from the paper cup into an old ceramic mug, and he sat on the edge of the bed and looked at a fist-sized peace sign medallion on a hemp necklace hanging from a hook near the door. The sun outside and the temperature according to a thermometer indicated a warm day, but Jason seemed to never get warm. He coughed, and he sat with his arms crossed thinking about drinking the coffee before him on the dresser scarred from old cigarette burns. He sat and he thought, and then he stood and reached for his keys. On the way out he took the peace sign medallion.

At the storage unit, he worked the key into the lock, and once inside he felt about for a dangling string to pull and activate the dim incandescent bulb. The front of the unit contained the cardboard boxes he had packed in his most recent long-term rental, the overpriced top-floor flat. Beyond the boxes, some items of furniture, an old dresser, a bed frame, and a leather reclining chair partially blocked the remainder of the storage that held what he referred to as useless antiques. Jason squeezed past the furniture and stood before an enormous black metal contraption with the word Beseler. On top of and beside the apparatus lay padded bags holding cameras of various formats, and around those in haphazard fashion trays, drums, and other souvenirs of an abandoned livelihood blocked the way to the large steamer trunk.

Upon opening the trunk, Jason smelled moth balls and saw clothing he had not worn in over a decade. The older ones had a distinctly western flavor, and as he examined those he smiled and thought about when he first moved to San Francisco and had been warned about wearing that type of clothing in the part of town called The Castro. More recent acquisitions offered greater warmth, and some of those items he set aside. Near the bottom of the trunk, he found the scarf and gloves that he sought, but coughing shook him, and he felt tired. While he sat in the leather recliner and looked at the immense Beseler enlarger, he thought about useless antiques. Something large in his pocket felt uncomfortable, and Jason reached inside and retrieved the fist-sized peace sign medallion. Rising from the recliner, he hung the medallion on the enlarger, put on the scarf and gloves, and left the storage unit.

Outside in the bright sun, Jason thought he must be the only person in the city wearing winter garments, but he did not feel self-conscious. He felt tired. With each step he felt more fatigue, and he wondered if he could control the coughing long enough to use public transit. The bus arrived, and after boarding and paying the fare Jason found an empty seat near the rear exit. For some reason the bus did not depart, and a heated conversation occurred at the front of the bus. The driver repeatedly said, "I can't. I can't. You can try to get it through the back door, or you can wait for the next bus." Other passengers began to grumble, and some shouted inquiries about the delay. Jason left his seat and walked to the front of the bus. Outside he saw a slight and bent aged Asian man with a little wheeled cart containing grocery bags. The driver tried to explain that he could not activate the ramp for the front door, but the slight Asian man did not understand. More passengers grew restless, and some offered unkind suggestions for remedying the delay. Jason stepped off the bus, hoisted the cart up the steps, and then helped the man step up. Before Jason could climb back onto the bus, the door shut and the bus departed.

Jason resumed walking, and with each step the return to his residence seemed more arduous. A few blocks farther on, he encountered a park, and at the bus stop across the street from the park he found a bench. He discovered that while sitting relieved some fatigue, the process of changing posture caused strain on his back, and he had to use his arms to steady himself while lowering to the bench. Once seated, he hoped he had a few moments before the bus arrived because he dreaded having to rise again.

In the park, a young woman watched two children playing. One child, a boy of perhaps three or four, played with a rubber ball. The other child, too young to walk and too young for Jason to discern a gender, sat on the grass near the mother and also played with a ball. The older child picked up and threw the ball then chased after it to kick it and begin the chase anew. Despite his discomfort, Jason smiled as he watched the boy in his endless pursuit of his glossy red ball. Most of his attempts to kick the ball missed, but one met the ball and sent it flying. The ball collided with a lamppost and bounced at an angle perpendicular to the sidewalk. As the ball approached the sidewalk and the boy ran after the ball, Jason's smile flattened, and as the ball reached the curb Jason shot off the bench and rushed into traffic coming from the left and the right. He scooped the ball as he ran, and once on the sidewalk next to the boy Jason tossed the ball near the mother and small child and pointed for the boy to follow. "Go get the ball, little hombre," he said, and then a coughing fit that caused him to bend in half took hold. When he regained his breath, Jason looked into the park and saw the mother gather her children to herd them farther into the park and away from the street. She cast a wary glance over her shoulder at Jason. "Yall are welcome," he said in a rasp. "Have a good day."

Back at the bus stop, the bench held others, so Jason stood and waited. He felt tired from the recent exertion, tired from the coughing, and tired from lack of food for several days. Usually he suffered from pain or nausea, but at this moment he felt both. Behind the bench, across the sidewalk, the exterior wall of an auto garage presented a flat stone surface, and Jason stretched out an arm against the wall while he tried to catch his breath and cope with the queasiness. The leaden sore weight of his legs caused him to turn his back to the wall and sink to the sidewalk. He sat against the building coughing while the bus came and went. "My life is a party. It's a never-ending party. Let's celebrate."

Using his arms and hands as much as his feet and legs in getting himself upright, Jason straightened, and he walked. "Oh yeah, my life is a party," he said while he passed through the door of a liquor store. In the wine section, he searched the bottom, the bargain shelves until he spotted the bigger-than-gallon bottles and selected a red variety, jug-like rising to a stem with a round hole of a handle. Jason wanted to drink immediately, but he needed more items for his party. Near the liquor store, he visited an Italian deli. While he pointed to foods in the glass counter—olives, cheese, pasta salad—Jason noticed what he thought might be disapproval in the deli worker's glances at the large jug Jason carried. "Well, you see," Jason began, "I'm havin a little party, and I have little money. Better wine would take up all the money for good party food. So I decided to get cheap wine and good food. Which would you choose?" The white-coated deli worker did not answer, but he did grin, and the portions he gave became more generous.

A ceramic mug of coffee and a half-full paper cup occupied the top of the dresser etched with burns and gouges, and Jason removed those before placing the party wares. He set a drinking glass beside the unopened jug of wine, and he placed the containers of hors d'oeuvres in front of the wine. Sitting on the edge of the bed, he surveyed the items. "Okay, a deal's a deal. I gotta eat one of each of these before having any wine." Jason sat motionless looking at the food and the big bottle of wine. "Okay, maybe just one drink first."

He watched the red liquid splash into the glass. Lifting the glass to his nose he smelled the grape. The first drink washed across his tongue, and upon exhale he felt the warmth spread through his body. With the second drink he closed his eyes, and with the third all the pain, sadness, and fear departed. Jason sank into snug solace.

He followed the woman with fiery hair and emerald eyes into the domain of weeping love grass. Down below the rim they passed the grove of cottonwood trees under Capitol Peak and near Fortress Cliff where the hoodoos stood as little chimneystack sentinels atop rusty ridges silhouetted against a cobalt sky. Spanish skirts clothed the escarpments. Red claystone swirled with snowy gypsum and rose to meet lavender mudstone with bands of yellow and gray. A hawk sailed overhead under distant rumbling from the anvil cloud with shooting sparks. He followed her, always following the ginger luminescent hair as she broke through the salt cedar lining a creek bed, and he followed, crept, along a narrow ledge of rock holding to a sandstone wall. Passing through a narrow opening at the end of a sharp bend, they entered the realm of giants, a bowl-shaped expanse bordered on all sides by mudstone hills draped with the multicolored material of Spanish skirts. Throughout the hidden bowl realm, mudstone columns supported enormous sphere and egg-shaped granite boulders. She found a patch of clover dotted with tiny blonde flowers, and in this verdant bed he joined her.

He woke sometime late in the night. His arms seemed inoperative or somehow blocked, and after a brief moment of mild alarm he understood that he had become wrapped in the blanket from the bed and rested on the floor between the bed and the dresser. The struggle to free himself and the onset of guilt coincided, and he felt confusion upon seeing a half-full glass standing beside a nearly full jug of wine placed near an untouched collection of hors d'oeuvres. The nearly full bottle and the half-full glass presented an incomprehensible scene for Jason, and he stared at the bottle for a long time before moving about and searching for one or more empty bottles. He looked throughout the room, including under the bed and in the bathroom, but he could not find additional empty wine bottles. He looked again that the half-full glass, and then he touched first his head and then other parts of his body in disbelief. He seemed completely devoid of hangover-like maladies, and aside from the grumbling emptiness in his stomach he felt no discomfort. He looked again at the half-full glass and despite mounting evidence could not make himself believe that he had consumed only two, maybe three drinks, not even a half glass.

"This is some magic wine," he said as he poured the half glass back into the nearly full bottle. After capping the jug he touched his temples again in a futile search for the headache that must arrive after imbibing. "Unbelievable." First with one hand and then with both hands he sampled the food. Unable to comprehend the presence of leftover wine, he turned his focus to the food, and as soon as one hand emptied bread to his mouth another provided cheese. No nausea curbed his appetite, but lack of intake over several days reduced his capacity, and with a filling stomach he felt another calm coming. The calm spread over him, and he closed his eyes. Using his outstretched hands he felt his way back onto the bed before collapsing. "Unbelievable. Magic wine. Unbelievable."

It seems more and more like this town is for younger folk. Maybe my current ill health has me thinking this way, but in looking around more people seem younger than me than older. Ten years ago it seemed like a pretty even spread: some younger, some older, and most right about the same. Now it seems like the majority is younger. And in thinking about how much has changed in body and waist size, then the time seems far longer than a decade, but in other ways it seems like time passed in secret. Familiar people, friends have moved on to different locations and different occupations. Some even became parents. Time is a heavy thing to think about.

There's too much time for thinking when staying cooped up inside, but that's got to be done, especially with this infernal cough that won't go away. Outside there's too many opportunities for booze. But I'm just not one for bed rest. A fellow that spends too much time in bed has too much time for talking himself into taking a drink. And a fellow outside has too many chances for acting on thoughts of hooch. After something that happened recently, more time needs to get spent outdoors in this pretty town. Something happened that's still hard to figure out, something that never happened before.

Being in a position to allow good things to happen ain't easy these days. On top of this cough that won't go away, there's pain. It just showed up here recently, and it doesn't stay all the time, but when it's here it hangs out in my back and chest, and it makes moving and staying still uncomfortable. It's best to try hard to ignore the pain just like the cough because it's temporary, and I'm just biding time till it goes away. When I can get some time away from the cough and the pain, good things happen. And the one that happened the other day came out of nowhere.

Happy accidents live in this town. That's something that got forgot over time. After first arriving here with a puny nine hundred dollars and the feeling of being filthy rich, amazing happy accidents happened all the time. Up on Twin Peaks waiting for the fog to break and allow some good shots, a landlord with a nice place for rent and an interest in photography started a conversation. Or at Fort Point, shooting pictures of old architecture got interrupted by a bump and into an angel from Wisconsin. But some fun times didn't involve meeting other people so much as making discoveries, important ones I might not be able to completely explain. The one the other day was like that.

Sometimes these happy accidents begin with a mistake. The one the other day started with getting on the wrong Muni train. That morning had been one of those where the booze craving drove me nearly out of my mind. Fortunately, the cough stayed scarce, so using public transit could be done without scaring other folks with contagious hacking. Despite having some place to go, passing by all kinds of things that reminded of hooch just seemed to make everything miserable. In one spot, three saloons sat near just as many if not more stores that sold to-go hooch. The early morning meant the bars hadn't opened, but the stores had business aplenty. It ain't until a fellow can't have hooch till he notices just how many places there are to get it in this town. Surrounded on all sides by devil juice temptation is just the way of this place. Sometimes it's hard.

Walking had been the intention, but public transit offered a faster way to get to the destination as well away from the growing spirit obsession. Just on the other side of the street, the stairs for the Church Street Station dropped down to the start of the happy accident.

Sometimes the stations can be packed, like that early morning. Seeing all those people congregated in one place put me in mind of some apologies and explanations yet to be offered, and I felt bad, anxious. The dread of the apologies gave cause for far-off nerves, but the persistent cough hit a lot closer to home. It's impossible to put folks' minds at rest about wellbeing while hacking my head off. The explanations will be easier once the cough has passed and there's something better to show for life. Then again, the longer it takes to make the contact the more the deck is stacked against me. After all, if a fellow ain't on a bender, then there ain't no other excuse—not that a bender is a valid excuse for anything—for not making some calls.

Over the course of a year, or even ten years, dozens, hundreds, maybe thousands of folks in this town get on the wrong train or bus. I've done it. Drinking encourages some things, like getting on the wrong train or bus, but it can be done sober too, just like the other day. After two or three stops in the wrong direction, I got off the train and could have just stepped back on a train going the other way but instead left the station and came out in the land that time forgot. West Portal all tucked in behind the big hills gets forgotten, at least by me and by the look of the neighborhood time too. The word quaint comes to mind, and while looking at the storefronts that probably ain't changed in a long time thoughts of booze got run off. Other locales in this town stick out, but West Portal always strikes me and makes me wonder why I don't spend more time there. While thinking about that, thoughts of the original destination got pushed aside. Those thoughts came back after a cup of coffee, unusually good coffee, and then the idea to catch a bus came. Getting back on a train seemed backward, so while enjoying that extra good coffee I took a chance on a bus.

Heading due west when the original plan was to the north and east meant that the bus ride had further mixed up the morning, but the scenery kept me seated. After a time, the bus turned north on Sunset Boulevard, and that's when the cloudless blue sky and golden sun took hold of the morning. Up from the south, that bus cut right through the Sunset District and the bright painted houses. The pastel blues, greens, and even shades of pink complimented the bold sky blue and the green strip in the divided avenue. I thought for a minute that the bus might take me back east, and it did for a while, but then it cut up north again right through Golden Gate Park.

The park is always something to behold, a place where one second there's a crowded noisy city and then the next there's trees, hills, and lawns. A thousand acres, more than a section and a half, amounts to a big spread, even by the standards of the land where I come from. Just that short drive from south to north is enough to shake a fellow into paying attention for a second, or in the case of the other day, to let me forget again for a minute that the progress went the wrong way for the original destination.

Off the bus in the Outer Richmond, the original destination couldn't have been farther away short of leaving the city, so it was about then that I abandoned the original plan. Strolling west under the clear sky and morning sun made it hard to picture the place in its usual coat of grey fog. That grand morning made it easy to forget about planned destinations, aches, pains, and a never-ending cough, but it didn't quite yet allow forgetting the friends awaiting apologies and explanations. On that walk west, possible excuses sounded empty and false. The truth didn't sound much better, and the tally of days since last drinking didn't amount to enough to be impressive, and even if they did, I'd still have to explain the silence since. From any angle, the prospect of making contact seemed a shameful ride, and that put me in mind of the cough and the pains absent that morning and the hope that they had finally gone.

The end of Geary Boulevard really amounted to a dead end. The street stopped at a bus stop in front of a line of trees. From behind the bus stop, a path extended through the trees, and it would be through there that the wrong train mistake would turn into a happy blunder, maybe the best accident ever had. But I didn't go down that path right away. I sat at the bus stop thinking. What in the world could be said to friends to explain how a fellow this age could get so deep in a bottle? To me, that kind of thing has no sensible explanation, no reason at all. I can't very well tell the folks that I've completely lost my mind, but that's what it amounts to. At my age, a fellow ought to know what's coming from deep in that bottle, and so if the fellow goes there he either wants that ugliness or he's plumb crazy. I sure don't want no more of the ugliness, so where does that leave me as to why I do those things? I must be unhinged, but that ain't the kind of thing you can call out to friends that care.

No bus ever came to that stop, and whether I waited there a minute or an hour ain't clear. All I could think about for a spell stuck on how to explain the shambles, and that thought came only after giving up trying to think of new ways to hide the big mess.

The path behind the bus stop led through the trees for a bit and then joined a wider dirt trail. Off to the side of the dirt trail a statue stood in the oddest of locations. Usually statues seem to be located near something else, like a building. But this one stood there beside the dirt path and nothing else. It stood by itself, like it didn't have to help out some other attraction but more like it was its own attraction and maybe that dirt road came later just so folks could come and see that one single statue. But then farther down the path more statues stood proud like they too gave center to their own worlds. Maybe the sun that had climbed up overhead gave everything a more cheerful feeling, but I think the statues got me to thinking that everything would turn out all right.

Near one of those statues, the grass made a good place to sit. Nice stone benches here and there would have made better seats, but the grass offered the perspective of the statue. Looking up at the sky and sun until brightness forced my eyes shut, I thought about the town full of so many surprises. That first arrival years ago had been for a temporary job, but that plan didn't last long after crossing the bridge. Just a couple of hours, just long enough to find cheap lodging in the Tenderloin and then walk over to Union Square and then up Grant through Chinatown, was all it took to get me thinking about staying longer. Been finding ways to stay ever since. San Francisco may not be the easiest—certainly not the cheapest—but after being here even a minute it's hard to think about living anywhere else. So sitting there by that statue I figured that as long as I can remain in San Francisco, life can be as good as allowed and better than deserved.

Farther down that dirt path, the special moment happened. Before that moment, I speculated about the reasons for spending so much time alone. Compared to most folks, maybe more of my time had been spent alone. Shooting pictures amounts to a mostly solitary activity unless taking pictures of folks. Seems like I spend all spare time alone, and lately without the booze for company being alone ain't no kind of fun. But running out to be with people just to be with folks ain't my style. Even with bars, the main attraction for me was the booze, not the people. Spending all that time alone and not talking to anyone because of hiding out drunk or being ashamed of having been drunk or even because of this cough that won't go away just ain't no way to live. Still, it's kind of funny in a weird way. I used to avoid folks so they wouldn't know about the drinking, but now it's mostly cause of this infernal cough.

Somewhere along the way, the dirt path opened to a grassy park, and beyond that stood a bench and a cliff. Sitting on the bench and looking straight out west at the Pacific Ocean, I caught sight of gray lumps on the horizon. That part of the world generally stays bundled in fog, but some days like that beautiful morning get so clear that the Farallon Islands can see right up to the beach, up the cliff, and beyond to the city. There in that blue and gold clarity, the thought of booze came into my head. Starting off with the usual thinking about what juice would go best with that particular moment, the thoughts went off to the side and on a route never rode before. Thinking about what flavor of hooch would best pair with the morning, I hit upon the notion that any hooch at all would just flat ruin the whole beautiful happy accident morning. That was the exact word, ruin, that came to mind. Never, ever did I feel such a way, never even dreamed of such a state. That realization hit harder than any rotgut liquor. I just flat never could have imagined the feeling, and I sat there on that bench until the sun shone straight into my face and reminded me to head on back. The thought never occurred that there could be places so good on their own that any amount of alcohol could ruin them.

But since there are such places, I aim to find them.

So when that Angel of the darker Drink
At last shall find you by the river-brink,
   And, offering his Cup, invite your Soul
Forth to your Lips to quaff—you shall not shrink.

Beauty and Warmth

Two people waited in line at the coffee shop when Jason entered. He had decided that this day would be a day free of ethyl alcohol, but he had already violated that decision less than an hour after making it. A persistent cough warranted use of cough medicine, and Jason took several times the recommended dosage. The thick red juice quelled the cough, improved his mood, and steadied his hand long enough to shave, and Jason did look well as he entered the shop. He displayed a fine suit and a head of full hair, coiffured. No signs betrayed him as a shiftless inebriate, and he fancied he looked much like the bankers and lawyers and such across town at that very hour in the Financial District. He watched as the two in front of him told the cashier their desires, and he wondered if the cashier, the same cashier that had sold him dozens if not hundreds of bottles of beer, would be surprised when he requested coffee.

Jason did not get to make that request, at least not initially. When he reached the counter in front of the cashier, she had already stretched into a nearby cooler and fetched a green bottle. That bottle rested on the counter in front of Jason. While the cashier waited for payment, Jason stared at the bottle and tried to understand how the event fit into his plans for a sober and productive day. Telling the cashier he had planned to refrain from alcohol that day would be awkward, so he thanked her. He thanked her and he requested a coffee, and while he carried the coffee and beer to a table he laughed at the idea of a single beer derailing his plans for the day. A single beer amounted to a drop in the ocean of his usual consumption. The single beer would not spoil his plans to stay sober for one day and in no time at all completely change his life. Those plans would remain in effect, and he could still have the beer.

The morning had begun with Jason disappointed to find himself in a sullied hotel room and not in the dream oasis where his mind had taken refuge in the night. Instead of golden sunlight filtering down through a verdant leafy canopy and dancing on the water before and after the little waterfall in the brook, he parted stained curtains to see a grey grimy window and beyond to drab liquid grey skies oozing down soot-stained walls across concrete walks and curbs down into gutters where all grey combined to black. He knew he had to get out of that cell, and he began preparations immediately, but before finishing grooming and dressing, the unshakable aggravating cough robbed him of enthusiasm. A dose of the red cough syrup changed nothing. A second had seemed to help a little, so he took big gulps until half the bottle disappeared and the enthusiasm for change returned.

At the table in the coffee shop, Jason laughed about the need to fear beer, so he rose from his table to purchase another because during the consumption of the first in the cool green bottle he decided that he could stay with weaker beverages, beer, and the day would still progress as planned, a day away from the television in the darkened hotel room.

Stepping out of the coffee shop into Polk Gulch, Jason contemplated going a little north to Nob Hill or going south to the Tenderloin. He knew that the museums, places of color, indoor sanctuaries from the rain, did not open until later in the day. No cultural attractions awaited him in the Tenderloin, but the Tenderloin abounded in places to buy cheap booze, even just beer, and he could pass the time, maybe just a couple of hours, while he awaited the opening of the museums and the start of a new happy productive life. While he contemplated options, he walked south. Riding the wind, the rain accelerated from drizzle to stinging drops that came at near horizontal angles. Jason opened his umbrella and pointed it slightly ahead as he leaned into steps.

After a side step and a shake of the umbrella, Jason stood in a dank room with fetid air. Soon dim shapes of a bar, patrons on stools, and a bartender emerged from the clammy murk. Jason took care to tap his umbrella on the bar floor before he approached the bartender and the other drinkers, though he soon remembered he entered a place where no one cared about decorum. So long as patron behavior did not involve overt violence, no one cared, and each customer of that establishment, each serious and daily drinker, let bygones be bygones in the never ending quest to satisfy their own unappeasable thirst. Jason took a stool, ordered a beer, and smiled when the bartender presented a can. First the smell and then the taste took him back to other cheap barley pop in other cheap dives. The wrinkled and worn patrons soon put Jason in remembrance of a particular cheap joint, a dive that almost changed his course.

Oak Harbor had been on the north part of a long-stretching island Jason briefly called home. He had left the pastoral southern part of the island and headed north for the day to Oak Harbor to see and photograph a bridge. He had no recollection of seeing a bridge over something called Deception Pass, but he had the most distinct memory of a juice joint that nearly set him on a different path. Stale beer from the tap cost a pittance, and as Jason watched the other tavern customers in their craggy and crumpled visages downing pint after pint, Jason saw his future. He saw where he headed if he maintained his course. He too in a few years could be wrinkled, disillusioned, defunct, and moments away from final organ failure and death. The thought of a wasted life shook Jason, and he abstained from alcohol for three days or perhaps even a week.

Jason's Tenderloin beer tasted flatter and more soured as he again made a connection between the flotsam patrons and himself. He still had some time to go to achieve the facial lines and creases, but he had already achieved much of the puffy booze hound bloating, and he already had the dour outlook. The vision of decay and surrender sickened Jason. Before him he saw the social extension of the grimy life he led in his own filthy skid row hotel room. He saw everything he hoped to leave behind. Jason drained the remainder of his can in one large gulp, and he took long strides to the door, exited, and took definitive steps away from the dive.

A few blocks away, he found another tavern with cleaner amenities and fewer sleepwalkers seeking a reliable and even buzz. He paid more for a beer that tasted neither flat nor sour, and he thought about the new life he would soon embark upon as soon as he stopped drinking. This day he would drink just enough to get by, just enough to make things enjoyable. This day would be a day of color despite the rain. And after this day he could resume the life he should have lived had he not gotten sidetracked by all those other things, things he could not name, just ancillary stuff that got in his way. Others blamed alcohol entirely for Jason's trouble, but he knew the true culprit to be the ancillary stuff. Regardless of where the blame originated, with hooch or with side stuff, neither mattered because this day would be free of both. This day would be full of color, purpose, and hopefully continuity.

Thoughts of color and beauty combined with multiple rounds of beer that tasted neither flat nor sour, and Jason had visions of a place to the west, a spot of beauty on the northwest corner of town in an area called the Presidio. Jason recalled multiple treks through the surroundings with multiple partners, all beautiful. He had not visited the Legion of Honor in a long while, but it had once been one of his favorite escapes. He recalled when he first came to San Francisco, back when he still made photographs for a living. Visits to the museum rejuvenated Jason in the time before all waking moments had been spent with libations. Just as his present airy thoughts of the museum lightened, he rose and moved through the door of the tavern. The rain increased in intensity, but Jason floated on thoughts of beauty and color to the west, and he floated into another tavern. Along with pints of amber beer he had smaller glasses of clear liquid, and upon leaving that establishment Jason exuded the red-faced heat of a drunkard. Cold rain splashed on his face, but Jason kept his umbrella at his side while warm from the booze and lost in the remembrance of past museum visits. He stumbled over a curb into the street nearly colliding with a bus, and in doing so he found his route to the west. The welcome buttery gleam of the bus sign read 38 Geary, and Jason climbed aboard.

Uniform grey skies and unremitting rain fell as Jason exited the bus in Outer Richmond. He took no notice of the cold and damp while he walked first north toward the museum before changing his course to southerly and drawing upon his encyclopedic knowledge of the city's saloons. In yet another, Jason thought more about beauty and the upsurge in his feeling of well-being. Pint after pint flowed, and Jason wanted to perpetuate the wave of good feeling. On his way back north toward the museum he stopped at a liquor store and bought several ounce and a half bottles of vodka. His corpulent leanings made his suit too tight for concealment of contraband in pockets, so he carefully placed each little bottle inside his umbrella before closing it. Jason held his umbrella in various poses to ensure no bulges betrayed his blissful cache. Satisfied, he walked on while the rain soaked his hair and turned his suit a darker shade.

The normally glorious façade of the museum matched the gloom of the winter weather, so Jason marched past while yearning for the color inside. And once past the grand doors, he felt an instant and immense sense of relief, warmth, and happiness. That sensation lasted only until he had paid his admission and been informed that he must check-in his umbrella. As

Jason took the little pink rectangular ticket, he tried to mutter feeble reasons he could not check his umbrella, but instead he placed the ticket in the pocket of his suit jacket and staggered away into the majestic hall. His first stop featured an enormous painting that stretched from floor to ceiling and many feet laterally. Color abounded inside the frames, but Jason focused on the red until most all he saw had a red hue. The misappropriation of his umbrella vexed Jason. He could think of little else, and the thoughts seemed to displace his previous keen passion for color, art, and new beginnings. Red ire fixed in his mind, he began to backtrack with the intention of retrieving his umbrella and leaving, but another area called.

In the museum café, Jason ordered two glasses of pinot noir. He watched as the young woman poured burgundy liquid into stemmed glasses, and he thought about the theft of his umbrella. With both stemmed glasses in front of him, he took one, tipped it to his lips and consumed it all. While the young woman looked on in confusion, he dropped the first glass into a nearby trash can and reached for the second. He drained the second in the same fashion as the first before heaving it into the trash can with such force that both glasses broke. Jason then started to deliver an obscenity about umbrella thieves but instead uttered a loud belch. On his way to the exit he continued to mutter what formed in his mind as stinging insults but emerged as inebriate slurrings. Jason stormed out of the museum back into the rain with no umbrella.

Islands, strips of light, first on Clement then Geary then Balboa and then Geary again provided beacons. Trudging wet into one pub he stayed long enough for single sometimes double libations before meandering out into the street and stumbling into another saloon. If intoxication still permitted speech, he kept the mumblings to himself. Reverting to habit, his auto-drunk controls governed his time and intake in bars in order to avoid being ejected and perhaps banned. A curdling mood, too, prevented his speech, and while the alcohol made him impervious to damp cold, it also decayed previous hopes for productivity and happiness. The sky and his mind darkened. Insatiable thirst and occasional lighting from tavern fronts composed the only sensations. Devoid of thought and hope he walked from one humming neon to another. Passing tires sizzled across wet asphalt. Occasional visits inside to artificial light and artificial sustenance in clinking glasses with amber fluids gave nothing. Without feelings of desire, he drank down the caustic liquid and breathed up fire.

49

North Beach still offered vice but with much more light. Flashing, ever-present, and multicolored light signaled the presence of places of diversion. Inebriation dulled both sensation and wishes. His foot slipped a curb and stumbling out into the avenue headlights blared, horns blasted, and his legs tried to keep pace with his forward leaning until he grabbed hold of a light pole near the safety of the sidewalk but still in the wet spray from passing automobiles. Wet and getting wetter he ceased to care. Holding the pole he swayed and wanted to sleep.

Up a long hill he saw a shaft of light, a tower illuminated. The white-golden radiance of the cylinder beckoned, and he strode toward it until the street narrowed and gave way to steps. Wet concrete steps, hundreds of them, stretched up toward the beam of light, and with no other thoughts he stepped toward the glow. Step after step weakened his legs unable to balance, but still he trod upward. Rain spattered his face and blurred his vision. Blinking and straining to see through eyes that no longer focused, he reacquired the luminance of his target, Coit Tower, and took another step and then another. A slippery misstep sent him first leaning forward, and after overcompensated reaction he titled far back while the rest of the world surged forward beyond his grasp. Still, he reached out a hand toward the pillar of light and saw it arc past the tower and disappear against the black void above. With nothing left to see, he closed his eyes and surrendered. Back, back he leaned, and his feet left the ground. He no longer felt heavy as he passed on backward into blackness.

III. Peninsula to Peninsula

Indeed the Idols I have loved so long
Have done my credit in this World much wrong:
    Have drown'd my Glory in a shallow Cup,
And sold my reputation for a Song.

Into this Universe, and *Why* not knowing
Nor *Whence*, like Water willy-nilly flowing;
    And out of it, as Wind along the Waste,
I know not *Whither*, willy-nilly blowing.

El Camino Real

His mouth opened a piercing shriek, and muscles strained. Pain and swirling apparitions shaped to dimensions. "Comanches!" he shouted. Wraiths blended, some horses—some human, and again he shouted, "Comanches, don't scalp me!" Outnumbered he struggled while a voice, multiple voices, pleaded with Mr. Spearman to remain calm. But he would not be fooled. Jason knew the Comanche intent for one such as himself taken on their land. With all his might, he pressed his hands forward into the red dirt south of Adobe Walls to raise his prone body, but other unseen hands burdened his back, and while his shaking arms refused to give up the fight, a figure in white thrust a needle. Shadows faded, and the world became white, clean sterile white, and Jason sank first into a paper sheet and then into comforting dark slumber.

Auditory sensations came and went, but he had neither visual reference nor the will to strive to see. Sounds, perhaps voices, preceded faint shadows and a slight red hue before silence and black solace returned. With each cycle, the sounds and the shades grew in strength and length. The first attempt to open his eyes met with painful searing white. Fear grew to terror, and Jason raised a hand to shield his eyes. Something protruded from his arm, and with his other hand Jason felt a tube attached to a hard, discomforting object stuck into his skin. As he used his hands to try to block the bleached light, he saw silver metal rails on either side, and he saw a clear hose coming from his arm and extending somewhere beyond the metal rails and into the harsh white. Antiseptic smells filled his nose as he fought to comprehend.

Cautious assessment with as little physical movement as possible revealed Jason shirtless but otherwise clothed from the waist down. He found his suit jacket draped over the metal railing of the bed, but he could not see his shirt. Dried and crusty redness adorned his chest and neck, and reaching up higher Jason found his head wrapped and padded in bandages. The antiseptic smell intensified as did his pulse and breathing, but Jason fought the compulsion to panic as he unscrewed the hose where it connected to the hard metal object stuck into his skin. With the hose detached, he tried first to move his legs, but the metal railing prevented this, so Jason struggled with his arms to surmount the railing. With an abrupt thud he found himself on a cold hard floor, and all the breath left his body. Dazed pain and fear gave way first to little breaths. Again respiring and able to again open his eyes, Jason reached up to the railing and snatched his suit jacket. It fell onto him, and keys and wallet scattered onto the floor. Jason replaced the items in the suit jacket pockets and then discovered that he could stand despite the throbbing pain in his head. Shirtless and clutching his rolled up jacket under his arm, he took tentative steps into the painful blinding white light.

Jason heard a voice shouting sir, sir, sir! And Jason quickened his pace into the blind white-out as the shouting grew nearer. A dark rectangular portal lay ahead, and Jason smelled damp air devoid of the antiseptic. He neared the portal, passed through, and saw a paved lot with two ambulances and standing human figures. More voices joined the chorus of repeated utterances of sir and stop. With a burst of speed, Jason fled past the figures near the ambulances first onto one street and then via right angles onto others, always choosing the darkest path with the least overhead lights. When the voices faded, when Jason felt confident they had abandoned the chase, he stopped, leaned against a stone wall, and tried to endure the throbbing pain in his head.

Shivering Jason put on his suit jacket over his shirtless torso, and he tried to hold the lapel tight up to his neck. The walking path of least resistance led downhill, and ahead the sky lightened in early dawn. Jason tried to discern his whereabouts, and sometimes he thought he recognized places, but the effort to seize the memory produced first confusion and then an uncertain dread or fear of what misdeed he might have recently committed. Wandering on toward the dawn he tried to recall, but his throbbing dizzying head made him stop and sink to the sidewalk. A few people walked past and looked at Jason, but none spoke. Jason tried to glean clues, and he tried to read lettered signs, but his vision lacked acuity. The borders of letters bled into their backgrounds. When the discomfort of the cold surpassed the head pain, Jason stood, walked, and turned another corner.

His first concrete realization came as Market Street. He looked across the wide thoroughfare. Cars, taxicabs, and railed streetcars passed, and Jason knew Market Street though not much else. Trembling and staggering he crossed the street at mid-block amid honking horns and shouts. Leaving the loud street, Jason walked again into a place of blinding light and made his way through confusing aisles of wares and found himself standing before a rack of garments. He touched an orange hooded sweatshirt, felt the thick cotton fabric, and craved warmth. Wincing as the cloth passed his bandaged head, Jason wore the sweatshirt over his suit jacket. He stood shivering until a voice asked if he intended to pay for the garment.

Jason followed the figure with the voice to a counter with a cash register. He discovered that placing the hood over his head helped with the harsh white light, but he still found the transaction confusing. After handing his entire wallet to the figure with the voice, Jason turned to leave and walked back toward the relative darkness from which he came. Before reaching the door, he felt someone grab his arm, and he felt a jolt of pain where contact disturbed the metal object still stuck in his skin. Someone placed something into his hands, and when the pain stopped, Jason realized he held his wallet, some cash, and a white paper receipt.

While walking toward the gray dawn, Jason became aware of the rain, and he pulled the hood forward so it obscured the bandages covering his head and most of his face, his field of vision limited to a few square feet of the sidewalk ahead. The lingering dread that he had done something terribly wrong, something illegal and likely violent, haunted Jason, but it did not grow into an intact memory. Memories of any kind stayed scarce. Jason walked to gain distance from whatever he might have done and distance from the horror of the place with blinding light. During a stop for rest under a storefront awning, he discovered that the sweatshirt had pockets, and he placed his cold wet hands inside. Still, he could not discern the words on the front of the orange garment. Black raised lettering spelled two, maybe three words, but all Jason could distinguish were the letters S, A, and N on the right side of his chest.

As he progressed toward the dawn, more pedestrians passed, and they seemed to be moving toward a building surrounded by lights. Taxicabs lined one side of the building, and after much thought Jason uttered,

"Trains. The station." Entering the concrete building full of light and people, Jason saw many doors with many parallel sidewalks running alongside trains. He followed a group through one of the doors and boarded a train. Slumped in a seat and leaning against a window, Jason checked the hood to ensure that it obscured his face, and he shivered. The train moved, Jason felt less cold, and his eyes closed. Sometimes the train rocked side to side, sometimes it jerked to stop, and sometimes a voice sounded over a loudspeaker. In between these sensations, Jason passed back into dark slumber. He felt pressure on his shoulder and heard a voice, "Sir, last stop."

Again on a wet sidewalk under a dim gray sky, Jason saw people going and coming from a building. Taxicabs lined one side, and a line of buses bordered the other. Jason walked down the line of buses and followed a group of people onto one. Again slumped in a seat and turned toward the window, Jason fell back into darkness before emerging in Amarillo. He thought he heard a voice say the word "Salinas," but with eyes closed he could see outside the window, and he knew he looked east from Texas Highway 87. He muttered, "We'll pass the Canadian River Bridge in a little bit. I gotta find a way to get east." Jason tried to open his eyes with the intent of leaving the bus, but he sank back into darkness and warmth.

The bus stopped moving, and when Jason won the struggle to open his eyes, he saw the other passengers disembarking. He too left the bus, and he stood in a large triangular area surrounded on all sides by buses taking on or leaving passengers. Rain fell and once again Jason felt cold as he walked. He felt a moment of panic and wondered about his location, but just as soon as it had come upon him the moment left him and he walked on dazed but comfortable. The rain no longer felt cold, and Jason's desired only sleep. He walked across a bridge spanning a narrow body of water and beyond he saw the old black locomotive. As he neared the dark metal, he whispered the words "Dennis the Menace Park," and the sky cleared to pour sunshine on a lanky preteen girl in a soccer uniform and cleats standing atop the locomotive. Jason yelled, "Vixen, get off that thing in those shoes. You're gonna fall!" The girl ignored him and ran back and forth along the length of the locomotive. The sound of a bat cracking against a baseball in the nearby park caused fans to cheer, and the smell of hamburgers drifted from the concession stand. Jason laughed in the sunlight, and he looked around for the girl's brother. He could not see the boy, but he shouted, "Fink, tell your sister to get off that thing before she falls.

Fink?" When Jason looked back to the locomotive the cold rain had returned, and he saw just a dark iron behemoth dripping rain with no girl atop.

Weak and shivering Jason sat on a wooden park bench and tugged at his hood saturated with rain. "That was a long time ago. Ten years? Fink and Vixen are gone." Rain fell on the empty park and splashed into Lake El Estero. The pain in his head returned, and Jason labored to push himself from the bench and stagger forward trying to avoid the muddy puddles along the walking path. Back across the bridge he passed buildings with tile roofs spawning little rivers and waterfalls. The wetness came through his clothing to his skin, and Jason's teeth chattered. Another park with a lawn and trees and benches stretched on the other side of a cobblestone street, and Jason took short steps unsure of the slick footing over the wet stones. He found a bench under a tree and sought relief from the rain.

A wave of warmth spread over Jason, and once again the sky cleared. Birds sang, and a man sat next to him on the bench smoking marijuana and eating almonds from a bag. "You want to see something?" the man asked. Jason looked at the man, and he watched as the man removed a ball cap and placed an almond atop his head in an unruly mess of copper curls. "Now be real still and real quiet," the man said. The park filled with golden warm light. A bluebird landed on the man's head, took the almond, and flew away. The man placed another nut on his head, and another bluebird snatched the prize. A third stayed longer, and Jason could see that more than blue made up the color of the bird. A jet black beak and ebony eyes stood out from the blue feathers with tufts of white, and when the bird spread its wings to take flight, Jason saw an undercoat of brown or perhaps golden feathers. Jason laughed with glee, but when he looked back to the man hoping for another almond and bird, he saw only an empty wet bench under gray skies and a dripping tree.

The sensation of warmth gone, Jason moved again through the rain. When he approached the harbor, he thought for a short moment that he heard first the barking of sea lions and then the clack of bocce balls, but when he surveyed his surroundings he saw no other people in the plaza. The constant rain overloaded many of the buildings' drain gutters, and sheets of water cascaded from roofs to pavement. Jason recalled earlier feeling like he must travel east to get to home and comfort, so he walked in the direction he believed to be east, toward the part of the sky that seemed darker.

A Moment's Halt—a momentary taste
Of BEING from the Well amid the Waste—
    And Lo!—the phantom Caravan has reach'd
The NOTHING it set out from—Oh, make haste!

HPE 625

Yearning to the point of seeing he dreamt of citreous sun over lemon morning prairie, but his real eyes revealed glossed indigo darkness cut by passing automotive lamps. Ahead in the undefined black a green rectangle made ethereal intermittent appearances to coincide with the auto lamps. Always to the left, the wind arrived and brought the sound of nearby but unseen thrashing forces in a maw seeking to devour. Arms outstretched for guidance and balance he neared the green, and passing light revealed white words and confusion: Moss Landing.

Swirling colors, all in the rainbow, adorned the periphery, but the emblazoned peace sign dominated the side of the Type 2. When the side door of the Microbus moved to the rear, so did the peace sign, and the golden light within spilled out onto the wet asphalt. The old air cooled engine sent metronome regular puffs turned taillight cherry before merging with the undefined black, and the rain made a timpani of the Volkswagen roof while everywhere else the rain descended soundless and forgotten. Youth and warmth beckoned from within, and two, maybe three voices rose in friendly greeting above the music, music from childhood and before, music of love and harmony with lyrics idealistic celebrating life without conflict. Swishing arms clearing glass and blinking amber light kept time while unsure he took tentative steps toward the van.

An image from memory superimposed and blended with the image of the Microbus, and he said aloud though unsure, "The last known photograph." Two figures, one male and one female, stood beside a Volkswagen van with Texas license plates and a newly hand painted peace sign. The wet cold version overpowered the vision of an aged yellowing photograph, and again he heard the beckoning from within the box on wheels.

Pulsating amber light reflected from the wet pavement and illuminated still falling rain. The music from within grew from a distant undefined noise to something almost recognizable with a repetitive line, "I hum the miles where arroyos crack." Headlights tore a path through the rain, and occasional diamonds flared from the beams. The amber pulsating light and the searing white light of the headlights made him shut his eyes. He still heard the music, but his trembling limbs no longer carried him. Through closed eyes he saw the photograph, the last one known.

During many years of carrying the photograph, he never remembered where he had found it. It had always been there. Its existence predated his memory, and he learned early to keep the photograph and questions to himself. Grandparents appeared injured and unable to talk when he displayed the photograph, so he treasured it alone. Over time the attributes of fading color and winkles joined the paper print, and his childhood obsession to enter the picture began. Before he could drive a car, he pleaded with relatives and friends to drive him to the river breaks north and east of town because he had become certain that the badlands in the background, devoid of the white dolomite boulders but with the rich russet soil, must be those to the east. Many times he saddled horses and ventured east. Too far north along the river bed he fought quicksand. Too far south he faded into the flat treeless featureless plain between Isom and Panhandle, the domain of the antelope. The middle path, the treacherous route down into tributary valleys, up onto ridges and mesas, down again into rain cut ravines, ran through private lands, and to the consternation of county authorities and grandparents he became an expert fence cutter. He never found the exact spot, never found his parents, but he learned the river breaks.

Yearning to the point of seeing makes dreams of citreous sun over lemon morning prairie, but real eyes reveal glossed indigo darkness cut by passing automotive lamps. Ahead in the undefined black a green rectangle makes ethereal intermittent appearances to coincide with the auto lamps. Always to the left, the wind arrives and brings the sound of nearby but unseen forces thrashing in a maw seeking to devour. Arms outstretched for guidance and balance he nears the green, and passing light reveals white words and confusion: Moss Landing.

An orange man with a big head materializes in the van, and Travis giggles and points, "Man, your head is huge, man." Gracie tells Travis to

59

shut up while she closes the van door, and she takes a seat beside Joel who says nothing but looks from the orange man to Travis and back and might be laughing on the inside too except for fear of Gracie. She introduces, "My name is Gracie, and this is Travis and Joel."

Joel interjects, "Her name is Grace, but she thinks that's pretentious."

"I'll show you pretentious, you little maggot!" Gracie grabs Joel behind the neck and pulls him from the bench seat face-first to the floor where she sits on his back and lightly raps on his head with her bunched fist. "How do you like me now, Joel? Huh, stumpy?" Joel laughs and tries to cover his head, and Gracie addresses the orange man with the huge head. "Sorry about that. Sometimes these guys have no manners at all. I'm Gracie. My seat here is Joel. And Isabel is driving. Say hi, Izzie. We don't have to worry about Travis over there. He's tripping on acid, and I'm not sure he's with us right now."

The orange man gazes at Gracie and sees her long willowy frame and milky complexion at odds with the jet black hair. She hypnotizes him with her black pupils fringed by auburn hazel and circled by first jade then sapphire. She tells him to take off the orange, and he does, and all pause in discomfited silence and behold the helmet of gauze. The silent man formerly of orange has no shirt under his suit, but a dried rust crust adorns his ashen neck and chest. Gracie moves from atop Joel and commands Joel to replace the orange with a dry blanket. After draping a wool Native American style blanket over the man's shoulders, Joel hangs the orange sweatshirt by the hood and tries to spread the rest of the garment to speed drying. Joel asks, "You like baseball?"

The man does not answer, and Joel and Gracie exchange glances. Gracie inquires, "So where are you headed?"

"Freeland."

Again Joel and Gracie exchange looks, and Gracie asks, "Did you say Freeland?"

"Freeland. I don't remember passing Clinton. I don't remember the ferry. Freeland."

"We're going to Santa Cruz," Gracie says. "We came a long way. Have you ever been to Santa Cruz?"

The man does not answer. He stares ahead, expressionless at first, and then his gaze rests on an object near the hanging orange sweatshirt. The man's mouth opens as if to say something, but he closes it again, extends an arm, and points.

"You want your baseball hoodie back, dude?" Joel asks.

The man shakes his head and appears to smile. "Nikon FM2. Nikon FM2."

"Oh, that's my old camera," Gracie says. "It's broken. The arm thingy that makes the film move is jammed."

"Film advance . . . Film advance lever," the man says with growing delight. He points to the orange sweatshirt and says, "I get it now. I like baseball. San Francisco Giants. I remember now."

The man becomes orange again, and the orange man with a big head says over and over that he remembers as he dissolves and disappears.

Yearning to the point of seeing he dreamt of citreous sun over lemon morning prairie, but his real eyes revealed glossed indigo darkness cut by passing automotive lamps. Ahead in the undefined black a green rectangle made ethereal intermittent appearances to coincide with the auto lamps. Always to the left, the wind arrived and brought the sound of nearby but unseen thrashing forces in a maw seeking to devour. Arms outstretched for guidance and balance he neared the green, and passing light revealed white words and confusion: Moss Landing.

Two silver poles supported the green rectangle, and he extended wet shaking hands to grasp a pole and preserve balance. From both directions headlights followed the beams they projected, and some illuminated the green rectangle while others drew attention to the void beyond the road. The sound of wind and waves frightened him because he knew—for an instant—the water surged on the wrong side of the road for venturing to Freeland. He should have passed Clinton long ago at the top of a hill he never encountered, never climbed. The green rectangle presented the only tangible reality, and he grasped the pole with both hands while staring at the black void beyond the road, beyond the headlights.

Invisible rain soaked until blinding light assaulted his world. He shut his eyes and still saw painful red. First he released the pole with one hand and covered his eyes, and then he lost the second grip while stumbling backward stunned by the light. Away from the green rectangle swallowed by the light, he saw the source of illumination. A put-putting box with wheels and dual eyes and adorned with a hand painted peace sign targeted the green rectangle. The peace sign shifted to the rear of the box, and golden light fell from within to merge with the flashing amber light and turn the wet pavement into a luminescent multicolored pallet.

"The last one known," he said. After years of childhood and adolescent searching for a spot in the badlands, he turned his older, cleverer attention to the print itself. The square format with a wide depth of field revealed that the shot came from 126 film, likely from a fixed focus camera. The Agfa print paper revealed little in the way of pinpointing a date, but it did pique an interest in photo reproduction. For years, with every improvement, every new acquisition of gear, he did his best to faithfully reproduce the aging photo. In time, he had dozens and hundreds of images of a Volkswagen Type 2 with a hand painted peace sign.

And for years he studied the photograph for clues to his origin. He searched for similarities between his facial attributes and those displayed by the man and the woman in the photograph. Where he could see no evidence of emotion or thought, he inserted some. For much of his life he viewed the figures in the photo as a man and a woman, but later with his own aging he viewed the figures as a boy and a girl. They stayed eternally young while he aged, even though he knew what came soon after the scene in the picture. Their end came soon after his beginning, so he came to know them through stories told by mourning relatives looking for blame to assign. From the paternal side, blame rested on the girl who lured away their special boy. From the maternal perspective, the fault came from the boy with off-kilter political notions and a desire to go west. So they set out west seeking like minds and better climates, and they never came back except in the last known photograph. It was through that image that he came to know his parents.

Yearning to the point of seeing makes dreams of citreous sun over lemon morning prairie, but real eyes reveal glossed indigo darkness cut by passing automotive lamps. Ahead in the undefined black a green rectangle makes ethereal intermittent appearances to coincide with the auto lamps. Always to the left, the wind arrives and brings the sound of nearby but unseen forces thrashing in a maw seeking to devour. Arms outstretched for guidance and balance he nears the green, and passing light reveals white words and confusion: Moss Landing.

An orange man with a big head materializes in the van, and Travis giggles and points, "Man, your head is huge, man." Gracie tells Travis to shut up while she closes the van door, and she takes a seat beside Joel who says nothing but looks from the orange man to Travis and back and might be laughing on the inside too except for fear of Gracie.

The orange man with the huge head grins and says, "Nikon FM2! I remember."

Gracie takes the camera by the strap and hands it to the orange man. His grin widens to a genuine smile as he turns the camera over and inspects the exterior surfaces. "I had one just like this," he says as he removes the lens and then opens the back of the camera. He tries the film advance lever, but it moves only a little before stopping firm. "I see what you mean. Got some kind of jam here." He places the camera in his lap while he digs in his pockets before producing a coin. "Let's see what we can do here." On the bottom of the camera he works with the coin and then moves the film advance lever before tripping the shutter. He does this three more times. "Yep, I think we got it fixed. Mine had the same problem once. The autowinder got things out of whack, and when I tried to use it without the autowinder it jammed just like this one."

With the camera in his lap, the orange man's head nods and his eyes close. Gracie asks if he's all right, and his head jerks upright and spreads a smile. He holds the camera up and says, "I remember! I had one just like this one. It was with me in Mexico when I got those gems, those three little gems. I was lost on a dirt road trying to find my way back to Lajitas, and I saw them up ahead. I grabbed for the right lens, and it happened to be on the FM2. I shot two maybe three times at the three little girls on that yellow sandy dirt. They didn't have no shoes. Just those dresses and their raven dark hair. One was green and one was red and one was blue. Little gems. Gorgeous little barefoot jewels. I remember."

His eyelids droop, his head nods, and the camera falls to the orange man's lap. Gracie touches his shoulder, and he says, "I'm so tired, so tired, but I remember." The man pulls items from his pocket, including a wallet and a hotel room key. He looks at a card from the wallet and says, "Yep, that's me. I remember." Struggling to focus his gaze, the orange man looks at Gracie. "You're an angel. Beautiful." Again the orange man searches his pockets until he finds a pink rectangle of paper. "This is a claim ticket. Take it to the Legion of Honor." The orange man gives Gracie the ticket. "Take that to the museum, and they'll give you a fine umbrella. It'll go great with your hair."

The orange man begins to fade. He smiles, his eyes droop shut, and as his head nods and sinks toward his chest he diminishes and then rises as orange smoke. As he drifts in a long carroty trail out a partially open window, he says over and over, "I remember now. I remember."

It must have been about a ten-day adventure. Rent at the skid row hotel had been more than a week paid up front, but it fell three days behind by the time I got back and saw some ire in the face on the other side of that half door and metal grate. Seemed like the slumlords was fixin to haul my stuff out of the room and pitch it. That sort of thing must happen a lot in places like that grimy hotel.

But my bunk ain't in Polk Gulch no more. Being banged up and not too sure my brain worked right meant a need for a little better, cleaner at least, place to stay, so I found a new place over in SOMA. And the spot has a dandy view. The window faces Howard Street right near 5th Street, and out the window and up the hill north or northwest the big buildings downtown stick up in the sky. Might be something to behold in summer fog season, but that's a long way off, and for now I'm just glad to have some break in the rain. Seemed like it rained forever, but it's mostly clear now, though a little too cold to call comfortable.

How it all came down is still a mystery. Regular thoughts and such came back at the hospital in Santa Cruz, but disagreement over the details remained. In fact, my version of events got me an unwanted but probably necessary extra three-day stay. When the docs had almost decided to turn me loose, somebody got interested in the kids I asked about so goodbyes could be said. Me getting irritated about them saying the kids didn't exist caused extra interest. They claimed not to know no such folks as a black Calvin, no Filipino Marvins or Lesters, and no Mexican Julio. That caused me considerable vex, at least when single subjects could be remembered and understood for more than a minute or two. But the hippie kids most probably fetched me that extra three-day stay in the booby hatch, and I stayed pretty bent out of shape and mad about it while there, but in looking back and seeing the situation from the doctors' view it had to be the safest thing to do, and I'm thankful even though no such thing got said at the time.   The craving for alcohol is still here, but the shaking is gone, so I'll get by. For now, staying off the hooch will be easy cause I'm still scared. There's a strong feeling that things come real near an end, like I might have been done in to death, but somehow that didn't happen, and now is the time for being careful. My head still ain't working right. It's more than a half-bubble off level most of the time, and the hooch, as much as I pine for it at times, would probably be enough to do me in for good. Now ain't the time to be taking no chances. And then there's the cough that just won't go away. The docs at the hospital down in Santa Cruz offered to look into the matter of the cough more than once, but at the time getting out of the hospital seemed more important than any kind of cooperation. Now it seems like the cough has gotten worse, and that scares me.

So that, fear, is a big feeling right now, but so is sadness. Just like they said those hospital kids didn't exist, the docs also said the hippie kids didn't exist. They didn't come right out and say the hippie kids wasn't real, but when they said their records of how the situation ended up at the hospital in Santa Cruz differed a considerable amount from my story, that's pretty much the same as saying the hippie kids wasn't real. The doctors kept saying that some cops or deputies found a fellow wandering in Watsonville, and an ambulance toted him to the hospital. That ain't the way I remember it, but in the interests of getting out of the nut house a fellow sometimes has to go along and stop asking about hospital kids or hippie kids. And that made me sad. Anybody that says bad things about the kids of today don't know the same kids. They saved me.

When my head is right and not gazing off yonder at nothing, the biggest thing felt is shame. The more pieces of what might have happened that come together, the heavier the shame. Turns out, the advice from countless old timers that a fellow can crawl so deep in a bottle that he can't get out is true. And it turns out, under all them bandages twenty metal staples held together the back of my scalp. I got so deep in a bottle that I broke my own head. Them staples didn't feel like much going in—at least not in a clear memory—but every single one caused all kinds of pain coming out. Those strips of metal could have got took out at the same hospital that put them in, but the shame at that first hospital piled up into a mountain, even though the memory of being there ain't too sharp. Over across the bridge at a hospital in Oakland a pretty blonde doctor took some pliers and did away with them twenty metal staples forming a question mark on the whole back of my head.

Despite the headaches, scattered memory, and the scar, it seems like the knob will hold together, and eventually hair will cover the scar. My head will look regular, but it still don't seem to work normal. So every day has to be took real easy. Sometimes a strong urge says to rush out and get back to work right away to somehow make up for lost time or even to show some remorse for all the trouble, but for now my head ain't right, and it has to take it easy. There ain't much to do other than sit and look out the window or maybe watch TV. Most entertaining things require some sort of attention, and there ain't no attention to spare. A time or two of trying to see shows didn't amount to much because the mind drifted and lost the trail of what went on with the characters on the screen. Reading more than a few words at a time without losing interest don't seem possible. So the only thing to do comes down to walking when the cough ain't so bad that it keeps me inside, and the new neighborhood has the best paths for slow walking. SOMA lays flat, not Panhandle flat but flatter than the rest of town. When nothing else comes to mind, which is most days, there's the Mission District and Mexican food. It ain't TexMex, but it's cheap, and it keeps me full.

The hardest part of every day is the shame. Shame comes from all directions. There's the general drunkard shame from things remembered clearly as well as them hazy thoughts of embarrassing things that might not have happened but probably did. Sometimes adding up all the people put out by my idiot adventure gets me down and real sad. There must have been folks that saw the fall or my crumpled bloody outcome. Then there must have been folks that got me to the hospital and folks in the hospital before the running off to who knows where on the way to Santa Cruz. And then there was all them folks, real and imagined, at the hospital in Santa Cruz.

All that's bad, but it ain't the worst of the shame.

Usually having no family means that nobody finds out about the dumb boozer things. And my friends, the closest thing I got to family, don't know about this most recent wreck. But then they don't know much about me at all anymore. I ain't made no calls in months, and I been dodging their calls for just as long. The plan was to call after getting some time away from the bottle, but after this busted head and with this cough going on, there ain't no chance to make no calls. Thinking about them folks hearing the way my life has turned out is so heavy that it just crushes me and pushes out everything else. Sometimes the coughing and the pain gets me scared and makes me miss the folks even more than usual. Maybe it's those times that I feel the saddest about the docs saying that the hospital kids and hippie kids didn't exist.

In that hospital in Santa Cruz, I didn't know what went on at first, but while coming and going from sleep to almost awake somebody, one of those kids, always seemed near. That kid Calvin loved his television basketball, and he explained the teams and the players. Mostly we'd talk about basketball, but sometimes he'd tell me about growing up in Oakland. One time he told me about a favorite uncle from Texas. This uncle of Calvin's was a dipsomaniac—Calvin's word. One time he came up some stairs at a BART station in downtown Oakland, and up top in a nearby park some Chinese women did their slow motion karate dancing the way they do, and they said the same word over and over. Calvin's hungover and probably still drunk uncle was absolutely sure those young women chanted a word that to us means a specific part of a woman's body. Calvin laughed real hard when he told me that story, and hearing it did wonders for my attitude.

Getting out of the rubber room might not have happened if not for that kid, Julio. He didn't have preferences for television but instead always had his college books. That kid was smart, a real strategist. His idea convinced the doctors to turn me loose. When the docs talked about their concern over my drinkin, I showed them brochures for folks who want to stop imbibing and promised to visit each and every one at least once before taking another drink. It must have worked because they let me go.

Those Filipino kids helped a bunch too. They worked the night shift. Marvin taught me to play a kind of card game, a kind of poker called Texas hold 'em. His cousin Lester came from a tougher background. He told me stories about stuff he had to do to get away from crime and such popular with his running buddies. He said he had a wife and a daughter, but none of them kids looked old enough to be a parent. Even after thinking over and over about them hippie kids and them hospital kids, it's still a mystery why they acted so kind to an old burnt out drunk. I told the docs what they wanted to hear, but really there ain't no doubt them kids was real. Things can't be imagined any other way.

Some things remembered can't be real, but that doesn't stop me thinking about em. While in and out of my mind, some lines, lines maybe from a song or something, kept running through my head at the same time as a picture of a place that looked like Tule Canyon. Driving on some road alternately paved and dirt I passed through narrows with giant red rocks stretching from the canyon floor to the sky, and it put me in mind of the part of Tule Canyon off Highway 207 northwest of Silverton and east of Lake Mackenzie. The tune of the song sticks with me just as much as the scenery, but of the words all that stays on is "I hum the miles where arroyos crack." There's no telling where the vision came from or why it sticks with me even now.

Shame is the main thing felt, but it stays at odds with something new: loneliness. Booze kept me from feeling lonely while wallowing in self-pity and feeling sorry for reasons that seem downright stupid now. It's like back in little league baseball or some sport when one of the other kids got hurt. If the kid cried, a coach came over and yelled, "Git up and git back in the game or I'll give you something to really cry about." After all that boozin and moanin I finally gave myself something to really cry about. It might be a little bit funny except for the shame. And it's the shame that keeps me from being around other people much. Talking to anybody makes the shame sharper and heavier, so it's best to avoid conversation. To me, it's obvious that I'm just a screw up drunkard, so they must see it even clearer. The thing to do is keep to myself and when the cough ain't too bad to pass the time with walking.

Still though, it's hard to go a whole day without speaking to anybody. There's always a need to go to the store for something, and there's two little stores close by. One is run by a Chinese couple and the other is run by a Middle Eastern, maybe Arab couple. Both those stores stand just around the corner from my new place, and they might be the only stores in town where I've never bought booze. One day in the Arab store I didn't have the right amount of money for the goods on the counter, mostly candy to take the place of alcohol. I was fixin to put some back, but the Arab fellow behind the counter said not to worry about it and to just bring it next time. Maybe that sort of thing is still common back in rural Texas, but it sure ain't a regular occurrence in this city. For some reason, that fellow's kindness made me feel the shame even worse. And over at the Chinese store another thing happened. Almost every visit includes buying buttermilk. It's one of those cravings that came after giving up the strong drinks. At the cooler, no buttermilk stood behind the glass. Maybe that caused a sad look on my face because the Chinese lady yelled something real loud and real fast at her husband in the back of the store, and buttermilk got to the counter before I did. It took a whole bunch of determination not to drop tears right then and there. That nice Chinese lady mistook the fellow that needed the buttermilk for a decent person.

Things like that make me want to be as nice to people as possible. Right now, the nicest thing is stay out of people's way and get myself back together. So when going out for walks it's important to look respectable. That will do for now, but one of these days I'll have to face the shame and call the friends who've been neglected and hid from for so long. Apologies and maybe somehow explanations will be necessary, but then this situation don't got much in the way of a complicated explanation. Drunken stupidity is the explanation. But that's too much to face now. So I'll lay low, stay out of people's way, and get well. Then I'll get back to work and see if anything can be fixed. In the meantime I'll walk, just walk.

The Moving Finger writes; and, having writ,
Moves on: nor all your Piety nor Wit
    Shall lure it back to cancel half a Line,
Nor all your Tears wash out a Word of it.

Equinox

Jason looked at a card resting on the dinette next to the big jug of magic wine, and he wondered when he last saw a postcard. It used to be that he saw them often and even sent a few, but in more recent times with the adoption of computer communications worldwide he saw less and less until he forgot them. The one on the table displayed Jason's name and address in beautiful calligraphy, and in turning it over Jason viewed again the hand-drawn image that had amused him ever since he received the card. In the foreground, a man in a suit delivered a sly smile and a wink while gesturing toward a long-haired man wearing a poncho and a peace sign. Photographers surrounded the man in the poncho, and the Golden Gate Bridge and the Transamerica Pyramid held prominent places in the background. "Thanks, Bobrick," Jason said while returning the card to its place by the magic wine.

The early hour complicated Jason's plans for the day, though his plans consisted only of getting outdoors in the city. The cough that had plagued him persisted, though it seemed to wax and wane in severity. He intended to get out as soon as possible, but he knew few establishments would be open for business for at least another couple of hours. Still, he looked forward to getting outside. The weather had been pleasant for a long stretch of days, and Jason found staying warm easier, but the more the weather improved, the more his coughing ailment seemed to worsen. He could not recall ever having an infirmity that lasted so long. Each day Jason expected an improvement, and when the recovery did not happen he thought it would follow the next day. Fresh air and sunshine would provide the cure. Though sunshine remained hours away, fresh air could be had as soon as Jason departed the residence.

Before reaching the door, he extracted keys from a jacket pocket, and he looked at the oddity of a keychain. He had been given the keychain when he rented the unit, and he had intended to replace it because he thought the practice of walking around town with a clearly labeled key to a residence an imprudent custom. A palm-sized green plastic shamrock displayed in faded gold lettering Chrystal Rose Bungalows and the address including the unit number. He wondered why a shamrock advertised the apartments. Perhaps rose shaped fobs had been unavailable. He also wondered about the use of the term bungalow, since that meant separate structures, but perhaps the fact that the units each had outdoor access was enough in the crowded city to merit use of the word.

Well before dawn he turned the corner to pass first the Chinese store then the Arab store. Turning northeast he used a narrow alley as a shortcut to 4th Street and a coffee shop that opened before the rest. With steaming coffee and no destination, Jason stood alone at a dark and quiet intersection. Commuters had not yet started to crowd the sidewalks, and automotive traffic had not yet become fierce and noisy. A slight breeze felt cool, and Jason looked to the east, but no signs of the coming dawn lightened the sky. With no destination, Jason moved southeast along 4th Street. He enjoyed the coffee and turned a corner.

The earliest signs of dawn came as Jason neared the ballpark. The northwest facing portion of the park presented a wall of brick red. Nearby to the southwest, the train station and yard prepared for the morning rush. Locomotive engines and floodlights drew in the first commuters. The light before dawn revealed few clouds, and Jason continued touring the streets of SOMA without any planned goals. Inside a tavern not yet open for business, antique motorcycles hung from the ceiling and occupied prominent places near windows. He remembered his more reckless days of two-wheeled transportation, and he recalled how the choice between booze and motorcycles meant the end of his riding days. Jason also recalled his more reckless days of imbibing at that particular tavern. He looked from a vintage Harley-Davidson to an even older Indian, and he smiled a little before moving on.

The abundance of large red brick buildings amid the newer construc-tion betrayed the district's history as a light industrial and warehousing area. Florists, bakeries, dry cleaners, and the like occupied portions of gargantuan stone block structures that once held items of larger, heavier, and dirtier natures. In another repurposed structure, high-priced residences portioned an old factory with smokestack still intact into lofts for the affluent with eccentric tastes.

By the time the sun passed the horizon, Jason stood across the street from a drab gray building. He stood and looked at what he regarded as possibly one of the ugliest buildings in the city. The concrete structure appeared to have been built by an unimaginative child using gloomy blocks, and the entire lackluster gray bulk seemed devoid of color. Despite its ugliness and resemblance to a fortress or prison, Jason had a fond sentimental regard for the drab gray building. It held a special place in his personal history.

A sign above a row of windows read Transbay Transit Terminal, and Jason chuckled as he remembered first setting foot in San Francisco. Many years earlier, Jason had arrived on a bus in Oakland. The driver had told the passengers the break would be short, so Jason left the bus and stood outside the station in Oakland for fifteen minutes. Warm, sunny weather just the sort Jason expected in California held on the east side of the bay. Shortly after the bus departed the station, it reached the Bay Bridge, and Jason saw The City for the first time.

As he sipped his coffee that morning and remembered a summer afternoon many years previous, Jason recalled that the bus had released the passengers inside the building, and he had come outside, just past the monolith that still stood ahead of his position across the street. He looked at the monolith with the pointed top, and he laughed while thinking about his wardrobe wholly unsuited for the climate. While he had brought a lot of luggage, almost all the space had been occupied by cameras and other photographic equipment. As he recalled, he had brought a couple of pairs of jeans, a couple of shirts, and that one second-hand tweed jacket just in case he ever had to dress up. Jason's laughter turned to coughing, but once he regained composure, he remembered that he had heard that the building before him, the Transbay Terminal, his spot of arrival, would be demolished. A moment of melancholy seized Jason as he thought that the end of the building's existence somehow also marked an end for him. He thought the destruction of the building much like the burning of boats or bridges. If the portal granting city access and exit must be destroyed, at least at the time of destruction Jason stood on the right side of the portal and remained in the city. The sobering thought ended the laughing for a moment, but Jason thought again about his first arrival, and he thought about his first words to the locals.

After carrying his luggage outside the building to the monolith, Jason asked a nearby police officer where to catch a taxi. Jason also asked, "Is it always so cold here?" The police officer simply laughed at the question. The cab driver responded with another question, "Have you ever read Mark Twain?" Jason continued asking the same question, until a man who gave Jason keys to lodging in the Tenderloin answered, "Yes. It is always this cold here." With that information and with his luggage safely stored, Jason put on the second-hand tweed jacket and began walking in the new city.

He had a camera with him that first day as he always had a camera nearby back then, but Jason could not remember having taken a single shot. He had been so captivated by the new city that he strolled on in wonderment. His first pass up Market Street from the Civic Center toward the Financial District also gave Jason his first introduction to the summertime fog. The world had been brilliant blue when he arrived, but minutes later the sky had turned a grey-white chalky mix, and mists of fog floated between the tall buildings and wraithlike hovered over sidewalks and streets. Turning off of Market Street, Jason soon found himself in the expanse of Union Square flanked on all sides by retail establishments.

From Union Square, Jason found Grant Avenue, and he hiked until he saw a roofed gate at the corner of Grant and Bush. Staying on Grant, he passed under the gate into China. On either side of the narrow street, scores of retail stores and restaurants crowded each block, and Jason passed by occasionally touching his camera but never lifting it to obscure his view. Block after block, curio shops bordered restaurants and often supported second stories with residences or other commercial establishments. The density of people and things in Chinatown seemed higher than anyplace Jason had ever encountered, and he marveled at the complete lack of wasted space.

Wet chalk air had not been an image that Jason expected when he decided to take a job in California, and as the fog increased onward up Grant Avenue Jason found the same excitement he experienced at an earlier age when visiting amusement parks. Just as he had not known what ride or attraction lay ahead in the parks of his youth, he had no way of knowing what the next block of Chinatown might offer. And so when Chinatown came to a subtle end, Jason had not noticed the exact spot, but he thought it had been somewhere around the last wide street he crossed. On one side of the large street, the usual sights of Chinatown, including dragons and Chinese letters, had been intact, but once across the street traits of Chinatown ceased. Some buildings and other structures such as light poles displayed small Italian flags.

A distinct absence of flat ground amazed Jason. Side streets flowed up impossible inclines, and the foundations of buildings followed those same lines. Like in Chinatown, the premium put on space in North Beach left no square inch unassigned. Streets narrowed, and the bay windows on so many of the buildings jutted out over sidewalks. Fog flowed down streets and turned in swirl and eddy investigating even narrower side streets and alcoves. Along a broad avenue, fog shrouded a bookstore, and farther along the avenue cut through a park with a tall church on the north side. Twin church spires rose and disappeared into the fog.

The chill of the fog prompted Jason to enter one of the stores that displayed the Italian flag, and once inside he smelled the warm aroma of roasting coffee beans. A tall woman with long dark hair, dark eyes, and slender angular features captivated Jason. He stood and gazed at the woman unable to speak, and the woman returned Jason's smile. He caught another glimpse of those mysterious sable eyes when she handed him a tiny ceramic cup on a tiny saucer and a tiny paper cup with a tiny spoon. Jason took his gelato and espresso to a little table near a window, and he looked out at the fog floating over Columbus Avenue. There at that little table with Italian coffee and ice cream, Jason had worked with a pencil and paper and begun to plan ways to remain in the city beyond the dates for his contract work.

Standing before the Transbay Transit Terminal in the early morning light, his coffee no longer steamed, but he could still taste that espresso from many years ago. He could not taste the gelato, but the idea of gelato beckoned, and he wondered if places in North Beach sold ice cream so early in the morning. He thought surely they must have it available even if people did not customarily order it for breakfast, and he turned away from the drab gray building while thinking about North Beach. Jason stopped and tuned back toward the Transit Terminal, and he wondered if that would be the last time he saw it.

Near Market Street the wind picked up, and Jason had to lean while wondering whether to go back down Market to Grant Avenue or simply to continue up Front Street and later try to find a way to get a few blocks west. He chose the Front Street route, and when he reached the midway point across Market Street the sudden urge to cough surprised Jason. It surprised Jason in its abruptness and force. The coughing that morning had been milder than previous days, and Jason continued to hope for the signs of recuperation. This bout of coughing marked a departure from any course of improvement, and once across Market and safe on the sidewalk Jason extended an arm to brace against a building. The coughing continued, and Jason hacked into a handkerchief while growing ever more exasperated at the coughing's persistence and refusal to be satiated. The clanging bells of a vintage railed streetcar concealed the sound of Jason's insistent barks, and while he caught his breath for a moment he looked up Front Street to the giant Financial District buildings and then back across Market into SOMA. He thought perhaps that morning did not present the best time to go in search of Italian ice cream, and so he continued along Market Street.

Sometimes Jason's desire to take in air conflicted with his body's desire to expel air, and Jason felt as if he choked or drowned while he coughed and coughed, and he could not understand why the hacking would not stop and allow him to breathe. Muscles in his back cramped, and a stabbing pain assaulted his upper right chest. Jason held his left hand to his chest and tried to cover his mouth with his right hand and a handkerchief. While coughing, Jason felt something collide with the handkerchief. When he removed the handkerchief from his mouth and looked, he froze. Before he could contemplate his disbelief, another bout of coughing seized control of his whole body, and Jason sank to his knees on the Market Street sidewalk. In brief moments in between coughs, he removed the handkerchief from his mouth and looked. He could not understand what he saw, and he doubted the reality of what he saw. Gasping and teary eyed between coughs, Jason stared at the handkerchief and whispered, "Oh no. Oh no . . ."

IV. Sanguine

Heav'n but the Vision of fulfill'd Desire,
And Hell the Shadow from a Soul on fire,
   Cast on the Darkness into which Ourselves,
So late emerged from, shall so soon expire.

There was the Door to which I found no Key;
There was the Veil through which I might not see:
Some little talk awhile of ME and THEE
There was—and then no more of THEE and ME.

Lazaretto

The first seventy-two hours passed without holdup or creeping monotony because fear had overpowered impatience. Since then and the lack of a positive result to the skin test, time had crawled. Dread of the seventy-two hour mark had sped time, but longing for escape seemed to stop time altogether and made Jason wonder if he would ever get the all-clear, even though that breakthrough, if it came, remained at least another day away.

A graying sky betrayed the coming dawn, but streetlamps remained on. Jason looked through the window and saw the parking lot attendant still in the closet-sized box near the entrance to the lot, but later that attendant would abandon the box and stand near the gate directing traffic as he did every morning. The kitchen light of the ever-present neighbor had come on a couple of hours earlier, as it did every morning. Traffic and the associated noise increased as it did in the hours and minutes before daylight. This morning, like the several preceding, opened on schedule and with the false promise of adventure, false for one cloistered and ill. Jason had come to resent the dawn. At some point anger had replaced fear. In the previous days, Jason had observed every detail of the mornings because he feared his last morning might occur soon. But later Jason resented the dawn that taunted him with sunlit visions of outdoor splendor.

Since that first instance when he thought he saw the tell-tale sign of death, calamity, or at least consumption, all of Jason's priorities and concerns had been reordered. He thought he worried about drinking, yet in the time since the arrival of the gruesome symptoms he had not seriously considered imbibing. Jason also believed that he owed some friends apologies and explanations, but since the confinement the unease and dread he felt at the idea of having to explain his life, his shortcomings to friends seemed a small trifle by comparison to the prospect of a grave illness. All of these sources of anxiety had been replaced with fear, which evolved into resentment over confinement.

The visit to the hospital came after a period of dread and doubt. The walk there had been easy enough, and he had been treated well while there. But making the decision to go and then following through had been the hard part. In Jason's experience, hospitals came in two forms: the emergency room where throughout his life he had gone or been taken for brief repair visits, and some other entrance where people went in but never came out. They went, stayed in a bed for a time, and then died. All of Jason's relatives had gone that way, so he had gone to the familiar and safer emergency room. Since then, he spent much time in quiet observation.

The abundance of time allowed Jason to get to know one of his neighbors. Though he had not spoken to the man, Jason probably came to know the man as well as anyone, for the man never seemed to go anywhere. He remained always at his residence. Early in the morning before dawn, the glow of lights behind a curtain and shades marked the start of the neighbor's day. From mid-morning until noon, the man sat in a chair just outside his apartment door. Sometimes he read a newspaper, sometimes he drank coffee, and sometimes he did both, but every day he sat in the chair just outside his apartment door, and he did so at nearly the same time every day. Jason thought about his own condition of confinement, and he thought how he longed to leave his own apartment. He could not imagine choosing to stay in the same few rooms every single day, and he wondered what kind of person could endure such an existence, but the man's physical attributes gave no clues. The man appeared average. He stood at average height, he had a typical middle-aged man's haircut, and he wore clean clothes that fit, though nothing about them could point to a preference for a particular style or even color. The man seemed like a ghost tied to a particular place.

Jason, too, seemed like a ghost. He spent most all his time looking through a window at a world he yearned to join but could not. In the first three days, the prospect of release had been overshadowed by the fear of alternatives in the opposite direction. Not until the third day had passed and no reaction to the skin test had developed did Jason begin to form plans. The first plans came as lists. Jason had lists that required visits to grocery stores, dry cleaners, cobblers, and various other merchants and providers of services. The lists mimicked the string of tasks he performed back when he had been a regular, productive person, the type of person he hoped to become once again.

After the initial appearance of the gruesome symptom, he had been so shocked that he doubted his own perceptions. He slept little that first night. Each cough, no matter how slight, merited close inspection. But two days passed without cause for fear except for the constant coughing. Nothing troubling came with the coughing. And then on the third day, when he had dismissed the first occurrence as a product of imagination and fatigue, the symptom returned and came in such abundance to remove doubt. The evening had passed with little coughing, but during the night Jason felt as though he could not get enough air. He went for a walk hoping he could find breath easier outdoors. Violent coughing returned, and it brought confirmation of the symptom. Jason had stayed in his apartment the entire next day. First fear for himself and then fear of being a carrier of something deadly paralyzed Jason. He knew he must seek help, but the prospect of visiting a hospital frightened him nearly as much as the shocking new symptom. The chance of infecting another person frightened Jason the most, so he made plans to visit the hospital.

He relied on three handkerchiefs. Two rested in his hands or in side pockets for quick access. The third he tied around his face in bandit fashion. Early morning before dawn had seemed the best time to walk to the hospital and encounter the fewest people en route, so he had left well before dawn. He kept to the least traveled streets and alleys as much as possible, and he took frequent breaks. As he neared the hospital and delayed entering for a bit, he felt self-conscious about his homemade mask, but the emergency room staff showed no reaction. Before he described his problem verbally or on paper, Jason had asked for a surgical mask, and the nurse behind the counter showed no reaction while she provided the mask. It seemed to Jason that the request must be commonplace.

Wearing a surgical mask and feeling less embarrassed, Jason tried to describe the reason that brought him to the hospital. He mentioned the persistent cough, and he mentioned the latest symptom. That latest symptom had been the one he most worried about, but the hospital staff received the news in much the same way as if he had delivered a weather report. They even had a single word name for his symptom. Jason saw them write the word on his paperwork before a nurse escorted him to another room to deliver the biggest shock since the arrival of the gruesome symptom. In the room, the nurse measured Jason's vital signs, and when he stepped on the scales he thought the machine malfunctioned. It showed his weight at a level it had not been in over twenty years. Jason knew he had lost weight because his clothes had a more comfortable fit, but he had not thought he had lost a fifth of his total weight.

"I won't be calling myself the fat man anymore," Jason said.

"Why is that?" the nurse asked.

When Jason explained that a few weeks ago his normal weight had been nearly forty pounds heavier, the nurse made a note in his paperwork and then directed Jason to wait in another room. His wait seemed short before another nurse appeared and escorted Jason to a room with a large x-ray machine. After the x-rays, the nurse directed Jason to yet another empty room. While he waited alone in the room, he wondered about his condition, but he feared asking questions. Certainly the latest symptom could be only the harbinger of grave news, and he dreaded hearing it. When a woman from the county health department arrived, Jason listened. She explained that in order to best diagnose his problem as well as protect others, he must remain in quarantine for a few days while providing specimens for tests. The word quarantine troubled Jason, and sensing his apprehension the woman clarified that Jason would not be committed to a ward or otherwise incarcerated. The quarantine could take place at Jason's own residence.

At first, the prospect of a long wait in his own residence seemed positive, even comforting. Glad to get out of the hospital and relieved that the staff at the hospital had not seemed exceptionally alarmed at his condition, Jason got through the first few hours of his quarantine with relief. The relief turned to boredom, and the boredom turned to fear. After the skin test failed to yield a positive result, the fear turned to resentment, and over time that resentment turned to anger. He often looked in the mirror for long moments, and he saw his grey skin and hollow sunken eyes. He thought about the rapid weight loss, and he thought about how prior to the arrival of the latest symptom he had considered his biggest sources of concern excessive drinking and inadequate communication with his friends.

The latest symptom had changed his entire sense of priorities. The latest symptom had been something he never anticipated. Even describing it had seemed difficult, as if no one would believe him since he could not make the symptom appear at will. Saying it aloud had been hard at first, but when Jason said, "I'm coughing up blood," to the first nurse at the hospital, the nurse appeared friendly but unmoved and unsurprised. Jason thought the man could not have appeared less troubled had Jason said the reason for his visit resulted from a mere hangnail. While the hospital staff seemed unbothered by Jason's gruesome symptom, they did express compassion and concern, and for that Jason remained grateful, though at times good will got pushed aside by the resentment at being confined.

By midmorning the neighbor who always remained at home sat in his chair outside his door reading the newspaper and drinking coffee. Jason watched from his window and thought how much farther he would go than just outside his door if only he could get the all-clear. He also thought about all the wonderful and forgotten places to get coffee. As he watched the neighbor, Jason drank coffee too, and he tried to list his favorite places to get fresh brewed coffee, but over time his list seemed to give preference to places for their great distance from his residence rather than for quality of beverages only.

During the afternoon, Jason sat at the dinette table and looked at the still full jug of magic wine. For a brief instant he smiled. First, he felt a bit of pride at not having consumed the wine during his long hours confined, and then the anger returned and turned upon Jason. Simply not doing something known to be harmful to oneself is no reason for a sense of pride, he thought. Nevertheless, Jason looked at the magic wine with broiling indignation and thought that if all efforts at regaining health failed, he still had the magic wine he could drink with wild abandon.

Evening came and passed without a call or another visit from a county worker. Jason counted the days, and he determined that if the same time arrived the following day and the county authorities had not found cause for further detainment, he could be free as early as the next morning. He tried counting the hours, but that proved discouraging, so he settled on telling himself over and over "morning after next." When that morning came, he would be free to leave the residence.

That evening, though, Jason did not have the freedom to leave his residence. As evening dwindled into night, he looked through the window and watched the last of the pedestrian commuter rush clogging the sidewalks. They made their way to trains, buses, and parking garages. He thought about the days past when he had regular commutes. If the commute involved a train, that meant drinking on the evening trip and unfortunately more often than not drinking on the morning trip to work too. Drinking or not, he had resented the trips, and that evening confined to his apartment he could think of few things more liberating than the joy of riding a train or bus. Any kind of movement, he thought, must be better than this hum drum crawl of time toward an uncertain prognosis. He determined to escape those walls at the first opportunity.

Night came, and after a couple of hours the glow of light behind his neighbor's curtains and shades went dark. The parking lot attendant took refuge in the closet-sized box. Jason remained at the window of his darkened apartment, and he looked toward the tall buildings bursting with light. Light and life abounded outside. Inside the apartment, weak light from outside mingled with the black shadows. He thought about the remaining time, perhaps as little as a day. He wondered what he would do when given the all-clear, and his dreams of release focused on his residence door. His single-most intense desire centered on passing through that door.

Then again, he thought, the determination from medical personnel could require more confinement or medical treatment. That prospect inspired cold fear. Jason wondered if he could face such a situation and concluded that he would have little choice. He had not had much choice regarding the quarantine. Back when Jason had a variety of choices, he chose to drink.

In the dark early hours, the traffic noise ceased and few pedestrians passed. Unable to sit any longer, Jason paced about. He stood for a time in front of the door he so longed to pass through, and then he walked back to the window. One way or another, this has to end, he thought, and he determined to escape those walls at the first opportunity.

I sometimes think that never blows so red
The Rose as where some buried Caesar bled;
That every Hyacinth the Garden wears
Dropt in her Lap from some once lovely Head.

Lone Blush

Jason did not wait for daybreak. Well before dawn, he turned the corner to pass first the Chinese store then the Arab store. Turning northeast he used a narrow alley as a shortcut to 4th Street and a coffee shop that opened before the rest. Confinement had been frightening and infuriating, and fear of it, loss of freedom, surpassed Jason's concerns for his current state of health. He departed the rental unit with a long list of tasks, and after getting coffee he started with purchasing groceries. And simply because he had not been forbidden or otherwise restricted, he had skipped over the closest stores and chosen one unnecessarily far from his residence.

The pain began in earnest as soon as he left the grocery store. Carrying the grocery sack, though light, produced sharp pain in the middle of his back, and he tried carrying the bag in a variety of postures, switching from arm to arm. Joining the pain in his back, an ache began in his upper chest and then seemed to spread everywhere when he coughed, and from time to time the coughing made it necessary to set the bag on the ground and double over while convulsing took control. Near a crosswalk, the coughing would not stop, and he looked in vain for a place to set the grocery bag. With each cough, air left his body, and he longed for the cessation of rasping and hacking so that he could take in a breath, but the break did not come. More and more air went out, but none came in, and as he waited for the light to change so he could cross the street, his vision narrowed to a tunnel. With no air left in his lungs to force out, his diaphragm kept up the convulsing, and Jason wondered if he would pass out before the light changed. Lack of air and a growing doubt that he would get breath in time caused a lapse in judgment or outright panic, and Jason walked into the

85

street clutching the grocery bag at his chest with both arms. Midway across the street, he had a sense that a car neared, and he felt the rapid movement of air as the car sped past, and he also felt the long overdue inrush of air into his lungs. The relief was fleeting because no sooner had his lungs expanded with the dear air than his body forced it out again with urgent hacking. As the last of the air left him and he felt his chest about to implode, Jason tripped over the curb and reached out just in time to place a hand on the sidewalk. Groceries spilled across the sidewalk, and Jason crawled through them.

On hands and knees Jason coughed while he retrieved groceries and returned them to the bag. With the violent coughing, the blood returned, and with the straining and longing for air Jason's vision took on a red hue. He feared making another spectacle, and so he decided to take a route through the park, carrying groceries from one bench to another. At the first stop, he sat on the bench, coughed into a handkerchief, and waited for normal breathing to return. When he could breathe in and out at somewhat regular intervals, he rose from the bench and took slow careful steps. All movement produced aches and fatigue. Near the edge of the park, severe full-body convulsive coughing took hold, and Jason looked back into the park at the bench he had just left. The coughing too severe and the distance back to the bench too far, he coughed while vision again went red. He dropped the groceries to the grass and then fell to a sitting position beside them. For a moment he tried to replace the items but then directed his narrowing tunnel gaze to the grass before him while he yearned for the return of air and normal breathing.

Well past the point of impatience, his longing for air progressed to fear. No previous bouts had been so severe, and with each cough the blood that had been sporadic became constant, and sometimes the outward coughing did not synchronize with the desperate inhalation. Jason coughed, and Jason choked, and while the periphery of his vision grew ever narrower he believed he would choke on his own blood and die, drown right there. His eyes grew wider in terror, but the tunnel of vision grew narrower.

Jason sank into grass that ceased being grass and became sticky clay mud that started where bluebonnets stopped twenty feet before the shore of the little pond behind the farmhouse. He heard the flapping of clothes on the line, and he rolled over into a prone position in the mud. The mud covered him, and he knew he would have to find a way to wash it off before returning to the farmhouse. He pressed his hands into the mud and rose just enough to see past the patch of wildflowers, and two bonnets, a baby blue one on his grandmother and a pink one on his favorite aunt, hovered about the clothesline. He remembered his ongoing directives and one from earlier that morning: Don't leave the house without a hat. Don't go near the pond. Don't shoot or otherwise disturb the goats.

"Jason!"

He heard his name shouted, and he knew his favorite aunt had discovered his inability to leave the goats alone. She might not know about the hat and the pond, so he stayed quiet and sank onto the mud.

"Jason!"

He felt himself lifted up from the grass, and he heard her voice. He saw the torn orange leggings, and he saw the fleecy pink sweater. Through the rasps and wheezes he struggled to say, "You're still clashing, baby girl."

"Oh Lordy. What have you done to yourself? Oh Lordy."

She pushed him about, and she retrieved spilled groceries, and she lamented what he had done to himself. When she touched his head, he remembered his aunt's directive: "Don't go out in that sun without a hat. You'll bake your head."

She said he would bake his head in the Texas sun, but he worried more about the slingshot than the hat. She had said that one more transgression against the goats would mean the seizure of the wrist rocket, and he feared the loss. This one had surgical rubber, and he did not want to lose it and have to go back to making slingshots from tree branches and tire inner tubes. This one was store bought, and he had to keep it. He had also grown weary of hearing what grand slingshots his uncles had made from tire inner tubes. Surgical rubber beat any other, and if only he could get up and out of the pond mud, he could stash the coveted bean shooter before she took it.

"Oh Lordy. I can't stay here with you, baby. I have to go." He felt her push and pull, and breathing came easier as she leaned him against a tree. He tried to form words, but the coughing returned and red vision narrowed to black. He felt her reach into a jacket pocket, and he knew she must be searching for the slingshot.

Again he pushed up from the mud, and he could see the colored bonnets moving back and forth by the clothesline. As long as they remained by the clothesline, he stood no chance of making it through the pasture and into the woods to stash the slingshot. Just ahead of his position in the pond mud, the prairie grass began, and bluebonnets dominated the nearest section of grass. Blue and blue-violet petals climbed up the stalks until the white tip-tops. Occasional five-petaled Texas yellow stars mingled with the bluebonnets. In the patch of blue with occasional yellow stars, a single stand-out, a lone Indian paintbrush, not the usual reliable red but a riveting shade stood in shocking pink defiance. Not even the color of the rest of its tribe, the flushed and glowing nonconformist unleashed its beauty amid the blue clan. Jason's attention focused solely on the shocking pink angel until another spectacle demanded consideration. A scissortail, Oklahoma bird aerobated overhead. With the forked tail, the carefree bird performed maneuvers impossible for any other creature, and Jason sank into the real blue and snickered sleepy, whispered to the real blue pond mud, "We're in so much trouble." Fickle bluebonnets changed their hue to suit the drifting clouds, but the solitary blossom stood firm in riveting, shocking pink.

His head baked in the Texas sun. Pond mud dried to his skin. The scissortail performed above the patch of flowers, and Jason looked ahead to the shocking pink flower set apart from the others by the force of her flamboyance. Jason could remain in the pond mud and get caught. If he ran, he would most likely be seen, caught, but a chance or impatience tempted Jason. The woods offered freedom to move, but the mucky patch between the pond water and the prairie stagnated. Rays from the sun's stern glare heated the mud and forced out all the air. Jason struggled to breathe while he clung to his slingshot, and he looked ahead to the bonnets hovering by the clothesline, and he knew he ran short of time. He baked his head under the Texas sun, and the Texas sun exploded into innumerable pieces to rain down golden meteors on the patch of bluebonnets. Bits, little buttery shards of the sun rose again as coreopsis, tickseeds, and Jason burst from the real blue pond mud into the verdant field dotted with sapphire, ruby, gold, and the single lovely shocking pink seraph.

Legs and arms furious pumping, his strides lengthened, and the time he spent in contact with the ground shortened to brief instants just as the balls of his feet touched the prairie and propelled him again in near flight. The tree line of the woods grew closer, and Jason rejoiced as he left the airless pond mud and moved into the rich atmosphere of the prairie. Air filled his lungs and powered his legs. He had never run so fast. No one could see him, and he could see no one. All Jason saw stayed framed in a gray tunnel aimed at the growing tree line. Feet barely made contact with the prairie. He spent most of his time at mid-stride, in flight, and he saw beyond the top of the tree line to a black expanse dotted with silvery lights. When the tree line stood before him and the time to decide came, Jason chose against hiding in the woods and instead jumped. He leapt with all his might and flew over the wood's canopy and into the expanse with silvery dots.

The gray tunnel widened and revealed green grass all around where he sat leaning against a tree. Short shallow breaths began to deepen, and his vision lost the red hue. In and out slowly he savored the air, and he wiped away tears spawned by violent coughing and straining for ventilation. An open newspaper rested in his lap, and his legs crossed at the ankle. Rather than the victim of near suffocation, he appeared at leisure, almost posed. He clutched the tree while he stood, and then he reached into a jacket pocket in search of a handkerchief. The pocket did not hold a handkerchief. Patting the rest of his pockets revealed that Jason had somehow lost everything he thought he carried. Checking twice confirmed the empty pockets, and Jason began to curse, but coughing commandeered his voice, and when he raised a hand to cover his mouth he felt something odd about his wrist. Inside the cuff of his jacket a pink ribbon held a palm-sized green plastic shamrock flush to his wrist, and the chained key dangled down his sleeve. Jason pulled one end of the ribbon, and the entire keychain fell to the ground. With the key and ribbon stored in a pocket, Jason began the journey to safety.

The absence of a full sack of groceries made walking somewhat easier, and Jason did not have to stop for every bout of coughing, though he took frequent breaks. Milestones in the form of street corners, shaded spots, and the sought after benches broke the journey into smaller portions. A quarter mile remained, but Jason breathed better. A slow amble on the inside of the sidewalk where an arm against a building could provide support for the violent coughing bouts eliminated the need for rest stops. Breathing came easier, but the aches increased. Each cough tore apart his chest, and the agony centered in the middle of his back made standing upright uncomfortable and any other position excruciating. After rounding a corner, Jason caught sight of his objective, his rented apartment, and he told himself that with each step and each cough he grew nearer. He held on long enough, and he reached in his pocket for the key as he neared the door. While he slid the key into the lock, he heard someone speaking. Jason turned to see the neighbor who never left home carrying a grocery sack.

"Excuse me, sir. Your grocery delivery came to my place."

Jason said thank you as he took the groceries. The average looking man asked, "Are you all right? Would you like me to carry those inside?"

Jason claimed to be fine and thanked the man for his offer to assist. He carried his groceries inside, set the sack on the dinette, and closed the door. The knife-like pain in the center of his spine made sitting difficult. Jason lowered himself part way and then fell the rest of the way into a chair at the dinette. After reaching inside the sack twice to take items and place them on the table, Jason felt something odd in the bag. From the bag he removed an item he did not purchase but thought he remembered seeing though he could not remember when. A plastic pink zippered pouch had been inserted into Jason's bag of groceries. The color of the pouch fascinated Jason. It went beyond pink, past hot pink, blazing into the realm of shocking pink. He opened the zipper and looked inside the pouch to see his wallet, his pocket comb, other keepsakes, and jewelry he forgot he wore.

Jason sat staring at the shocking pink zippered pouch next to the jug of magic wine and a hand-drawn postcard, and for a moment he did not know what to think. A moment later, he wept.

It comes from all sides. That's what he said to me. Good thing the usual impudence had been toned down some by genuine admiration, and the question came out as, "Is it true that the two most important things a plumber must remember is that it rolls downhill and never bite your fingernails?" Maybe the usual gall showed through some, but he smiled when he answered, "Kid, it comes from all sides, all directions."

That sure is true. Not long ago the biggest worries concerned vexed roommates and landlords. Then a knock on the head gave a much bigger worry. That cause for fret stayed in first place only so long before worrying about drinking the way other folks had for years. Somewhere in there, the friends owed apologies and explanations bothered me plenty, but then that cough came. After that, the coughing up blood, or hemoptysis as the medicos call it, pretty much trumped everything.

Somehow this morning here in this hospital bed a memory returned, a memory of an angry woman years ago calling me a drifter. She didn't like some name that had been flung at her, something bad, something hurtful, so she turned about and yelled drifter. She spat the word like a weapon, and the more of my beer drinking and laughter the more of her angry yelling drifter, just the word with no other explanation. At the time it seemed a funny thing to holler. To a person raised on cowboy movies, it didn't seem much of an insult.

Nurses come in and out, and sometimes they speak, but I'm not sure I'm always awake when they do. Asked what's the matter with me, they usually say something about how the doctor will be in later, but sometimes they also say stuff about my horse and how he's just fine outside the little hospital, Plains Hospital, in Isom, and that's how I know later that I've not been awake entirely. When awake for long enough to get clear ideas, thoughts go to that pink friend that saved me, and thoughts turn to worry.

She said over and over that she couldn't stay, that she had to go as if being chased. To be sure, not being able to breathe made for a bad situation. She fixed it as best she could, and then she disappeared without hanging around for the thanks owed. After this hospital, I'll find her and thank her, and if she's in any kind of trouble it'll get fixed. Nobody better be chasing her. That just ain't acceptable. But right now, there ain't no way to get up and out cause nobody is saying what's wrong with me. If they don't tell soon, I'm fixin to get up and out anyway.

Chico ought not be waiting outside. That horse just does whatever he wants. We're pals and have been for a couple of years now. I was just a little kid, eight, when we met, but that was a couple of years ago, and we been best pals ever since.

When the bad coughing comes, somebody pushes me over on my side. It's been happening so much I don't even care to notice who's doing it. After and sometimes during the coughing, they take away the pillows turned red. The pillows look just like second base after drinking too much tomato juice before a game. Me and Chico had been down at Dixon Creek that morning, and when we got back to our grandparents' house before the game, I found the juice and then drank the whole big can and then had two snow cones before the team went out on the field. After the first batter struck out, I walked about four or five big steps over to second base and let loose all that juice. That's what the pillows look like before they take them away.

Maybe she was right. Maybe I am a drifter. The idea seemed silly when she said it, when I drank the beer and laughed at her. How can a fellow be a drifter when he lives in the same city for so many years? Drifters move about from place to place. They don't know nobody, and nobody knows their names. But then it's almost like that for me here in this town. My folks are all back in Texas, and the only people that know me around here are women that don't want to talk to me or who I'm too ashamed to talk to after they seen me drunk a few too many times. Maybe I am a drifter, and maybe that ain't such a good thing to be, cowboy or not.

Chico ought not be waiting outside. That horse is going to get me in trouble, not as bad as those times of leaving school and getting caught riding him, but he could get me in trouble or worse yet get hisself in trouble. He don't show no sense when it comes to cars. How did he even get into town? I don't remember riding him into town. Too much trouble got flapped up the last time. Somebody must have forgot to lock the gate at the livestock pens. If the cattle got out too, there will be no end to the trouble.

What my pink friend might have been running from has me uneasy.

She said over and over that she couldn't stay, but she stayed long enough to save me, and she got the groceries home. She didn't have to do none of that, and if it put her in danger she shouldn't have. There's gratitude for being saved and all cause drowning in blood ain't no kind of good, but she didn't have to go and put herself out like that. If she got herself caught by whoever she ran from cause she stopped to help me, I don't know what I'm gonna do. For one thing, after getting out of here I'm gonna find who chased her and put a stop to that. People ought not be chasing aunt Gladys in her pink bonnet.

Something is in the way of getting up to the window to see if Chico is outside. He ought not be here. I need to get up to that window, but something keeps me from moving from this bed. He ain't supposed to be here. That horse is gonna get me in trouble.

The thought, a bad one, came. When that doctor comes and tells me what is wrong, he might well say it's something he can't fix. And if he can't fix it, then what can be said to the folks in Texas? The fall and the broke head still ain't been explained. This situation is bad.

She kept yelling drifter like it was the worst thing a person could be. At the time, it sounded like a compliment compared to all the other bad and true things that could be said of me. It seemed funny that the worst she could come up with was drifter. It don't seem funny now, and it ain't certain that drifter don't suit me. Being in the same place for a few years ought to mean a fellow can't be no drifter, but maybe she meant it in the way a drifter ain't got nothing steady. I ain't got nothing steady except the worry that the folks in Texas will find out what a mess I've become.

Up and out that window and Chico is waiting for me. We'll head west over by Golden Gate Park and then up to the Presidio where maybe there's a cutoff to the highway between Isom and Pampa and then off on that trail to Dixon Creek and maybe further north and east into the river breaks. Chico stepped on to that sandy trail leading down to Baker Beach, and ripples spread out from his hoof. I jumped down real quick to look, and sure enough it was quicksand. That's all right cause we can turn off here and make it through that thicket of eucalyptus trees and get on the shortcut to Texas. We didn't want to go down to Baker Beach anyway. Nearly lost in the thicket, we found our way again when we seen the fountains. We're the only ones that knows about them ancient fountains even though my uncle's house is just beyond this bunch of mesquite. When we clear these mesquite thorns, we'll cut across the back part his place by the stock tanks and sneak on down.

This last time someone came and pushed me over and took away the red messed pillow, they didn't bring one back but instead wheeled in a different bed. There's more of them coming in, and one is working the bags and tubes attached to the needle in my arm. They're tugging me away from the red mess and onto that bed with wheels, and I'm starting to get mad. I'm trying to ask about Chico, but the words won't come out, and that's making me almost as mad as the hurt they're causing me by yanking me about. I'm trying to tell them they're hurting my back and chest, and I'm trying to ask about Chico, but all I can do is cough and choke, and I'm getting mad. I'm damn near mad enough to cuss.

We're through a doorway, and lights is whizzing by overhead, and I'm trying to yell, but all that comes is red sputter. We stop, and there's more fiddling with the bags attached to the tubes, and people are calling me Mister Spearman. Mister Spearman. That's what the coaches and principal calls me before they're mad enough to lay a board across my behind. These people around the bed are saying Mister Spearman it'll be all right, and I commence to giggling but it's just a bunch of red sputters.

Down past the fenced lots where we keep the livestock, there's a creek. It ain't got no name, and most of the time it ain't got no water, and it could be just a gully, but sometimes it's a creek. And next to the creek stretches a trail. What makes the trail is a mystery, and me and Chico is the only ones that use it. Maybe mule deer could use it too, though I never see any. That trail goes one way and another, and it leads right off the cliff down to Dixon Creek. Me and Chico take that trail all the time, but we don't never tell no one cause they'd call us crazy, but that's cause they don't know that Chico in his unshod hooves is as steady as a mountain goat. I've never seen a mountain goat, but that's what my uncle said one time about Chico, and he was right cause we fit right through that pass between the giant white boulders and make our way down to Dixon Creek.

After we get off the steep part and down to the flat area and before we get to the creek itself, we gotta pass through acres of mesquites, some of them taller than me and Chico put together. I been cut a thousand times by them thorns, but they don't bother Chico none. When we get out of the tall mesquites, we get into this high grass here, and this is the only place that scares me. I don't dare step off Chico in this patch. A rattler could be anywhere, and I've heard them plenty, but there ain't none buzzin now. Clear of the high grass, comes the dry sand, and this is the slow part. This sand looks just like the movies about the desert, but it don't go on forever like in the desert cause closer to the creek is the wet sand, and that's where the quicksand will be if there is any. There ain't no quicksand in this spot, so I'm gonna get down off Chico and let him go back to the high grass while I look around.

Again there's a white pillow, and it looks like second base, a regular second base and not the second base that time after losing the tomato juice. This place looks like the same room and bed from before those folks were fiddling with the bags attached to the tubes, but it's hard to tell because it's darker. Air comes in and out better now, and if the sputtering allows words to pass I could ask what happened, but I don't cause my throat is scratchy sore, and it don't seem like anybody is in this dark place anyway. The wanting to know what happened sinks under the heavy sleepiness, and it's so dark.

Me and Chico better be getting home. Sundown came and went a while ago, and if we ain't through the mesquite thicket before full dark we'll be sorry. Sneaking through the back part of my uncle's place near the stock tanks we see lights already on in the house. There is a pretty woman shaking her arms before a man on a couch, and the man ain't my uncle. This man has on the fanciest suit I've ever seen, but he puts his feet on the coffee table with a bunch of beer bottles like the one in his hand. The pretty woman looks mad or sad, but the man laughs. She shakes her fists and hollers drifter, drifter, drifter, and the man smiles and laughs and laughs, but he looks mean in his fancy suit. The pretty woman cries, and the man laughs and laughs.

I need to get up off second base and to the window before Chico gets me in trouble for being in town. After trying and trying to find the strength to get up, there's no change in the distance from clean second base to the window, and the only thing different is the new crying joining the sadness of the lady yelling drifter. If crying can happen, so can yelling. I yell, and fire rips through my throat even though words won't form. There has to be a way to get out of this bed. Got to tell that pretty woman I ain't no drifter, but maybe she's right about the drifter business. Got to tell that pretty woman sorry for making her cry and that I ain't worth crying over. But words don't come, only hollering and fire in the throat. Somebody is calling Mister Spearman again and working that line attached to the needle.

Mister Spearman is up and out the window and off with Chico.

The Worldly Hope men set their Hearts upon
Turns Ashes—or it prospers; and anon,
  Like Snow upon the Desert's dusty Face,
Lighting a little hour or two—is gone.

Pronouncement

White light illuminated Hyde Street. The morning's late April aureolin light he had earlier seen through the hospital window had matured to white and warmed Polk Gulch. Pedestrians passed in shirt sleeves and shorts, but he did not feel the warmth as he advanced down Hyde and turned left at Post Street on stiff legs that let his shoes scrape against the pavement. The slight breeze had no feeling in the odorless air devoid of sensation. All feelings of fear, anxiety, impatience, and even hope vanished with the doctor's grim news earlier that morning. Fear had grown in anticipation of the meeting with the doctor, and it had increased to the point that the dread of dire prospects produced such anxiety that fear itself became his chief ailment. But once the news came, he felt nothing. It manifested itself as calm, but a calm or tranquility did not describe his state of mind after the news. What he felt, if anything, settled as a numb nothingness.

He tried to recollect the revelation, but only bits came to mind. A mass. Growing fast. Prognosis. Cases like these. Not much time. Prepare. Not much time.

Trudging on in a state of numbness without feelings of any kind, he tried to comprehend the news but instead felt only the blunt shock much like the aftermath of a heavy physical blow that steals breath, balance, and purpose. Without orientation, he spun into Union Square with the dizzying replay of words like mass, prognosis, and terminal. The square swirled under him, and the words mass growing fast knocked him to the ground. Bewildered he sat on concrete and looked about for a place of safety and succor, and as watering holes came to mind and he measured distances to taverns, another thought, the first clear thought since the news, seized him, and he laughed. Snickers at first, then full-body guffaws shook. Struggling to knees first then feet, he fought for breath and through laughter he spoke.

"I have a golden ticket. For the first time in my life, nobody, absolutely nobody, could blame me for taking a drink. And I'll be damned. I don't want one."

He departed the square and took a zigzagging route toward an appointment at a lawyer's office near the Embarcadero. He had been told to prepare. Shoes no longer scraped the pavement, but the lack of sensation persisted. The time for feeling had passed. The time for hope gone. Everything over. Game over. He lost. Only minor tasks remained, and he consulted a list kept in a shirt pocket until he had to cough and exchanged the list for a handkerchief. Breath restored but devoid of desire, he marched on. He attended to the first step of preparation.

Upon leaving the attorney's office in early evening, he thought he noticed faint wisps of fog floating along the waterfront, and he knew he would never again see San Francisco's dense magical summertime world of white, and he felt a brief pang before the numb sluggish melancholy returned. Tasks remained, and he pressed on toward SOMA and the Chrystal Rose Bungalows.

The nearly full jug of magic wine still rested on the little dinette next to a shocking pink zippered pouch, and he looked at both as he passed by on his way to pull a suitcase out of the closet near the bed. After opening the suitcase, he extracted an ornate metal flask and set it on the dinette. For a moment he looked about the room appearing confused, and then he fashioned a funnel from a rolled piece of paper. With the flask full of the magic wine, he capped it and placed it in the suitcase. Then he placed clothing from the closet in the suitcase with the flask, and he took the pink pouch into the bathroom and filled it with toiletries before placing it in the suitcase. After a quick survey of the room and a long gaze out the window at the tall buildings, he left the apartment carrying the suitcase in one hand and the jug of wine in the other. The keychain with the shamrock fob clattered into the landlord's mailbox, and he tried to hurry away before getting a brief last look at the building on Howard Street and contemplating last looks.

Behind the donut shop he found the shopping carts covered with an old tarpaulin, and he called out, "Barry. Barry, are you here?" A groan came from a soiled bedroll. "Barry, I got something for you." After an interval with no response from the soiled bedroll, he placed the jug of wine on the ground. "It's a big jug, but go easy on it. It's magic. I won't be seeing you at the donut shop no more. I got to get on down the road. Take care, Barry. Don't take no wooden nickels."

He had a free hand for holding a handkerchief, but the weight of the suitcase still complicated his movement. When the suitcase grew too heavy, he stopped and set it on the ground, and sometimes he covered his mouth with the handkerchief and fought to clear choked passages and get air. After each break, he tried to set goals of a hundred yards or just to the next corner before having to release the suitcase and cough, but the intervals grew shorter until he reached the storage unit. Once inside, he snaked his way past the boxes, furniture, and useless antiques. From the suitcase he took the pink zippered pouch and the metal flask. He placed those in a small brown leather shoulder bag and then looked around for a change of wardrobe. One after another he looked at suits and sport coats, but all fitted a girth he no longer had. The only garments he found that came close to fitting his thinner frame rested in the bottom of the steamer truck. He looked at western wear he had not donned since first arriving in the city and selected a canvas jacket, two shirts with fake pearl snaps, and a couple of trousers. At the very bottom of the trunk he found a pair of boots with pointed roach killer toes and riding heels.

"These will come in real handy if I get an opportunity to ride a horse before I kick it. Maybe I'll die with my boots on."

He put on half the selections and put the other half in the leather bag. While putting on the canvas jacket, his arm collided with something hanging from the wall, and upon turning he saw a palm leaf cowboy hat. He put the hat on and backed out of the storage trying not to look at the rest of the useless antiques because he knew that nostalgia could only lead to regret, but something on the big black Beseler enlarger demanded attention. He took the peace sign medallion with the hemp necklace and put it in the leather bag along with the clothes, flask of magic wine, and pink zippered pouch.

Walking along Market Street did not present the best choice for one trying to avoid nostalgia and thoughts of never seeing The City again, but it did afford a flatter surface for walking than most of the other choices. Avoidance of hills and preservation of breath kept his mind occupied while he tried to think of a destination. He knew he had to leave San Francisco completely. He did not want the end to come in the city he loved so; better to be somewhere unknown to him and somewhere that regarded him as a drifter. The cough, though less frequent and regular, still came with enough violence and volume to make public transit an embarrassing trial.

With the Civic Center and the gateway to the Tenderloin to the left and SOMA to the right, he continued on Market Street and looked up occasionally for the fog he thought he had seen at the Embarcadero. Seeing the fog could be a fitting mirror, a similar ending to his beginning in San Francisco, but he did not see traces of white. He considered taking BART to Daly City or perhaps even San Bruno where he stood a better chance of seeing the fog, but the idea of avoiding nostalgia returned and so did the cough. Convulsing and holding the handkerchief to his mouth in a vain effort to muffle sound and hide shame, he found small reason to be thankful. The wide brim of the hat concealed his face.

Considering options for leaving The City, he thought of only two that did not involve public transit. He could walk south on the peninsula, or he could walk across the big red bridge to the north. Each labored step demonstrated the folly of walking out of town and sent thought back to the problem of public transit. The constant coughing would surely raise alarm and revulsion, so he pondered doubling up on handkerchiefs to further muffle sound. Perhaps the train afforded a better option than the buses. He would surely cough, but he could change cars periodically so no single group of passengers would fear contagion. The hospital staff assured Jason that he posed no threat to others, but he had seen even seasoned medical professionals recoil from his prolonged hacking, and the memory and resentment of the forced quarantine stayed fresh. The option of taking a train and frequently changing carriages might chafe a conductor, but it presented the best at hand, so he walked on toward the station for his passage out of the city and his acceptance of spending the last days as a drifter.

Only one train had a station in the city, and it traveled south. An Amtrak station at the Embarcadero used buses to convey passengers to the actual train station in Emeryville, and while he favored the wide variety of options in a nationwide train network, he knew he could not stifle the coughing for the long ride across the Bay Bridge to Emeryville. The other train ventured south to San Jose and sometimes a town or two past. He knew the route and the area well for it lay on the way to Monterey. Thoughts of Monterey made him stop.

Monterey housed memories of the folks in Texas from the days before they departed. He hoped he could find a way to head south but avoid Monterey. From San Jose, he could head west to Santa Cruz, but that town of wannabe hippies and fruitcakes amounted to a dead end at the ocean. If he could get from San Jose south to Salinas, he thought perhaps he could find a way to get to Bakersfield. Bakersfield with its love of country music and nearby oil fields could remind him of home, and perhaps that would be a comfort. Besides, he thought, Bakersfield might be the one place in California where his present attire would not draw attention. With a partial plan, he resumed his way toward the train station.

A peninsula, he thought, surrounded on three sides by water had probably once had more than one rail line, and he wondered why it had held on to only the one. In the days before the two bridges, the 1930s and earlier, boats must have supplied the majority of the traffic to and from the city. At the end of Market Street, the Ferry Building with its clock tower remained, but while it once served as a major transportation hub it later sent off one or two ferry lines and mostly served as a center for tourist-focused retail establishments. A vintage street car clattered by, and Jason thought about what San Francisco might have been like during the days of ferry boats and cable cars. A few cable car lines remained, though Jason had never actually ridden one. Up ahead, he saw the area where tourists waited in long lines to ride the Powell Line, and he thought he remembered hearing that the man who first designed the cable cars for San Francisco had been inspired by seeing a toppled horse drawn wagon dragging its fallen horses down one of the many steep San Francisco streets. Thinking about terrified horses being dragged made Jason shudder.

Jason returned to thinking about ferry boats, and it occurred to him that the ferries he had seen operating in the bay all had open and accessible decks. It could be, he thought, that if he could find passage on a ferry he could make his way out onto the deck and then cough all he needed in the open air and never bother anyone. He felt no hurry to reach the train station and leave the city, so he stayed on Market Street to investigate the possibilities of leaving on a boat.

Ticket in hand he sat on a bench outside the Ferry Building awaiting the arrival of the boat that would take him across the bay. When he saw the boat approach the dock, he stood near the back of a line of people waiting to board. Once the majority of people had passed the ticket agent, Jason joined the line. He boarded the boat through a doorway near a bar and concession stand, and he looked around for stairs leading to the outside deck. A few other tourists on the deck took photos in the fading evening light, and Jason found a seat at the aft away from everyone. After the engines started and shook the entire vessel, the boat moved away from the dock. Jason looked down at the white metal deck. He knew that if he looked up he could see the clock tower and all of San Francisco's waterfront area in splendid electric light. But he kept staring down at the deck.

V. Golden Gate

When You and I behind the Veil are past,
Oh, but the long, long while the World shall last,
   Which of our Coming and Departure heeds
As the Sea's self should heed a pebble-cast.

Some for the Glories of This World; and some
Sigh for the Prophet's Paradise to come;
 Ah, take the Cash, and let the Credit go,
Nor heed the rumble of a distant Drum!

Gettin on Down the Road

Outside the coffee shop with the big picture windows, Jason stopped and smelled the warm aroma and decided he had finished walking. He had walked the entire night, partly to get somewhere farther from the city but mostly to stave off the night chill. He had not worn cowboy boots in over a decade, and the ache in his feet spread up his legs to his back. At the curb of the sidewalk, a brick wall a couple of feet high lined a street flanked on both sides by a variety of retail stores. The beauty of the little town impressed Jason. He sat on the wall and removed his hat and mopped his brow while breathing deep in an effort to gauge his chances of getting in and out of the shop without falling into a coughing fit.

Back outside with a large paper cup of coffee, the brick wall offered a flat surface for sitting, but the back pain demanded more support. The tables and chairs outside the shop all had occupants save one chair opposite a table where a man dressed in black sat engrossed in a paperback. The man wore a black leather jacket with silver metal studs and zippers, black denim trousers, and black tennis shoes. His skin had a light pallor, but his close-cropped hair and beard stubble matched the black of his outfit as did the dark half-moons under his eyes.

Jason approached the table and asked, "You mind if I sit in that chair a little bit? I won't stay long."

The man did not look up from us paperback, shrugged his shoulders, and gestured with an upturned palm toward the chair. Jason pulled the chair away from the table and turned it at a right angle to the table so it faced the street. As he lowered into the chair, the back pain increased momentarily and he winced, but he remained otherwise silent and grateful for the absent urge to cough.

Next to the coffee shop, a movie theater still possessed an old-style overhanging marquee, and under the marquee stood a detached ticket booth. At the curb in front of the ticket booth, a red Volkswagen Beetle displayed a for sale sign. Jason scrutinized the taillights and other features and guessed it a late 1960s model. On the other side of the street, a store had the word newsstand on the exterior sign, but it looked more like the five-and-dime on Main Street of Jason's hometown. The street-facing window displayed a rack of paperbacks and magazines, another of greeting cards, and next to that various grocery products and children's toys.

A soft breeze blew, and Jason noticed the lack of hydrocarbonated fumes. He felt far from the city.

Jason tilted his paper cup to his lips and drained the last of the coffee. With both hands on the chair armrests, he pushed up a few inches, groaned, and fell back into the seat. He started to make another attempt, and the black clad man said, "You're not from around here."

"No. I'm not."

"Me either. Ohio. You?"

"Texas. But that was a while ago." The leather jacketed man studied Jason, and Jason said, "I better be gettin on down the road."

Again he started to rise when the man said, "Don't rush off. My name is Mike. You look like you could use another." Mike stood, took Jason's empty paper cup, and entered the coffee shop. When he returned, he put a full cup on the table and said, "I knew you weren't from around here because you asked if you could sit and you didn't talk constantly. These rich entitled jerks around here just talk and talk. They see me reading, but they don't care. They just talk and ask stupid questions. But what about you? What brings you to San Rafael?"

Jason looked at the new cup of coffee and then Mike. "San Rafael. Is that the name of this town? I'm just passing through. It was time to get out of the city."

"San Francisco? That's where I lived for a few months. I really blew that situation."

"This is sure is good coffee. Thank you."

"Yeah, this is a good place. But too many of these rich entitled locals just think they can come up and start yakking when I have things to do and things to think about. You live in San Francisco long?"

"A fairly long spell."

"Man, that must have been great. I was there just a few months and loved it until screwing up. I'm in the music business and moved out here for a job as a sound engineer. What line are you in?"

"I'm a drifter."

Mike laughed and said, "Aren't we all, brother. What kind of work do you do? What's your occupation?"

"Photographer."

"Man, far out. You're an artist. Cool, man."

"I'm not an artist. I used to take pictures. That's all."

"Yeah, cool. I started out as a guitar player, but got into production later. I loved my job and had a great place to live in North Beach and hadn't touched heroin in years."

Jason returned his coffee to the table and said, "Heroin? That's tough, pardner. Been known to have trouble with the bottle myself. How long did you say you lived in San Francisco?"

"A little less than three months."

Jason drank his coffee and watched people enter and exit the newsstand five-and-dime.

Mike said, "The folks at work were straight. Everything was cool, and then one Saturday in that park in North Beach, the one across from the famous bookstore, the idea of heroin came out of nowhere."

"Washington Square. You scored heroin in Washington Square?"

After a long pause and a smile, Mike answered, "No, I asked about it in the park, and some tweakers offered to sell me meth, which I declined, and then they told me where to get heroin."

"Did they tell you to get it in the Tenderloin?"

"That's the place. It didn't take long either. I used in New York and in LA but never found it easier than in San Francisco."

"I bet not, pardner. That Tenderloin is a great place for finding anything day or night."

Mike looked at the closed paperback on the table, shook his head, and said, "What a screw up. After hanging out in the city for another two weeks, mostly in the Tenderloin, that trashed my job and my place to stay. I came up here to go to rehab but stuck with it for about a month. I've been to rehab before. I don't need it again."

"Well, this seems like a nice little town."

"It is except for these rich entitled types. I thought I'd go back to Ohio, but my girlfriend back there split, so now there isn't much reason to go back, and I kind of like it here. It's close to San Francisco and maybe someday soon there will be more production work. Right now I'm working at a pizza joint a couple of blocks down. You ought to stop in some evening. Now I'm going to go to lunch. You want to go?"

"Appreciate the invitation, and I surely appreciate the coffee, but I got to be gettin on down the road."

"Are you sure? It's a free lunch. They serve it every day over a Saint Vincent's. It's just a block from here."

"I'm sure. But I probably could use some more sittin down before heading out. Is there a park around here?"

"Oh sure. My favorite park is close. It's just two blocks up that way." Mike pointed and said, "Just go here to the end of the block and take a left, go two blocks, and you can't miss it. Don't get caught there after dark, though. The cops here are generally nice, but they have some kind of thing against people in that park after dark."

"I'll keep that in mind. Thanks again for the coffee."

Jason followed Mike's directions and found the park. The entrance to the park also advertised a history museum, but the climb up the slight hill made Jason more interested in finding a place to sit than in learning about local history. A paved path led into the park amid tall trees. A row of benches faced a children's playground, and farther along the path a row of picnic tables stretched parallel to a stone and iron fence marking the park's boundary with the street. Jason approached one of the tables and started to take off his shoulder bag, but then he noticed a giant tree trunk rising from green lush grass. With his back resting against the tree trunk and his hat titled forward to cover his eyes, Jason sank into the grass.

Without anyone else in the park, and without the ever-present traffic noise of the city, the constant chirp and song of birds sounded loud yet soothing. Late morning turned to afternoon and then early evening, and the breezed seemed cooler as Jason drifted in and out of sleep. The sudden and unexpected sound of a voice jarred Jason awake, and as he jumped a bit his hat fell to the grass.

"You must be the guy from Texas."

Jason held his hand to shield his eyes, and he squinted and saw a slim black man before him. "Yeah, I'm from Texas." Jason took his hat from the grass, put it back on his head, and rose to a full sitting position still resting his back against the tree. The movement tested his sore muscles, and he groaned.

"I saw Angry Mike at Saint Vincent's, and he told me he met a guy from

Texas."

"Angry Mike?"

"Oh that's what we call him because I'm Mike too. He's Angry Mike, and I'm just Mike."

"Okay, Just Mike. Pleased to meet you. I'm Jason."

"So you're from Texas? That is so cool, man?"

"Why is that so cool?"

"I love Austin. Ever been there? I've been three times, not counting when we would go when I was a little kid. My dad was from there."

"What do you like so much about Austin? The music? The barbecue?"

Just Mike sat on the grass across from Jason and said, "Oh, man that's great too, but I like the water."

"The water?"

"Yeah, man. Have you ever been to Barton Springs?"

"Oh, that water. Yeah, I've been to Barton Springs."

"Hamilton Pool?"

"No."

"Deep Eddy Pool?"

"No."

"Hippie Hollow?"

"Nope."

"Krause Springs?"

"Yep. I've been there, but that's in Spicewood, ain't it?"

"That's right! Oh, man I love that place. And you're from Texas. That is so cool. Why are you all the way out here? Man, I'd rather be in Texas. Wouldn't you?"

"Maybe so. Ain't there no water around here that you like?"

"Oh sure, there's the Russian River up in Sonoma County. It's great in the summertime. Sometimes it reminds me of Austin."

"There's a place around here that reminds you of Austin?"

"I mean the swimming in the river up in Guerneville reminds me of swimming in Austin."

"Cause the water is cold?"

"No, it's not too cold in the summertime. It's great. The water is clean and clear, and there are woods and vineyards."

"I don't remember too many vineyards in Austin, but I did drink a lot of beer there. What's the name of the place again?"

"Guerneville."

"I'll have to check that out. In fact, I better be getting on down the road pretty soon."

"Right. You don't want to be in the park after dark."

"That's what I hear."

"It was great meeting you." Just Mike stood and said, "Don't forget to be out of the park before dark. The cops here are cool, but they don't like people in the park after dark."

"I'll keep that in mind."

Jason watched Just Mike walk down the path to the park exit, and he thought about the comparison of a location in Sonoma County to Austin, Texas. "Guerneville," he said. He decided that when he left the park he would visit the five-and-dime and get a map of Northern California. This Guerneville place presented as good a destination as any, and while he thought about what Just Mike said he also thought about Austin and his last visit. That had been over ten years previous, but he vividly saw giant pecan trees in front of the bricked entrance to Barton Springs Pool. Beyond the entrance, to the right, the pool stretched up-creek into the shallow end, and the hue of the water transitioned from a deep blue to lighter turquoise. Just ahead on the other side of the pool the diving board extended over the area of the pool where the springs gushed in millions of gallons every day. To the left, the deep end stretched in indigo blue before pouring over the spillway to Dog Beach. As his eyes closed, Jason drifted from Barton Springs west to Krause Springs and past the wind chimes and past the concrete pool down the winding stone path to the cool green water with the grotto.

Blinding white light jarred Jason, and he heard a voice demand identification.

"I'm sorry. I fell asleep. I'll be gettin on down the road. I'm sorry."

"Show some identification, now," the voice demanded. Jason squinted and saw a large figure silhouetted, and it appeared that a police car had driven into the park along the walking path.

As Jason reached for his wallet, he said, "I really am sorry. I didn't mean any harm. I can be on my way right now if that's okay with you." He handled the office his driver's license.

"Is this your current address in San Francisco?"

"Yes sir. Came up here for the day to see the town and that little museum there and accidentally fell asleep cause I've been working a lot of overtime. I need to be getting back home now cause I got to be at work early tomorrow morning . . . in San Francisco."

The officer handed back Jason's license, and Jason did not wait for further direction. He stood, grabbed his shoulder bag, and began walking toward the park entrance on stiff uncooperative legs. Near the park gate, pain in his back caused Jason to lean forward, but he kept walking. He tried to stifle the coming cough, and the back pain made him stumble. As he fell forward he put out an arm to catch the park gate, but he missed and fell forward to the pavement. Coughing and redness came, and while he tried to crawl on hands and knees his vision took on the red hue.

Jason heard the crackle of the officer's radio, and he heard the officer's request for medical assistance.

"You don't have to do that," Jason sputtered. "I'll be gettin on down the road. I'm going now. Please just let me be."

Think, in this batter'd Caravanserai
Whose Portals are alternate Night and Day,
How Sultan after Sultan with his Pomp
Abode his destined Hour, and went his way.

The Grand Ole Opry

Jason woke fully clothed except for his boots, and after sitting and turning sideways on the bed so his legs dangled toward the floor he saw his boots near the corner of the bed. A curtain surrounded the area of the bed, and after Jason put on his boots and moved past the curtain, he saw a larger room divided into curtained sections. Through the door, the hallway looked the same in both directions. A stark florescent corridor extended both ways, so Jason chose the right and walked until he found a counter with nurses. They took no noticed of Jason, so he waited a few moments, and when they still took no notice he said, "Sorry to interrupt yall, but I'd like to leave now."

Without looking up, one of the nurses seated at the counter asked, "What's your name?"

"Jason Spearman."

The nurse looked through a stack of papers, extracted one, and said, "Yes, Mr. Spearman. You've been sleeping a while. Are you feeling better?"

"I need to be gettin on down the road. Which way is out?"

"It says here that Derrick would like to talk to you."

"Don't need to talk to no doctors, but thanks anyway. Talked to plenty of them in San Francisco. I know what's comin. Please direct me to the door."

The nurse looked up at Jason and said, "Derrick is not a doctor. You really should talk to him, Mr. Spearman. If you go back to your room, I'll bring him by."

"And then can I go?"

"That's right. If you'll just go back to your room, he'll be by to talk to you."

Jason turned and went back down the stark white corridor. He crawled back into the bed face down, and he thought he ought to take his boots off, but the idea seemed too daunting so he left them hanging off the bed, and he fell back to sleep.

He thought he heard a voice, and he thought he felt the bed shake, and then he heard, "Mr. Spearman."

Jason turned to his side and then rose to sit in the bed. A stocky bald man stood before him and said, "Don't get up. Let me pull up a chair so we can talk." The stocky man reached outside the curtain and pulled a chair across the floor. After he sat, he said, "My name is Derrick, and I work for a non-profit organization here in Marin. We have a place where you can rest."

"Appreciate that, but I got to be gettin on down the road. There wasn't any need to for them cops bring me to this hospital. For me, there ain't a lot of time left, and I don't want to spend the little bit that remains in a hospital."

Derrick smiled and said, "The place I work for isn't a hospital. We call it The Hospice, but it's no hospital. It's just a place to rest."

"Hospice? Ain't that a place folks go to die?

"Some do. But we like to think of it as a place of comfort for people in transition."

"Like drifters?"

"Sure. Everyone is welcome."

"Appreciate your kindness, really. But it ain't time for a hospital just yet. I was just tired, had walked too far, and was just tired. If that cop had just let me rest, I'd have been on my way. I tried to explain that."

Again Derrick smiled. "Everybody needs rest sometimes. You ought to come see our place. You can rest, and if you don't like it you can leave."

"I am awful tired and could go back to sleep right now. You say I wouldn't have to stay no longer than I wanted to?"

Derrick shut the van door behind Jason, and as they passed along tree-lined roads Jason fought the desire to sleep. "It sure is pretty country around here."

"You're from Texas? Is that right?"

"Yeah. A long time ago. What about you?"

"I'm from Southern California, San Diego."

"How far is Guerneville from here?"

"Probably about fifty miles. It's up in Sonoma County past Santa Rosa."

Both sides of the road presented a wall of green, and Jason could not keep his eyes open nor could he think of anything more to say to keep the conversation moving. When he heard the van door open, he woke to see Derrick waiting to help him out. "Let me show you to your room so you can rest. We can do the paperwork later."

Jason followed Derrick out of a small parking lot in front of a stone building and around the building on a curving cement walkway. Well-tended lawns alternated with small cultivated patches, and some of them appeared to be little vegetable gardens. Behind the stone building extended twin lines of little cottages painted in pastel colors, and Jason followed Derrick into one of lemon chiffon. "You're here on the left." Derrick opened the door and motioned for Jason to enter. "Just make yourself at home, and when you're ready go back out to the main building near where we parked."

The room had simple decor, a single bed, a bedside table, and a wall locker. Jason dropped his leather shoulder bag on the floor, removed his hat and let it roll across the bedside table onto the floor, and he collapsed onto the bed. He thought he would remove his boots after just a moment of rest.

It seemed the door opened briefly as if someone looked inside from time to time, but Jason did not have the energy to open his eyes, or if he did he saw a closed door and no one else in the room. Once after thinking he had heard the door open, he opened his eyes and saw no one in the room but a tray of food on the bedside table. He thought this might have happened a few times, and one time he managed to sit up, eat a couple of bites of something white, and take off one of his boots before he fell back to the pillow.

The feeling of a breeze and the sensation of light helped Jason in the struggle to open his eyes, and after he rolled out of the bed and found his balance he saw the door to the room open and opposite the door an open window and a curtain fluttering. Except for the winkled bedclothes, the room looked clean, empty. He opened the wall locker and saw his leather bag on one shelf and his hat on another. He did not see his boots in the wall locker nor under the bed. After putting on his hat, he left the room and once outside saw the row of little cottages and the walkway to the stone building. Barefoot he made his way toward the building, but once inside he saw only an unattended desk.

"Hello? Anybody here?"

No one answered, so Jason walked back outside. The walkway continued on in a direction opposite the path to the cottages. After rounding a corner, Jason saw a small courtyard with a table and awning. Two people, a man and a woman well beyond middle age, sat at the table smoking cigarettes, and when the breeze blew in Jason's direction he sensed the aroma of marijuana. In the courtyard near the table but nearer still to Jason, a young man wore headphones and danced. The dance moves appeared jerky and repetitive, and though Jason could not hear the music the young man moved to, he did hear the tapping and scraping of the youth's shoes on the courtyard pavement.

Jason approached the dancing man and said, "Excuse me." When the youth continued dancing without answering, Jason shouted, "Hey, Michael Jackson. Hey!"

The young man removed his headphones, and asked, "How did you know my name was Michael?"

"It seems to be a popular name around these parts. Listen, I just came in . . . got here not long ago, and now I'm missing some boots. Who do I need to talk to about that?"

"Boots. Do you like my shoes?" Michael lifted his right foot to reveal a worn and dirty tennis shoe with metal plates glued to the toe and heel."

"Yeah, those are fine shoes, but about my boots now, who do I need to talk to about that?"

Michael smiled and seemed unaware of a pending question. The smoking man and woman at the nearby table looked at Jason, and the man said, "You say you're missing some boots?"

Jason approached the table. "Yeah. I came in here with a fellow called Derrick, and while I was sleeping my boots got took out of my room. Yall know anything about that or who I need to talk to?"

The woman said, "Oh, you're the new one that sleeps and sleeps. I'm Jolene."

"And I'm Porter," the man said as he extended his hand.

Jason shook Porter's hand and nodded at Jolene. "So it's Jolene and Porter? Is Dolly around? Yall think maybe she knows where I can find my boots?"

"Dolly? I don't know a Dolly," Jolene said. "Is there a Dolly here?"

Porter shook his head, and Jason said, "Nevermind about that. Do yall know anything about my boots or who I need to talk to? I went in that rock building, but nobody is in there. Now, I need them boots."

Porter said, "Loretta usually takes a break about this time in the mornings. She'll be back any time."

"Loretta, huh?" Jason asked. "What is this place? The Grand Ole Opry? Damn weirdest thing I ever heard." Jason began to walk to the stone building and then stopped. "Hey, if yall see Tanya Tucker, tell her that I'm here and that I've had a crush on her since I was five."

Inside the stone building, Jason again saw the unattended desk, but through the window facing the parking lot he saw a woman with long brown hair smoking a cigarette. As he exited the door to the parking lot, Jason again smelled the same aroma that Jolene and Porter's cigarettes produced. "Yall sure do like that weed around here. Might you be Loretta?"

"I am, cowboy, or should I say Mr. Van Winkle?"

"Jason will do. But more important than my handle, I seem to have lost my boots. Had em with me when I come, but they're gone now. You got any idea where they might be?"

Loretta took a draw from her cigarette, exhaled, and said, "Adam was the only person that went in your room during the days you slept, and he . . ."

"Days?"

Loretta laughed and answered, "Yes, you've been asleep for quite a while."

"Okay then, but what about my boots."

"Adam must have them."

"Why does Adam have my boots?"

"I don't know. We'd have to ask Adam."

"Where is Adam?"

"I guess he's in Mill Valley now."

"Is he coming back?"

"He'll be here for the evening shift," Loretta answered. "I'll tell him you're looking for him. Why don't you just relax. Lunch will be in a little over an hour. You can walk around and meet some people. There are usually some hanging out by the table in the courtyard. And you might want to shower and change too. If you need soap, towels, or anything just let us know. Somebody is always here at the desk."

Jason returned to the courtyard and found a seat near Jolene and Porter.

"Did you find your boots?" Porter asked.

"Adam has em."

"Oh, of course," Jolene said.

Jason looked at Jolene and said, "Of course."

"Can I offer you a smoke?" Porter asked.

"No, but thank you." Jason said. "I'm having a hard enough time breathing as it is."

Michael tap danced on the courtyard pavement, and when he let out a shrill shriek Jason jumped and looked first at Michael and then at Jolene and Porter. The older smokers remained mellow and unperturbed, and Jason looked down at his bare feet. He thought about Loretta's suggestion that he shower and change clothes, and as he readied to rise, Jolene said, "Don't look up. The esteemed professor is about."

Porter groaned an unintelligible curse, and Jason looked ahead to see a white haired man in a tattered gray tweed sport coat shuffling on the walkway between the small cottages. Jolene said, "This guy knows everything there is to know. He's a real super genius."

Porter added, "Yeah, and now that he sees a new face he's going to come over here and tell us all about it."

The man did come over, and after surveying the group and studying Jason a moment he said, "I am Charles, though many here call me the professor. You may do the same if you like. And who might you be, good sir."

"Might be just a drifter. What's in a name anyway?"

"Touche. Touche indeed, good fellow. I am a man of letters and have in fact written three novels, and the last was almost published. I am now writing an expose of the homeless situation in this county. I have shown it to many publishers, and they will compete for it. I expect more than a few people here to lose their jobs. I would very much like to hear your hard luck story, my good man."

Jason noticed Charles looking down at his bare bootless feet, and he said, "Well Charlie, there's hard luck stories and then there's . . ."

"Charles."

"Come again, pardner?

"My name is Charles."

"Oh dear. Well, pardon me all to hell." Jason said. "Anyway, Chuck, my hard luck story is just too horrible to share in front of civilized folk. Maybe another time. Right now I'm going to go and try to wash away some of my horrible forlorn anguish. I'll now take my leave and be gettin along."

After showering and changing clothes, Jason intended to return to the courtyard, but he thought he would rest a bit first. As he lay in the bed and as the curtain fluttered, he thought again about the place called Guerneville, and he thought about swimming in Austin. Once he had gone to Zilker Park intending to go to Barton Springs Pool. Before reaching the entrance to the pool, he saw Dog Beach below the spillway. He went to the edge of the water below the spillway and watched people and their dogs playing in the water. Lost in the reverie of other people, he nearly fell off the rock when an enormous German Shepherd collided with him while in pursuit of a ball. A Hispanic woman with chocolate eyes and raven hair apologized for her dog's rude behavior, and he sank into the chocolate eyes and into sleep.

He awoke to the fading light of evening, and the breeze making the curtain flutter felt cooler. Something different about the bedside table caught his attention, and upon focus he saw his boots. But the boots looked far different than the ones he remembered. The boots had a mirror shine from the formerly scuffed heels to the pointy roach killer toes along with new soles and new heels with flawless stitching. Baffled yet grateful, Jason pulled the boots to his chest and fell back to sleep.

There's freedom in knowing you're about to die. There's still plenty of regret when thought heads that way, but there ain't no point in going over all that again, so it's best to just leave the regret alone. All them things, them reasons for fret don't matter now. There ain't no time to change anything, and there ain't no time to make up for bad things already done, so the best thing to do is accept what you are and go along with it. I'm a drifter, and in what time is left I'm gonna get on down the road. If I can keep up a little bit of dignity, that's just fine, but mostly the main thing is just to not to get in anybody's way and to not to get tangled up in anybody else's business.

Falling into this hospice place was a bit of good luck cause I felt awful tired and needed to rest up. Can't stretch that luck, or I'll be back to doing what I've always done: taking people's good thoughts, making em think something special about me, and then letting em down. And just cause I don't aim to drink don't mean I ain't plenty capable of letting folks down. So the thing to do is get on down the road before things get tangled up. This could be an easy place to like. The weather is good, a little warmer than in the city. And all the people are nice. All of em are weird to varying amounts, but they're all nice too. A time or two I forgot the situation, and that's odd because most the other folks here are in tight spots too, but they don't talk about it, and that's fine, just the way it ought to be. They seem to want to have a good day every day, and that's just what they ought to do.

But then forgettin what's around the bend maybe ain't the best thing.

I ain't sure about much at all. It still seems like it ain't really happening. Those days leading up to when the doctor told me about the mass growing fast, I felt scared. To tell the truth, scareder than any time before. It ain't the first time I nearly died, but those other times happened sudden. If a fellow points a pistol at you, then you probably didn't have no time to think about it, or you wouldn't have been there. I sure wouldn't have if I'd have known what waited outside that bar. But it went down real sudden. And then it was over, and the chance of dying had blown off before giving time to ponder on it. That time the car crashed into the lake with all them hours wet and cold and wondering if I'd be found, the liquor kept me too stupid to be afraid. But this time it all happened real slow.

Plenty of time for thinking lay ahead before that meeting with the doctor, and the more thinking, the more fear. All that worrying before hearing from the doctor focused on the wrong thing. The possibility of death might have occurred to me, but that wasn't the fear that had me so bent out of shape. I spent all them long hours fearing what they might do to me in that hospital. For sure, that doctor was gonna tell me that they found the source of the problem and the way to fix it involved something real bad, painful. Looking back, that seems like a coward's way of thinking.

And then he said I'm gonna die.

Didn't see that one coming.

That first day might have been the easiest. I don't recall dropping any tears over the matter, and that might seem peculiar. I don't recall feeling much of anything except some shame way far back in my mind, and that shame told me there couldn't be no running to anybody for help after not being in no way reliable to anybody, so I just went and saw that lawyer. Since then I've felt free cause nothing really matters no more so long as I don't make a nuisance of myself. Things are just simpler this way. The game is lost, and I'm just running out the clock. Crying would be silly.

Not seeing certain people, knowing that I'll never see certain folks back in Texas could cause hurting, and thinking about it for even just a minute can bring heart crushing sadness like none ever felt, so I stay off that road. Every time pondering goes that way, so does the idea of what it would feel like if they could see what I've gone and done to myself, and that just makes me want to crawl off and be forgotten.

That Guerneville place sounds inviting. But putting too much stock in somebody saying a place out here in California reminds them of Texas could be downright foolish. There ain't no telling how many times I've been told a place has authentic Texas barbecue, but I can say for certain that the last time I had so-called authentic Texas barbecue happened the last time I visited Central Texas. Still, though, that Guerneville place is as good as any to aim for. The story to remember wasn't about it being like Texas. The story was that it had good swimming. Having some of that before the end wouldn't be half bad. That Just Mike fellow said the swimming in Guerneville reminded him of Texas. He said it reminded him of swimming at places in Austin. Don't know if he specially meant Barton

Springs or Krause Springs or some other place. If I had the choice, I'd hope for Krause Springs cause there ain't no prettier place. Thinking about it gives a sort of comfort.

There's freedom in knowing you're about to die, and for me a big part of that freedom is in not needing no sort of complicated plan. When it's more important to stay away from a few known places, that makes choosing where to go easier. It makes it a lot easier. There's a whole lot of road that don't go back to San Francisco or Texas, so gettin about ought not be any trouble. Later the physical part of moving about will get harder and then impossible. That's what the doctors said, and that's what they said to prepare for. Maybe by then I'll have found a place to hole up. If not, there's always tequila and crawling off in the woods dying dead drunk so the coyotes got something to eat. I been saying that to myself as a joke. Sometimes it's funny, and sometimes it ain't.

Sometimes guilt tries to take hold. Having a lawyer do the talking might not be the way regular folks let family know bad news, but then regular folks don't drink to no end instead of showing up at birthday parties and graduations and such. It'd be downright selfish to go back for this trouble after not being no help for any of their trouble. I been selfish my whole life, and there's one last chance to not be selfish, so I aim to take it. Ain't no point in thinking any more about it. It's hard, so the thing to do is just buck up and do what has to be done.

The folks here don't complain about dying or being sick. They whine and moan constantly, but I ain't never heard a one of em gripe about the big dark that's coming, and I can admire that. They mostly complain about each other, but it don't seem to have no real meanness to it. Even that professor pomp-ass that thinks he's so much smarter than everybody else don't seem harmful so much as a thorn that keeps folks from thinking about scarier things. And maybe from his angle, all that talk about high-falutin studies and writing, well maybe that's his way of not thinking about what's coming.

And that's another reason I can't stay too long in this place. First, caring about these folks ain't a good idea cause it'll just lead to hurt, and there ain't no shortage of that. Second, I don't want to forget what's coming cause every time I forget I'll get reminded. It's better to just stay on the same road and understand what's at the end. And at the end of this road is nothing, just nothing. And there ain't no reason to get scared of nothing.

Sometimes the idea of not seeing certain places ever again is stupefying, just hard to swallow. And it ain't just San Francisco. There's other places even harder to revisit. Dixon Creek may still exist, and it probably flows into the Canadian River like it did long before a boy and paint horse sneaked down there at every chance, but there ain't no way to bring back a particular paint horse. He's gone, and there ain't no way to bring back grandparents. Knowing that my own death is just around the bend don't change that. The horse and the grandparents was already gone long before that doctor said to prepare to die, but somehow there was still always the idea that again there would be a Dixon Creek with a paint horse and grandparents who said not to go there. Learning that death is coming soon somehow made it real that they're dead too, and I ain't going to ever see them again even though they're already gone.

Maybe some folks believe in a heaven because of fear of black nothing. Maybe some believe in it because that's what they've been told their whole life. But I wonder if some don't believe in it because it's just hard to comprehend not seeing people and places ever again. The folks that are already gone seem deader now that I'm almost dead too. And the living folks that I'll never again see . . . that just hurts so much that sometimes I want the blackness to hurry up and get it done. But then a second later I want every single minute I'm allowed.

There ain't no heaven, and it don't matter how much some folks believe in it. It just ain't there. It might be a comfort to believe that after the pain and all the coughing has passed and I'm quit of this place that I'll go through a gate and see Chico and my grandparents. Maybe if I had control of what I could believe in I'd believe in that, but then if I had control why not believe in being able to bring Chico back here to this time or all the time that went by since he died. It ain't possible to believe in heaven. Black nothing, not heaven is what is coming. Now maybe I ought to be glad that hell ain't coming neither, but then the fact is I am dying, and all I've ever done is let down folks. That's hell.

But that Guerneville place sounds worth seeing. For now the folks here are tolerable and even entertaining. There won't be no harm in resting up some more so long as I don't get tangled up in anybody's business or get otherwise attached to these comical characters.

It's strange, but even with all this going on I feel like my mind is getting clearer. Maybe my head is getting back to normal after the bump in North Beach. Maybe it's cause booze ain't messing up the circuits. Or maybe it's cause now that I'm dying things just got a whole lot simpler.

But helpless Pieces of the Game He plays
Upon this Chequer-board of Nights and Days;
    Hither and thither moves, and checks, and slays,
And one by one back in the Closet lays.

The Coughing Cowboy and the Reefer Man

Jason woke to another mild spring morning, and on his way along the path between the pastel colored little cottages he saw May morning sun turning dew droplets on blades of grass to citrine gemstones. A cloudless sky of pale blue promised yet another balmy day. Looking up at the baby blue and cyan in the east to darker shades in the west, Jason felt the urge to cough, and after searching his pockets he discovered that he had forgotten his handkerchiefs. Once back inside his room, he decided to leave his hat and canvas jacket.

In the courtyard, Jason encountered Michael wearing headphones and hopping about on his homemade tap shoes. Michael beamed at the sight of Jason, and after he ripped off his headphones he pleaded. "Jason! Let's do that move from yesterday. Let's do it now."

"Aw pardner, it's too early for dancin. I ain't even had any coffee yet. Maybe later."

"Just one time, come on."

Porter, Jolene, and others sat and smoked, and Jolene called out, "Come on, cowboy! Show us your stuff. Show us some dance moves."

Porter added, "Show us that Texas two-step."

Others added to the chorus of cheers and chants, and some clapped.

Michael tugged on Jason's sleeve, and Jason gave in. "All right. All right. Let's get that beat. Lemme hear the tune."

Michael placed his headphones near Jason's right ear, and Jason bent his knees to shorten his height and allow Michael to put his ear next to the headphones. They listened for a moment, and then Jason began to tap his fingers. "Okay, get ready, and one, two, three . . ."

Michael and Jason both sprang away from each other, and both

123

stomped in unison while Porter, Jolene, and the rest of the smoking crowd laughed and cheered. Jason tried to mimic Michael's jerky robotic arm movements, and he stamped his boots to the ground while swaying side to side. While Michael continued dancing, Jason stopped and put his hands on his knees and bent over with his face pointed to the ground. Michael noticed Jason's posture as not part of his planned dance step, and he put his hands on Jason's shoulders while Jason coughed. Jason fell forward to his hands and knees, and the crowd stopped cheering and clapping. Porter hurried to Jason, but Jason waved him away. Between coughs, he said, "I'm fine. I'm fine. I'm fixin to start break dancing. Here in a second, I'm gonna do that thing where I spin on my head."

Michael and Porter helped Jason to his feet, and Jason said, "I told you I needed my coffee first."

Porter continued to help Jason across the courtyard to where they sat with Jolene. Jolene offered Jason a puff of her marijuana cigarette, and Jason said, "No thank you, darlin, but tell me something, honey. Did you steal that man?"

"What man?"

"Dolly's man. You know, that man that talks about you in his sleep, Dolly's man."

"I don't know any Dolly, and I've never stolen a man."

"Well, that's mighty nice of you since you could so easily seeing how your beauty is beyond compare."

Jolene gasped and then laughed. "What has gotten into you, cowboy? You say crazy things."

"It must be your green eyes, honey. They drive me plumb crazy."

Jolene placed her hand on Jason's arm and said, "You sure are some sweet talker. You might be crazy and blind, but you sure do say sweet things to people."

Porter said, "Here comes someone you can sweet talk. The professor will probably write down your every word."

Jason and Jolene looked ahead to see Charles advancing in his broken shuffle, and Porter said, "Let's leave. I'm not in the mood for professor pompous today. Jason didn't you say you wanted some coffee?"

"Yeah, I said that, but I don't have the breath for walking right now, and the two of you better not leave me. Jolene, if you even think of leaving me alone with that pill I'll take back my proposal."

"What proposal."

"Why my proposal of marriage! How could you forget? Are you still stuck on Dolly's man?"

"When did you propose?"

"Just now. I'd get down on a knee, but I don't have the breath."

"What about Tanya Tucker?" Jolene asked.

"I hear she ain't the marrying kind."

Charles stopped his shuffle immediately in front of Jason and said, "Good sir. I would like to remind you that you agreed to tell me your story. I wonder if now would be a convenient time, that is if I can borrow you from the cannabis enthusiasts."

"Well monsignor, truth is me and . . ."

"It's Charles. I am Charles or the professor."

"Right, right Chuckie. But the deal is that me and these canvas enthusticans, as you call em, is talkin about something awful important. Fact is, me and this this emerald eyed beauty is gettin hitched. That is, if she'll have a broke-down lunger."

"Stop it," Jolene said. You're not broke-down. You're adorable."

Charles sat in a chair, opened a notepad, and extracted a pen from a pocket of his tattered tweed sport coat. "So your name is Jason. Might I get your surname?"

"Do you have to write that? I'm kind of on the dodge, you see."

"I just need to list something. Do you have an alias?"

"How about Blank?"

"Fine," Charles huffed. "We can leave it blank. Can you tell me about your upbringing?"

"I was born and raised in New York City. My parents . . ."

Charles frowned and interrupted, "New York? Your voice sounds entirely southern, Tennessee most likely."

"Why thank you, pardner. I worked hard on that. It's part of my cover, you see."

"Okay, New York. Please continue."

"Well sir, I was born in New York City, Brooklyn . . . no, I mean the Bronx. I mean I was born in Brooklyn but raised up in the Bronx. My parents was both scientists, medical research. When I was little, about ten I guess, I got bad sick. My parents thought I was dying from a special disease I might have caught on one of our missionary trips to Africa. Turned out it was just chicken pox but nobody knew that until after I had killed em."

"You killed your parents?"

"Both of em. One then the other."

Charles brows furrowed and his chin jutted out and he asked, "And you were just ten years old?"

"That's right. See, what happened was my parents gave me an experimental drug for the tropical disease they thought I had. During the night I went to seeing things that wasn't there, and I killed them with a pewter jigger."

"A jigger?"

"Yes sir. It's a thing for measuring booze, usually about an ounce or so."

"I know what a jigger is."

"Well, good. This one was sort of like a hammer or double tomahawk. It had a handle and two jiggers at the end. When I was seeing stuff, I thought my parents was giant redheaded flying centipedes, which really do exist and kill folks in Central Africa. Anyway, I beat hell out of the centipedes, but it turned out it was my parents. So the cops put me in a special jail in the Bronx. That's where I grew up, but I escaped at twenty-one and ain't never been caught since."

"If you escaped at twenty-one, that was some time ago. What have you been doing since?"

"Oh, hell, lots of things. For one, I picked up this here Texas . . . I mean Tennessee accent. I got it from a pastry chef back when I was in the kidnapping business. Her daddy was rich, see, and he owned some race tracks in Florida and about half of the ones in Kentucky. Turns out she had a master's degree in linguistics from NYU, and she coached me on how to talk like a Tennessean. Her daddy never did pay up, though. Cheap bastard."

"Did you kill her?"

"Naw, I ain't much of a killer except for my parents and a few Burmese pirates. Had to let her go. See, I went and let her in on the business on account of her being so smart, but I had to leave to pick up some emeralds in Venezuela, and while I was gone she met this fella that was half Chinese, half Irish. Nice fellow too, and they got married while I was in a Colombian jail and had twins, two girls. One come out white and the other full Chinese. Damndest thing. Now she owns a donut shop in Louisville, and both her daughters skipped elementary and high school and went straight to college, one to Cambridge and the other to UC Santa Cruz."

Charles looked at his notes, and tapped his pen on the paper. "You said you killed some Burmese pirates. Can you tell me about your time in the orient?"

"Oh, them pirates. Yes sir, killed a whole boatload of em. They was trying to take the rubies I had traded anacondas for, and I just couldn't let them do that cause I needed those rubies for . . ."

Charles interrupted and said, "Anacondas come from South America. Are you sure you don't mean pythons or boas?"

"I'm sure. I mean anacondas. Had one as a pet from when I was in Venezuela prospecting for diamonds . . . I mean emeralds, and while we was on our way to the orient she had a mess of babies, and I traded em for rubies. But about them pirates, they sneaked up on me while I was nappin in a hammock, and I didn't have no gun, but . . ."

A commotion among the smokers in the courtyard made Jason stop. Jolene put her hand on Jason's shoulder and said, "We'll be back."

Porter added, "And then we can go get coffee."

Jolene and Porter left the courtyard and joined a crowd near the stone building. Jason asked Charles, "What's all that about?"

"The weekly supply of cannabis has arrived. And these mindless rats want their cheese. You we're saying that the pirates were upon you while you slept. Please continue."

"Maybe later." Jason walked toward the crowd, but he stopped several yards back. As the crowd thinned and people walked away, Jason saw something peculiar about the person distributing little green bags, but he caught only brief glimpses because as soon as the crowd parted enough to give Jason a line of sight it shifted again and blocked view. When all but a few of the group had departed, Jason saw the person of everyone's interest. A short snowy headed and bearded man took little plastic bags from a soiled leather backpack.

Jason approached the man and said, "So you're the reefer man?"

The white haired man handed a bag to Jason and then reached in the backpack for another and looked for the next person. Jason extended the bag back to the man and said, "What am I supposed to do with this? Did you get your buddy's car locked up again? Am I supposed to sell this?"

The man froze for a moment and then looked at Jason. Jason asked, "Is it true you're one of the original Haight Street hippies?"

The man remained frozen. His eyes widened, and his mouth hung open, but he said nothing.

"Don't tell me you already forgot your weed slinging picture selling buddy, Bobrick."

"Jason . . . but . . ." Bobrick uttered. "What are you doing here?"

"Well, a minute ago I was dancin. After that I was telling my life story to a puffed up piece of . . ." Jason stopped when he noticed Bobrick's troubled look. He appeared shaken, near tears.

"Oh, I guess I do look a little different." Jason said. "Hey pardner, buck up. It's all right. I shoulda told you. If it makes a difference, I didn't tell anybody except a lawyer."

Bobrick let his leather backpack fall to the ground, and Jason bent to grab it. "I remember this. Whew, it still has that earthy smell."

Bobrick took the pack and then gave small bags to the few remaining people. "Jason, what is going on? How did this happen?"

"You got a minute? There's a coffee shop across the way over next to the grocery store. Can I buy you a cup?"

VI. Big Green

Would but the Desert of the Fountain yield
One glimpse—if dimly, yet indeed, reveal'd,
    To which the fainting Traveler might spring,
As springs the trampled herbage of the field!

And this reviving Herb whose tender Green
Fledges the River-Lip on which we lean—
   Ah, lean upon it lightly! for who knows
From what once lovely Lip it springs unseen!

The Farm

Pain made getting out of bed difficult. Jason wished he had more clothing as he put on the canvas jacket and reached for his hat. Outside, an overcast sky offered dreariness without the promise of rain. Increased pain in his chest and back made walking a challenge, and Jason hoped the pain would ease as the day progressed. In the courtyard, Jolene and Porter huddled together while they smoked. No one hopped about on homemade tap shoes.

Jason sat near Jolene and Porter and asked, "Where's Michael?"

Jolene answered, "The ambulance came for him last night."

"Well, I'll be damned." Jason said. "How old is that kid? Where are they keeping him? I'll go see him."

"No need," Porter said.

"What?"

Neither Porter not Jolene answered. Both gazed ahead at the ground.

After a moment, Jason said, "Yall excuse me, please."

In the room in the lemon chiffon cottage, Jason reached into the bottom of his leather bag and extracted his ornate metal flask. He looked at it a moment and then shoved it back in the bag. Then he shoved in the shocking pink zippered pouch and his clothes from the wall locker. He slung the bag over his shoulder and left the room.

At the coffee shop, Jason accepted the cup and then took it to a table outside. When a large and new Mercedes Benz parked in front of Jason's position, he took no notice until he saw a mass of white hair emerge from the driver's side. Bobrick joined Jason at the table and said, "I can't tell you how glad I was to get your call."

"You sure made it here fast. Is that your buddy's car, the one you got locked up down in San Francisco?"

Bobrick laughed. "No, no way. That's Eleanor's car. She owns the land where I live. She owns a lot of land. She inherited it and a lot of money, and she's into all sorts of causes. That's all she does is host meetings. She lets me live there because she thinks I'm an organic farmer. She knows about the kind bud, but she thinks I do it organically."

"Do you?"

"Brother, I use whatever makes the kind buds the biggest and most potent. Are you ready to go see my farm?"

When they turned west off the major highway, Jason said, "These are some big trees."

"They get even bigger where we're going."

"How far did you say your place is from Guerneville?"

"About ten miles as the crow flies. What made you change your mind about coming to stay at my place? Did something happen at The Hospice? You seemed pretty determined to stay there last time we talked."

Jason watched the big trees rushing by and said, "It was time to go. That's a place where folks go to die. But I don't want to spend what time is left being surrounded by other people's suffering or complaining about mine. You do understand this visit is just for a little while, and then I got to be gettin on down the road, right?"

"I understand. Can I ask you another question?"

"Shoot, pardner."

"When are you going to tell your family in Texas?"

Jason watched the flash of green at the side of the roadway, and after a while he said, "Done told a lawyer and paid him. Once I kick it, he has the information for the bank account and storage in San Francisco. He'll pass those on to the folks in Texas."

Bobrick continued driving without reply, and Jason watched the big trees. "You're thinking that having a lawyer tell the folks ain't no way to break the news," Jason said. "But you don't know the whole situation."

"Brother, I don't judge."

"That's much appreciated. But you must be thinking that ain't no way to go about things. But as things is, you see, I ain't never been nothing but a disappointment. Folks who depended on me found out that the only thing I could be counted on for was drinking and being loyal to the bottle. Plenty of times instead of helping out, I was off somewhere drunk. So now that I've ended my life, I can't go back. They'd do anything for me, and then I'd die and disappoint em again. Can't do that."

"You can't say you never helped anyone. You helped me out of an impossible jam the first time we met."

"That was a fun day."

"And I'm glad you changed your mind and decided to come stay at the farm," Bobrick said.

"We really did sell that whole bag of weed down in the Haight, didn't we?" Jason laughed and said, "We did all that, and not a single cop took a close look. You still have that serape?" Jason's laughter increased until it turned to coughing. He bent forward in the seat and covered his mouth with a handkerchief. When the coughing subsided, he sat back in the seat and titled his head up and toward the window taking in shallow and difficult breaths.

"Are you under a doctor's care?" Bobrick asked.

"Well, I got that hospital appointment in a few days."

"Don't worry about that appointment. You'll be there. Are you taking anything for the pain?"

"The doc offered me a prescription, but I didn't take it. After spending most of my life liquored up. It'd be a shame to spend the last of it drugged."

"Have you considered cannabis?"

"I have a hard enough time breathing as it is. Don't need to be inhaling no smoke."

"You don't have to smoke it. There are edibles and tinctures. I have plenty of kind bud if you ever want to try any."

"I'll keep that in mind, pardner. Sometimes a big jug of wine or a bunch of shots of tequila sounds good, but my drinkin days are over. All my days are soon to be over."

"Is that an absolute certainty?" Bobrick asked. "Isn't there any chance you can recover?"

"Sure. There's a chance. But as I understand it from what the doctors told me, that chance is about the same as getting dealt an unbeatable hand of five card stud as soon as you sit at the table. Now I ain't much of a gambler, but I know when chances are so slim they ain't even worth thinking about."

The rural road curved and descended and climbed, and Jason said, "You weren't kidding about the trees getting bigger." Jason leaned toward the window trying to look up to find the tops of the trees that seemed to meet over the road. "I don't believe I've ever seen trees this big. Back where I come from, some of the mesquites and junipers we call trees you'd call bushes."

"We're almost to the farm. There's something I need to tell you about before we get there. It's about Eleanor, the owner."

"Does she keep her face in a jar by the door?"

"What?" Bobrick asked.

"Oh nothin. You was saying?"

"Yeah, Eleanor is the owner, and she means well, but she can come across as meddlesome to put it mildly. She absolutely does mean well, though she has some strange notions of how to save the world. She knows you're coming, and she knows you're ill, so we can count on her being around at times. I just thought I should warn you and tell you to try to remember that she has the best of intentions always."

"I'll keep that in mind."

Bobrick steered the car off the rural road onto another smaller paved road that led into the trees. A few hundred yards from the rural highway, they passed a gate. Just beyond the gate stood a house, and in the paved driveway stood and old Jeep. Bobrick parked the car in front of the Jeep, and said, "This is the old carriage house. It's been converted more than once over the years. The main estate house is farther down this road, but Eleanor just uses it for meetings and parties. There are people out here every day for all of her causes, but she lives in Santa Rosa these days."

Jason got out of the car and walked over to the Jeep. "This here's the real deal, ain't it?"

"Yeah, it's a Willys postwar civilian model. I got it about ten years ago, and I've been doing my best to get it completely restored. It's not totally street legal right now, and I don't have the headlights connected yet, but it runs great, and I use it every day here on the property. Come on in and I'll show you the house."

Jason followed Bobrick inside, and he saw that much of the original space of the carriage house had been preserved. Most of the house still consisted of a single room where kitchen blended with living area. Across the ceiling, a large beam extended the width of the house, and a fan with pulleys and weights dropped from the beam. "Is that one of those old fans from before electricity?" Jason asked.

"It sure is." Bobrick pulled one of the weights, and the fan began to spin. "See over there where the ceiling is lower? That's where the place has been converted to a kind of loft. There are two bedrooms and a bathroom up there. You can take the bedroom on the right. The stairs are over by the far wall. I need to take Eleanor's car down to the main house. Make yourself at home. I'll be right back, and then we can go see the farm."

Jason looked about the main room and saw many items he always wanted but never got around to acquiring. Though the converted carriage house had a fully modern kitchen, it also contained a variety of antiques and oddities. Opposite the kitchen in the living area, a pot-bellied wood burning stove stood where a fireplace might be in another home. Jason opened the little iron door and saw ashes from a previous fire. He followed the smokestack to where it exited through the ceiling. He thought about turning the crank to the Victor Victrola phonograph, but the 1970s jukebox beckoned. Jason looked behind the machine and saw that the power cord extended to the wall, and the temptation to play a selection could have been overwhelming but for the many other treasures in the room. Near the counter dividing the kitchen and living area, a mechanical pachinko machine from the same era as the jukebox stood on a sturdy table. The temptation proved too much, and Jason pressed down the lever and released it. A little metal ball shot upward then danced down through the pins before disappearing. Before he succumbed to playing with more of the wondrous toys, Jason went up the stairs, found the room Bobrick mentioned, and left his shoulder bag on the bed before going outside and looking at the Jeep.

Jason had managed to walk around the vehicle only once before he saw Bobrick approaching along the narrow paved road. "You have the vehicles and toys I've always wanted," Jason said. "Is any of that stuff inside yours, or does it go with the estate?"

"Oh, it's all mine. You'd be surprised what you can get when you have a knack for fixing things and when you always have kind bud to trade. Most of that stuff didn't work or was broken somehow and came from people who liked kind bud but were short of cash."

"That's impressive. I didn't have no idea you were so handy with fixing things."

"I'm an electrician by trade, but I've always tinkered with stuff. I have rent paid on this carriage house in perpetuity just for the kitchen remodeling. And of course Eleanor pays me for the work on the estate. I fix most everything, and she lets me farm the kind bud and even sell to her friends."

"Her friends like the reefer?"

Bobrick laughed and said, "That whole rich do-gooder society of hers runs on kind bud. Speaking of which, let's go see the farm." Bobrick got in the driver side of the Jeep, and Jason approached the passenger side when Bobrick said, "Do you want to drive?'

Jason jumped into the driver seat and didn't wait for any instruction before he started the engine, put the transmission in gear, and started to ease out on the clutch. "Take the road down that way. We'll pass the main house soon," Bobrick said.

Jason slowed the Jeep as they passed by the main house and said, "Yall call that a main house, but where I come from we'd call it a mansion or a castle. Course we ain't got nothin like that where I come from." Jason noticed all the high-value cars parked outside the main house. "Is one of those meetings you mentioned going on now?"

"Yeah, it's a save something or an anti-something. I don't keep track. The road is going to curve a little to the left and then a hard right, and then we'll be at the greenhouse."

Jason followed Bobrick into the greenhouse, and he saw rows of green plants, but the giant tank full of goldfish impressed Jason most. "This thing is about the size of one of our stock tanks back home. Why do you have so many big goldfish in it? You don't eat em, do you?"

"No, I don't eat them. One of Eleanor's environmentalist friends talked to her about aquaculture, so she asked me why I didn't use that method. I told her I'd give it a try if she'd pay for the equipment. I'm still evaluating it. See these pipes here? These take the water with the fish waste to these planters here. It's supposed to be a self-sustaining method. So far it seems to be a great way to dispose of fish food. Now over here is my pride and joy."

Jason looked at the plants stretching up almost to the roof of the greenhouse and said, "Those are big as little trees."

"Yeah, those are some of my sativa strains. It's going to be a hell of a crop this year."

"Follow me in here, and I'll show you more of my hydroponic operation." When they reached a doorway, Bobrick stopped and handed Jason some blue sunglasses. Inside the room, powerful high intensity lights hung over a sea of smaller plants. "These are hybrid strains mostly, and I use a few different hydro methods, but most of the operation is a drip and deep water culture set up."

"I have no idea what any of that means, pardner. But it sounds impressive. Where I come from people farm in the dirt."

Bobrick said, "Then let's go see the fields."

At the Jeep, Jason started to get in the driver seat, but a sudden bout of coughing caused him to double over. When he regained his breath, he said, "I believe you better drive."

Bobrick steered the Jeep back toward the carriage house, and said, "We can see the fields when you're feeling better. You can get some rest back at the house."

"Can I play with some of them toys too?"

The Revelations of Devout and Learn'd
Who rose before us, and as Prophets burn'd,
   Are all but Stories, which, awoke from Sleep
They told their comrades, and to Sleep return'd.

The Fruitcake

Jason wrapped the dishtowel around the handle of the percolating coffee pot on the stove and moved it to the counter, and as he poured coffee into a cup Bobrick entered the carriage house.

"Hey pardner, you're just in time."

"I forgot about that old thing and haven't used it in ages."

"Well sir, after the last couple of mornings of bad coffee, it's time to go back to more familiar ways. I've made many a cup of coffee in percolators just like this one but don't understand these more modern ones, especially that fancy glass French contraption of yours."

"The coffee you've been making the last few days was fine."

"Then you're a man of low standards when it comes to coffee, or I've become more picky since this is the closest thing I do to work all day. Are you sure there ain't nothing I can do to help you out in the fields?"

"I'm sure," Bobrick said. "Just keep relaxing. Just keep enjoying your walks in the woods, and if you need to go into town for anything, just let me know. We'll arrange a ride or lend you a car. And that reminds me of something I need to talk to you about. You have that doctor's appointment this afternoon, and I was planning on taking you, but Eleanor says she wants to."

"The lady that owns the place?"

"That's right. She's coming by this morning to meet you, and then she'll be by again later to take you to the doctor. I'm sorry about that, but it's her car I was going to borrow. She loves feeling like she's helping."

Bobrick removed jars containing marijuana buds from a satchel and placed them on the counter. He took smaller, more decorative jars from the cupboard and set them alongside the larger jars. As he filled the smaller jars, Jason asked, "Is that from the fields?"

"No, that harvest won't be until the fall. This is from the hydroponic garden. Eleanor is having a couple of meetings tonight, and these are samples. After the meetings, some of her friends will likely stop to buy more."

"So these friends of the lady that owns the place get together, talk about saving the world, and get stoned?"

Bobrick laughed. "That is absolutely correct. For the most part, they're a bunch of idiots with too much money and time on their hands, but they bring me a regular stream of cash."

A knock sounded at the door, but Bobrick continued filling jars. "That will be Eleanor," he said.

The door opened, and a short and plump woman entered. She had silver-gray hair that she wore unbound, and it stretched straight and long down her back almost to her waist. "Good morning," Eleanor said, and as she approached Jason and passed Bobrick she patted Bobrick's shoulder. She wore sandals and a loose and billowing peach blouse she tucked into a long denim skirt. "You must be Jason. I'm so happy to meet you. I heard about that wonderful thing you did for Patrick in San Francisco. It's just terrible that those police bothered him at all. We're all lucky he had a friend like you. Thank you."

"Well, I ain't sure wonderful is what I'd call what we done, but thank you anyway. Pleased to meet you."

"I understand that you have an appointment later today. I'll be back later to get you and hope to have a surprise for you. Call it a welcome gesture and an expression of gratitude for the kindness you showed our Patrick."

Eleanor joined Bobrick at the counter, and said, "I'm so glad you have more. We ran out yesterday at the anti-BPA, and tonight we have the anti-GMO. We'll surely need more." Bobrick put labels on the decorative jars and then gave them to Eleanor. As she neared the door, she said, "I'll see you later, Jason. I look forward to our little trip."

Once the door had closed after Eleanor, Jason said, "Bobrick, there's a couple of things I got to ask you. First, and tell the truth, was that your mama? Are you actually the son of rich parents and still living at home?"

Bobrick frowned and said, "I'm from Stockton, and I'm far from being the son of rich parents."

"All right then. The other question is what did you tell her about what happened in San Francisco? From what she said to me, you couldn't have told her what really happened."

"I told it exactly as it happened and had to tell it a hundred times. She asked me to tell it over and over, and then she made me go to her save the world meetings and tell each of those groups. She loves that story. I'm surprised she didn't ask you to tell it, but she might ask you about it when she gives you a ride today."

"Hope not. Ain't no good at telling stories, at least not truthfully anyway."

After Bobrick left to tend his crop, Jason finished the rest of the coffee, washed the percolator, and fell asleep. He woke to Eleanor knocking and then entering the room. After following her outside and getting in the passenger seat of the Mercedes, he said, "Appreciate the ride. Don't expect no good to come of this appointment, but it was already set, so I figured I'd keep it."

"Oh, it's my pleasure. I'm delighted to meet a friend of Patrick's. I need to make one very brief stop along the way, and it's nearby."

Before they had traveled more than two miles, Eleanor turned off the road and parked in front of a building. A sign on the building said Animal Hospital. "I'll be just a minute, and then we'll be on our way."

After they resumed the route, Eleanor said, "As I said, I'm delighted to meet a friend of Patrick's but thrilled to meet the person who got him out of that unfortunate situation in the city. You must be a creative and resourceful person."

"Don't know about that and don't know how you can be so impressed with me and Bobrick committing crimes down in San Francisco."

"Committing crimes? Why it sounds like it was the police who committed a crime in bothering him. What crimes did you commit?"

Jason said, "Bobrick told me he told you that story a dozen times, and he said you made him tell it at all your save the whales meetings. What more can I say?"

"I do not have save the whales meetings, though, of course, I think whales are magnificent creatures."

"Me too, of course."

"I do host several very important meetings. We have an anti-BPA group, an anti-GMO group, and the Organic Coalition. That's the group that hopes to have only organic produce sold and served in Sonoma County."

"What's BPA?" Jason asked.

"I don't recall what the letters stand for, but it's plastic for drinking containers."

"What's the other one, G-something?"

"GMO," Eleanor explained, "Stands for genetically modified organism."

"Sounds to me like yall hate affordable groceries. Is that about the size of it?"

"Why no. It has nothing to do with that. Our groups promote healthy choices."

"Choices? That's funny to say cause it sounds to me like you're trying to limit choices. Sounds to me like you're trying to keep poor folks from getting groceries they can afford. Do the folks in your groups hate all poor people?"

Exasperated, Eleanor exclaimed, "No, no we want to protect all people."

"Oh, maybe I misunderstood. Seeing how none of that stuff yall are against is actually harmful for anyone, I figured yall didn't like it cause it don't cost enough."

"Not harmful? That's preposterous!"

"How many people in your groups are scientists?"

Eleanor remained silent a moment and then said, "I don't think we have any scientists."

"But you probably have scientists from universities and such come to your meetings and talk, right? Surely you wouldn't go and spend your money and time without checking with experts, right? You wouldn't have all those meetings just cause someone in the group said plastic is bad, right?"

Eleanor did not answer nor did she appear to be about to answer, so Jason asked, "And about them groups that have opinions on crops and food, how many farmers you got in your groups? You ever have any farmers come talk or maybe even agricultural scientists? My grandparents was farmers before moving to where I was born, and I'm pretty sure they'd be all for anything that helped the crops."

"Several of our members grow vegetables, and all of us shop at the farmer's market."

"That's real good, but that's gardening, not farming."

Eleanor did not reply. She drove the car and did not take her eyes off the road. After several minutes of silence, Jason said, "I shouldn't have said all that. What do I know, anyway? I'm just a drifter who's about to die, and so I was just havin some fun. Didn't mean to offend, especially after your kind hospitality. Besides, I ought not let my life-long feud with hippies get me wound up."

"What have you against hippies?"

"My parents was hippies."

Eleanor laughed, "Well then, of course you feud. How then did you ever become friends with Patrick?"

"Ole Bobrick made me feel bad about running my mouth just like I done with you a minute ago. I made some nippy comment about him looking like a mountain man."

"He does look like a man of the mountain. But why do you call him Bobrick?"

"Oh, he didn't tell you all the story, I see. I was walking around San Francisco trying to find something to do other than drink and on my first days away from the hooch, and around a big rock stood a mountain of white hair, and it gave me a start. I said something about it, something that riled him some, so when I first asked his name he said he was Bob. Later he told me he was Patrick. So now he's Bobrick."

"Would you believe that when I first met him he had very short hair?"

"Then you've known him a good long spell."

Eleanor looked ahead at the road and appeared to be struggling with a calculation. "Wow. It has been a long time. It's been over fifteen years. He worked for an electrical company, and he came to do some work back when I lived in the house and back when my son was still alive. My boy was also named Patrick, and he used to follow Patrick, Bobrick, everywhere. He found everything Patrick did fascinating. Little Patrick was still in the first grade, and he wanted to be an electrician like big Patrick. That was so long ago."

Eleanor steered the car near the front doors of the hospital and said, "I'll be here when you're finished. Good luck."

Jason got out of the car and paused a bit before entering the hospital.

When he came back through the same doors, he did so with haste. He pushed the door so hard that it flung away from him. Jason noticed the Mercedes parked nearby, and when he got in the car he said, "Hope you didn't wait here the whole time."

"Oh no, I attended to several errands."

After several miles and no conversation, Eleanor said, "I hope you didn't get bad news."

"Nah, they didn't tell me anything that hadn't been said the hospital in San Francisco."

"It must be frightening."

"Sometimes. To be honest with you, ma'am, I don't know how I feel most of the time."

"Have you tried any alternative medicine?" Eleanor asked. "I know several herbalists, and one of the members of our group is an acupuncturist."

"Now that's a fine idea! I'll get stabbed up like a pin cushion, eat the right weeds, and while I'm at it a chiropractor can twist on my backbone till it's a knotted lariat, and then I'll be just fine again. We can go get a tequila and beer after. Yee haw!"

Eleanor laughed and said, "I take it that non-traditional methods are out with you. That's okay. That's your choice."

"I'm sorry. Don't mean to be so sarcastic all the time."

"That's quite all right."

"Can I ask how your boy died?"

Eleanor's lips tightened, she took a deep breath, and then she said, "He rode his bicycle off the estate and onto the main road. He wasn't supposed to do that, but he was a headstrong boy. Patrick was the first to see him. He was on his way to the house to fix something, and he arrived at the accident. Little Patrick had already been taken to the hospital by the time I found out."

Miles of enormous trees passed before Eleanor spoke again. "Patrick took it hard. He had grown fond of my little boy. He quit his job. He just stopped going to work after the accident. Of course, I couldn't live in that house anymore, but I heard that Patrick had been seen there often. He started going to the estate every day, and when he finished the electrical work, he worked on other things. He's still doing it."

When they arrived at the carriage house and Eleanor stopped the car behind the Jeep, Jason said, "Thank you for the ride. It was nice talking with you."

"Thank you too, Jason. And don't forget that I have a surprise for you later today. It might be ready now. I'll check and be back."

Inside the carriage house, Bobrick sat at the kitchen counter and used tools on what appeared to be some metal mechanical object. When Jason got closer, he saw two spheres, one large and one small, connected to the same metal stand and supported by multiple metal braces. As he watched Bobrick test moving parts, Jason realized the larger sphere represented the Earth and the smaller the moon. He read the yellowed and faded words terrestrial globe, and he asked, "How old is that thing?"

"I'm not sure. A friend of mine found it among family stuff and traded with me."

Jason looked closer at the globe, and said, "From those boundaries in Europe, this thing must have been made before World War I if not way before that. Wow."

A knock at the door preceded the door opening and the shout, "Surprise!"

Both Jason and Bobrick turned to see Eleanor standing in the doorway. Eleanor pointed to the ground, and Jason looked down to see that Eleanor held a leash connected to a collar on the neck of a dog. The thin dog held its tail between its legs and shook. It had a pointed nose and a multicolored coat that began as black and white on the face then tiger striped to mid-back and then a chaotic mixture of spots near the hind quarters and rear legs.

Jason looked at Bobrick but said nothing.

Bobrick said, "Eleanor, I'm not sure this is a good idea."

"But of course it's a good idea. This adorable dog needs a home, and she can be a comfort to Jason. Jason, you like dogs, don't you?"

Jason tried to speak, but his mouth just hung open. He blinked hard a few times and said, "I ain't sure that's a dog. It looks like a psychedelic appaloosa."

The one main thing that had to be avoided has gone and happened. The biggest hindrance to being a drifter is getting tangled up, tangled up in the business of somebody else or just tangled up. Dropping off that dog amounts to about the most senseless thing a person could have done. You don't give a dying man a dog. You give him a big jug of wine or a kind word to two. You don't give him a dog. Senseless and downright selfish is what it amounts to. With all that yearning to do something kind for the dying man, there just wasn't any thought whatsoever give to what was best for the dog. And that just burns me up.

I ought not have hollered and taken so much of it out on Bobrick that first day the dog came. The person that deserved the hollering, Eleanor, had already cleared out by the time my wits returned. She just blew in with that word surprise and then blew back out to one of her meetings of idiots. I had about half a mind to head on down there to her estate house and give her a piece of my mind, but Bobrick kept saying to calm down and that we'd figure something out.

What I should have done was get on down the road right then and there.

But I didn't, and so now there's this dog to look after. She ain't no trouble at all, and she's a real fine dog. But that ain't the point. The point is that now this dog is gonna go and get attached to someone who is gonna die on her and leave her alone. Some folks must be plumb stupid not to know that being left hurts a dog just like it does a person. And that just burns me up.

She is a good dog, though. If I wasn't dying, I'd be mighty proud to have her. But there ain't no use in thinking about that cause it just leads to everything I been trying to dodge, not getting in folks' way and not getting tangled up in nobody else's business. This is a damned sorry state.

Before Eleanor went and did that stupid thing, a fellow could almost forget about dying. This place, this estate and the country around it is some of the most beautiful land I've ever seen. The trees are even bigger than the ones up in Washington State, but here it don't rain as much. In fact, it hadn't rained in a good long spell of a week or more. It feels hot to me after all them years in San Francisco, but if I think about Texas, especially Central Texas, I remember what hot is. Folks down there used to say they had four seasons: December, January, February, and summer. But here the temperature is bearable. It's gets a little warm in the afternoons, but the mornings, evenings, and nights are fine.

These trees are something else. Trails through these woods let a fellow like me from the flat land of the High Plains get lost in a hurry. There ain't no landmarks in these woods, and most of the time you can't see in a straight line more than a few yards. Back home you can usually see for a couple dozen miles. The woods can be dark and spooky too. A couple of times thoughts of death combined with the gloom and shadows of them woods, and I couldn't get out and back to the estate fast enough.

One of the many things I'll regret not seeing again is the fog in San Francisco, and up until coming here to this estate I thought white walls of cotton air happened only in that city. That ain't true at all. Sometimes the fog out in them trees is as thick as it ever was in the city. It floats in among those trees and makes things wet, and the temperature drops a considerable amount, and I start to shivering and thinking on getting on back to the carriage house for my jacket but usually just stay out there shivering cause it's such a sight. When just a kid, I read stuff about characters like Robin Hood who lived in a forest. This place is sort of how Robin Hood's forest might have been, all green and not too warm or too cold. But I never could have imagined trees so big and so tall. Robin Hood didn't have no trees this big.

Turns out, that Guerneville place ain't so close after all. I asked Bobrick about how to get there the other day, and he said something about having to go all the way back to Santa Rosa and then west on a river road. That surprised me cause he had told me that this place was ten miles from Guerneville, but then he explained that it's ten miles as a crow flies. That don't make no sense to me since where I come from a place is as far away as it takes to get there, but then the folks up here are as different to me as the trees.

One thing that ain't all that different, though, is that folks up here got pain and the stories to go with it. What Eleanor told me about her boy dying and how Bobrick came to live here is one of them stories. There ain't no other kind of pain as bad as that. It's one thing for a regular person to die, but a child dying has to be about the worst thing there is. Take a fellow like me and let him die, and the world keeps turning. Maybe some folks are sad. There won't be too many of them in my case, and that's good in some ways. It's a strange comfort to me to know that I ain't leaving too much behind. But when a young person or child dies . . . well, that just takes away any reason to keep doing much of anything. I admire Bobrick and Eleanor for being able to find ways to keep going. Bobrick fixed up the estate, especially this carriage house, into a real fine spread. Eleanor became the queen of saving the world idiots. I'd have probably drunk myself to death or at least into a hospital or jail. Most folks are stronger than me.

I've thought a lot about that hospice place. Leaving there without a word might have been rude after all their kindness that didn't cost me a dime, but there wasn't nothing to say. Michael was too young for passing on, and the rest of us folks just waited our turn to follow him. I didn't want to be part of that. It had come time to be moving on while there still was time.

Time keeps moving, and it's more noticeable than ever before. Every day could be the one when things take a turn for the worse and I won't be able to get out of bed. Thinking that way has me studying about next stops on down the road. It sure would be nice to get to see that Guerneville place while so close, but with death coming a destination don't really matter so much as keeping moving and dodging getting tangled up. And that's what has me so vexed about the dog. I got to find a place for this dog before leaving, and that's a chore I ought not have been saddled with. Eleanor is the one that knows everybody, so maybe she can find a place for the little dog. Then again, the folks she knows are fruitcakes, and they'd probably decide this dog needs some kind of fruitcake food. Maybe we can put the little dog with some normal folks, but in this country that might be a tall order. Kids that would let her sleep in their beds would be good. She's a sweetheart, and she deserves the attention.

The way that little dog looks took some getting used to, but she won me over, and now she's a beautiful creature. Bobrick found out from Eleanor that the little dog is a whippet. I hadn't ever heard of them dogs and hadn't ever seen one. She's just like any other dog but prettier than most.

The day after the dog come, I was still vexed thinking about ways to get out of here. That's when I realized this place is a little bit of a trap. It ain't a trap like jail or something, but being on this estate off a country road that leads one way back to Santa Rosa and another way off somewheres deeper in the woods makes getting out of here on my own kind of a challenge. I can't walk that far without resting. When hiking in these woods, there's almost as much resting as walking. The day after the dog come, a notion I'm none too proud of entered my head. It sure would be a lot of fun to take one of them fancy cars from the meetings at the estate house. It ain't that I'm a thief at heart so much as it is the hankering for being on the road in a fine automobile at least once before dying. I ain't had no need for driving in a lot of years, never had a car the whole time in San Francisco, and maybe I just miss that feeling of driving like on them Texas Panhandle roads that went on and on. Still, that'd be a rotten thing to do to Eleanor and Bobrick after all they done for me. Even if the dumb old bat did dump a dog on me, stealing one of her friend's cars wouldn't be no kind of good.

But it's good for everybody around that my mind is still clearing. If I'd have taken a notion a few weeks ago to boost a car, it might have happened even though I never was a thief. But then I never was coughing up and out my life either. One time years ago while locked up for some drunken brawl, a car thief shared the cell, and he turned out to be a nice entertaining fellow. He'd be tickled to know about the notion of taking a car that didn't belong to me. But these days thinking seems to be a little clearer, so I ain't gonna steal. What I have been doing instead is surprising enough. Bobrick has quite a few books and magazines around this place, and I've been reading some. It's been ages since reading without getting confused or bored. The other day I took one of his science magazines, sat on a rock in the woods, and read till my behind hurt.

Here lately, there ain't no need to take stuff to read in the woods since the little dog goes with me. It sure is pleasurable to walk with that little dog. At the same time, though, it's worrisome. I'm already attached to her, and there ain't nothing to be done about that, but she can't be getting the idea I can be counted on, that I'm gonna be around. Every look at that sweet little dog is both happiness and sadness. She has a way of making me feel like she thinks as highly of me as I think of her. But she also makes me feel like I'm responsible for her, and that can't go on. At my best, I wasn't no good at responsibility, and now that I'm dying ain't no time to start being dependable, even if that had been an ambition.

That ain't my ambition. The only goal is to get on down the road without getting tangled up. But I'm gonna miss that little dog.

A Book of Verses underneath the Bough,
A Jug of Wine, a Loaf of Bread—and Thou
　　Beside me singing in the Wilderness—
Oh, Wilderness were Paradise enow!

Solstice

A focused wet spot woke him, and when he opened his eyes he saw the moist round black orb with two holes. "Good morning, baby girl," Jason said. A pink tongue moved across his face in a wide swath. The little dog stood her two front paws on Jason's chest, and she bent her head to look down directly into his eyes. "Did I oversleep? Do you need to go outside?"

The dog jumped off the bed, and once Jason reached the door to the bedroom she dashed down the stairs. She did not wait for Jason to open the front door wider than necessary for her to slither snake-like out onto the porch and then dart onto the grass. He found the percolator, but before he could pour in either coffee or water he heard the scratch at the door. While he made coffee, she sat on her hind legs and watched. "Are you hungry, darlin? Just a second, and I'll fix you something to eat." She had finished her breakfast before his coffee brewed, and she waited for him on the couch.

Jason sipped coffee and read the local newspaper while she rested her head between extended paws. As he turned the pages, her eyes moved back and forth, and she inched closer until her paws touched his thigh. He moved his hand lengthwise up and down her back. When he set the coffee and newspaper aside, she raised her head to resemble a long-nosed sphinx, and Jason said, "All right, honey. Let me get some clothes on and then we'll go."

As Jason neared the door of the carriage house, the little dog spun in two complete circles, and Jason laughed. Once outside on the estate grounds, she pranced sometimes to his left and sometimes to his right and sometimes ahead but never more than a few yards away. Occasionally she stopped to let Jason catch up. As they traveled down the long lane of the estate and passed the main house, Jason saw a Mercedes parked outside the house, and he quickened his gait. He pointed to an opening in the tree line and called to the dog, "Let's take this trail. I don't want to run into the surprise lady this morning. We can take the other trail later."

The little dog followed Jason to the tree line and between two enormous Coastal Redwoods that stood as a gate to a trail that meandered into the green shadowy woods. The morning fog had cleared early, and the lawns of the estate stretched under brilliant golden sun, but under the canopy of the redwoods a dimmer, cooler realm enveloped Jason and the little dog. She led the way, and he followed her past the colossal trunks, past ferns of many types, and over lush beds of sorrel. Rustling in the branches above prompted the dog to look up, but just as often a rustling in the bush caused her to shoot ahead and stick a pointed nose into a fern and then emerge with a dew laden face.

When the level ground began to descend and the trail switched back one way and then the other, Jason had to slow his pace and pay more attention to his footing. She waited with patience for him to catch up before again springing surefooted on downward to the sound of a brook. Beside the stream, he found mossy boulders and looked around for one with less green. While he sat and breathed irregular with intermittent coughs, the little dog stepped into the clear water that rose halfway to her chest. She lapped water, and when she lifted her head upright drops rejoined the brook. With perked ears she looked down into the water at flitting minnows. Back and forth to each bank she walked, and when she shoved her head into yet another fern Jason said, "You better be glad we ain't in Texas, girl. The way you're poking around is just the perfect way to run into a cottonmouth." The little dog looked at Jason while he spoke and then resumed her hunt. "Bobrick said there ain't no snakes to worry about out here, but if we was back where I come from what you're doing would have me worried some."

Sunlight filtered down through the branches in beams, and where those beams met the brook the ripples generated by the little dog's exploration sparkled. Jason looked on the ground near the bottom of the bolder where he sat and found a handful of pebbles. He tossed one ahead of the dog's position, and she bounded to where she had heard the plop of rock meeting water. After a couple more times with similar results, he could not stifle his laughter any longer, and when he chuckled she trotted to him, stood to put her front paws on his lap, and licked his face when he bent toward her. "I was just playing, baby girl." He scratched her behind the ears and then ran both hands up and down the length of her back. "Are you the beautiful baby girl? I think you are." He felt the water soak through his clothes and looked down to see the wet marks left by her paws, and he asked, "Are you trying to drown me, honey? Ooh, that's cold. How do you stand that water? You better get out of there. We better get moving."

She again led the way on the trail as it rose up away from the brook. Once the trail returned to level ground, and after a few hundred yards, they began to see the brightening shade of green where a clearing stretched on the other side of the tree line. The little dog ran into the small meadow and then whirled around waiting for Jason to emerge. Less than a hundred yards across, the meadow constituted enough of a break in the canopy to permit full sunlight, and the temperature rose. Jason sensed a shadow moving across the grass, and he looked up to see the wings of a gliding bird. "What kind of bird do you think that was? A hawk? An eagle? I don't know what birds fly around these parts, but I bet it's a turkey buzzard, and I bet it's looking for us." She watched Jason as he spoke, and he continued, "That's right, it's a buzzard. No! It's a pterodactyl, and it's looking for you. It's gonna get you. It's gonna get you." The little dog whirled in circles as Jason's voice rose, and he laughed.

On the other side of the meadow, the trail continued, and Jason felt grateful for the shade after only a little while in the sun. At times Jason had to pay close attention to the forest floor because the narrow worn path gave the only indication of a trail. The view above ground on all sides looked the same with gargantuan tree trunks rising from the ferns. Jason thought back to years past, to young adulthood and even earlier, when he spent more time outdoors. He had hiked through the canyon lands of the High Plains, and before that he had ridden a paint horse through badlands. He had not encountered anything like the verdant forest, and he would not have been able to imagine such a place. Despite the captivating beauty, he felt tinges of apprehension at the unfamiliar and felt relieved to see the lightening of the approaching tree line and boundary to the open ground of the estate.

As the little dog approached the edge of the woods, Jason called to her, "Hold up, baby girl. We'll be in view of the big house, and we don't want to run into any of them fruitcakes." Once Jason got nearer the end of the redwoods, he indeed saw the estate house, but he did not see any cars parked outside. They walked out of the woods onto the estate lawn, and turned to walk toward the carriage house before Jason stopped. "You know what, tiny darlin? I ain't been aching that much today. I believe I can walk some more. Let's go say howdy to Bobrick." Past the estate they reached the greenhouse and the point where the estate road ended. Jason looked around, but he did not see the Jeep parked anywhere nearby. He started to turn back when he noticed tracks leading toward the woods and a break in the trees. "Those tracks are about the width of a Willys Jeep. Let's see where they go."

They followed the tracks that extended into the trees, and at times it seemed the tracks might disappear into the forest, but after a series of curves the tracks led to an open area. Jason saw the Jeep first, and then he saw the crop. He had expected to see parallel rows like with most other crops, but the plants, some over six feet tall, grew in a random pattern. The little dog zipped in among the cannabis plants with a purpose, and Jason followed. Soon he saw Bobrick kneeling and working on something at the base of one of the plants.

"Howdy farmer," Jason called out.

Bobrick stood, turned, and smiled. "How did you get out here? Did you walk all the way?"

"Yep. I followed the little darlin. So this is your freaky mind blowing garden? Is it a lot of work tending this crop?"

"Not too much work. I was repairing the drip emitter for this irrigation line. The real work will come with the fall harvest."

Bobrick walked to the Jeep, opened a cooler, and dug through the ice. He extracted two bottles of water and handed one to Jason. The little dog whined, and when Jason looked at her he saw that she stared fixed on something in the distance. Her ears pointed forward and all her muscles seemed tensed. After a moment, Jason realized that a squirrel on the ground thirty or forty yards away held her attention. "You want that squirrel, baby girl? Well go get it. Get it!"

The little dog shot forward with blinding swiftness, and both Jason and Bobrick looked on shocked to see a dog run at such speed. Her spine seemed elastic as it bent to permit a stride of impressive length for such a small dog. The squirrel became aware of the approaching dog, and it turned to run to the nearest tree. When close enough, the squirrel vaulted up onto the tree trunk, and that should have been the end of the chase, but the speedy little dog seemed capable of flight as she too shot into the air and made contact with the tree trunk with all four paws. At the same instant, she snatched the squirrel from the tree, and on the way back to Earth she shook her head with the squirrel flapping to pieces.

Jason stood stunned for a moment and then looked at Bobrick speechless, and then he ran a few steps toward the little dog and her prey before stopping and bending at the waist to cough violently. Bobrick jogged to the dog and coaxed her to abandon her kill and return to Jason. Once she reached Jason, she stood on her hind legs with her front paws on his shoulder as he bent and coughed. She licked his ear, and through coughs he managed to say, "Keep them jaws away from me you little killer," and he reached an arm out to pet her while he continued to cough. By the time Bobrick had rejoined them, Jason had caught his breath, and he asked, "Have you ever seen anything like that? I wouldn't have told her to go after it if I'd have thought there was a chance she'd catch it. You ever seen a dog do that?"

"I've never seen anything like that. I've seen fast dogs but not that fast. And the way she jumped up in that tree was unbelievable. Are you okay?"

"I'm fine," Jason said. "Just forgot I can't run. That's all. Had no idea that was even possible. Won't be telling her to chase after nothing no more. That's for sure."

Jason groaned and reached an arm around to press on his lower back as he crouched and walked away from Bobrick.

"Are you sure you're okay?" Bobrick asked.

"Just need to find a place to sit."

"Sit in the Jeep. I can give you a ride back to the house."

Jason climbed into the passenger seat of the Jeep, and Bobrick got in the driver seat. "You sure you're okay? You want me to wait a minute before we go. The path back to the road is a little bumpy in places."

"Yeah, maybe just a minute. I just over did it with that running is all. I'll be fine."

"I saw Eleanor earlier," Bobrick said. "She said she had to go meet someone at the university. I don't know which university, but she also said that the meetings were canceled tonight, which is unusual. She seemed a little upset about something, but I didn't pry. One thing she did say, though, is that she is looking for a home for the dog."

Jason did not reply right away. He looked ahead at the marijuana plants, stopped holding his back, and sat up straight in the seat. "Well, yeah, that's best."

"I asked her to hold off on that."

"Oh?"

"I understand your reasons for not wanting to get tied down with the dog for both your plans and for what's best for the dog. I like the dog, and she seems to like it here. If you have to leave, for whatever reason, she can stay here with me. And if you want, or can, come back, she'll be here."

Again Jason looked ahead and then said, "Okay then."

"You ought to pick a name for her, though. Besides, I can use some help keeping those squirrels from stealing my kind bud."

Shocked, Jason looked at Bobrick and asked, "Squirrels eat marijuana?"

Bobrick burst into laughter and said, "No." He continued laughing as he started the Jeep and then steered it along the narrow path through the woods.

A wet spot again woke Jason, and when he opened his eyes he saw the little dog staring down at him, and when he rose to a sitting position on the couch he saw the magazine he had fallen asleep reading hours earlier. "You need to go outside, little darlin?"

Jason opened the front door and let the dog out. He picked up the magazine that had fallen to the floor and tidied the couch before walking to the door to look for the dog. He could not see the dog in the night, so he called out, "Baby girl." After several moments the dog still did not come, so Jason turned to go back into the house to find a flashlight. He heard what sounded like a simultaneous bang on the front door and a yelp. When he opened the door, he saw the little dog standing on the porch. "Did you run into the door, honey? Are you okay?" As Jason bent closer to the dog she rose on her hind legs and licked his face. "Okay then, baby girl, let's go to bed. I'm tired."

VII. Pearly Hiatus

Why, all the Saints and Sages who discuss'd
Of the Two Worlds so wisely—they are thrust
    Like foolish Prophets forth; their Words to Scorn
Are scatter'd, and their Mouths are stopt with Dust.

Then of the THEE in ME who works behind
The Veil, I lifted up my hands to find
    A lamp amid the Darkness; and I heard,
    As from Without—"THE ME WITHIN THEE BLIND!"

Bent Out of Shape

Sunlight beamed through the window and warmed a square patch on the bed. Jason opened his eyes and pushed away the blankets. He saw the little dog at the foot of the bed. She rested with her hind legs under her and with her fore legs extended. "No wakeup call this morning?" Jason asked. The little dog looked toward Jason for an instant but seemed otherwise frozen and stoic. "All right, then. Let me get some clothes and boots on, and we'll see what's out and about today."

While Jason dressed, the dog remained motionless in the bed. By the time he had reached the bedroom door, he expected her to have shot past him on her way to the stairs, but when she stayed in the bed, he said, "I guess somebody is still tired after all that squirrel killin yesterday. I'm gonna go see about the coffee, and you come on down when you're ready."

After preparing the old percolator and putting it on the stove, Jason looked out a window and considered another morning without fog. He knew the day would be hot, not Texas hot but hot nonetheless. He looked in the cupboards and in the refrigerator while thinking about preparing a lunch to take on a walk in the cool woods. After the hissing steam and spattering sound, he removed the percolator from the stove. He found the morning's newspaper that Bobrick had already perused, and he took it and a cup of coffee to the couch.

With his coffee cup empty and nothing of interest left to read in the paper, it occurred to Jason that the little dog had still not come downstairs. He climbed the stairs and entered the room to find her still in the same position in the bed. She looked at him as he entered. "You feeling okay, baby girl?" The little dog looked away and began shaking. "Oh no. What's wrong honey?" Jason reached to pet the dog, and then he saw the spot, the hole between her withers and shoulder on her side that had been hidden from him when he woke. The red hole measured more than an inch in diameter, and as he bent close to inspect he saw that the skin parted to reveal muscle tissue. "Oh no. No, no. What did you do, honey?" Confused, he noticed a surprising lack of blood on her fur or on the bedclothes.

Jason ran into the bathroom and wet a towel. He ran back to the dog and started to apply the towel and then reconsidered disturbing the wound. "You wait right there. It's gonna be okay." He ran down the stairs coughing along the way, and then he stopped at the front door. On the floor near the door, faint rust spots had a duller appearance than the rest of the floor, and when Jason touched them he knew he had found blood. He opened the front door and looked at the exterior. Nothing appeared out of the ordinary until he inspected the weather stripping at the bottom of the door. A sharp piece of metal protruded a mere fraction of an inch beyond the edge of the door. "Damn! Damn, damn." Jason remembered the crash and the yelp the night before when he had called the dog inside.

Back up the stairs and in the bedroom, Jason pet the dog and inspected the wound. He knew he could not treat it. The severity required a veterinarian. "It's gonna be okay, baby girl. I'm gonna go find Bobrick, and we'll get you patched up."

Outside the carriage house, Eleanor's Mercedes stood parked behind Bobrick's Jeep. Jason ran in the direction of the main house, but after a few strides and some violent coughing he reduced his pace to a fast walk. He flung open the door to the house, stepped inside and yelled, "Hey! Anybody home? I need some help here. Hey!" He walked through the rooms of the house continuing to shout and cough, but no one answered. Back outside he hurried in the direction of the greenhouse. Once inside the greenhouse, he shouted, "Bobrick." Jason walked through the tall plants to the back of the greenhouse and found the door leading to the hydroponics room. He beat the door and yelled, "Bobrick. Patrick! I need some help."

With no assistance available, Jason returned to the carriage house. His coughing had increased, and he doubled over and hacked. Blood came, and Jason said, "Not now." He placed an arm on the trunk of Eleanor's Mercedes and tried to breathe. After another bout of coughing and gasping for air, he stood and examined the space between the Jeep and Mercedes. The space separating the vehicles amounted to less than a foot, not nearly enough to maneuver the Jeep around and free of the Mercedes. Jason tried to open the driver-side door the Mercedes. "Why would she lock her car out here?" He walked around to the passenger door and found it locked too. He leaned close and peered through the window. Another fit of coughing caused Jason to crouch and hang onto the car for balance. When he caught his breath and while still on slightly bent knees, he succumbed to frustration and delivered a left hook to the passenger side-view mirror. The entire mirror assembly tore from the car and flew through the air. With his hand dripping blood, Jason climbed into the driver's seat of the Jeep.

He hit the ignition switch and then stomped the clutch and put the vehicle in reverse. While he revved the engine, he let out the clutch abruptly, and the Jeep smashed into the Mercedes. Jason looked back and saw that the bumpers did not match. The Jeep bumper tore through the grill and wrinkled the hood of the Mercedes, and Jason pressed the Jeep's accelerator pedal to the floor. More of the grill and hood crunched, and the Jeep's tires spun in the driveway, but the Mercedes did not move.

Jason climbed out of the Jeep and walked to the front door of the carriage house. Coughing and kicking, he assaulted the door until he fell. From his knees on the porch he reached out and tugged on the weather stripping. He tore half of it away from the door at a right angle before the sharp metal cut into his palms. Once back on his feet, he entered the house and stopped at the foot of the stairs to catch his breath. He climbed the stairs one step at a time breathing as best he could and trying to calm himself before reaching the bedroom, and with each grasp of the handrail he left a bloody print.

The little dog still rested on the bed and shook. "I'm sorry, baby girl. We're on our own. There's a vet up the road. Eleanor stopped there the time she took me to the hospital. It's gonna be a long walk, but I'll carry you, darlin. Don't you worry." Jason picked up the dog and held her to his chest while he maneuvered backward out the bedroom door and turned to face the stairs. As he descended the stairs, his back seized, and he started to feel a loss of control in his arms, but with no way to set down the dog he quickened his pace and took two steps at a time. At the bottom of stairs when he bent to put down the dog, he lost his balance and fell forward, but he managed to roll to the side and avoid falling on the dog. Her shaking increased, and she whined while she licked Jason's face. "Oh honey, don't you worry about me. I'm fine. And we'll get you fixed up too." In standing he felt again the pain in his back and chest, and when he coughed he expelled blood that dripped down his chin. Jason ran a sleeve across his chin and picked up the dog.

The front door opened wide when Jason kicked it, and he made no attempt to shut it after he passed through clutching the dog to his chest. He took long strides up the estate road toward the gate leading to the rural highway, and at the gate he bent and set the dog on the ground while he crouched over her and coughed. When he again hefted the dog, he felt stabbing in his back and wailed as he stumbled backward. Once again in control of his footing, Jason walked along the rural road. He found maintaining a straight path impossible, so he crossed to the left side of the road so he could see oncoming traffic. No traffic passed, but the realization that cars would pass encouraged Jason for he thought someone might stop to offer help.

With each step he worried more about the little dog because he could see from the redness spreading on his shirt that her wound had started bleeding again. He worried about the wound so much that he stopped thinking about the amount of blood that he expelled, and as he walked on he coughed and the redness ran down his chin and neck and onto his shirt and onto the dog's back. He had not worn cowboy boots in many years, and he thought perhaps they contributed to the unendurable pain in his back, and he thought about stopping to take them off, but he continued trying to walk straight and staying on the side of the road.

When riding in the car with Eleanor, the topography of the roadway had seemed insignificant. But while carrying the dog and looking ahead to where he hoped to see the animal hospital, he saw the road descend from view and then reappear in the distance. The heartache from seeing the upcoming inclines made him cry out and sputter more redness. The man who had not shed a tear at hearing of his own forthcoming death yelled out but not in lamentation so much as in anger and in an attempt to keep his airways clear. He tried to talk and comfort the dog but words came as gurgles. With each step toward the bottom of the small valley, he knew he would have to make upward steps again, but he tried not to think about the additional pain to come as he focused on the current pain in his arms, chest, and back.

The sound of a car approaching from behind enlivened Jason, but as the car swooshed past he tried to shout an insult that arrived as a spattering that added to the dripping flow from his chin. At the bottom of the valley, he prepared for the exertion of the climb, and he heard a car approaching from the front. This one too passed, and the anger helped Jason take long deliberate strides. He determined to not look up and gauge the insurmountable distance to the crest of the hill but instead to just take each step without thought of progress. He looked down at the dog's back dripping with gore and saw pointy roach killer boot toes extend along the pavement. He stepped two strides and then looked up just long enough ensure that no car approached and to realign himself with the side of the road. Then he took three steps and looked up again. One, two, three, four look up, look down, one, two, three, four.

Once beyond the crest, he saw the animal hospital, and he crossed to the right side of the roadway. Less than a hundred yards remained, and Jason could no longer feel the pain in his arms and chest because the pain in his back pushed out all other awareness. Coughing and gurgling, he took in only short breaths mixed with blood that choked, and his vision narrowed and took on the familiar red hue. He knew he had to hang on a little longer, and when he reached the door to the animal hospital he discovered that it opened outward. If he put down the dog, he knew he could not lift her again, so he managed to extend and open his right hand just enough to grasp the door handle. He took a step back and then used his heel to further open the door.

Two steps away from the front counter, he stumbled, but he got the dog over the table top where she landed on her paws in front of a shocked receptionist. Jason grasped the counter with one bloody hand while he reached back with the other to retrieve his wallet, which he slapped down next to where the dog stood. He took a half step back and then lost his footing and fell backward. Though the fall onto his tailbone must have hurt, Jason laughed a gurgle as he rolled to his side and began to crawl back toward the door. Still laughing and sputtering, he used the door handle to pull himself to his feet. Outside the animal hospital, he staggered and he aimed for the inviting cool green of the tree line. He sensed the fall forward, but he did not feel the force of the pavement as it met the side of his face. Jason laughed sputters of victory.

> I sent my Soul through the Invisible,
> Some letter of that After-life to spell:
> And by and by my Soul return'd to me,
> And answer'd "I Myself am Heav'n and Hell."

Lost Moon in the Darkroom

Light of differing shades alternated with darkness, and sound interrupted silence, and through it all he passed unburdened, indifferent. At times he thought he heard voices, but he could not understand what they said, and he did not care. Momentary fleeting still images on print paper appeared in the developer, and then all went black again. Distant voices sounded, and sometimes the darkness lifted. The light beamed down from the bottom of the enlarger onto the paper before a click and the return to darkness. Multiple unseen whispers preceded the click and the ray of light shining downward on the paper before the second click and the darkness that turned to faint pink. He saw his hands grasp the edge of the paper, and then he felt the corners of the print paper as he let it slide into the liquid. Shadows appeared on the paper, and he strained to discern an image before all went again black.

From the dark, voices brought the vinegar of stop bath and later the ammonia of old fixer, and he felt about in the darkness searching for trays or the base of the enlarger or any fixed point to give a reference for the way out, but in every direction the darkness remained empty. The familiar odors faded and so did his interest. Voices sounded, and differing shades of light came and went, but he floated heedless and content.

A slight pain, an annoyance pressed into the bridge of his nose and below his mouth, and for eons he wanted to touch his face and make the annoyance go away, but he lacked the ability to move his arms. Over and over he thought he had succeed in moving an object from his face and relieving the pain, but the pain returned, and he suspected he dreamed. An unseen voice and perhaps unseen hands made the annoyance on his face stop. He tried to inquire, but he could not form a question in his mind. He knew only that he had the feeling that he should ask a question.

The 120 film resisted going into the reel more than the smaller and easier 35mm, so he moved slow and careful to avoid a crimp. He reached about for the developing tank, but he felt nothing. And then he realized that he had lost the reel. For undetermined lengths of time, years perhaps, he reached in the darkness searching for a metal reel containing film and the stainless steel tank to hold the reel. He knew there could be no light until he found the reel and tank, so he alternated searching with content waiting in the darkness.

Voices approached in the darkness, and he fought to open his eyes, but he could not tell if he succeeded. The desire to inquire again came to mind, and he fought to form a question. When the sound came it passed not through his voice but through a painful dry rasp in his throat, barely more than a whisper. He asked, "What are the charges?" No answer came, but he thought he heard the faint crackle of a radio, and he tried again. "Has bail been set?"

He sensed the nearby presence of the enlarger, and he knew that if he could activate the light then he might get his bearings enough to get out of the darkroom. He might also ruin film, so he waited. The timer switch did not activate, or it did not exist. He could not be sure. So he waited on the darkroom floor. If only he could activate the enlarger, then maybe he could find the door. But he could not find the switch. He found only an easel alone and nowhere near the baseboard. Years passed and frustration built, and the pain, the annoyance, above his nose and below his mouth returned. He could not find the metal reel or the tank.

Over and over he tried to climb the stairs to help the little dog. He saw her in the bed shaking, but when he tried to climb the stairs to be near her he lacked the strength or he could not find the stairs or the stairs vanished. He saw the little dog in the bed shaking. He saw the red hole. But he could not see the stairs. Crying out for help did not matter. In place of sound, a dry raspy pain seared through is throat, and he could not find the stairs. The little dog shook. Over and over he saw the red hole, but he could not find the stairs to climb. Anger turned to desperation, and he fought to get clear of the pain above his nose and to find the reel and the tank and to climb unseen stairs to the little dog. The dry raspy pain in this throat caught on fire, and then the sound came. Soon other voices joined, and the little dog stopped shaking, and the stairs ceased to matter, and the darkroom's soft pink light faded to blackness.

An odd shaped plastic dome covered his mouth and nose, and when he tried to pull it away he discovered elastic straps. While sliding the painful mask up over his forehead, the elastic straps dragged across bandages taped to a cheek and above an eyebrow. The pain above his nose subsided, and he felt air cooling the wetness as he opened his eyes. A white ceiling met a white wall with a window. Content with the knowledge that no jail house confined him, he slipped back into darkness.

The sound of voices made him consider opening his eyes, and after many failed attempts he pulled his eyes apart a sliver and saw a bright room where the surprise lady talked to a nurse. Of their own accord, the eyes shut while he sank away from the annoyance above his nose and below his mouth into the soft, dim pink light of the darkroom. The developing tank stood beside the sink, just where it should have been and just where it must have been all along. Soft and comforting, the surprise lady's whispers washed over him.

The sensation of lateral movement and a clattering noise made him think he ought to open his eyes again, but before he gained adequate motivation the sensation of movement ceased. Other noises continued, like the unmistakable clank of metal on metal, but he chose to believe the noises did not concern him. An abrupt yet brief downward motion coupled with a thud helped him to pry open his eyes. A different room with brighter light and no window surrounded him, and the infernal mask no longer pressed against his face. He tried to utter a question but the effort proved too daunting. A voice spoke, and though he knew it addressed him he could not understand the message beyond the part that said not to worry and that he would be asleep soon. Another voice near and clear asked, "Mr. Spearman, can you count backward from ten?" He giggled at such a silly question, and he did not count at all.

Light of differing shades alternated with darkness, and sound interrupted silence, and through it all he passed unburdened, indifferent. He did not care until the annoyance pressed into the bridge of his nose and below his mouth, and he fought to make the annoyance go away until unseen hands made the irritation on his face stop. Soft and comforting, the surprise lady's whispers washed over him.

The little surprise led the way between two enormous Coastal Redwoods that stood as a gate to a trail that meandered into the green shadowy woods, and he followed her past the colossal trunks, past ferns of many types, and over lush beds of sorrel. Rustling in the branches above prompted her to look up, but just as often a rustling in the bush caused her to shoot ahead and stick a pointed nose into a fern and then emerge with a dew laden face. When potential prey caught her attention, she moved ahead in a gait that made her seem to float. She did not bounce as she walked, and she stayed ready to spring ahead.

Level ground descended, and the trail switched back one way and then the other, and she waited with patience for him to catch up before again springing surefooted on downward to the sound of a brook. The little dog stepped into the clear water that rose halfway to her chest. She lapped water, and when she lifted her head upright drops rejoined the brook. With perked ears she looked down into the water at flitting minnows. Sunlight filtered down through the branches in beams, and where those beams met the brook the ripples generated by the little dog's exploration sparkled.

She again led the way on the trail as it rose up away from the brook. Once the trail returned to level ground, and after a few hundred yards, the brightening shade of green marked the boundary where a clearing stretched on the other side of the tree line. The little dog ran into the small meadow and then whirled around waiting for him to emerge. Her pointed nose tapered to soft white fur that gave way to black fur that surrounded her wide and dark eyes. The tips of her upright ears tilted forward, and down past the neck that alternated in random patches of black, white, and gray her withers and the tiger stripes began. The tiger stripes faded beyond mid-back where the chaotic mixture of spots took over the hind quarters and rear legs. A thin, wire-like white s-shaped tail extended behind her, and she looked ready to run. She whirled in circles while he laughed, and together they ran through the meadow and back into the woods.

A sharp voice commanded, "Mr. Spearman, you have to keep that mask on."

He opened his eyes long enough to see a figure moving about the room. He let them close again to harsh red light, and he saw the little dog in the bed shaking. He saw the hole in her side and he saw her shaking and he wanted to help. Over and over he saw the little dog shaking and the red hole until with a huff he opened his eyes and tore away the mask.

No one else occupied the room, and he managed to keep his eyes open. After a while, the room turned from uniform gray to a contrast between the white moonlight streaming through the window and the black the moonlight could not reach. He could see the effect of the moon though he could not see the moon directly, and he wanted to see the moon. When he tried to get out of bed, he became aware of the tangle of cords. He found the one attached to his arm, and he traced it up to a bag hanging from a metal rack. With his legs hanging off the bed, he inched closer to the side while grasping the pole of the metal rack. Legs did not want to support his weight, but the metal rack assisted, and he took short steps toward the window while dragging and then leaning on the tall metal pole. At the window, he caught the direct shine of the moon, and for a time he had to squint. White silver light inspired almost a smile before legs gave way and only the drag of his hand sliding down the metal pole slowed descent. The meeting with the cold floor revived memories of a recent tail bone injury, yet he still found reason for amusement when he discovered that the garment he wore had no back and offered no barrier against the frigid surface. The impossibility of rejoining the bed made effort pointless, so he scooted across the smooth cold floor to where the moonlight made a square, and he laid there until angry voices came and jostled.

Pink light grew brighter until he opened eyes to see a ceiling joined to a wall and window streaming sunlight. He removed the mask and heard a voice, "You're awake."

He turned his head to the side and saw a white headed and bearded man sitting in a chair beside the bed. "Bobrick," he rasped.

"I hear you're giving the staff quite a bit of trouble."

"Little dog . . ."

"She's fine. She's fine, brother."

"Where?'

"She's back at the house. She's fine. She runs. She plays, and she sleeps in your bed. It just took a few stitches. She's fine. How are you feeling?"

"I'm so sorry . . . the car . . ."

"Don't worry about it, brother." Bobrick said. "It's already in the shop getting fixed. Eleanor has a loaner and says she's thinking about getting rid of the Mercedes anyway. Says she wants something less pretentious."

A nurse hurried to the bedside and barked sharp, "Mr. Spearman, you must keep that mask on." The nurse replaced the mask and left the room.

Jason removed the mask, and asked, "Little dog is okay?"

Bobrick laughed and said, "She's fine, but you scared everyone else nearly to death. The sheriff got involved for a little while. The people at the animal hospital thought you and the dog had been shot or hit by a car. But she's fine now. She'll be glad to see you. Eleanor has been arguing with the hospital staff about bringing the dog here."

"Eleanor has been here?"

"Every day, brother. She feels terrible about what happened."

"She feels terrible? I tore up her car. Please tell her I'm so, so sorry."

"You'll be able to tell her yourself, but I'll warn you she won't listen to that. She feels like it was her fault for not looking after you better."

"But. . . I tore up the car. I'm sorry . . ."

Bobrick put his hand on Jason's arm, "Hey. That's enough of that. It's all okay. The dog is fine. Eleanor will be happy you're awake and talking. Just concentrate on getting well. And you probably better get that mask on before the nurse comes back."

I got a real knack for certain things. Disappointing folks is a specialty of mine. Even without my main tool, the booze, a masterpiece of a mess comes natural. Friends Bobrick and Eleanor gave me kindness and tried to help me and got tore up property in return. But that ain't even the best part. The real amazing accomplishment, the masterpiece part, is that they think the whole thing is their fault. Even without the booze, I am one scroungy sorry degenerate ungrateful bum.

I never should have called Bobrick after running into him at that hospice outfit. Come to think of it, I shouldn't have been there in the first place. Tangled messes start with taking somebody's kindness. If that man's offer to go stay at that hospice hadn't been accepted, there wouldn't have been no run-in with Bobrick, and he'd have remembered me as that crazy fat man who helped him out of a tight spot down in San Francisco. He wouldn't know anything about no shriveled up dying drifter. Eleanor wouldn't have got her property tore up, and there wouldn't be no little dog that got hurt, scared half to death, then abandoned. That's how these tangled messes get started. I accepted the kindness of that hospice place and then went one worse by accepting Bobrick's kindness.

Well, I learned this time. There won't be no more tangles.

Finally, that damned oxygen mask is gone. Maybe it wasn't no longer necessary, but most likely they just got tired of fighting about it. That infernal thing didn't help me breathe none, and the irritation grew and grew until it pushed out thought of everything else. If they hadn't stopped telling me to wear it, getting on down the road would have come about pretty soon even if it meant crawling out. And if anybody had tried to stop me, I'd have give em a left hook.

The left hook never was one of my best punches. Truth is, in all them years at the Boys Club, I got more practice in taking punches than throwing them. While in and out of being awake after they brought me to this hospital, some dreams featured the Boys Club in Isom and getting beat on, and that's how things usually went back in those days. Lots of boys that boxed with me went on to the Golden Gloves, but I just kept getting better at taking punches. I loved boxing at one time and even had ambitions to get good at it for a little while. And for most of my life I might have been real tough when it came to brawling between stumbling drunkards but never no count against somebody that really knew how to box. But that Mercedes didn't know how to box, and the left hook throwed at that mirror would have made even Joe Frazier hisself proud.

I ain't proud of it, though. Downright stupid and probably half-crazy is what that stunt amounted to. Some kind of rage came up all the sudden. Sure, the worrying about the dog had me riled, but plenty of dogs been in worse shape, and I've sure been in worse shape myself. Where that anger came from is a mystery. Anger hadn't been a part of me for a long time, but it sure was that day. Even when that doctor in San Francisco said to prepare for dying, I didn't get mad. After getting a little bit of a handle on the shock from the news, I took care of business, seen the lawyer, and got out of town. I didn't go to crying or getting mad about it being unfair. I don't feel like I done much complaining at all, so where that anger come from is a mystery.

But all the time now, complaints take up most of the mind, and more of that peculiar anger is chomping at the bit trying to get out of the gate. It's always over little things, first that mask, then over being out of bed. Now it's mostly over the needle they still got stuck in my arm and attached to them bags. In answer to the question of when they're gonna take it out, all they say is that it's up to the doctor to decide, and here recently I've been telling them that I've got about half a mind to take it out myself. Once in a while, one of them nurses pops off some bossy stuff, and that suits me fine. She can go ahead and start a ruckus and then see what happens. Instead of hoping not to see the rude nurses, I particularly enjoy when the disagreeable ones come. It's some kind of sick fun to start the insults right as soon as they step in the room. There's one that vexes me so much I've had thoughts about slapping the ugly right off her face, but I'd rather not spend what time is left in a jail house.

Just don't know where this anger has come from.

Not everything around here makes me mad. A good lot of it makes me ashamed. Eleanor visits every day, and that's something to both look forward to and dread. She's always so cheerful and kind, and she's always asking if she can do or get anything for me. I'm real careful in answering cause she'd up and get anything asked for. That lady is such a sweetheart.

All she wants to do is kindness for folks. Why she has took such a liking to me I'll never understand. There must be something broke with her thinking.

Bobrick comes too most days. It's easier talking to him. He really don't judge, and that's a relief sometimes. Other times, it just makes me feel worse about the whole sorry mess. Most of the time, we don't talk about heavy things. Mostly he tells me what Eleanor is up to and how the little dog is doing. He seems particularly concerned, or at least curious, that Eleanor went and canceled them meetings at her estate house. He said he asked about it a time or two, but Eleanor said only that she had canceled meetings until further notice. He said she seemed annoyed about the subject, so he didn't ask too much more, but he stays curious. And I got to admit to having some curiosity too.

He says the little dog is doing fine. Sometimes thinking about her hurts real bad. But I'm going to have to stop that. There ain't no point in it cause I ain't gonna see that little dog ever again. I'm gonna have to just put her out of my mind. Bobrick don't know yet, and I ain't sure how or if I'm gonna tell him, but he and Eleanor are wrong in thinking that after getting out of this place I'll go back to that estate. Eleanor thinks that way for sure cause she's even said as much. Bobrick ought to know I'll be gettin on down the road. If he don't know, then I don't know how or when I'll tell him.

Now and again the nurses get on to me for being out of the bed. It ain't so much that I'm restless that makes me get out of the bed. It's more the fear that when ready to use my legs they won't work. So regular exercise amounts to walking around the room dragging that pole with bags and sometimes hanging onto the bed while bending knees just to make legs work in pushing me up and down. The strength is there, but I'm short on the stamina. There probably ain't nothing to be done for that, so I'll just have to take what comes when it's time to go.

Another thing that has me puzzled is that my appetite has come back. Even before the worst part of this sickness, I didn't have no appetite, but now there's hunger all the time. It seems like an odd waste of time for a dying man to want to eat. Asking them nurses if an appetite is a sign of anything is pointless cause it's impossible to get a straight answer out of these people unless it's a yes or no question, and then the answer is pretty much always no unless yes would be more unpleasant. Probably my body just now realized it's dying and is trying to do something about it, so I ain't gonna put no more stock in being hungry. I'll eat even though the food here has about as much taste as clean air. Besides, it's something to do to pass the time.

It don't look like I'll ever get to see that Guerneville place after all. Ten miles as the crow flies is too close to the estate, and getting on down the road needs to amount to farther than ten miles. There ain't gonna be none of the mistakes again. There ain't gonna be no more tangles. And that means I'll have to find a place without too many dealings with the same folks every day. In a lot of ways, The City would be the best place for being invisible and not dealing with folks. With so many people all around, nobody notices any one in particular. But I just can't face dying in San Francisco. There's too much there that's meant a lot to me. An unfamiliar place is best. California has other cities, and maybe I'll end up in one. But smaller towns might be all right too, just so long as I don't get in nobody's business and they stay out of mine. I ain't particular.

The way out of this hospital might not be so simple. It might involve walking out with them trying to get me to stay, or it might be more along the lines of sneaking out, and that might be best cause part of me would enjoy a confrontation. There ain't enough physical strength for confrontations, and there ain't no spare time for a trip to the jail house. Sneaking out might be best, but that could be tricky since the only part of this hospital that's familiar is this room.

And then there's the question of whether to tell Bobrick. For certain, it would be a bad idea to tell Eleanor. She don't need that kind of worry. Telling Bobrick might be the right thing to do, but it would also be hard cause it would mean having to say goodbye. Maybe a clean break without a word to no one will be best.

Texas ain't ever far from mind. The hardest thing is getting used to the idea that I'll never see them places again. It just don't seem possible that when this coughing business has passed there won't ever again be no Canadian River Valley or Palo Duro Canyon. I keep having to tell myself that I'm dying, but them places ain't. They'll go on and on, but I just won't see em no more. Sometimes when the pain ain't too bad, daydreams can come, and some of em is beautiful and silly. Hours get frittered away thinking about being in Texas with that little dog that liked walking with me on the estate. We go all over the Panhandle in a pickup truck. And then something here and now interrupts the pictures and reminds that none of those adventures with the little dog can ever happen. It's enough to make me more than a little mad at how the mind can drift. It's hard to do anything about being mad at myself, but there's always some nurse around that gives me good reason to be mad, and sometimes I let em know.

A better thing to contemplate is California. It's a plenty big place, and there might still be a little time to see some of it. The aim ain't to see the famous places. The unfamiliar places is a better thing to aim for. And in this big state, there's plenty of new places to go. There's more cities. There's more forests. And there's mountains, deserts, and farm country. It shouldn't be no trouble getting someplace new and drifting out without so much shame. It starts with picking the right road. If a road goes someplace I've already been, then I'll have to find another. If a road goes somewhere I ain't ever heard of, that might be the best road of all.

And that inverted Bowl they call the Sky,
Whereunder crawling coop'd we live and die,
    Lift not your hands to *It* for help—for It
As impotently moves as you or I.

Tarantula Hawk

The motor hummed while the top half of the bed bent upright but not enough to suit Jason. After the motor stopped, he took the pillow and much of the bedclothes and bunched them in a wad to put behind his lower back. A knock at the door got his attention, and he turned to see a young man push a cart into the room.

"Hector! My amigo, what's for lunch today?"

"Sandwiches, I think. But I found some extras for you."

Hector placed a tray on the table beside the bed and removed the lid, and then he reached back in the cart and produced two small containers of dessert to go with the one already on Jason's tray.

"You're a good man, Hector."

"Thanks, but don't get caught with that extra cake today."

"Oh? Is hatchet face working today?"

"I don't know, but just in case . . ."

Hector wheeled the cart back into the hall, and Jason pulled the tray from the table and placed it in his lap. He ate the extra cake before consuming the rest of the meal. After putting the tray back on the table, he turned so that his legs bent off the side of the bed, and he used his arms to slow the slide off to the floor until sure of his footing. He found his trousers and took them to the chair while dragging the IV pole. Once he had both legs in his pants up to the knees, he stood and tucked in the hospital gown, careful to ensure that it overlapped in the back. Boots rested underneath the bed, but Jason thought about the difficulty in getting them off again, especially if in a hurry, so he left them and dragged the pole with bags to the door. On the way, he muttered about not having a pole and rack mounted on wheels.

Through the door opened only a hand width, Jason watched the people passing in the hall. Most of the people not in hospital staff clothing came from the left. He stuck his head outside the door and looked right, then left, and then he hefted the pole with both hands and walked out of the room turning left down the hall. After a section with rooms on both sides of the hallway, the passage opened to an area with windows on both sides. The windows to the right showed a parking lot, and those to the left revealed a landscaped area with a lawn, flower bushes, and a small fountain. Beyond the area with windows, a walled hallway curved to the right and opened into a large foyer with rows of chairs. Jason walked a few feet into the lobby until he could see large sliding glass doors, and then he turned back to the hallway.

When he approached the room, an overweight nurse with an abundance of facial makeup bellowed. "Why are you out of the room? You're not supposed to be out of bed."

Jason feigned fright and said, "Oh! I thought you were a tarantula. Back home there some that look just like you with big fat dirty brown hairy bodies. Do you have any kin down in Texas?"

The nurse pulled the door open as Jason passed, and she began to lift the pole with bags, but Jason said, "Could you keep your fatness and your stench away from me? I know you probably had a tough time at the roadhouse last night, but that ain't no reason to take it out on me. You ought to go back when fellows are drinking more. You'll have better luck then. Some of them drunk cowboys will ride anything."

"You're supposed to be in bed!"

"Oh, I'm heading that way. You can go bother somebody else, but you better find a place to hide before a tarantula hawk gets ya."

Jason pulled the chair away from the bed, positioned it facing the window, and sat. After a few moments he turned to see the nurse still in the doorway. "Are you sweet on me, honey? That's awful cute, but you can run along now." He heard the door slam, and he laughed.

He flipped a few pages of a magazine Eleanor had left earlier that morning, and then his head began to nod. A light knock at the door raised his head, and a young woman he had not seen before wheeled in a cart with food trays. "You picking up lunch trays? Oh, dinner? I must have dozed for quite a spell." Jason shoveled mashed potatoes with no flavor and another vegetable with the texture of wax, and though the chicken also lacked taste he ate that too. As he moved the empty tray to the table, a second knock sounded.

"Bobrick! Good to see you, pardner."

Bobrick entered carrying a leather bag, a canvass jacket, and a palm leaf cowboy hat. "You got the bandages off."

Jason touched the slightly swollen area on his face and said, "Yeah, it's healing up pretty good. But then I wasn't gonna win no beauty contests no how."

"I brought the rest of your stuff like you asked and encountered Eleanor on the way. I told her having your things would be a comfort to you."

"That's good. Eleanor came this morning."

"That is the reason, right?" Bobrick asked. "You want these things just to have around for comfort?"

"Sure thing, pardner. Tell me, how are the crops doing?"

"The crops are great. Another bunch of kind bud is due from the hydro in a few days, and the outdoor and greenhouse fall harvest is going to be huge. But I may have no customers."

"How's that?"

"Remember how I told you that Eleanor had canceled the meetings and seemed kind of irritated about something? It seems that until further notice means forever."

"Come again?"

"It shocked me too," Bobrick said. "It seems someone told her that no scientist or farmer would support what those groups are all about, so she went to the university to ask some scientists to come address the groups, but she couldn't find any takers. Then she went back to the groups and said no scientists agreed with the causes, and of course the members all agreed that the scientists must be getting paid off by the evil corporations. Eleanor didn't buy that, so she told them they can have their meetings elsewhere from now on. You have any idea who might have put that bug in her ear about scientists?"

"I . . . I was just having fun one day, just pokin. She ought not listen to me. She really canceled them meetings? Don't know what to say about that."

"Well, I do." Bobrick laughed and said, "Good riddance. I told her years ago those people were weird, but then left it alone because they made good customers. Whatever you said made her think, and now maybe she'll put her good intentions to better use."

"What are you gonna do about the customers?"

"Some or even most of them will keep coming by. Also, I might be able to get a deal supplying a dispensary."

"A dispensary? Hope it ain't down in San Francisco. I won't be around to help get your car out of hock this time."

"Maybe next time you can go with me. You can do the driving. And that reminds me, when looking in your room for the lawyer papers you said you need—they're in the bag with your other stuff—I ran across something else interesting." Bobrick produced the peace sign medallion on the hemp rope. Both men laughed, and Bobrick said, "Remember how you told the crowd I couldn't talk? That still makes me laugh. It was like a signal not to say anything, like I was just a wooden Indian outside a cigar store."

"Only our cigars were green."

"And there's something else you should see." Bobrick pulled two new western shirts out of the bag. The shirts still had the tags, and pins held them together in squares with the fake pearl snaps running down the front. "When I ran into Eleanor on my way here, she asked me to bring these to you. She said they arrived after she had already visited you this morning."

"What is Eleanor doing getting me shirts?"

"The one you were wearing during the . . . accident . . . Well, that shirt is gone. Eleanor saw part of it the ambulance crew cut off you when they picked you up at the vet clinic. It shook her up. She found another one in your room and then tried to find some in the same size and brand. She said she finally found some at a store in Salinas. If she hadn't, she'd have probably found a way to get some from Texas."

"Don't know what to say. She shouldn't have done that. She's such a sweetheart. Where'd you say she got em?"

"Some store down in Salinas. They mailed them."

"Salinas, huh? Ain't that where they have the California rodeo? Or ain't it roDAYo the way yall say it?"

"Like I told you, brother," Bobrick said, "I'm from Stockton, so I haven't had much occasion to say the word at all."

The young woman pushing the wheeled cart returned for the empty food tray. After she left the room, Bobrick said, "I better be going soon. Any word on when the hospital might release you? The little dog will be happy to see you. You ought to think about giving her a name."

"Can't get no straight answers out of these people. Leaving a fellow in the dark seems to be one of their favorite ways of torture."

"When you find out, let us know. We'll have you out of here the instant they release you. Take it easy. I'll try to come again tomorrow."

Bobrick had reached the door when Jason called out. "Pardner, hold up just a minute." Bobrick turned back, and Jason continued. "Don't know how to tell you this, but I won't be coming back to that estate, and there won't be no reason for you to come here tomorrow."

Bobrick looked at Jason then looked at the floor and nodded. "Are you taking off? Releasing yourself?"

"I figure it's about time."

"Are you sure? I can understand you not wanting to return to the house, but shouldn't you stay here? Maybe they can help you. Maybe they can increase your chances of . . . Or maybe buy you some more time."

Jason smiled and said, "Pardner, there ain't nothing these folks can do for me anymore. And it's time for me to be gettin on down the road. Didn't want to just head out without saying anything, not after all you and Eleanor have done for me. Please tell her how much I appreciate her kindness."

"Sure. I'll tell her. It would be better if you stayed and told her yourself, but I'll tell her."

"Oh, and one more thing. You ought to call little dog Elly. Between me and you, it could mean she's named after Elly May Clampett, one of the best parts of television when we was kids. Or it could be short for Eleanor."

Bobrick smiled a little and then turned and walked out of the room. Jason watched the snowy mass of hair disappear into the hallway, and then he looked out the window at the late July evening.

After sunset, Jason stood from the chair and dragged the IV pole into the bathroom. He set aside a hand towel and a large pile of tissue paper. Slow and careful he removed the tape that kept the IV attached to his arm. He draped the hand towel over the area of his arm with the IV, reached under the towel to grasp the needle with a thumb and finger, took a deep breath, and pulled. His bent arm held the towel in place while he let the IV fall into the sink. After a few moments, he substituted the pile of tissue for the hand towel, and then he went in search of his boots and to have a look at his new shirts.

VIII. Flatland

Yon rising Moon that looks for us again—
How oft hereafter will she wax and wane;
   How oft hereafter rising look for us
Through this same Garden—and for *one* in vain!

Ah, by my Computations, People say,
Reduce the Year to better reckoning?—Nay,
'Twas only striking from the Calendar
Unborn To-morrow and dead Yesterday.

No Creek

Jason could not recall ever having worse coffee, and he worked on finishing his second cup. The all-night gas station, besides offering horrible coffee, had provided some information about the town. A couple of different maps showed that he had landed in the southern part of town and that the little locale stood like an island surrounded on all sides by agricultural land. Not much else worthy of a mark on a map existed between the municipality and Davis to the northeast and to the southwest Vacaville, from where he had come after hitching a ride for the fourth time. Neither of the maps indicated a creek in or near the town, and though the reason he had stopped in the town rested on its name and the possibility of a creek by the same name, he decided to stick to his plan to seek the unfamiliar in his ongoing effort to spend his last days free of entanglements.

Upon securing the ride with the friendly trucker, Jason had intended to go all the way to Sacramento, the trucker's destination. But about thirty miles before reaching Sacramento, Jason saw a sign for an upcoming location. He had asked the trucker if it might be possible to be let out early, and the trucker kindly agreed but warned Jason of the lack of sights and services. But Jason saw again the sign with the word Dixon, and he confirmed his desire to be dropped in the little town.

The first glimmer of dawn appeared outside the gas station, and Jason decided against a third cup of burnt sour coffee, but he did ask the attendant if she knew of any creeks in or near the town. The attendant said she did not know of anything other than farms in the vicinity, so Jason left the station and walked east toward the dawn and away from the interstate highway. A residential neighborhood extended to the north, and on the right side of the road agricultural land extended as far as Jason could see, though he could not tell what sort of crops grew. After a few hundred yards, the farmland ended, and houses populated both sides of the road. Farther on, the houses gave way to commercial buildings with retail establishments, most still closed at the early hour.

Turning north Jason entered what he guessed to be the town center. Some of the buildings, like small strip malls, looked new, but others appeared far older than anything Jason remembered from his own small hometown. In one of the newer looking strip malls, Jason saw a donut shop and entered. He asked for two donuts and a cup of coffee, and after paying for the items he asked the cashier if he knew of any creeks in or near town. The man did not know of any creeks, but he told Jason of a few municipal parks.

After leaving the donut shop, Jason walked north on a wide street. The small commercial zone gave way to more industrial surroundings, and Jason passed twin parallel railroad tracks. A nearby grain elevator reminded Jason of every small town in the Texas Panhandle. The rising heat of the morning sun also made Jason think of August mornings in Texas, and he knew that later in the day he would be glad to have his hat. Already the heat had become uncomfortable, and he remembered passing a small park not long before the tracks. He turned back.

A park bench offered repose after many miles with little sleep, and Jason dozed in the shade until the shade moved and direct sunlight and heat prompted him to leave. Back in the area of retail shops, he moved on without purpose until he passed a laundromat. Inside the building, he found a restroom, double-checked the lock on the door, and took off his clothing. After a quick wash at the sink, he put on clothes from the leather bag, including one of the new shirts from Eleanor. With his shed clothes in a coin operated washing machine, Jason found a spot under a ceiling fan. The cool air made him want to doze again, so he stood and walked about. He thought about looking for a newspaper or magazine, and then a bulletin board caught his attention. Local advertisements, some in English and some in Spanish, advertised services like babysitting, lawn maintenance, house cleaning, and handyman services. A few of the religious oriented announcements again reminded Jason of small town Texas. Near a top corner, a particular handwritten flier interested Jason. It said simply "furnished mobile home for rent" and included a telephone number and address. He copied the address.

Again seated under the fan, Jason contemplated remaining in the little town. He tried to list positive qualities, and anonymity came to mind first. He had never heard of the place, and he guessed that few outside the region had. It seemed like a quiet town, just the kind of place to get some rest and stay out of entanglements. In thinking of negative qualities, he could not list any that might pertain to a dying man. While he moved his clothes from a washer into a dryer, he thought about what might be required to rent a place, and then he returned to the restroom and shaved.

Upon leaving the laundromat, he noticed the temperature had continued to climb, and he realized that aside from a short time at the estate in Sonoma County his California experience had been limited to San Francisco and Monterey where the weather stayed perennially perfect. He had not anticipated such hot temperatures, and it amused him to think that in all those years of falling homesick for Texas he had remembered the heat but in a romanticized way. When exposed to real heat, he remembered home in a more realistic manner, and he adopted the slow walk necessary under searing sun.

Jason had no idea which way to go in order to find the address he copied, and as he walked back in the opposite direction he had taken to get into town he passed back through the area with retail establishments and restaurants. One establishment had a weathered red and white sign with black letters. The only legible part of the sign said "Drive In," and when Jason saw the rectangular building with an awning displaying the words burgers, shakes, tacos, and fries, he also caught the familiar aroma of grease. At the little sliding window he asked for traditional fare, the same as he would have at any similar place in any of a dozen little Panhandle locales. While he waited for his order, he found concrete benches and tables next to the area for cars to park.

He had visited countless drive-ins in little Texas towns, and tried to recall if he had ever arrived at one as a pedestrian. He could not think of a single occurrence, and he laughed at the thought that back in his hometown walking, for anyone beyond teen years, had been considered suspect behavior. Once his order of soda, burger, and fries became ready, Jason took it to the concrete table, and he immediately noticed a difference in the portion size between those he remembered and the one he had. The one before him seemed tiny compared to Texas-sized burgers, but too his delight the flavor met expectations.

More than the heat and the food and the reduced population kept Jason in mind of Texas Panhandle towns. There at the concrete table at the drive-in, he realized that perhaps the feature that kept sending his mind back to places like Isom, Pampa, Dumas, or Hereford could be found at ground level, specifically the ground itself. In all his time in California, flat ground had been a thing of memory. Amid the tall buildings of San Francisco, the ground always climbed or descended depending on which direction one moved. The town of Monterey had less drastic grades but no more abundance of flat land. In Sonoma County, the hills had immense trees or lush grass. For at least as far as Jason had seen in his time since dawn, Dixon had plenty of flat ground.

Before leaving the drive-in, Jason approached the window and asked for directions to the address he had copied at the laundromat. The window attendant took the address to the cook at the grill, and some debate ensued. Another person from father back in the kitchen added to the discussion before the attendant returned to the window. Jason memorized the directions and headed back in the direction of the railroad tracks. Shortly after crossing the tracks, he felt the urge to cough, and like many bouts it started small and grew in severity. He had to hold onto a fence as he fought to maintain breath and keep the handkerchief over his mouth. Jason had not experienced a bout that severe since earlier in the night before accepting the ride that brought him to town. He hoped he could stave off further attacks until at least after he inquired about the furnished mobile home for rent.

Past the railroad tracks, past the warehouses, and past the auto salvage yard, he followed the directions memorized at the drive-in. After the salvage yard came yet another junkyard and then the orchard, which preceded the auto body shop. Farmland reached all the way to the road before giving way to more warehouses that marked the final landmark before the address. On the west side of the road, opposite the address, a dwelling stood surrounded by cars, trucks, and a dune buggy, all in various states of repair. The place resembled one of the auto salvage yards as much as a residence. The address Jason sought bordered the east side of the road.

A dirt road extended from the paved road and then branched at near right angles in both directions. The center of the property featured a wood-frame house flanked on both sides by two mobile homes. Of the four mobile homes, three appeared in good repair, but the fourth, the northern most, had broken windows. Outside one of those rectangles with shards of glass, a screen bent outward attached only at the bottom. Black smudges in stark contrast to the mobile home's white paint stretched from the broken window to the roof. The dwelling lacked a front door, and overflowing garbage cans and rolls of old carpet joined the scattered remains of a wooden porch. Beside the battered and burnt structure, just to the south, a parked camper trailer provided a barrier between the junked box and the other three cared-for domiciles.

The other three mobile homes, though old, wore bright ivory paint under shingled roofs. Wood skirting lined the bottoms, and each had a small wooden porch, some with lawn chairs. Two children's bicycles, one pink and one purple, rested against the side of the home closest to the damaged building, and the home farthest to the south had a chicken wire enclosed vegetable garden.

Jason guessed the address referred to the wood framed house, and as he approached the front steps, the door burst open and twin metal poles emerged. A moment later, the twin poles developed into a step ladder carried by a rotund woman in shorts. Jason stepped back to give the woman plenty of room, and he said, "Good afternoon."

The woman stopped, leaned the step ladder against the house, and scrutinized Jason. "Can I help you with something, cowboy?"

Jason saw the woman's fading and thinning short brown hair that might have once been red, and he saw the amber spots on her flushed and wrinkled skin where it emerged beyond her over-sized and worn out t-shirt. "Yes ma'am. I saw an ad about a furnished mobile home for rent. The ad had this address."

"That's old information. That one isn't for rent anymore. It was, but it got torn up, and I haven't finished fixing it yet. I'm going over there now. I'm Maddie."

Jason removed his hat with his left hand and extended his right toward Maddie, but she turned to pick up the step ladder. "I'm Jason. Please to meet you ma'am. You say the mobile home is not for rent?"

Maddie walked toward the burnt mobile home, and Jason followed. "That's right. I let some no good bum stay there, and he and his buddies tore it up. He still hasn't paid me a cent of rent not to mention the cost for the damages, and now he lives right across the road." Maddie pointed with her free hand to the run-down building with all the cars.

"I'm sorry to hear that, ma'am. What about your other ones, are any of them for rent?"

"Nope. That one has a retired couple. They're rarely there. They prefer their RV. I got a postcard from Idaho last week. A nurse and her husband the welder rent that one. And the one just this side of the one I'm fixing, the one that was for rent, has a family with two kids. The dad is in the air force. I'm not sure what the mom does."

"Would you happen to know anybody else nearby that's looking to rent a place maybe for the short term?"

Maddie stopped walking and turned to look at Jason. She looked from his head to his feet and then back to his head. "What do you do, cowboy?"

"Ma'am?"

"For work. You do have a job, don't you?"

"Yes ma'am. I'm a photographer."

"Knock off the ma'am business, cowboy. I told you my name is Maddie." She resumed walking, and Jason followed.

"All right then, Maddie."

"Where's your camera, cowboy?"

"Well, Maddie, it's in San Francisco. I'm taking a little bit of a vacation. I've been livin and workin in San Francisco for a long time, but I'm originally from a small place. I just wanted to take some time off from the city."

Maddie positioned the step ladder against the burnt trailer near a broken window. She climbed onto the ladder, removed glass shards, and tossed them into a pile. "What are those marks on your face? Did you get in a fight?"

"No ma'am . . . no, Maddie. I started my vacation in Sonoma County about ten miles as the crow flies from Guerneville and got jilted by a motorcycle. So I'm trying to start my vacation over in a quieter place."

"What brings you here?"

"I've never been here, but it reminds me of where I come from in the Texas Panhandle."

Maddie moved the step ladder to another broken window, and said, "Well, that's an interesting story, but I don't have anything for rent right now."

"That camper trailer has an electric cord and a water hose running to it. Is anyone staying in it?"

"My son-in-law . . . ex son-in-law stayed in that while he worked on fixing this place, but he got a good job down in Fresno."

"How much would you rent that for?"

Maddie climbed down from the step ladder. "You're a persistent

186

cowboy, aren't you? I'm not even sure it's legal for me to rent you that camper, and I like to check references first, especially after what happened to this place."

"Legal? I don't think it's a matter of being legal. If I was to stay here at your place as your guest in that there camper, then there wouldn't have to be nobody looking into whether we traded money. As for references, I can head to the closest bank and bring you back a pile of references. Just tell me how many references you want for that camper for a week or a month, and I'll give em to you upfront, in advance. From the looks of this tore up trailer, you could probably use a pile of references. Am I right, ma'am, Maddie?"

Look to the blowing Rose about us—"Lo,
Laughing," she says, "into the world I blow,
　　At once the silken tassel of my Purse
Tear, and its Treasure on the Garden throw."

Delta Breeze

Of the few items that Maddie's ex son-in-law had left behind in the camper trailer, Jason appreciated the drip coffee maker and the radio the most. He used the radio only in the evenings, and he started his mornings with the coffee maker. He had bought some paper filters and coffee, and after several mornings of practice he had learned to make robust coffee to suit his taste. The camper's little air conditioner, which barely cooled the metal box under the best of circumstances, already had a hard time that morning. The previous days had been hot, but Jason could tell this one might be even Texas hot.

Jason finished the last of his morning's coffee, rinsed the cup, and cleaned the coffee maker. When he stepped outside, the sun still hung low enough in the sky that the camper provided some shade. As soon as he stepped into the direct sunlight, he knew it would indeed be a Texas hot kind of day. At the road, he turned left, but first he looked at the junkyard house across the way, and it seemed the collection of beer bottles kept growing. They littered the ground around the various cars, trucks, and dune buggy. Jason felt glad that he no longer spent his days and nights consuming mind-numbing booze and that he no longer contributed to such ugly refuse.

Past the warehouses, past the orchard, and even with the junkyards, Jason moved in his slow but steady hot weather walk, and his palm leaf hat absorbed the sweat. No breeze cooled his walk, and Jason tried first ignore then estimate the level of humidity. He knew the level felt far higher than the Texas Panhandle but much less than Central Texas. In trying to find other ways to think about and tolerate the rising heat, Jason decided that in his present condition he need not worry about the effects of sun exposure. He rolled up both sleeves past his elbows.

At the donut shop, he purchased two donuts and a large coffee to go. He had thought about trying to find a thermos so he could transport his own coffee, but after brief consideration he had decided that he would not enjoy carrying the thermos and his coffee, which, while effective at waking him in the morning, did not meet the standards of coffee for sipping enjoyment. Grease had saturated the paper bag with donuts by the time Jason found the shaded bench at the park. While he consumed the donuts and enjoyed the coffee, he wondered how much longer he should stay, and he wondered if he should worry about falling into a routine. A routine could establish familiarity, and people often felt comfortable asking questions of familiar people. Getting too familiar could lead to entanglements. But so far no one had asked him anything.

A squirrel hopped out of a tree, ran across the grass, and leaped into another tree. Jason thought about the little dog in Sonoma County, and for a moment he smiled. The temperature in the shade became uncomfortable as the sun continued to heat the morning, and Jason left the bench. The town's tiny library sat on the south end of the park. Jason went inside the small stucco building, felt the relief from air conditioning, and found the periodical section. He glanced at the covers of a few magazines until one made him stop. A photography magazine's cover displayed a twin lens reflex camera much like one he had used for many years. That camera still resided with his collection in storage in San Francisco. Jason started to open the magazine, but then he noticed words advertising other articles in that issue, words like digital and pixel and others he found foreign and intimidating. He put the magazine back on the rack and chose a day-old copy of the New York Times.

Jason tuned the big pages one by one, and he saw headlines for stories of national and international interest, events of which he had been unaware. Each time he began an article, he read only a few lines before his mind drifted to a fast little dog. After a while, he turned the pages at regular, robotic intervals but did not read stories or even headlines. When the air conditioning had made him forget the exterior heat, he rose and left the library.

Every parking space at the drive-in held a car, but no one sat at the concrete tables. Jason sat at one and waited until no line formed at the ordering window. He ate two cheeseburgers but left a third in the bag for later. He finished his soda and kept the cup and remaining ice, and when he passed the park he filled the cup from the drinking fountain. The rest of the walk progressed in a slow hot mirage without interruption except for the time just prior to the second junkyard when he felt the urge to cough. In preparation for the calamity to come, he set his cup of water on the ground, but he coughed for only a few seconds before the difficulty passed. He thought about how the coughing bouts came less frequent and less severe, but he knew better than to believe in signs of improvement.

A street before the last group of warehouses led a block off the main road and offered the closest retail establishment of any kind to his rented camper trailer. He entered the liquor store and walked along the rows of glass doors, past dozens of brands of refrigerated beer, to the last door. He chose a six-pack of soda pop. To make carrying the paper bag with the soda pop easier, he placed his left-over cheeseburger in the bag atop the cans of soda, and he discarded his empty water cup before setting off on the final quarter mile to the camper.

Before he turned off the main road onto the dirt road leading to the mobile homes and the camper trailer, he heard the shouting. About the time he identified the voice as Maddie's, he saw her standing before a large man while shouting and gesturing with her arms. The man towered over Maddie. He had close cropped black hair, and tattoos climbed his neck onto his face. After delivering a foul stream of profanity, the man got into a shiny coupe. The coupe roared up the dirt road toward Jason, and once even with Jason the man made the car swerve and accelerate to spray dirt and gravel all over Jason. Unable to open his eyes in all the flying dust, Jason heard the laughter. When he took his hat off and dusted off his shirt, Jason looked back toward the road and saw the coupe cross over to the junkyard-like residence and stop. Maddie met Jason as he approached the camper.

"Are you all right, cowboy? That's the knucklehead that tore up my mobile home and didn't pay me. He came over because he heard I was looking for a lawyer. Can you believe he threatened me? When I said I could call his parole office, you should have heard what he called me."

"Are you gonna do it?"

"What?"

"Call his parole officer."

"I might. It probably won't do any good. I called the police a while ago, and they told me it was a civil matter. They said I'd have to take him to court for the unpaid bill. It would probably cost me more than I could get.

190

That knucklehead has been nothing but trouble, and I have work to do."

Maddie walked away, and Jason continued to the camper. Inside he found the temperature hotter than outside. He turned on the air conditioner, but the feeble output did not bring the temperature to a tolerable level. Soaked in sweat Jason stepped out of the camper, and he thought about returning to town or simply trying to find some shade. He noticed above the door of the camper a roll of canvass material wrapped around a spool that ran nearly the length of the trailer. He tried moving the arms attached to the spool, but they moved only a few inches. After working the arms back and forth a few times, he stopped and walked toward the burnt out mobile home. He found Maddie on the back side standing on a step ladder and removing more broken glass.

"Can you believe what they did to this lawn? This was the one out of all four that had decent grass, and they would drive their cars around the side."

"That's a shame. Can I borrow a screwdriver for a little bit."

"Ha! A tenant who wants to fix something himself. Now that's a first. Over at the house in the garage there's a tool box toward the back. Take what you need, but don't forget to put it back."

With the awning functional and extended all the way, the area in front of the door and nearly the entire length of the trailer stayed under shade, and Jason knew it could stay shaded all day because the door faced north. On his way back from replacing the screwdriver, Jason saw an old folding metal chair, and he took it to the camper. Seated in the shade, he thought about turning on the radio or going to get a newspaper but instead dozed.

The sound of tires on gravel and laughter woke him. Jason looked up to see a young girl on a purple bicycle being chased by a younger one on a pink bicycle. They rode up and down the dirt road in front of the mobile homes and occasionally made brief forays onto the blacktop of the main road. The older girl, always in the lead, had a svelte frame and waist-length raven hair drawn in a ponytail. The younger, far shorter girl had a plump body and the same raven hair but with frizzy curls. She lacked the older girl's poise and control of her bike, but she made up for it in tenacity. "I'll catch you!" the younger hollered while the older slowed a bit and then pedaled ahead before the younger could draw even.

The older girl turned back where the dirt of the property met the pavement of the main road, and she took a wide loop that sent her past the camper. The younger followed, but when she passed the camper she noticed Jason sitting under the awning, and she slowed and turned back. She rode a couple of figure eights in front of the camper before rolling up to the edge of the awning, stopping, and getting a toe on the ground to help steady the wobbly bike.

"I've never seen you before."

"And I've never seen you," Jason replied.

"I'm Ada. That's my sister, Val. We live right there. Do you live in that?" Ada pointed to the camper, and Jason began to answer, but Ada continued, "This is my bike, but it's not as fast as Val's because hers is really a boy's bike. I don't want a boy's bike. This one is better. Do you have a bike?"

"No, I don't have a bike."

"Do you have a car?"

"No car either."

"We have two cars. That one over there is my mommy's, and my daddy has his at work. He's in the air force. Are you in the air force?"

"No, I'm not in the air force."

The older girl arrived and chastised her sister. "Ada, leave the man alone. You talk too much. I'm sorry my sister is bothering you, mister."

Jason smiled and said, "She's fine. She's telling me about bikes and the air force, and she said your name is Val. Mine's Jason. Does Val stand for Valerie?"

"Valentina."

"That's a beautiful name. Very fitting."

Valentina looked at the ground and smiled a thin line. "I . . . uh . . . like your hat."

"Why thank you, Valentina. You sure have pretty hair. It's as long as some horse's tails. Very pretty."

Valentina again looked pleased but embarrassed. "Where did you get that hat?"

"This old thing? I got it in a place called Alpine way out in West Texas."

"I have a hat," Ada said. "It a cap, though, not a cowboy hat."

"It was nice meeting you, mister," Valentina said. "Come on, Ada."

"It's been a pleasure meeting both of you."

Valentina pedaled away, and Ada followed. Jason watched the girls return to their game of chase, and he admired both Valentina's lithe athleticism and Ada's cheerful determination. The heat that had made dozing easy earlier just made everything sticky. Jason removed his sweat-soaked hat and pushed his hair back before donning the hat again. He thought he felt a slight movement of air but attributed it to wishful thinking. A moment later a gentle breeze accelerated to a blast. Jason stood and walked away from the awning. He looked up at the sky expecting to see the signs of a blue norther. He did not see the signs, and he realized that the wind came from the wrong direction, but he remained certain a storm approached. He turned to go back to the camper, and a gust caught his hat. The hat flew a few yards and settled on the ground, but before Jason could reach it another gust lifted it, and this time the hat rolled along the ground. Jason took quick steps, but he knew he could not run and expected to lose his hat as it neared the end of the property. A purple flash whizzed past, and Jason watched Valentina draw even with his hat and lean over to snatch it, never missing her peddling rhythm.

"Wow. A little Comanche," Jason exclaimed.

As Valentina handed Jason his hat, Ada slid to a stop next to them. Jason said, "Thank you so much. I'd have never caught it. You girls might want to get home. I think it's gonna storm."

Both girls laughed, Ada the loudest and most animated. Valentina explained, "That's not a storm. That's just the Delta Breeze."

"Okay then," Jason said. "I better get that awning rolled up before it rips to pieces."

After Jason got the awning secured, he opened all the windows on the camper trailer and left the door open. He continued to sit outside and wondered how much the temperature had dropped. Soon he began to shiver, but he remained outside and thought how much more comfortable this cool wetter air would make sleeping.

A car arrived at the girls' mobile home, and a man in an air force uniform got out. Valentina parked her bike, and Ada dropped hers, and both girls hugged their father before running inside. The man in the uniform waved, and Jason waved back before going inside and turning on the radio.

Maddie said when her husband bought the house the land around had nothing except almond orchards. She said that around the whole town there wasn't nothing but almonds and walnuts, and around the house it was all almonds. Tom, her husband, worked for the railroad and bought the house with plans to put in the mobile homes for rent. She said he had big plans for how they'd collect the rents and not have to worry in their retirement. First, he bought the house and fixed it up, and then he put in the mobile homes. They were all set for a comfortable retirement, and Maddie quit her job just before her husband took sick and died at 56. She spoke about him in the sour way she talks about everybody, but I could tell she missed him.

Dixon must have been something to see with all them orchards. It would be nicer with more orchards and less junkyards now. From what Maddie said, the town traded the orchards for more houses, junkyards, and liquor stores. Whether that's the truth or if it's just the way she remembers it, the way she talked about Dixon back when her husband still lived sure made it sound like a peaceful and beautiful spot.

This turned out to be a good place to stop, and I don't regret it, but avoiding getting tangled up is still a hard chore. When that knucklehead yelled at Maddie, that was hard to stay out of. He's lucky I ain't drinking no more. Or I'm lucky. He's a big mean looking loudmouth. But he sure did have a nice car.

Them girls, though, that's where the real tangles come from. They're hard to avoid. And when they do come by and talk, especially that littlest one, it's hard to remember the aim to stay away from people and conversations. Every day starts with the determination to do whatever it takes to avoid talking to them little girls, and I'll be damned if the little one don't see me and come right over and sit down. They are about the cutest little girls ever seen. That littlest one is a real fireball full of energy and joy. The older one seems to be more of a thinker. She's quieter. That's for sure. But she's also quite a little athlete. In some ways, they couldn't be more different, but they're both going to grow into gorgeous young women. I can't imagine what it must be like for their parents. They must be awful proud.

And them girls is the main reason to be thinking about moving on. The cough ain't been too bad lately, but there ain't no way to avoid what's coming, and that's not a thing for little girls to see or even know about. It's time to be making a plan for moving on before things get bad again.

With all the worrying about keeping dying a secret from other folks, there ain't always time for thinking about how to feel about it. But I do think about it, especially here lately in the evenings. I think about it, and I'm scared. Knowing that dying is gonna be never ending nothing don't matter. It's still a scary prospect, and maybe that's cause nothing is damned near impossible to comprehend. Even in a little spot like this, there's plenty to regret not seeing again. There won't be no more little girls on bicycles, no more orchards, no more cheeseburgers, and no more junk-yards. Junkyards might seem a funny thing to miss, but when you come from a little oil patch town like Isom, if there is such a thing as a town like Isom, then junkyards ain't so unusual. Sometimes I get to thinking about never seeing anything again, and I get scared.

Putting in all this effort to keep folks at a distance is another odd thing. Most folks when they die want to have others near. They think it's a comfort. To me it's the farthest thing from a comfort there is. I'm dying, but the other folks have to go on, and I don't want to have to worry about them, and I don't want my dying to cause them sadness. Dying is scary enough without the sadness.

But then at the same time, there's this yearning to tell someone about the fear. I catch myself wanting tell someone that I'm dying and I'm scared, but then, of course, that's about the most foolish thing. For one, it would waste that other person's time. If I'm dying, then I'm supposed to be scared. There ain't no point in talking about something that's obvious and can't be changed. Another reason talking about dying is foolish is cause it makes other folks feel low. First they feel sympathy for the one dying, then they get reminded that everyone dies, and they feel scared for themselves. There ain't no point in making other folks feel low when there ain't nothing they can do about it. But knowing all that don't keep me from wanting to talk about it from time to time.

Sadness and fear ain't the only thing to feel. For some reason, I ain't been able to let loose of the anger that was getting to me in the hospital. It might have gotten worse. The same things that cause the fear and the sadness cause the anger. It starts as feeling sad and then goes to feeling afraid and ends up being mad enough to fight anybody over anything. It's a good thing I ain't drinking, and that's another strange part of what is going on.

There's all kinds of good reasons for not drinking. For the longest stretch, it felt good to be quit of the booze, but here lately my mind plays tricks. Sometimes in town there's thinking of finding a bar, and the thoughts are so powerful that out of nowhere comes the smell and taste of beer and liquor. Other times a notion forms of bringing a pint or two back here. When those girls go in for the evening, there ain't nobody around to see me drinking out there in that Delta Breeze that comes some evenings. And that's when the worrying starts. Cause if there's one true thing about staying off the booze, it's that if the only thing keeping me from it is somebody else's feelings, then I ain't far out of a bottle. So mostly when my mind heads that way it's helpful to think about what a hangover feels like. In my present condition, there ain't no way I could weather a real hangover.

I sure do miss that little dog. The other night I had a dream about her so real and so clear that it woke me. She chased a roadrunner and kept up. That road runner was just like in memory. When it ran, it flattened like a dart. When the little dog ran, she doubled in half and then sprang out straight in them long flying strides. If there ain't no roadrunners in Sonoma County, she must have been in Texas. Waking up and knowing that little dog wasn't near gave a real heavy feeling. Doing things with that little dog, little things like walking and petting, made for such pleasure. I miss her, and it hurts. And when I think about what she might be doing now, that's when it really hurts. Ain't no way she could understand me going away. I can handle being alone, but thinking about her alone and confused tears me up. And when I get tore up sad, being mad ain't far behind. Sometimes I get so damned mad at Eleanor for bringing that little dog that I forget about all the kind things Eleanor done and just get burnt up mad about the dog. What she done with the dog was worse than that knucklehead spraying me with gravel as he roared out of here in his fancy car.

Being mad puts me in mind of my hometown being strange. But understanding how strange didn't come until after getting far from the place. Folks in that town fight a lot. They always did. Back a long time ago, that place got so violent that the army had to come to town. Somehow the place stayed mean. And it wasn't just the roughnecks doing all the fighting and carrying on. Everybody did. There ain't been much fist throwing to speak of since leaving that place, but knock-down-drag-outs used to be a common thing for me. For some reason this dying business and being mad about it puts me in mind of them times, and I don't like it.

Stopping in this little place wasn't a bad idea, but the time here is almost up. Too many things make it about time to be gettin on down the road. Them girls don't need to see a man dying. And nobody needs to see what can happen if the anger takes hold or if I take to drinking or both. But leaving in a rush without a word like at the hospice place and in some ways like in Sonoma ain't no kind of good. Things got to be done more orderly with some manners. I ain't one for real goodbyes and don't aim to become that way, but there has got to be a way to do things with some manners. This camper is paid up till the end of the month. That might be a good time to go. Maddie ain't one for pointless conversation, but she might appreciate a note just saying thank you. Them girls deserve something more than wondering why an adult up and left without saying a word. If I done that, they wouldn't know how much I appreciated them stopping by on their bike rides. I could leave some little gifts or trinkets or something so they'd know I didn't just leave without thinking of em.

There's a train that runs north and south, and it stops in Davis. Davis ain't too far to walk. The train runs all the way down to Los Angeles, and it runs all the way up to Seattle. But with winter coming, heading north ain't a good idea. It gets cold up in Seattle, not cold like a Panhandle blizzard, but it stays cold, and it's always wet up there. All of that Southern California country is foreign to me, but it's got to be at least as warm as San Francisco in the winter. Probably it's even warmer. The coughing ain't like it was when I left San Francisco. That might mean that my body is just giving up and not trying no more, but it also means I can be around folks a little longer without worrying that a coughing fit will sneak up on me. And on them trains folks can get up and walk around, so that might be the best thing to do. The rent is paid until the end of the month, and then I could walk up to Davis and catch a train all the way down to Los Angeles. All that country in and around Los Angeles is stuff from the movies. The closest I've been is Big Sur, and that might as well be in another state it's so far away. The name of the train is the Coast Starlight. From Davis, that Coast Starlight goes all the way down to a city so big I'd just disappear and be forgotten. That sounds like something a bona fide drifter would do, especially a dying one.

And this I know: whether the one True Light
Kindle to Love, or Wrath-consume me quite,
One Flash of It within the Tavern caught
Better than in the Temple lost outright.

Knucklehead

The shade under the awning offered shelter from the direct afternoon sun, but Jason still found the heat insufferable. He wished he had stayed in town after lunch. Somehow immune to the heat and fatigue, Ada and Valentina played their game of chase on their wheeled mounts. Jason resolved to do his best to ignore the heat and yet still hope for an evening Delta Breeze. On one of their passes by the camper, Ada stopped her bike and then walked it on tip toes under the awning.

"Jason, do you know how to ride a bike?"

"Oh sure. I had one at your age and another one at your sister's age."

Ada lifted one leg over her bike and let the bike fall on its side. She sat on the ground next to the bike and looked up at Jason sitting in the folding chair. Her wiry chaotic frizzy hair sprouted in all directions, and when she looked up with her brown round cherub face Jason noticed a dark spot just to the left of her constantly moving lips. He did not ask, but he suspected that she did not like the dapple, and that made him smile because he knew that when she became a little older other young women would be envious of the beauty mark.

"When you were a kid, were there mountain bikes? I want a mountain bike and so does Valentina."

"Don't remember any mountain bikes."

"But you had a bicycle? Did you ride it every day?"

"Most days. Rode my horse more than my bike."

Ada's deep brown eyes widened, and she asked, "You had a horse? Really?"

"Sure. My folks had lots of horses, and I rode all of them. When I was your sister's age, or maybe a couple of years younger, I got a very special horse."

"Wow! I want a horse so bad. I want . . ." Valentina stopped her bike near Ada's fallen one, and Ada said, "Val, he said he had horses when he was little."

"Really?" Valentina asked.

"Yep, really."

Valentina's shyness vanished, and she said, "I love horses! I want one. Daddy said we might get one someday, but we would have to live in a bigger place."

"Well, your Daddy is right. You couldn't just keep a horse outside with your bikes."

"What kind of horse did you have?" Ada asked. "What's your favorite horse? Did you have a pony? Did the horse let you ride it, and did it run, and . . ." Valentina nudged Ada with a bike tire and made a shushing noise.

Jason said, "We had all kinds of horses. We had quarter horses, of course. But we also had a few appaloosas. My favorite was a paint horse."

"Do you have any horses now?" Ada asked. "Can we ride them?"

"Don't have any horses now, but . . ." Jason felt the urge to cough, and he fought to stifle it.

"I want a horse so much," Ada said. "I would feed it and pet it and we'd be friends."

"You young ladies will have to excuse me," Jason said. "I have to go inside for a little bit. We can horse talk later."

As soon as he shut the camper door, Jason began hacking, but he tried to muffle the sound with his hand. When he saw that the girls had remounted their bikes and ridden away from the camper, he let loose, and the coughing dropped him to his knees. After the bout, he stood and then sat at the dining area couch that converted to a bed. He looked at his hands with curiosity because he did not see blood or even traces of blood. After a few deep breaths he stood and turned to the door to get out of the hot camper.

As he neared the folding metal chair under the awning, he looked ahead and saw the girls near the paved main road. They sat on their still bikes near the shiny coupe, and Jason saw the driver, the same man that had verbally assailed Maddie days earlier. Jason stood still, and he listened. He heard the man's words, and he wished he had not. He thought he must have misheard, misunderstood what the man said for no man would ever say such things to girls so young. When he saw Valentina command her younger sister to go back to the house, and moments later when he saw Valentina crying and riding directly to her parents' mobile home, he knew he had not misheard. Ada lagged behind as usual, and Jason walked out into the sun to meet her. "Is everything all right?" Jason asked.

"That man said something gross. I'm going to tell my Daddy when he gets home."

Jason found speaking difficult, so he put his hand on Ada's shoulder. "Okay, hon. You better get to your house and see that your sister is okay."

As Ada pedaled away, Jason looked toward the road and saw the shiny coupe parked near the junked cars and dune buggy. The large man with the tattoos got out and accepted a beer from one of the other men standing around the cars. Jason walked toward the road, and then he stopped. The sun beat down, but Jason felt only shock. He could not think, and he became aware of the shaking. His arms shook, and his knees shook, and when he raised a hand and looked at it he could not hold the hand steady.

Jason slammed the door to the camper and paced back and forth. The camper permitted only three steps in any direction, and the constant turning made Jason dizzy. He sat at the dining area couch and stared at the sink while he shook. Sweat flowed down his face, and Jason took off his hat and placed it on the fold-out dinette table. He stood and turned the tap above the sink, cupped his hands, and threw water onto his face. No urge to cough burdened Jason, but he breathed fast as if he had been running. And no amount of breathing seemed to deliver enough air.

In the bottom of his leather bag, near the peace sign medallion, he found the ornate metal flask. Pouring the magic wine into an open mouth, he over-poured and a stream trickled down from the corner of his mouth and along his neck. He waited a few moments, but the magic wine did not render any miracles. Jason finished the rest of the flask's contents in a few large gulps, and then he tossed it back into the leather bag. After smashing his hat onto his head, Jason left the camper and walked toward the road. At the edge of the pavement, he stopped for a moment and watched the large man and his compatriots. Jason turned left and walked along the main road.

When he approached the counter at the liquor store, the cashier asked, "No cola today?"

"No thank you. Could I get a pint of tequila . . . make that two pints."

Outside the liquor store, Jason pulled both pints from the paper bag, shoved one pint in a back pocket of this trousers, and let the paper bag fall to the ground. He uncapped the bottle and took a long drink. By the time he returned to Maddie's property, he had finished half the pint, and he stood at the road watching the large man and his buddies drinking beer and working on cars. The men took no notice of Jason.

In the metal chair under the awning, Jason stared at the men across the road. He drank the tequila at a slower rate, and he kept the bottle hidden under his shirt in case the girls came outside. By late evening, no Delta Breeze had arrived, and the heat continued despite the fading sun. When he finished the bottle, Jason went into the camper.

Jason resumed his pacing, but this time he did not get dizzy. He seemed to get angrier, and sometimes he made a fist or two fists and held them to his temples. Jason flung his hat across the camper, and he looked outside to see darkness. Night had come with no Delta Breeze, and the camper's little air conditioner had little effect on the intolerable heat.

He unscrewed the cap of the second pint and kicked the camper door open. Under the awning, he took another drink, capped the bottle, and shoved it in his trousers' back pocket. From across the road he heard a loud radio, and as he walked away from the camper toward the dirt road leading off the property he saw some exterior floodlights. His boot collided with something, and he almost tripped. When he bent down he saw a half piece of broken brick, and he picked it up.

Before crossing the road, Jason stood in the dark beyond the range of the floodlights. He saw one person, the person he sought, crouched and working on the dune buggy. Jason waited, but he did not see other people, so he crossed the road. As he neared the crouching figure, the blaring music concealed the sound of his boots on the gravel. Jason looked at the back of the man's head, and he thought about what the man had said to the girl. Sweat snaked down Jason's forehead across the bridge of his nose and onto his face. Jason lifted the brick above his own head as he focused on the head of the man couched at the dune buggy. A yard away from his target, Jason felt the brick slip from his fingers and fall to the ground.

The man at the dune buggy stood and turned to face Jason while Jason still had his right arm over his head like a shocked frozen dancer. The man who liked to say vile things to young girls stood four or five inches taller than Jason, and his weight exceeded Jason's by at least sixty pounds. He looked at Jason with confusion, and he too froze.

Two jabs, a double jab, shot from Jason's left arm, and as he saw the man's head tilt back twice he launched an overhand right that met the left underside of the man's chin. Jason tucked his own chin almost to his chest and stepped forward throwing alternating hooks. The man staggered backward until he fell, and then Jason heard the clatter of metal on the concrete beside the dune buggy. A bright silvery revolver lay just a few feet to the man's right, and Jason stepped and bent to pick it up, but something grabbed his left boot and prevented forward progress. Jason stumbled, and his knees and hands met the pavement at the same time. He turned to see the man hanging onto his left boot, so he rolled to his left and stomped with his right. The first kick missed, but the next two caught the man directly on the top of the head. Jason scrambled on hands and knees to grab the revolver, and then he twisted around and smashed the pistol across the top of the man's head until he felt like his arm could no longer lift the gun.

On wobbly legs, Jason stood. He coughed and feared that he might not regain his breath. While he bent to let one knee touch the ground, he did his best to control his breathing amid the coughing, and he kept the revolver pointed at the motionless man. Once again in control of his breath, Jason stood. Blood pooled around the man's head, and Jason saw blood on his own right hand and the revolver. He had not planned the event beyond the initial assault, and he had not envisioned being the one standing after an altercation. He tried to think of his next move, but blaring music prevented clear thought. Jason found the box from where the music came, but he did not understand the controls. For an instant he thought about shooting, and for a moment he thought about kicking, but then he found a power cord and jerked until the music stopped.

Jason stood over the man and tried to think of a plan. He saw a red tool rag nearby and used it to clean the blood from his hand and the revolver and then tossed the rag at the man. The rag landed near the man's head, and Jason said, "Get up. You awake? I said get up." The man remained motionless, and Jason reached into his back pocket for the pint of tequila. He took a long drink and recapped the bottle. He could simply leave, but he knew he could not stay in the camper trailer any longer. He might have a hard time making it far out of town by daybreak while depending on the kindness of strangers for rides.

Jason looked around while he took another drink of tequila. He stood before the dune buggy and next to the shiny coupe that had thrown gravel on him days earlier. As he started to open the door to the coupe, he heard groaning. Jason whirled around and pointed the pistol. The man clasped his hands to the top of his head and continued to groan. Jason took two steps and thought about putting one of his pointy roach killer boots at the man's temple, but then he stopped and returned to the coupe. He reached inside and pulled the latch for the trunk.

With the pistol pointed, Jason commanded, "Get up. Get up and get in the car." The man lay on the ground with his hands clasped to his head. Jason kicked him in the stomach and again yelled for him to get up. The man removed his hands from his head to cover his midsection, but he did not get up. Jason took a drink of tequila and then poured some on the man's scalp. The man howled and shrieked.

"Get up and get in that car or I'll give you another drink."

The man pushed himself up off the ground while Jason pointed the pistol. "Get in the trunk or I'll shoot. I ain't wasting no more of this tequila, knucklehead. Hurry up." The man bent over the trunk face-first and seemed undecided how to get in. Jason kicked him in the upper thigh. "I said hurry up. There's a can of gasoline over there. You want me to clean your head with that?" With his knees tucked up in a fetal position, the man lay sideways in the trunk. Jason stood over him, poured the remaining tequila on his face and scalp, and then slammed the trunk lid on the screaming and screeching.

IX. Quicksand

Of threats of Hell and Hopes of Paradise!
One thing at least is certain—*This* Life flies;
   One thing is certain and the rest is Lies;
The Flower that once has blown for ever dies.

We are no other than a moving row
Of Magic Shadow-shapes that come and go
    Round with the Sun-illumined Lantern held
In Midnight by the Master of the Show.

They Drive by Night

Jason started the shiny coupe and then looked at the controls and the lights on the dash. Except for the Jeep in Sonoma County, he had not driven a car in over ten years, and he had never driven a car as modern as the shiny coupe. Screaming still came from the trunk, and Jason yelled, "Quiet down. If I have to open that trunk lid, you're gonna be sorry." The screaming stopped, and Jason moved the gear selector and steered the car around in a big loop until he faced the paved road. He drove across onto Maddie's property, around the burnt out mobile home, and he parked in the back where Maddie had shown him that knucklehead and his friends had damaged the lawn.

Inside the camper trailer, Jason dropped the revolver on the foldout dinette. He paced, and then he washed his face in the sink. When a coughing bout came, he braced his arms against the sink, and when the coughing passed he reached for a towel. "Now that's something," he said. "Even after all that, not a speck of blood. None." The surprise faded when he again saw the revolver on the dinette table. After more pacing, he picked up the revolver and opened the cylinder to see six bullets. "Three fifty-seven magnum. Polished nickel. Four inch barrel. Real pretty."

He put the pistol in his pants waistband and made sure his belt stayed cinched enough to hold it and his shirt tails long enough to conceal it. After putting on his palm leaf hat, he found his leather bag and packed it with everything he had brought. Rickety steps as he exited the camper told him he could not yet drive the car, so went he back in the trailer and started a pot of coffee. While the coffee brewed, Jason walked around to the back of the burnt out mobile home and saw the shiny coupe where he had parked it. No pleas, threats, or incoherent hollering emanated from the trunk, so Jason went back to the camper and used an electrical extension cord to bring the radio outside next to the folding metal chair. He found a Sacramento station with a solid signal, and he turned up the volume just loud enough that if someone came to the camper trailer the radio could be heard but not noises from the shiny coupe trunk.

Jitters kept him from sitting in the folding metal chair and sipping coffee, so Jason used the chair for a place to set his mug while he paced in front of the camper, stopping occasionally for large gulps of coffee. He turned off the lights inside the camper, and he walked the length of the trailer again and again while he muttered. The alcohol and the adrenalin kept a detailed plan from forming. Only one thought, that he needed to get far away, came with clarity, and he decided maybe that would be enough for the short-term. He sat in the chair, sipped his coffee, and tried think of what evidence might cause trouble before he could gain distance.

Jason sprang up and set his coffee mug in the chair. He took a straight-line path for the residence across the road. Under the blaring floodlights, he looked for the pool of blood, and when he found it he looked around for ways to conceal it. Inside the cluttered garage, he sought something to pour on the spot. After he gave up that search, he looked for something to place over the spot, like a toolbox. He found a large metal box, and while moving it he noticed a nearly full quart of beer. The beer flowed out of the bottle in a stream and made the blood pool widen and lighten. Jason looked for more beer or liquid of any kind, and then he remembered the gas can. The gasoline spread over the concrete near the dune buggy, and under the floodlights the dark outline of the blood pool faded. He hoped that when the gas dried if any blood remained it would turn a rust color and draw little attention. After finding the switch for the floodlights, he hurried back to the camper.

The awning crank made a loud high-pitched creak that Jason had not noticed during the daytime, so he gave up stowing the awning and hoped Maddie closed it before the next Delta Breeze. After pouring another cup of coffee and cleaning the coffee maker, Jason rechecked the camper to ensure order and tidiness. He stowed the radio inside the camper and sat in the folding metal chair. He felt like the alcohol had worn off, but he knew most of that feeling came from fear. Car lights on the main road slowed near the entrance to Maddie's property, and Jason's heart beat so hard he thought it might stop. When he saw the car turn onto the property, he jumped out of the chair and dashed around the side of the camper. Fighting the urge to cough, he forced slow regular breaths and watched the car park in front of the bicycles. Ada and Valentina's father got out of the car and went into the house. When Jason did not see lights come on, he hoped that meant the girls slept and would not tell their father of the incident with knucklehead until at least the morning.

A thumping sound followed by muffled screams made Jason take his leather bag and walk toward the shiny couple. When he rounded the burnt out mobile home, he heard knucklehead beating the inside of the trunk and screaming. Jason tapped the pistol against the trunk lid and said, "You better stop that right now, or things are gonna get real painful for you. You think that tequila hurt? I got something a lot worse. Make one more noise and we'll find out what this here acid will do. Keep quiet and we'll see about letting you out and sending you on your way."

The hollering and banging ended, and Jason got in the driver seat. Still not ready to drive, he tried to think of a destination. Putting distance between himself and the place across the road with the gasoline soaked blood stain seemed most important, but Jason had no idea which way to go. If he could get the car and its trunk contents away, then the discovery of a crime would be delayed, but the challenge of getting himself away from the car remained. If he could leave the car somewhere, somewhere it would not be discovered right away, then maybe he could get far away before the altercation, the felonious assault became known. But that still left the contents of the trunk in question. If he left the contents in the trunk, that might amount to murder. If he opened the trunk just as he planned to leave, he might be able to outpace the knucklehead but probably not the cops once they had some kind of description. And from the way the tattooed tough guy wailed and carried on, Jason knew he would tell the cops all he could.

Frustration made the interior of the car feel stuffy, so Jason got out and paced circuits around the vehicle. He noticed that his steps got more definite and controlled, and in front of the car he practiced standing on one foot and extending his arms to the side. Years before, before he moved to San Francisco, field sobriety tests under the authority of law enforcement had been a frequent occurrence, and he remembered many of the trials. When his coordination seemed sufficient, he got into the driver seat and said, "All right, knucklehead, we're gettin on down the road. I sure do like this car. A Buick, huh? Always liked em, never could afford one. And then when I could afford one, I lived someplace where just having a parking place was too expensive and cut into my drinkin time. So I'll just enjoy your Buick. How will that be, knucklehead?"

Jason maneuvered the car around the mobile home and steered onto the dirt road leading off the property. When he had moved just past the camper trailer, he stopped. Jason saw the bicycles, and he closed his eyes and shook his head. He moved the gear selector to park, got out of the car, and looked around on the ground until he found a fist-sized rock. On the porch near the purple bicycle, he placed his palm leaf hat and weighted the brim with the rock.

As Jason turned onto the paved road, he asked, "Hey knucklehead, you ever heard of a place called Guerneville?" Though no sound came from the trunk, Jason continued, "I hear there's a river there, and it's real good for swimming. How bout we take this Buick over there and turn it into a submarine?"

A ruckus ensued with shouting and banging, and the shouting included plenty of profanity, though not many of the words formed into coherent messages. However, Jason did clearly hear the words "you're dead."

"I'm dead? I'm dead, you say? Well, knucklehead you got that right. But let me explain something to you."

Jason jerked the wheel to the right and turned down the street where he had bought tequila earlier that day. After a half block, he stomped on the brake and then the accelerator pedal. Back and forth he spun the steering wheel before slamming on the brake, putting the car in reverse, and accelerating enough to brake, turn the wheel, and make the car whip around. "Hey, what do you know, knucklehead? I can still drive. Do you like bouncing around in there?" Jason listened and heard only whimpers. "We can do that again any time you want. Just go to hollering again, and we'll go to bouncing."

Jason resumed his route on the paved road, and when he had to stop at a traffic light, he said, "That sure is some fancy pistol you got. A polished nickel 357 magnum. Shiny, shiny. You think you're some kind of pimp or something? I grew up around guns. Most Texans do. I ain't touched one in fifteen or twenty years, but I can still shoot well enough to ruin your day. Why did you pick such a flashy gun anyway? I can understand the flashy car but not the gun. The flashy ones don't shoot no better, you know. Idiot."

After another traffic light, the homes and buildings of town stopped, and the dark of the agricultural fields began, and Jason knew he had passed out of Dixon and headed south without a known destination. The darkness and the smooth motion calmed Jason, and he turned on the radio and searched for music. He thought how the flat land in all directions reminded him of drives in the Panhandle, long aimless drives when there had been little else to do.

The remnants of the alcohol and the comfortable interior of the Buick coupe made Jason feel sleepy, so he increased the volume of the radio. He saw an intersection ahead, and as he approached he looked ahead, left, and right, but no landmarks emerged in the darkness, so Jason chose left. To combat the growing desire to sleep, Jason yelled, "Hey knucklehead, this is some fancy car. It rides smooth like a Cadillac. Why does a man with such a nice car have to go around being such a nuisance? Just so you know, this ain't about you spraying gravel all over me. You know what this is about, don't you?"

No answer came from the trunk, so Jason yelled again. "Maybe you don't know. Maybe a turd like you goes around being such a nuisance that you don't even keep track. Well, I'll tell you what this is about. Remember what you said to them little girls this afternoon?"

Still no sound came from the trunk. "You hear me, don't you? And you remember what you said. I don't understand a filthy scrounge like you, but that's why you're in the trunk, for what you said to them girls."

The lights of a town shone ahead, and the fear of attracting the attention of police made the drowsiness go away. After a short time, the car passed through the town and over a long bridge and back onto a dark flat road. Jason changed the radio station just for something to do, and then he saw a sign and turned off the radio. "Whoa! Did I read that right? Is that an actual place?" Jason stayed alert watching for more signs, and then he shouted, "Knucklehead! Sing with me. I'll hum a tune and then you join in with me." Jason hummed and drummed on the steering wheel, and then he burst out with more yelling than singing. "Things got bad, and things got worse. I guess you know the tune. Oh lord, stuck in Lodi again."

Indeed the Idols I have loved so long
Have done my credit in this World much wrong:
Have drown'd my Glory in a shallow Cup,
And sold my reputation for a Song.

The Man Who Cheated Himself

After Lodi, the route changed to southerly, and Jason struggled to stay alert. A road sign indicated that the lights ahead belonged to Stockton. "Stockton! Fat City," Jason said. "I don't suppose you follow boxing, do you knucklehead? What am I saying? Of course you don't. From the way you fight, you've never even heard of the sport. That's too bad. There's a fine boxing movie from this town, one of my favorites. Stockton, Stockton, Stockton . . . Hey, I got two friends from Stockton. One, you don't deserve to hear about. The other would be real tickled at this situation." Jason turned on the radio and lowered the windows. He shook his head and rolled his shoulders and got ready to pay extra attention to driving in a better lit and more trafficked area.

Past Stockton the darkness of agricultural fields resumed, and Jason turned down the radio. "Yep, ole Johnny would be amused at this situation. He came from around here, and he made a top-notch car thief. You listening to me, knucklehead? Johnny stole hundreds of cars, and they caught him for only one, down in Fremont and only cause he accidentally ran over the owner. I spent a few months locked up with Johnny. He'd be entertained by this mess even though he might not give me credit for thieving. This amounted to more of a carjacking, right knucklehead? This wasn't Johnny's kind of deal. He wasn't no kind of violent cause he didn't have to be. He was a charmer, even in jail. Folks just liked Johnny. But then even Johnny would have got burnt up at what you did. I should have kept up with ole Johnny."

For a while the lights of Modesto helped Jason cope with the fatigue, but he knew he could not go much longer. He thought about stopping for coffee, but the risk of noise from the trunk made him keep driving. In the span between Modesto and Turlock, his eyelids grew heavy, and more than once he caught himself dozing. After one such lapse, he saw that he had let the car drift out of the lane, and the shock prompted him to yell and then slap his face and shake his head. He thought perhaps if he could find a more rural route he might then also find a place to park the car long enough to get some sleep. In Turlock, he chose a due south route.

Soon after taking the route south, the dark, flat agricultural land stretched all around, and Jason looked for a place to park the car. Plenty of dirt roads passed by, but they lacked lights, and at highway speed Jason did not see them in time to turn. He slowed as much as possible without arousing suspicion, but he could not find a suitable spot before passing through a small town. After the little town and with more determination, he examined the dirt roads branching from the rural highway, and when he saw yet another little town in the distance he also saw a dirt road larger than the rest. As he approached, he noticed that just ahead, just over a bridge spanning a small river or canal, another dirt road departed from the highway. He crossed the bridge and turned right. The well-graded dirt road gave a rougher ride than the highway, and Jason expected knucklehead to start hollering again, but no crying or threats came from the trunk. Off the road to the left, a large structure or perhaps multiple structures stood in faint silhouette against the lights of the nearby town. Jason parked near the structures at a point concealed from the highway, and he turned off the car's engine. He hoped to be gone prior to dawn in order to avoid being seen by farmers or whoever might be associated with the fields and the large structure too short to be a grain elevator and too big to be a barn.

The big framework of wood and metal shielded the car from the rising sun, and when Jason woke he saw direct sunlight illuminate the ground all around except in a cool band encompassing the car. He had slept far longer than he intended, and he looked ahead and behind the car in a flash of panic. He did not see any people or any vehicles, but he did feel the throbbing pain in his head. The large structure that he had parked near appeared to be some sort of grandstand topped with floodlights like those used at sports stadiums. Curiosity demanded investigation, and when Jason stepped out of the car he felt the nausea. A hangover had manifested itself during the night, and Jason knew this one, after so long away from the bottle, would be severe. After a few steps, a coughing fit seized him, and while he felt glad not to see any blood he winced at the pain the coughing produced in his head and neck.

The contour of the wood and metal reminded Jason of the underside of the bleachers at the little rodeo arena in his hometown. The farther he walked around the structure, the more convinced he became that he stood on the outside of a rodeo arena, but the circular nature of the structure confused Jason. Rodeo arenas had straight sides, sometimes with a curved far end. He tried to think of what sports might use circular arenas, but none came to mind. When he found a break in the structure blocked only by a chainlink gate, he turned to look inside and his mouth dropped in astonishment.

Jason looked at the soil floor of a bullring. Advertising banners lined the circumference of the ring. And above the wall lining the edge of the ring, amphitheater style seating rose. Jason wanted to see more of the ring, but the pounding in his head and his aching muscles signaled an even worse hangover to come. He remembered the contents of the coupe's trunk and the need to avoid attention. On the way back to the car, he considered for an instant tying the knucklehead to one of the beams supporting the ring's seating before roaring away in the shiny Buick. Then he considered inviting knucklehead into the ring in order to finally settle the matter. The thought made Jason laugh, and the laughter further hurt his smarting head.

Heading south on the rural highway, Jason squinted in the late morning sun. The intense light made him want to completely shut his eyes and hide from the pain in his head. In addition to the headache, muscle pain, and nausea, Jason felt intense remorse and shame. He thought the time away from heavy drinking had made him less susceptible to overindulgence and rash, destructive actions, but his present inspired thoughts of self-loathing. He considered stopping to purchase beer, just as a medicinal aid for the tequila induced pain, but after further consideration the thought only added to his feelings of disgrace.

The car provided a diversion from Jason's thoughts of worthlessness. The fuel gauge indicated a more immediate need, and Jason weighed risks against necessities. He needed gasoline, and he could certainly use some coffee, aspirin, and water. But if noise from the trunk alerted others to its suspicious contents, Jason could be spending the rest of his time incarcerated. In that event, the best case scenario would involve death before trial. Knucklehead had been quiet all morning, but that did not mean he would continue to remain silent if he heard other people and potential salvation outside. While Jason contemplated options and solutions, he noticed signs for a truck stop. A few miles later, he saw the large awnings and signs for a gas station and convenience store.

As he entered the station, he reviewed his plan. He parked the car at a gas pump on the end and went inside to pay. Only one person blocked him from the cashier, but the transaction seemed to take a long time as Jason watched outside. He looked at the other people pumping gas, but nothing in their actions indicated curiosity about the shiny coupe. Jason added fuel to the Buick's tank and then replaced the nozzle in the pump. He started the car and moved it to the far side of the truck stop, finding a parking spot some distance from the gas pumps and away from any other cars. Back inside the convenience store, Jason got a cup of coffee and a bottle of water. On the way to the cashier, he noticed a rack of brochures, and he stopped. Setting his coffee aside, he snatched a brochure from the rack, and his eyes widened as he turned it over and viewed a map. Jason shoved the brochure in his shirt pocket and selected two more bottles of water and a sandwich before approaching the cashier and asking for aspirin.

He parked as far away from the headquarters building as possible and hoped knucklehead remained quiet. When the park ranger took his camping fee, Jason asked for quiet spot. He said he had just one night away from the city, did not mind hiking to see the best scenery, and hoped for a place with the least amount of noise. The park ranger said he knew just the site, and he circled an area on the map he gave Jason with the receipt. Jason found the spot and parked the Buick. He had passed several RVs, camper trailers, and tents on the way, but no other people camped within sight of the Buick. Jason thought about trying to eat the sandwich but took a nap instead.

The evening sun shone through the windshield, and when Jason opened his eyes he found that his head did not hurt so bad. He finished one of the bottles of water and got out of the car. A strong sustained wind came over the grassy hills. Jason took another bottle of water, sat at the site's picnic bench, and looked at the shiny Buick coupe. He started to take a drink then recapped the bottle, drew the pistol, and walked to the car. With the revolver pointed at the trunk, he released the lid and chunked the bottle inside. He heard a thud and a groan as he slammed the lid.

"So you're still alive in there? Not that I give a damn. I'm just not sure I want to add murder to the charges just yet."

Jason returned to the picnic bench and looked at the lake in the distance. Then he turned back to the car and said, "So you're supposed to be some real tough hombre? Did you get them tattoos in prison? You're a pretty mean character when it comes to mouthin off to old ladies and sayin filth to little girls. But you didn't hold up so well against a broke down old drunken lunger, did ya knucklehead?"

For the first time in a while, Jason thought he heard verbal sounds from the trunk. He walked closer and put his head close to the car. "Oh my, are you crying? Why, you're bawling like a baby, aren't you? Did you know you made that little girl cry? I bet you wouldn't have cared a bit at the time. Do you care now? Do ya?"

From the picnic bench, Jason watched the sun approach the horizon and reflect from the lake. He turned back to face the car. "You know, tough guy, you wouldn't last two seconds in my hometown. Any average joe hanging out on Main Street could whip you. And that ain't saying nothing about the roughnecks. They'd have tore you up, even with your shiny pistol. What's a grown man need with such a shiny gun? One of my grandmothers used to carry a pistol cause she used to have to work long hours. She also carried brass knuckles, knucklehead. Even the old ladies in my hometown could whip you, and they would have the way you act."

Jason paced about the campsite and picked up a handful of pebbles. He skipped the little rocks across the hard-packed ground. "I'll tell you one thing, crybaby. I've been a scroungy unreliable bum most of my life, but at my worst I never even thought of something like you done. You go around cheating old ladies and scaring little ones. Mostly I just let the bottle help me cheat myself and waste my life. Ain't we a couple? One of us is gonna die for sure, so that takes care of half the problem. I ain't sure what's gonna happen to the other one. But you just go ahead and cry your heart out. You got all night to cry all over your sorry self."

There ain't no way to describe this mess without using a heap of profanity. A fellow all bloodied up is in the trunk of a car. It started with assault, which got done first with fists and then a deadly weapon. Then came some gunplay, no shootin . . . yet, but gunplay happened. Assault with a deadly weapon turned into kidnapping. And since the car is stolen, that probably adds grand theft auto to the mayhem. And all this come about from trying to stay out of other folks' business.

After a lifetime of drinking, you can bet there's a tall heap of stuff I ain't proud of. But this tops the long list. This is real felon kind of stuff. This ain't just another drunken brawl with a lot of noise, missed punches, and rolling around in the alley until the cops come.

Over and over the mind goes thinking of everything and trying to figure out where it all went so bad. After first going over events, it seemed like the minute knucklehead got in the trunk marked when the real crime started. The scuffle gave no choice about grabbing the gun, and of course he had to get knocked over the head, which was a whole lot better than shooting. And maybe the punching could be self-defense except that it happened at his place while intending to hit him with a brick. The real mistake, the start of this whole sorry business goes back to those two pints of tequila. It wouldn't take no prosecuting Perry Mason to see the whole thing as deliberate. Ain't nobody in the world would believe that this poor cowboy minded his own business and the situation got throwed on him. Things went from pouring hooch on my anger to pouring it on his bloody head.

Now I got to figure a way out of this. I've tried and tried to think of an answer that don't involve killing the knucklehead.

Things surely would have been ugly when them girls told their daddy what the knucklehead said. He might have gone over there hisself. But the outcome might have been different. The daddy might have got hurt. Being good at brawling ain't the first thing that comes to mind when thinking of somebody in the air force. That daddy might have walked right over and gotten stomped, and that could have hurt the girls even worse. Thinking that way feels better for a time, but it don't take much more thinking to see that the whole sorry business should have been handled a better way.

That air force daddy might have been smart, and maybe he might have talked to Maddie. They could have called the cops and the knucklehead's parole officer, and maybe the knucklehead would be going back to the place where he got those tattoos. Every which way of looking at this mess just shows that what I done was a crime with no excuse.

And now I got to figure a way out of this.

Hearing what that vermin said to Valentina, seeing her cry, and thinking about how her daddy would feel kept going through my head while drinking that tequila. It still goes through my mind, and I can't make it stop. Being a little kid and hearing a big mean looking adult say something vile, something about the little kid herself, had to be terrifying and confusing. And being a daddy, a daddy that has to leave to go make a living, a daddy that can't watch over his girls every minute of the day but one who still has to protect them somehow . . . I can't imagine what it would feel like to have a beautiful little girl, a little girl he loves more than anything in the world, tell that some no good scrounge said some filth. Imagine being a daddy and knowing that somebody might hurt the girl. Those thoughts just won't stop, and it's a toss-up whether I want to cry or commence to knocking that knucklehead with his pistol some more.

There's a good chance them girls might not tell their daddy. Even if that little Ada said something, the daddy might not think much of it if Valentina said it wasn't nothing worth concern. And something about that little girl makes me think she might do just that. She's a shy one. She's the kind that might let something bad happen and not say anything. She'd just go on being hurt and scared. Every day she saw that rotten snake she might be just terrified. Maybe no choice but to do what I done could have been made. And then there's Maddie. Maddie couldn't never get her money from knucklehead. The best she could have hoped for was more cussing, and she could have gotten a lot worse with him around. Maybe there wasn't no other choice.

This all come about from trying to stay out of other folks' business.

All my life, I didn't have time for all sorts of things. Didn't have time to finish school. No time to listen to other folks' problems and no time for keeping in touch. Always short of time. But this time it's the truth. There really ain't much time. I'm dying. I ought to be somewhere quiet and take things slow and easy just like trying to get a car into town when it's low on gas. There ain't no fill-up station for me, though. Taking things slow and easy is for getting every last second out of life cause these really are the last gulps of gas without no refills. But this ain't slow and easy. This mess would whittle time off anybody's life. How this wrecked body held up is a mystery. Less than this has put me in the hospital of late, but I ain't even been coughing that much. Instead of resting quiet, there's been assaulting, kidnapping, and stealing cars. The only good thing that come of it is that I've been so busy worrying about getting caught that I forgot to be scared of dying.

But I am still scared of dying. That black nothing is coming, and no matter what anybody does it's gonna get here in its own time. Can't out run it, and the doctors can't fix it. Black nothing is coming. Nothingness is an impossible thing to comprehend, and it scares me.

That don't mean, though, that I'm feeling any sympathy for knuckle-head and the possibility he might die. To think about him dying and whether it's right or wrong, I have to pretend like it's other folks. Thinking about the real him and what it felt like hearing what he said to Valentina after hearing him cuss out Maddie makes the thought of him dying seem not at all sad. On the contrary, it seems real fitting. Big Sur ain't far from here. It's just south of Monterey. A car could go off one of them cliffs, and it could take a while for anybody to get down to it and look at it real good. Then that leaves the problem of hitchhiking and whether I could get far enough away before anybody got a good look at the car and found what's in the trunk. Or there's this big lake nearby. It might be hard to sink the car enough to be out of sight, but if it could be done that might be better than a flying jump off a cliff. But that still leaves the problem of how to get on down the road.

And then there's the whole business of murder.

Acting as judge and jury and giving some no good scrounge a whooping is one thing. But it's something else to be a hangman. Maybe right when it happened, right when he said that to Valentina, if I'd have been holding his pistol then probably I'd have shot. Maybe during the fight if he'd have been hitting me instead of just hanging onto my boot I could have used the gun for more than a club. But having time to think about it and sinking a car in a river with him crying like a baby in the trunk ain't just killing. It's murder. Forgetting what the cops and judges would say, it still comes back to what I got the stomach for, and I ain't got the stomach for murder. Thinking about him dying ain't bothersome at all, but thinking about me taking on authority that don't belong to me and taking another person's life without no court or judge gives a real sickening feeling. Feelings like that are for letting folks know some things are just wrong.

There has to be a way to get away from this car. One of the first ideas that didn't involve killing was to leave the car way out somewhere where he'd have to hike out. But then I'd have to hike out too or steal another car. And stealing a stranger's car wouldn't feel right. I'd be too worried that maybe it belonged to a little old lady or an elderly man or worse a mama and daddy with kids. Another thought involved leaving the car at a bus or train station, but if knucklehead didn't get discovered in time, we'd be back to the business of murder, and if he did get found right away, then the cops would know to check the buses or trains.

Now if I could get down to Los Angeles, I might be able to ditch the car, make sure knucklehead has a way out, and disappear into that giant city. It'd be like letting a minnow loose in the ocean and then trying to find it again. Even if the cops wanted to come looking for me, they'd have to find me before I die. How long off the black nothing is ain't known, but finding out who pistol whipped an ex con wouldn't be something the cops would get too feverish about. In some ways time is against me, and in others it's on my side.

With all this fightin and car thievin, I haven't been thinking as much about the folks in Texas. It's a relief they won't see what become of me. I'm still sad about not seeing Texas again, but I'm getting more and more sad about wasting all these past years in California. Turns out, this state is a whole lot more than San Francisco and Monterey. All that time, a big green woods stood to the north, and little towns that get as hot as Texas but have evening Delta Breezes hid over by Sacramento. If that ain't mind blowing, what about that bullring? I would have thought the nearest bullring was down in Mexico, but that just goes to show how much I don't know about this place. All that time got spent crying about missing Texas when it could have been used in exploring California, which is every bit as amazing as Texas or anywhere else.

I'm looking forward to being in Los Angeles, but I'm also a little bit wary. I don't know nothing about that country, and I could fall into trouble before getting situated right. The best thing to do will be to get rid of the car as soon as possible, get rid of it in one part of the city and get to another real quick. The problem is not knowing one part of that city from another. We're still about five or six hours away, so once we get headed that way, I'll have plenty to think about.

On the way, I got to decide if this Buick goes off a cliff, gets put in a river, or gets left somewhere with knucklehead alive. There's a lot to think about.

Oh Thou, who didst with pitfall and with gin
Beset the Road I was to wander in,
    Thou wilt not with Predestined Evil round
Enmesh, and then impute my Fall to Sin!

Vertigo

In the early hours of darkness, the ailing and whimpering woke Jason. He shivered, put on his canvass jacket, and started the car. After a few minutes, he turned on the car's heater. The interior of the car warmed, but perhaps no warmth reached the trunk. The moaning continued, and Jason said, "You need to quit that. It ain't doing nothing but putting me in mind of using your fancy pistol. I ain't fired this thing yet, and I'd like to see how it shoots. We can pop that trunk lid and give you something to cry about. You ain't even been in there but twenty-four and some odd hours anyway. How bout this, every time you carry on we add another twelve hours before turning you loose. How bout that?" The fussing stopped, and after another few minutes Jason turned off the car heater and engine and went back to sleep.

Just before dawn, the cold woke Jason again, and while he ran the heater he listened to the radio and ate the sandwich he had purchased the day before. Most of the effects of the hangover had passed, and Jason thought about his options. Heading south to Los Angeles seemed best. Perhaps along the way he would decide what to do with the car and its captive contents. He needed to find a place where discovery of the car could be delayed long enough to gain some distance. Bus and train stations seemed too obvious, but if he could find a location near a transit center or simply near a place with a large pedestrian population, he intended to take the first opportunity. Jason tried to think of viable locations, but he had never been south of Big Sur, and he lacked a detailed map.

Just after peeking over the horizon, the sun turned the grassy hills auburn. The indigo lake reflected images of neither the sky nor the few cloud puffs. In time, the hill's red tint subsided and mellowed to amber, and by the time the grassy mounds turned khaki Jason steered the car onto the paved highway.

At the truck stop, Jason took his time sipping coffee from a paper cup and alternating between looking at a map and watching the Buick. None of the people at the gas pumps seemed interested in the shiny coupe parked as far as possible from the entrance to the convenience store. Jason stopped by the rack of brochures where he had seen the one advertising the camping area, but this time no brochure promoted a ready and relevant solution.

When he left the truck stop and headed west, the temperature had climbed, and Jason said, "It's gonna be another hot one today, knuckle-head. You'll be missing the cold night real soon now."

An hour after the truck stop, a road sign indicated a town ahead, and something about the town name caused Jason to turn off the radio while he tried to concentrate. "That's got to be it. It has to be the same place. If they filmed that movie there, and if it ain't too far from the highway, I got to see the place." Jason watched for signs mentioning the mission, and he steered the shiny coupe along the little town's picturesque streets. Some of the wood-framed buildings looked like they had not changed in over a hundred years. Buildings with Old West frontier style facades bordered older stucco Spanish Mission style buildings, and somehow to Jason it all seemed authentic. Except for the occasional traffic light, the town seemed like it had frozen in style a long time ago. When he saw the white top of an old-style building, he turned left onto the next street and found a plaza with grass and trees and flanked by a long white building with columns and arches. At the next block, Jason made a U-turn and reversed direction. He drove slow and looked at the old building, and as he turned right to go back the way he had arrived he said, "It sure don't look like in the movie. I just can't picture Jimmy Stewart standing out there."

Before he reached the highway, Jason saw a sign that advertised homemade hamburgers, and he followed the sign's directions to a restaurant. He parked on the street and walked a half-block to the restaurant. With a paper bag and a paper cup, he got back in the car and turned on the radio before reaching into the bag for the burger. After the first bite, he wished he had bought two. He ate the long rectangular fries three at a time, and took another giant bite of the burger. During a gulp of soda, he noticed the odor, faint at first then strong enough to induce gaging. For a moment, Jason froze unable to chew and incapable of swallowing. He knew the stench came from the trunk, but before he could do anything about it he had to deal with the too-precious-to-waste burger. Jason finished the burger and fries outside the car, and then he circled the car slowly to gauge the power of the graveolence. Near the trunk, he almost fell down and turned to cover his face. He looked up then down the street relieved not to see any other pedestrians.

He drove as fast as he could in the little town, and when he reached the highway he went a few miles over the speed limit with the windows down. Jason felt relieved that he did not have to breathe air that had passed near the trunk, but he thought about the particular odor, and he worried that its repulsive nature came from more than mere feculence. Knucklehead had cried out hours earlier, so he had to still be alive, and if he had died in the meantime, surely putrefaction could not have produced an odor so soon, not even in the hot trunk. Assuming that knucklehead remained alive, the only way to rid the car of the odor involved removing knuckle-head, at least temporarily. Jason discarded that option, and a moment later he realized that he must also discard his plan to drive the car to Los Angeles. He needed a closer, more immediate option, and so when the rural highway met a larger one and Jason saw signs indicating south to Los Angeles and north to San Jose he chose north.

"Hey knucklehead, I didn't get your real name," Jason said. After a moment with no reply, Jason shouted, "Knucklehead! How'd you feel about getting out of that trunk?" The lack of a reply caused Jason's breathing and heart rate to increase, and then he noticed that he exceeded the speed limit. He slowed just as he entered the outskirts of Gilroy, and he yelled, "Knucklehead, ole buddy, so do you want me to drop you somewhere or would you rather I just give you the car back?" Jason turned the radio up to full volume for a few seconds and then back down. "We're in between Davis and Sacramento now. I was gonna take you back to your place in Dixon, but if you want I can turn around if there's anything you want in Sacramento. You want something to eat? Or we could get your head looked at. Just say the word. Okay, knucklehead?"

Twenty minutes seemed like hours, and as the Buick passed through Morgan Hill Jason yelled, "Hey, now you need to speak up back there if you want out. If you're just gonna sleep, then I'm gonna go on about my business, and I'll check in on you later. But if you want out of that trunk now, you need to speak up."

Jason looked around the car's interior. He had to get his belongings and get away from the car at the first opportunity. Except for an empty water bottle, all he had to leave with included his canvass jacket and leather bag. Preferable places to ditch the car did not come to mind, so Jason stayed in the left lane and drove as fast as the law allowed. South of San Jose, the traffic backed up, and Jason had to reduce his speed by half. He hoped not to encounter gridlock, and he wondered whether he could endure the smell if he had to spend time in the car without motion.

North of San Jose, Jason rejoiced when he saw free moving traffic, and he matched the speed of the fastest moving cars. But around Fremont, Jason looked in the rearview mirror and began changing lanes to the right. Off the expressway, he steered onto a wide boulevard and then into the parking lot of an auto parts store. Forgetting about fragile lungs, Jason ran into the store and then returned with a can of spray lubricant and a pack of red automotive rags. Once back on the expressway, "I just remembered something, something damned important. There's plenty of time for talking in jail, and one of the things my car thief friend Johnny told me was to never, never steal a car without WD-40 on hand. Well, now we got some."

In Oakland, Jason chose the wrong exit and had to drive through Chinatown to find his way back toward his intended destination. At an intersection choked with pedestrians, Jason held his breath and hoped no one noticed the stench from the trunk. When the light changed, Jason turned right and discovered that he had made a mistake again and entered a one-way street going the opposite direction as his objective. While looking for corrective measures, Jason noticed an empty parking spot adjacent to a park, and he stopped the car. With a red rag in one hand, he sprayed the dash with WD-40 with the other hand, and then he rubbed the rag all over the dash and all controls. When he believed he had covered every surface of the interior he might have touched, Jason got out of the car and polished door handles and the trunk.

Back in the driver's seat, Jason spread a rag on the passenger seat and then took the revolver from his belt. He emptied the bullets and laid them on the rag. One-by-one he polished each bullet with an oily rag, and then he wrapped the bullets in a dry rag and shoved them in a pants pocket. Jason shined every surface of the revolver with the oily rag and then laid it on a dry rag while he dug in his leather bag. When he found the peace sign medallion with the hemp necklace, he untied the hemp line and then retied it around the trigger guard of the revolver. After a look around the car, Jason put the empty water bottle, the can of WD-40, and all but two red rags in his leather bag.

Driving with the two rags between his hands and the steering wheel, Jason passed back through the northern part of Oakland's Chinatown looking for the least legal place to park. He found a spot and parked the shiny Buick coupe so that it blocked two cars and partially blocked the lane. "Hey, knucklehead," he shouted. "Now is the time to make a ruckus if you want out of there. You can scream and cry all you want. Adios!" He hung the revolver on the hemp rope from the rearview mirror, and he leapt out of the car and ran to the end of the block, turned west, and remembered his fragile lungs. Resisting the urge to sprint, he stepped quick to the end of another block, crossed Broadway, and then descended into 12th Street Station. Before reaching the ticket kiosk, Jason stopped at a garbage can and discarded the rag full of bullets.

He took the first train that arrived at the station and found an empty seat. He tried to catch his breath while not appearing to breathe heavy, and he mopped his forehead with a handkerchief. After the train departed and then stopped again at West Oakland Station, Jason knew the next stop would be Embarcadero Station, San Francisco. He calculated the distance and fastest route to the nearest tavern.

X. Backtrack

Waste not your Hour, nor in the vain pursuit
Of This and That endeavor and dispute;
    Better be jocund with the fruitful Grape
Than sadden after none, or bitter, Fruit.

For "Is" and "Is-not" though with Rule and Line
And "UP-AND-DOWN" by Logic I define,
   Of all that one should care to fathom, I
Was never deep in anything but—Wine.

Stumble

The clink of empty bottles signaled the beginning of his day as he swung his legs out of bed and tried to keep his eyes tight shut and hidden from the afternoon rays streaming through the tattered curtains. He opened one eye halfway while he sat on the edge of the bed and reached among the mostly empty bottles looking for a full one. Once found, the bottle refused to give up its metal cap, so Jason used the bed frame for extra leverage in prying off the top. While he sat on the edge of the bed and while he drank the beer, his eyes grew accustomed to the light, and he found two more unopened bottles. When only half remained of the third and last bottle, he stood bent and unsteady and searched for his clothes.

Wrinkled, unshaven, untucked, and uncombed he stepped through the doorway onto the Tenderloin sidewalk and winced when the metal gate slammed loud behind him. He held a hand above his eyes while he plodded two doors over and into a store with an array of liquor bottles behind the counter adjacent to the glass coolers of beer. At the counter, he asked for aspirin. Squinting, he ambled to the end of the block and crossed the street.

In the dank room with fetid air, he opened his eyes without pain, and soon dim shapes of a bar, patrons on stools, and a bartender emerged from the clammy murk. He sat at a stool that wore torn red vinyl, and he reached into his pocket for the aspirin. Without a word, the bartender placed a can of beer on the counter, and without looking up Jason placed a bill near the can. The bartender took the bill and replaced it with smaller notes and some coins. Jason used the flat sour beer to wash down the pills, and then he drank the remainder of the can. When the empty can vanished and a full one appeared in its place, Jason added notes to the pile of bills

229

and coins on the counter. They repeated the exchange several times until Jason stood, took all but a couple of the notes, and stepped out into the sun.

A block away from the bar, Jason entered a small corner convenience store, and he took four 16 ounce cans of beer from the cooler. After paying, he stowed the cans in the pockets of his jacket and rambled along the sidewalk droopy-eyed with a listless stare. His path went southwest in a stair-step fashion from Turk to Jones to McAllister to Leavenworth. He cut through UN Plaza and passed through Fulton between the library and the museum. He found the little wall in the grassy area of Civic Center Plaza near the line of flags. At a spot offering a clear view of the Texas state flag, he sat and opened a beer.

The gilded dome of city hall gleamed in the October Indian summer sun, and tourists and locals alike sported shorts and short sleeves. Jason stared a few feet ahead at the grass. When he drained the first can, he put it on the ground and stomped it with a boot heel. A couple holding a map and a few other brochures approached Jason, and the man asked, "Sir, can you tell us how to get to Market Street?" Jason stared at the grass, and the man continued, "Sir?" Jason belched and crushed another beer can. When he had crushed the fourth, he stood and reversed his stair-step course through the Tenderloin.

On the sidewalk a few yards ahead of Jason, a man and woman tussled over a backpack. "My backpack!" the woman yelled. The man bellowed, "Gimme back my wallet."

"I don't have your wallet. Give me my backpack." As Jason came within a few yards of the disturbance, the woman called out, "Mister! Please help me. He won't give me my backpack. Can you call the police?"

Jason stepped out into the street and walked past the fighting before climbing back onto the sidewalk. In the dank gloom of the tavern, he saw his previous stool occupied so he took a stool at the end of the bar. He put a bill on the bar, and the bartender took it and delivered a can. An emaciated and tired black woman worked her way down the bar asking patrons, "Baby, do you want a date?" When she came to Jason, she just sighed and left the bar. After a few exchanges of bills for cans, Jason left the bar and walked less than a block to another saloon and found a seat near the jukebox.

He ordered a bloody mary and a beer, and when he had finished all of the beer and half the blood mary, no one had yet played anything on the jukebox. Jason took his empty beer glass to the bar and leaned far in to get the attention of the bartender. After she filled his glass and took his money, he gave her a couple more dollars and pointed at the jukebox. She asked, "You want me to play something?" Jason nodded. "Anything in particular?" Jason shook his head.

After the last of the songs for his money played, Jason had another bloody mary and several beers. No one else played the jukebox so he meandered out and back to the dive with cheap beer but no music. His usual seat stood empty, so he sat and dropped a bill on the bar. In a few large gulps he drained the can and walked out into late afternoon. At the nearest store, he bought a quart bottle of malt liquor and moved along, often stopping to lean against buildings while taking drinks from the bottle. At UN Plaza, a young man played a guitar near the fountain, and Jason found a seat on the steps facing both the fountain and the guitar player. Other youths joined the guitar player, and he stopped playing. Jason stood and stumbled away to the west.

At the spot on the wall facing the Texas state flag, he sat and gazed at the grass, and his eyes drooped and followed the grass to a thicket of mesquites that grew into redwoods where a little psychedelic appaloosa dog bounded down to a sparkling brook. He followed the dog down and through the brook and up a winding path that led to a meadow. The little dog reached the meadow first, and she whirled in circles waiting for him to join her. He emerged from the tree line at the same time a paint horse came from the woods at the opposite end of the meadow. The three took a path with the little dog in the lead, and they passed stone statues and fountains. Ahead the giant trees gave way to mesquites, and the path widened and took on the rust color of the broken arroyos peppered with the enormous dolomite boulders. Single file—dog, horse, and Jason—they walked the switchbacks winding down to the canyon floor that opened to the bluebonnet-filed prairie opposite the pond near the farmhouse. Two women tended clothes on a line, and he tried to call out, but no words came before the dog raced after a jackrabbit and the horse trotted into the red oaks and disappeared. He stood alone on the edge of the mesa before the clouds of the blue norther, and he knew that in a moment the frigid blast would catch him out, unprepared and unprotected. Closer and closer to the edge of the mesa he stepped. A couple of junipers grew from the crags at the edge before the slope grew too steep and plunged down to the black depths with no bottom. He stepped past the junipers and sank down into the black that did not end.

Jason opened his eyes and felt the grass where he had stomped cans earlier poking his face. He pressed his hands against the grass, raised some, and then fell back. After rolling onto his side he reached out and grasped the wall and used it to pull himself to his knees. High-level clouds had moved in and brought the dusk early. Amber street lights tempered the coming gray, and he moved east between the library and the museum. People and things passed in a haze while the air felt cooler. He stopped and grasped the edge of a garbage can while he tried to recall a vision, some picture that had recently come through is mind. He caught fleeting images of familiar and welcome scenes and beings, but the harder he gripped the metal and the tighter he squeezed his eyes the farther the images retreated. Defeated, he let loose of the can and staggered left and then right before gaining balance and a straight path. With the departure of the tantalizing pictures, the drab gray devoid of desire returned, and he pressed on to the place without feeling or memory.

In the dank place with fetid air, he joined his kind with their craggy and crumpled visages. A bill on the counter turned into a can of sour and flat beer, and each swallow washed away desire and fear. Side to side he moved in comforting sway to the tuneless atmosphere, and with another bill came another can until in jerky robotic agitation he pressed his hands against the counter and rose from the stool. His boots slid across the floor toward the door.

Nighttime in the Tenderloin abounded in electric multicolored light, and he passed down the sidewalk often stumbling off the curb into the street or bouncing a shoulder off a building. People passed, and some spoke, perhaps to Jason, but he glided along in a crooked daze without aspiration or apprehension. An uncaring navigator guided Jason to the place two doors away from the metal gate. Two doors from the metal gate held an array of liquor bottles behind a counter adjacent to glass coolers of beer. Jason shuffled toward the final stop that held the key to the black dreamless night.

Ahead on the sidewalk a panhandler performed for pedestrians and asked for change. Jason's autopilot sent him on a vector away from the obstacle, but the panhandler anticipated the maneuver and moved to intercept. Jason tried to switch direction, but the nimble grifter countered, and Jason knew he would just have to try to push through like with the faster Boy's Club fighters who cut off the ring. Head down gruff and scowling, Jason stepped through, but not before the panhandler delivered a missive.

He said, "Smile, brother. You ain't dead yet."

The directive stopped Jason, and he turned back to face the street sage. Jason tried to speak, but his mouth barely opened and no words came. Stationary and befuddled, Jason fought for clear thought. None came, and the panhandler had moved on to his next prospect. Jason resumed course until he arrived at the place two doors from the metal gate.

Something interrupted his design, and Jason stood outside the store trying to regain his autopilot. Inside, the glass cooler stood adjacent to the counter with the bottles, and Jason had a vague sense that he should go inside, but something impeded his advance. People passed by in both directions and had to step around Jason's place in the middle of the walk. He took short unsure steps inside and stood in front of the glass cooler. A voice asked if Jason required assistance, and Jason continued gazing at the frosted glass door. Again, the voice asked if he need help finding anything, and the louder tone prompted him to move away from the cooler and deeper into the store. With a wispy idea that would not coalesce and vision that lacked acuity, he fought to understand what he sought so that he could see it. At the bottom of a shelf on the farthest aisle from the cooler, he saw it, and he bent to pick up a can of shaving cream.

Would but the Desert of the Fountain yield
One glimpse—if dimly, yet indeed, reveal'd,
   To which the fainting Traveler might spring,
As springs the trampled herbage of the field!

Smoke Stack Library

He thought he dreamed of smoke, but when he sat up in bed in the darkness the burning sensation in his nostrils confirmed the reality. Reaching across the room to the wall he felt for the light switch, and once the long florescent bulb flickered and grew to a glow he expected to see a cloud-filled space to go with the sharp sensation in his nose and itching eyes. Instead he saw the room as he remembered it, but when he reached the window and started to open it the alarm sounded, and soon thereafter the sound of panicked voices came from the hallway. Jason put on his pants and looked around for the rest of his clothes. He found his shirt, put on one sleeve, and then put on his jacket. After grabbing his shoulder bag with one hand and his boots with the other, he stepped into the hall and joined other confused hotel guests in various states of dress. The far end of the corridor had more smoke than the near end, and rolling gray clouds crawled along the ceiling. Jason found the stairwell. Outside, he sat on the street curb in the predawn dark, put on his boots, and walked away amid the sound of approaching sirens. He hoped he had a place to stay at the end of the day.

Across the street and down the block, Jason stopped and took off his jacket. He straightened and tucked his clothing, and he tried to think of what to do. He had not planned on rising so early. In fact, he had not planned at all. The nature of the sky stayed obscured by the abundance of electric street light, and when Jason reached Geary and Van Ness he still could not tell whether the day would bring a cloudy or clear morning. For lack of any better idea, he walked west on Geary. Just beyond Japantown, he passed The Fillmore and thought about healthier and louder days with gorgeous companions. He crossed under an elevated pedestrian walkway and tried to remember the last time he had been to a concert. Later, a large hospital complex reminded him of things he had recently decided to try not to think about. At Masonic, he saw the all-night diner and went inside.

A smiling Asian woman escorted Jason to a table, left, and then returned with coffee. A different Asian lady refilled Jason's coffee and took his order. When she returned with pancakes and bacon, she refilled his coffee again. After he finished the breakfast, he pushed a jelly packet around the table with a straw until the Asian lady returned and left a paper ticket. Jason left a few bills on the table, took the ticket to the register with more bills, and shook his head when the cashier offered his change of coins.

Outside the diner, Jason stood and wondered where to go. He saw a northbound bus approaching on Masonic, hustled to the stop, and wished he had accepted the coins from the diner cashier.

The bus rattled north for several blocks and then cut west into The Presidio before turning east on Lombard. The dawn had not yet arrived, but already traffic filled the road. Jason got off the bus, crossed Lombard, and continued north. Once away from Lombard and in the Marina District, the traffic noise decreased. Street lights illuminated the pavement, and for all Jason could tell from the sky it could have been any time of the night. Two-story and taller apartment buildings flanked the street to the east and west, but at Marina Boulevard the vista widened to a larger area of black punctuated by distant points of light. Jason knew that some of the points he saw came from places like Alcatraz and from farther still points on the Marin side of the bay. He walked across the grass of the Marina Green and found a bench facing the bay. Not much of a breeze moved, but somehow the air felt cooler so close to the water.

To Jason's right, the sky lightened, and after several minutes he could see that the morning would be clear. Soon outlines and then shapes appeared in the bay, and when the sun surpassed the horizon the golden hills of Angel Island climbed from the inky water. To the left, the red towers of the bridge emerged from the black. Joggers and bicyclists passed in both directions behind the bench, and Jason shivered in the cool wet air. He got up, shouldered his bag, and followed the green to Marina Boulevard around the huge lawn of Fort Mason.

The southbound bus on Van Ness had no seats available. Every single seat held an occupant, and additional passengers stood in the center aisle and hung onto the overhead rail. For every foot of ground the bus gained, it stood motionless for several minutes on the clogged route. Some passengers that got off at a stop and continued walking south overtook the bus a block or two later. Jason heard the grumbling, saw more passengers give up and exit the bus, but he remained clutching a strap suspended from the rail above the seats. A seat came available next to Jason, and he offered it to an elderly Asian woman.

At Van Ness and Market, Jason exited the bus along with about half the other passengers. They scattered in all directions with most going down the steps of the nearby Muni station. Jason found a coffee shop then carried his steaming paper cup along Market Street to Polk before turning left. At Civic Center Plaza, Jason turned east, and he took a moment to pause at the Texas state flag. When he finished his coffee, he crossed Larkin and entered the imposing gray block library.

He took a crowded elevator to the 5th floor, and in the periodicals section he found back issues of *The Oakland Tribune* and *The Sacramento Bee*. Upon his return to San Francisco, searching the contents of the two dailies had been a regular occurrence, but since he could not recall when he had stopped, he checked issues dating back to within a few days of his return. *The Tribune* had articles about violence and crime in East Oakland and in West Oakland. *The Bee* had similar stories about crime in various neighborhoods and outlying towns. But neither featured any mention of a Buick taken from Solano County or its abducted owner. And neither mentioned a car found in downtown Oakland illegally parked with a dangling firearm and a man in the trunk.

Jason stepped inside a taqueria as one of the first customers of the day, and he watched the assembly of the massive burrito. He walked while he ate, pausing occasionally to peel down the foil wrapper as the burrito got shorter. Near Buena Vista Park, he stopped at a hill thick with trees and bushes, and he thought about a day many months earlier. She had tumbled down that hill through the bushes with her clothes and wig a mess, and her belongings had scattered on the sidewalk in front of Jason. She had a strange sense of color coordination, and she had needed a shave. He smiled and entered the park.

Trees formed a canopy above the paved walk with parallel polished marble drain gutters. No one used the tennis court with a vista of the city from Mission Bay to Nob Hill. A squirrel dropped from a tree, ran across the court, hopped onto the fence then onto a tree branch. Upward the path twisted through the trees, and when Jason reached the grassy patch at the top he stopped and held his hand to his chest. He had not coughed once during the climb, and he felt no pain. The absence of the cough and the lack of pain shocked him. Had he not been lost in daydreams, he would not have chosen such a steep path. While grateful for the respite from affliction, he knew better than to hope.

Another hill to the south with a fist-shaped rock outcrop appeared through a break in the trees. He remembered encountering a snowy-haired mountain man with curious wares. He closed his eyes, and he giggled a little in remembrance of some hijinks that day, and he whispered, "Harry the Hippie."

A nudge at the back of his leg cut short the nostalgia, and Jason turned to see a large German Shepherd. The dog, black except for brown areas on its face and legs, held a stick in its mouth and looked at Jason. Jason said, "Howdy there, handsome fellow. What are you doing here by yourself?" The dog dropped the stick, barked at Jason, and hopped so its front paws landed near the stick. "I suppose you want me to throw that? All right, then." Jason flung the stick, and it landed in an area between two large tree trunks. The dog ran and pounced on the stick before loping back and dropping it at Jason's feet. Jason bent to pick up the stick again when he heard a shout.

"Neo!" The dog turned for an instant in the direction of the shout and then looked back at Jason and then the stick.

"Are you Neo?" Jason asked. "Are you about to get in trouble?"

A woman in tight athletic clothing came up the steep path to the top of the park, and Jason saw first her hair. The fiery red hair looked like shiny new copper wire in the afternoon sun. She wore it in a ponytail that stretched halfway down her back. As she approached, Neo picked up his stick and walked to her, and when she bent to attach a leash to Neo's collar she smiled at Jason and displayed bright green eyes. Ochre spots dotted her bare arms and face.

She said, "I'm so sorry if he was bothering you."

"Not at all. He's a real nice fellow."

"He's just a little over a year old. I shouldn't have let him off the leash, but he wanted to chase a squirrel, and he didn't come back."

"Oh, those squirrels are always starting trouble."

"Thanks for understanding. Come on, Neo."

"My pleasure. Take it easy, Neo. Good luck with them squirrels."

Though he had not noticed the solitude at the top of the park before the appearance of Neo, with the departure of the redhead and the dog, he felt alone. The grassy area so often full of people, especially in sunny weather, lay empty, and the surrounding woods with shadows reminded Jason of the long, long sleep to come. Distant sounds of traffic on Haight Street came up through the trees, and he took long strides down the path toward the noise and life. On the paved path with marble drain gutters to each side, Jason stopped in surprise when he saw two bicycles coming up the steep grade. A young woman led the way, and a young man followed. Just as the young woman passed Jason, the man called out, "That's all I got. I have to stop."

The woman stopped, dismounted, and turned back to the man who stood beside his bike and panted. "Oh, come on," she said. "We were almost to the top."

Jason addressed the woman, "Can I ask a dumb question? Are those mountain bikes?"

The petite woman in the skin-tight clothing and tiny billed cap said, "That's not a dumb question at all because these are hybrid bikes. They're a cross between mountain bikes and street bikes. Are you interested in cycling?"

"Well, mostly I wanted to know what a mountain bike looked like cause some friends of mine talked about em."

"The biggest difference is that a straight mountain bike has bigger tires."

"Thank you, and yall have a good day."

Off Haight Street at the base of the park on the long lawn, a man tossed a ball for a dog, and several individuals and couples lounged on blankets. People waited at the bus stop, and tourists moved in both directions on both sidewalks. Nearby a couple picnicked, and the woman sent peals of laughter across the lawn. Jason thought about which way to go. East led back downtown, and west led toward the intersection of Haight and Ashbury. He decided to go west to see the intersection and think about a special friend. He wondered if this visit would be his last, and he wondered if he had a place to stay for the night.

After all that business about gettin on down the road, the road led me right back to San Francisco. In a way, it's like coming home. I wish the first weeks of my homecoming hadn't been blind drunk, but they were, and there ain't much use grieving over it. It's done, and this time it's done for good.

The trip with the shiny Buick is still hard to think about, so it's best not to do it much. I'm sorry for what I done, and that's also hard to think about. To be genuine sorry, a fellow has to know what he'd do different. After studying the different courses, I'm still not sure it could have happened different. When looking at things like they happened to other people, strangers, then the best thing would have been for me to tell the girl's daddy what I saw and heard and offer to tell the same thing to the police. But then there's the tequila part of the story to figure. Drinking that tequila amounted to the first and biggest mistake, but it happened, and if tequila has a part in the story then the thing to do different would have been to keep a tighter grip on that brick until ready to use it.

One good thing come of all that thinking about doing things different with the knucklehead. After a lot of tussling with the idea of taking different trails in that sorry situation, I came to see that things is already done, and there ain't nothing different to be done. Somehow that got me thinking about the folks in Texas. Things can't be changed just to make them easier to explain. If that was possible, I'd change the fact that I'm dying. But all I can do is take the sorry mess and try to make the best of it with them in mind instead of thinking so much about my shame. It ain't happened yet, and it may not, but I've been thinking about calling the folks.

I had a teenage friend that killed hisself. And I remember wondering why he didn't talk with me first. We was tight enough that if he'd have been in a hard place I'd have helped. Other kids had also been friends with him, and we talked. We talked a lot about how he didn't tell nobody, and he didn't leave no kind of note. The bunch of us saw things as kids do. We didn't understand a lot, but we kind of got to thinking that maybe he didn't think as much of us as we thought of him. I wouldn't want my folks to think a thing like that.

Maybe to see how calling the folks would go, I called Bobrick but didn't tell him about the shiny car and ain't got no plans to tell him or anyone. We didn't talk about the thinking on calling the folks in Texas either. We just talked about his doings and Eleanor's, and he told me the little dog is fine. The conversation gave the opportunity to mention being sorry for the way things turned out, and now that I'm back in San Francisco it's clear to me that a fellow can't run from stuff like this. He understood and didn't judge, and while that used to make me feel worse, it kind of made me feel better this last time, and maybe it's what has me thinking about something I might be fixin to do.

Running from things or finding ways to ignore things is a specialty of mine. That's what drinking amounts to. The drinking again after coming back to San Francisco might have been a way to dodge thinking about the situation. After that business with the Buick, it seemed the end, the black nothing had come. Even so, somehow I stayed off the hard liquor. Beer will get a drunk on just as good as whiskey if there's enough beer, and somehow having only beer seemed less like drinking at the time. Mostly it was just a real even buzz all day long every day. I'm still not sure how the drinking ended when it did, but I'm glad it's quit. It'd be a shame to waste the last little bit of time.

Hopefully that business with the knucklehead is over. Nothing about it came out in the papers. Maybe over in Oakland finding a car with a gun and a fellow—or a body—in the trunk is nothing unusual, but the situation and the fear of consequences caused considerable fret. If he made it out all right, and if he goes right back to Dixon, he shouldn't be in no shape for a while to bother nobody. And if he or his friends want to come looking for me, that'll be fine. Even I don't know where I'll be from one day to the next, so they should have a real fun hunt. Something tells me, though, those kinds of scroungy bums are tough only with old ladies and girls. And while the anger that led up to that situation is mostly gone, if the knucklehead or any of his friends want to play, I won't run. A gun can be had faster and cheaper in the Tenderloin than any place I've ever called home. Guns ain't my style. I never cared for toting them back in Texas, so I don't imagine I'd get one here. But if knucklehead and his friends want to come calling, we can have some fun. Chances are, though, that mess is over.

Aside from the drinking and the assault and the kidnapping, maybe one of the biggest mistakes made during that odd trip involved camping at that state park. Now there's a record of me with that car, and that wouldn't be no kind of good if cops or anyone else goes to hunting for clues. That thought didn't occur at the time, but it should have. That mistake might pose some trouble if I live long enough. But then maybe nobody is going to bend over backwards trying to figure out what happened to an ex con no good bum. All I wanted back then was to stay out of other folks' business and wallow in my shame alone and just die. In looking back, it seems kind of funny that a ruffian worse than me got me to caring about other folks again.

The other day I caught a glimpse, maybe real or maybe imagined, of somebody. It happened somewhere just to the east of Van Ness, and the fast glimpse took the form of somebody in a pink fuzzy sweater. After such a quick flash, there wasn't no way to be sure if it had been real or just something I wanted real bad to see. It seemed for an instant like a pink sweater over brown skin and under real big hair, like maybe a wig. As soon as she appeared, she disappeared around a corner, but after running up to that corner and turning around nobody in view looked like her. That made me sad. It would have felt good to see her and thank her. I won't never forget what she done that day and wish I could tell her that her kindness got put to better use, but I'd settle for just saying thank you.

Them little girls come to mind more than that no good scrounge with the fancy car and pistol. I miss that quiet thoughtful Valentina and that feisty Ada. For no longer than I knew them, they sure do stay on the mind. Maybe it's them that has me thinking so much about the folks in Texas. I wonder what them little girls thought about the disappearance of the man in the camper with no goodbyes and just a hat on the porch. Thinking about it hurts a considerable amount. So does thinking about the folks in Texas. Maybe saying nothing and hiring a lawyer to tell the bad news is a lot like my friend that killed hisself and didn't leave no note. Maybe there's time to think of some different choices.

But before telling anyone anything, I got to know the story myself. What happened to the cough is a mystery. The cough still comes often, but there ain't no blood with it. Maybe that's supposed to happen. Maybe it means the end is close. For sure, I ought to know what is happening before calling any folks. It runs contrary to my usual way of thinking, but maybe heading over to the hospital might not be a bad idea. If I could get a handle on how much time is left, I might be able to do something better with it than just run out the clock. After having done it for a time, that way of drifting seems wasteful.

Bad news is easier to handle when there's already an answer for it. And that's why I got to figure what to do before asking questions at a hospital. If they tell me what's expected, that the end could come at any time now, then I have to know what to do. Other places like that hospice might be an option. Even that very one would be fine, but I might have wore out my welcome in leaving without a word. The hospital might tell me that more time is left. If they do that, I'll have to figure something better than running around with no plan. Maybe I could rent another place like that Chrystal Rose Bungalow. Then the rest of the time could be spent quiet right here in The City.

Running all over might be tiresome, but that shiny Buick coupe rode real fine. That was some car. In thinking a lot about that car, I've taken a few extra trips in my mind. It's a pleasure to think about driving a car like that all the way to Texas. With a car like that, a fellow could take all the time he wanted along the way finding bull fight rings, beautiful lakes, old Spanish Missions, and who knows what else. That might seem a strange thing to daydream about, but it probably don't do no harm so long as I remember that it's just a dream and not something to believe in.

More than likely, the folks at the hospital would tell me they have no idea how much time is left. They didn't provide too many straight answers any of the other times, and maybe that's a kindness. After all, if you don't know something for certain, you don't want to tell a dying man something he'll count on just to be let down in his last days. With that in mind, I wonder if going to the hospital wouldn't be a waste of time for everyone.

Then again, the folks in Texas—if they get called—will want answers. Anybody would. One of the first things they'll ask is what the doctors say. If the answer is anything less than clear, they'll ask when the last doctor visit happened. I can't very well tell them that it was a couple or more months ago back before becoming a car thief. They forgive a lot, like the constant drinking, and they'd probably even forgive the car thieving under the circumstances, but there ain't no way they'd stand for hearing that despite knowing that I'm dying I ain't even bothered to check with a doctor in a long time. So before any more notions of calling the folks, a doctor better get seen first.

I'll study on it some more.

Would but some winged Angel ere too late
Arrest the yet unfolded Roll of Fate,
    And make the stern Recorder otherwise
Enregister, or quite obliterate!

1 in 649,740

The hospital's location meant that no matter what bus he rode, he would still have to walk a block or two unless he first walked several blocks in the opposite direction as the route to the hospital to reach the nearest stop for the 27 Bryant. He chose instead to play a game of dodge the rain. To give himself an advantage over nature, he had left extra early. In his second coffee shop of the morning, he sat near the window and watched people hurry by on the sidewalk huddled under hoods or umbrellas. The rain seemed unusual to Jason in that it lacked frigidity or dreariness. He watched out the window and noted that the rain came down in an even drizzle, and no wind gusts jerked and tore umbrellas or sent spray into the faces of the hooded. He would not have called it a warm rain, certainly not like those of summertime Central Texas, but he did think it tolerable where it had wet his hair and soaked through his shirt. The effects on his feet, however, he did not find tolerable, and he looked down to see his boots split at the seams between the uppers and soles and with the outside corners of the heels worn away.

Hopping to avoid puddles, Jason turned left off Taylor Street onto a minor street or alley to cut through to Jones. The narrowness of the lane and the height of the buildings provided some cover from the rain, so Jason took his time. He found it strange how some rainy days could bring discomfort, even misery, yet others came as welcome, even soothing. The steady drizzle collected on the buildings' masonry exteriors, pooled in crevices, gathered on outcroppings, and washed down in a clear veneer. A thin unbroken stream came from the corner of a metal fire escape ladder, and while Jason watched the thin line to where it hit the black asphalt and exploded into tiny diamonds he heard the hiss of tires on busier streets on the other side of the protective buildings.

After entering the hospital, Jason crossed the wide foyer to the rest-rooms. He used paper towels to absorb excess water in his hair, and he dried his face. He ran a pocket comb through his hair and then stopped for a moment to look in the mirror. "Well pardner, you sure do look the part of a dying man. Lost some weight and some hair too."

He passed the gift shop and found the elevator. The first available car had too many people, so Jason waited for the next. He thought that of the several days that he had come to the hospital in the last week, this day, the day he ought to be the most nervous, he felt the least concerned. He had prepared himself for the grim news he expected, and going to receive it amounted to a mere formality. The elevator arrived, and he rode up alone.

Jason found the door he sought, and on the other side he found a small waiting room with a sliding glass window at the far end. On the other side of the window, a receptionist sat at a desk and moved about papers. Jason approached the window and waited until the woman looked up from her papers. "I have an appointment today."

"Last name?"

"My name is Jason Spearman, ma'am. I'm a little early, so there's no hurry."

"Great. Then have a seat, and I'll call you."

Another man, a much older man, waited in the small lounge. He had a well-groomed appearance with only a little neatly combed snow white hair on an otherwise bald head. The frames of his gold wire rimmed glasses covered only the top half of the lenses, leaving the bottom half suspended.

Jason admired the man's style. He wore black wingtips, and his navy three-piece suit had subtle burgundy pinstripes. The white shirt made the coat and tie all the more striking, but the part of the man's ensemble that impressed Jason most rotated in the man's hands. He pulled the brim of the dark fedora with one hand while the other provided drag against the outside edge. Jason liked the fedora, had always wanted one, and thought about his grandfather's collection. His grandfather had hats for all occasions, and they ranged from the permanently sweat-stained to the pristine that spent all time off-the-head in protective boxes. His grand-father had not been a wealthy man by any standards, but he lived a long time, and he took care of the hats he acquired over a lifetime. Jason would have liked to have inherited those hats, but his head had not grown to a sufficient circumference, so the hats went to an uncle that could put them to better use.

The older man's legs shook, and sometimes one of the heels of his wingtips tapped the floor. He had a slight tremor in his hands as he rotated his hat, and the man's gaze never left the same spot straight ahead of his position in the waiting room. Jason remembered a visit to the same waiting room months earlier. He too had been nervous. He had feared hearing that he required some painful and invasive procedure, but the news he received had been far worse than any he imagined. Jason wondered if the man feared hearing bad news.

"I sure do admire that hat," Jason said. "Is it a Stetson?"

"Yes, it is."

"Thought so. I always liked them and always wanted one. I've had a lot of hats, but they were mostly straw or palm leaf. Never had a Stetson, though."

The man gave a hint of a smile and then resumed looking ahead. He stopped rotating his hat and held it brim-down in his lap.

"So, you here to see the doc?" Jason asked. "He's a good one I hear."

"No, I'm here with my wife. She's seeing the doctor now."

"I see," Jason said. "I've been coming here for months. I was in sorry shape when I got here, and I know I still look a sight on the outside, but the doc here got me all fixed up on the inside. Things are probably gonna come out okay. Yep, he's a good doc. Been married long?"

"Thirty-seven years," the man said. He had a grin when he looked at Jason, "We got married late according to our families. We were both well into our thirties, and I married an older woman. A whole three years older."

"Any kids?"

"No kids. We wanted to for a while, but . . . but we did travel a great deal. And we lived overseas on a few occasions."

"Overseas? Now that's something. I've done a fair amount of traveling, but I never made it overseas. Yall still like to travel? I bet when you get this situation taken care of you can do some more traveling."

"Sure. Maybe." The man looked ahead.

The door next to the receptionist opened, and a short slender woman with glasses and wispy white hair stepped into the waiting room. A nurse followed the woman and spoke to her. As soon as the older man saw the woman step through the door he shot out of his chair and stood at attention. The woman gave the man a smile while she listened to the nurse, and the man resumed rotating his hat while he waited for the woman to join him. As the couple exited the waiting room, the nurse called out, "Mr. Spearman."

She escorted him to a room with a couple of chairs and a desk. The lack of an examination table surprised Jason, but he said nothing, and when the nurse left the room and closed the door, Jason pulled one of the chairs closer to the window and sat. He thought about a time months ago he had been in a similar room. That room had an examination table, and Jason had been clothed in a hospital gown. He had been frightened back then. He had been terrified. While he sat in the chair in his own clothes, he looked out the window and wondered what he could find to do after the doctor told him what he already knew. He thought perhaps he could go to a museum if the rain persisted. Jason thought about the last time he had gone to a museum, and after wincing in embarrassment he began to laugh. He stopped chuckling when the doctor opened the door.

The doctor said hello, and then he sat at the remaining chair at the desk. He carried multiple folders with papers, and he put the folders on the desk, opened them, and spread the papers. Jason watched the man younger than himself. He thought the man did not look old enough to be a doctor, and he tried to remember the doctor that had given him the news months earlier. Jason could not remember the face, only the words. This younger doctor studied one of the folders for a considerable length, appeared dissatisfied or annoyed, and then looked at another folder. He clicked a retractable pen and put it in a shirt pocket before returning to examining the first folder. After opening a third folder and looking at it alongside the other two, the doctor let out a long sigh, pulled the pen from his pocket, and clicked it repeatedly.

"Pretty ugly stuff, huh doc?" Jason asked.

"I'm looking at your recent scans and bronchoscopy and comparing them to the ones from six months ago. There's a striking difference."

"Bronchoscopy? I've ridden some tough broncs."

The doctor did not laugh or react at all. He continued looking from the contents of one folder to another.

Jason said, "I imagine they have gotten a lot worse. I didn't make the best of effort to take care of myself."

"Oh they're not worse at all. In fact, the recent bronchoscopy revealed nothing, and the scan shows only the slightest abnormality and even then only from a top view."

"Not worse? Are you saying it's better then?"

"Certainly the recent results are better than the earlier ones."

"What does that mean, doc?" Jason asked.

"I don't know."

"Okay, does that mean it's not the kind of cancer they told me it was?"

"Cancer?" The doctor gave Jason a shocked look. "Certainly not. Cancer doesn't do this."

"Doc, I don't understand what you're telling me. What does *do this* mean?"

"The mass has all but disappeared." The doctor shuffled the papers in one of the folders and extracted a sheet. "The recent blood work looks good. A little bit of an issue in liver function but still within normal range. Some of the other samples indicate a slight infection." The doctor scribbled on one of the sheets of paper. "We can give you some antibiotics for the infection. Any allergies?"

Jason looked at the doctor and shook his head. "No. No, I don't have any allergies. Doctor, I don't understand what you're telling me. You say it's not cancer, but I was told it was. Are you saying it's not . . . are you saying it's not . . . terminal?"

"Terminal?" The doctor chuckled a little bit then saw the grave afraid look on Jason's face. "No, this is certainly not terminal."

The young doctor kept talking, but Jason felt as if the room spun under him. He grasped the chair under his thighs with both hands, and he breathed long deep breaths while staring at the floor. The doctor closed the folders and gathered them into a single stack, which he placed under his arm. When the doctor rose from the chair and opened the door, Jason still sat in his chair staring at the floor.

"Mr. Spearman?"

Jason looked up at the doctor, and then he stood on wobbly legs. He followed the doctor into the hall, and the doctor said, "Check with the receptionist on your way out, and she will give you the prescription for antibiotics and set your next appointment."

In the small waiting room, the receptionist handed Jason a small slip of paper. He took it and put it in a shirt pocket. "When would you like to set the next appointment?" Jason did not answer. He looked to the part of the room where he had spoken to the older man earlier in the day. "Mr. Spearman?" Again Jason seemed oblivious to the woman's words. "Okay, then, why don't you call, and we'll set the appointment."

Jason staggered into the hall and in the direction of the elevator. He started to reach out to push the elevator call button, but then made an abrupt turn and walked along the hallway wall looking at doors. When he found the door to the stairwell, he rushed through and ran down half a flight before collapsing to sit on the steps. First a few tears appeared, and then sobs burst. He crossed his arms atop his knees and buried his head. From deep in his midsection convulsive sobs began, rose through his chest, and erupted from his mouth. Jason, who had not cried at hearing the news months earlier that he would die, wailed at the news he would live. All of the fear, shame, and regret he had held back flowed out and down the concrete steps.

Outside the even drizzle had increased to big soft drops, and when they landed on Jason's face they mingled with the tears that gushed forth along with the uncontrolled laughter. He advanced down Hyde and turned left on Post on spring-loaded legs that kept him aloft and only briefly in contact with pavement. Without orientation, he sprang into Union Square with the dizzying confusion of too many thoughts at once. Bewildered he turned and spun in circles stomping his worn boots into puddles. When he stopped spinning he bent forward, placed his hands on his knees, and tried to catch his breath amid the laughter.

"Ain't this something? The doc tells me I'm gonna live, so I run out in the rain and try to get pneumonia."

Jason stood straight and let loose his loudest whooping yeehaw.

XI. Blue Garden

WAKE! For the Sun, who scatter'd into flight
The Stars before him from the Field of Night,
    Drives Night along with them from Heav'n, and strikes
The Sultan's Turret with a Shaft of Light.

Up from Earth's Center through the Seventh Gate
I rose, and on the Throne of Saturn sate,
 And many a Knot unravel'd by the Road;
But not the Master-knot of Human Fate.

Erelong

He tied a double Windsor knot because he thought it went best with his shirt's collar and because he had run out of other things to do. After re-reading the previous day's newspaper, he had spread it on the table and used it as a surface for shining shoes. In between glances at the clock, he worked with care to get the wingtips to gleam. The hands of the clock did not move fast enough to suit him, and he wondered if the clock had stopped, so he checked another timepiece, sighed, and went to the closet to choose between newly tailored suits. His showering and shaving had not helped the clock hands advance as far as he thought they should, so he stood before the mirror and tied a double Windsor because he thought it went best with his collar and because he had plenty of time.

With no place to go, he stepped outside, closed the door, and double-checked the lock. The warmth of the Indian summer still held, and the morning, or the early hours of the night, offered only a mild chill. He walked west on Bush Street glad that all the bars had closed but wondering what, if anything, remained open. After Van Ness Avenue, even fewer cars passed on the one-way track, but abundant street lights kept most of the sidewalk under a soft glow in between large buildings of various ages and styles. Sometimes newer block-like apartment buildings faced across the street to older wood and masonry structures with bay windows. At Presidio Avenue, the residences stopped, and a large paved lot with dozens of municipal buses extended to the south. Past the bus lot, he turned south on Masonic Avenue, and as he approached the all-night diner he hoped he had not arrived before the day's newspaper.

After the waitress whisked away the breakfast dishes and replaced them with the bill, he sipped the remainder of his coffee and held the rectangular piece of paper in his hand. He stared a long time at the hand-written scrawl, perhaps because he had no newspaper to read, and he thought about what to do with the coming day. The tasks on the lists he had made for the previous several days had all been fulfilled, and he had run out of lists and ideas. The day after getting the shocking news from the hospital, he had gone to his storage unit, selected a couple of suits, a couple of sport coats, and some trousers. He took them to a different tailor than the one he had used for years because he did not want to explain the dramatic weight loss. Though the fee to the new tailor had included extra for a rush job, the alterations still took a few days, and in that time he had visited a barber and a dentist. He had also secured a month-to-month residential rental at a nice and obscenely overpriced converted hotel in the southern fringes of Nob Hill. The second chance, the disappearance of the gruesome cough and constant pain, came as a surprise, a shock, and he did not want to waste it. Every single thing he could imagine needing to make the most of the new life he had acquired or arranged. But the new life had not started. All of his days since the news at the hospital had been the same, just a continuation of the old life. He did not know what the new life would be like or what moment would mark its beginning, but he wanted to be ready. So he sat ready with a slight tremor in his hand and a shaking leg that made the heel of a wingtip tap the floor underneath the table.

"Sir, is there a problem with the bill?"

The unexpected question caused him to jump a bit from his seat at the booth, and he answered, "No, not at all. Not at all. Thank you very much."

After leaving a few notes on the table, he took the bill to the cashier, and he accepted coins as change. Outside the diner, dawn had not arrived, and it did not appear to be coming. He went south on Masonic and contemplated continuing on to Haight but turned west on Fulton. He tried to enjoy the quiet of the early morning, but he felt anxious and frustrated. The urge to drink had not afflicted him. On the contrary, thoughts of alcoholic beverages, when they came, arrived as repellent and nauseating. Every change he thought necessary for taking advantage of the new life had been enacted, yet the new life did not arrive. He simply had a nicer place to sleep and better fitting clothes, but he walked on in the old life. He had no idea where to search for the new life, but he turned into Golden Gate Park at Arguello Boulevard, and he walked around the Conservatory of Flowers to follow the main park road a while before cutting between the art museum and the science museum.

He ran out of park at Lincoln Way at the same time as the sky toward downtown began to lighten. A mere block ahead, the intersection of 9th and Irving, offered coffee shops, places to sit and read the day's paper and pass or waste time, but he turned west and walked on the sidewalk between the dense green of the park and the long line of cars parked parallel to the busy street. He knew the road ended a few miles ahead at Ocean Beach, and he hoped he found a path to the new life before then, but before him an empty sidewalk stretched on and on. One after another, he passed cars taking up every spare inch of room along the edge of the sidewalk, and he stared unfocused in the distance hoping to find an objective, a task, a sign, or anything to interrupt the listless wasting of time.

First the shape of a vehicle caught his attention, then the peace sign between a curtain and inside the rear-window glass made him stop. The two-tone sea blue and white rectangle surprised him, and he stepped closer while the first rays of dawn superseded the weak glow from the overhead street light. From the chrome wheel covers and white-walled tires to the subtly curved roof, the van appeared in perfect condition as if it belonged more on a showroom floor or museum rather than parallel parked alongside a busy city street. The front of the van displayed the two-tone colors with the VW symbol in blue matching the color of the bottom half of the bus while the white of the roof narrowed to a point just above the front bumper. He waited for a break in traffic and stepped out into Lincoln to get a better view of the front and side of the van while he tried to count the windows. The abundance of windows and the split windscreen revealed the microbus as older than most he saw and perhaps as old as the one in a photograph he treasured throughout childhood. He squeezed between the rear of the van and the bumper of the car behind, saw the Kansas plate on the van, and stood back on the sidewalk outside the double side door.

A noise came from inside the van, and he started to step away, but as soon as he took a single stride back away from the vehicle one half of the double side door opened and an amazonian goddess wrapped in a quilt jumped out onto the sidewalk. She stood at least six feet tall, and at the top she sprouted thick sandy ringlets, some that jutted out and upward like defiant dreadlocks and others that extended down her shoulders and back as relaxed and darker corkscrews. Intense blue eyes peered out between errant ringlets and she issued the single-word question, "What?"

He stood captivated by the ultramarine pupils and the smooth fair skin, and he stammered, "I . . . I was just looking at the van. I didn't know anybody was inside. Sorry."

Perhaps satisfied with his answer, her eyelids drooped and she yawned, covering her mouth with one hand while the other held the quilt together at her neck. In a continuation of the yawn, she stretch the arm that had held the hand to her mouth high into the air, and she sighed as she stretched. Her bare arm displayed more of the fair skin with a slight golden tone, and he knew he should be moving along, but he said, "You have the most amazing hair I've ever seen."

She giggled, tousled her hair with her free hand, and sat inside the open half of the van's double door. She reached inside the van and then dropped a pair of sandals on the sidewalk and stepped into them. He saw her strong yet shapely legs emerge one then the other from beneath the quilt, and he felt uncomfortable for an instant and said, "I didn't mean to wake you. I was just admiring the van, and . . ."

Another noise, a voice, from inside the vehicle sounded, and the amazon said, "No, no it's okay. Just someone admiring the bus . . . and other things."

Again he said, "I didn't mean to wake anyone, but this van . . . just gorgeous. Perfect. Well, better be getting along now."

"It's okay," she said. "We thought you were going to hassle us about moving it."

He started to ask for clarification of her statement, but she disappeared inside, and in her place a tall young man stepped out onto the sidewalk. "Good morning. My name is Wilson. You like these old buses?"

"I'm Jason." He extended his hand to meet Wilson's, and he noticed both Wilson's height, which rose well over six and a half feet, and his thin wiry frame. Wilson sported short spiked hair dyed green. Jason said, "This one is amazing. It's one of the oldest one's I've seen in a long time. You don't see too many of the split screen models anymore, and this one is in mint condition. Is that the original paint?"

"It's the original colors." Wilson answered. "I do body work, and this van belonged to my granddad. He'd say it still does belong to him."

"Well it's a beauty."

"Yeah, but it hasn't been running so good lately, and for the last few days it hasn't started at all."

Jason asked, "Is that why she said yall thought I came here to hassle you about moving it?"

Before Wilson answered, the amazonian goddess reappeared wearing faded denim bib overalls and a tattered football jersey. Wilson said, "This is Laura."

Laura smiled at Jason and said to Wilson, "Honey, I want some coffee. Do you have any change?"

Wilson dug in his pockets and handed Laura a handful of coins and a couple of notes. Laura looked at Jason and asked, "Would you like some coffee?"

"Well, sure, but only if you let me buy." He handed Laura a note, and said, "I like mine black. Of course, I can run and get the coffee too. It's the least I can do after waking yall."

Laura smiled again and headed in the direction of 9th and Irving. Wilson said, "I haven't been able to get it running for several days. The part store gave me the wrong part." He reached inside the van and retrieved a metal cylindrical object. "I asked for a single port intake manifold for this engine model, and they gave me the dual port manifold for the wrong engine. Can't believe I didn't notice until after getting back to the bus. Engine work isn't really my thing. I'm a body guy."

Jason looked at the van and said, "I always wanted one of these but never had one. Had a Beetle for a while, and they have the same engines, but I didn't do too much work on it."

Wilson put the part back in the van and came back to the sidewalk holding a glass smoking pipe. He lit the pipe, inhaled, held his breath, and then offered the pipe to Jason. Jason said, "Appreciate the offer, but I'm fine."

Wilson exhaled and asked, "You sure? I grew this myself."

"You grew it in the van?"

"No, back home. It's as good as any California stuff."

"I have a good friend that's a farmer," Jason said. "He might argue that point."

Laura returned with three cups of coffee. After giving Jason a cup, she gave a cup to Wilson, and he gave her the glass pipe. She started to light the pipe, but Wilson put this hand on her arm and said, "Wait."

A three-wheeled parking enforcement scooter passed on Lincoln Way, and it slowed as it drew even with the van. Once it cleared the van and continued down Lincoln, Laura lit the pipe, and Wilson said, "They'll be all over us today. I have to get this thing moved somehow."

"Is that what Laura meant when she said she mistook me for someone fixing to hassle you about the van?"

"Yeah, we've had to move it all over town to avoid tickets, and one of the meter maids even threatened to put a boot on the wheel," Wilson said. "I don't know what we're going to do. We can't stay here, but we're trapped here."

"This place didn't turn out like we expected," Laura said.

"You mean San Francisco?" Jason asked.

Laura looked at Wilson as she exhaled, though neither responded to Jason's question. Wilson took the pipe from Laura, and while he lit it Laura said, "We used to dream of coming to San Francisco and seeing famous places like Haight-Ashbury. When we both decided to drop out of school, he did a bunch of work to the bus, and we took off. Haight Street isn't what I expected. And for most of last summer it was so cold."

Jason burst into laughter and spilled some of his coffee that ran down across his fingers grasping the cup. He switched hands and held the wet hand away from his suit. "I'm sorry. I'm not laughing at you," Jason said. "What you said about San Francisco sounds a lot like something a fellow said years ago after he got off a bus downtown. And as for the Haight, that famous Summer of Love lasted only a few months by all accounts before the place became a grimy hangout for junkies and muggers. From what I hear, it's a lot better today than it used to be. I've heard that even real-life hippies came here and were shocked just like yall."

"And now we're here and can't afford to get the bus fixed and get out," Wilson said.

"What did you say is wrong with it?" Jason asked.

"It had some carburetor problems. So that's why I got those parts, but since they're the wrong ones, I put the old parts back on, and since then the bus hasn't started at all."

"That kind of work is way out of my league," Jason said. "I wish there was something I could do to . . ." Jason stopped speaking, looked at the van, and then looked at the pipe in Wilson's hand. "Oh, wow, yeah, maybe. Should have thought of that sooner. Gotta get to a phone. Can you hold this?" Jason handed his cup to Wilson. "I'll be right back. Yall don't go nowhere." Jason laughed as he ran across the street in the direction of 9th and Irving.

As then the Tulip for her morning sup
Of Heav'nly Vintage from the soil looks up,
    Do you devoutly do the like, till Heav'n
To Earth invert you—like an empty Cup.

Golden Goat Rodeo

Jason crossed Lincoln at a slower gait than when he departed, and he headed for the VW van. He approached Laura and Wilson, and Wilson gave Jason his cup of coffee. "I barely caught him," Jason said. "Any later in the morning, and he'd have been out in the fields. My friend knows how to fix anything, and that's what I called to ask about."

"That's great," Laura said. "We wondered where you ran off to."

"Well, I called about the van, but I need to ask Wilson here a couple of other questions. Did you tell me earlier that the reefer you're smoking is some you grew yourself?"

Wilson hesitated and then said, "Yeah, I grew it back home. I don't see why anyone out here where it's practically legal would care about that."

"Bear with me a minute, pardner," Jason said. "My friend is a farmer, and he's in the middle of a harvest."

"What does he farm?" Laura asked.

"Dope. Or kind bud as he calls it. I asked my pal about the VW, and he had more questions about the van than I could answer. You think you might be able to help me understand the problem better?"

"Sure, man," Wilson said.

"Well, then the fastest way to get your van fixed might be to talk to my friend," Jason said. "I can't remember some of the questions he had, but if you come to the phone with me, we might be able to get this thing fixed soon."

Wilson started to follow Jason, and Laura asked, "What about the meter maid?"

"She has a good point," Jason said. "Yall got something to write on and something to write with?" Laura reached in the van and found a pen and piece of paper. Jason wrote a number on the paper and handed it to Wilson. "My friend's name is Bob . . . his name is Patrick. Just tell him that you're Jason's friend with the van, and yall talk. I think he can help."

Wilson crossed Lincoln Way and went off in the direction Jason had gone. Laura sat on the edge of the van just inside the side door while Jason stood on the sidewalk drinking cold coffee. "So you find San Francisco a little bit disappointing?" he asked.

"It's just not what I expected. And it's so expensive. It's not a good place for living in a camper van."

"No, it's not, and it might not even be legal here. But don't sour on California just yet. I love San Francisco like no place else, but it don't exactly fit yall's needs right now. You might find there's some other places out here that are even better than whatever you imagined California might be." Laura smiled a little, but Jason saw that she still seemed doubtful. "Where bouts in Kansas yall from?"

"I'm from Garden City, and he's from Liberal."

"No foolin? Been to Liberal lots of times. It ain't that far from the part of Texas I'm from."

"Really?" Laura asked. "With that accent, I'd have thought you lived here all your life." She giggled and went inside the van. When she came out she held a plate and asked, "Would you like a brownie?"

Jason took one of the brown squares, and Laura took one for herself before putting the plate back in the van. She returned to her seat at the van door. Jason bit into the brownie and noticed an unfamiliar, earthy, and slightly bitter flavor, but he ate the brownie while admiring Laura's natural, seemingly effortless beauty. He took another bite of the odd tasting cake square and stifled a laugh at the thought that he would probably eat a rock if she offered it to him.

Wilson approached Lincoln, and waited at the corner of 9th for traffic to clear. He wore a smile as visible from a distance as his green hair. He rounded the back of the van, and before Laura could inquire he exclaimed, "We're all set. It's fixed!"

Laura stood and started to ask for more information, but Wilson embraced her and laughed. When he released her, he took a step toward Jason and said, "Mister Jason, you just saved us." Wilson extended his right hand, and Jason had to transfer the brownie to his left before shaking hands.

"Did Bobrick tell you how to fix it?" Jason asked.

"Tell me how to fix it . . . no. He's going to come and get it, and he's going to fix it, and he gave us both jobs and a place to stay!"

"Oh, the farm . . . the harvest, of course," Jason said. "That's why he asked those questions about your reefer growing." Jason finished the last bite of brownie.

Laura asked, "What are you two talking about?"

Wilson answered, "Jason's friend is on his way right now. He said he's going to borrow a truck and tow us back to his place where we can stay in the van or in a house—our choice—and in exchange for helping with his harvest he'll fix the bus."

"He's on his way already?" Jason asked.

"Yeah. He said he would be here within two hours."

"He must really need the help," Jason said. "Yall are gonna like ole Bobrick."

Wilson stepped into the van, and he called to Laura still out on the sidewalk. "Laura, which brownies are you two eating?"

Laura leaned into the van and said, "That plate. There."

"Those are the hash brownies."

"So?" Laura asked.

"He doesn't partake."

Laura looked troubled, and Wilson stepped out of the van onto the sidewalk. Jason asked, "What's with the sour faces?"

"Man, I don't know how to tell you this," Wilson said. "She gave you a hash brownie. I make them from my stuff back home. They're powerful.

Jason chuckled and said, "I've been a drunk most of my life. I've been sideways from tequila and upside down from other hooch. I really don't think a little piece of cake is gonna give me no worries."

"It probably won't hit you for a while, even an hour maybe," Laura said. "You could go home before it kicks in."

"I'll be fine, darlin. Don't you worry."

"Okay then," Wilson said. "But if things start getting weird, remember it's just the brownie, and it will wear off eventually." Wilson joined Laura where she sat on the edge of the van at the side door, and he ate a brownie.

Jason noticed the parking enforcement scooter return. It stopped even with the van, and Jason said, "Yall, don't get up. I'll handle this. "Jason walked onto Lincoln Way, and he leaned down to see inside the scooter window. "We got a tow truck coming. It should be here any time now." The scooter moved on, and Jason returned to the sidewalk snickering. "Tow.

TOW. TaOwah. Tow."

"Are you okay?" Wilson asked.

"I'm fine. That word sounds funny. TaOwuh."

Wilson smiled at Laura, and said, "You better sit down." He guided Jason to the edge of the van next to Laura.

Jason held a leaf by the stem and moved it back and forth. "It's so green. Wow. Whoa . . ."

A big pickup stopped even with the van, and over the loud clatter of the diesel engine, Wilson said, "I think this might be your friend."

Jason stood and rounded the back of the van. He did not recognize the vehicle, but he saw the snowy mass of hair in the driver seat, and he approached the driver-side window wearing a droopy grin. "Bobrick . . ."

"You're looking good, Jason. I see you went back to your stuffy style of dress, and you're looking healthy, except . . . Have you been drinking?"

"No, pardner, I have not been drinking."

"Well, we need to get this thing moving quick. I can't back up the street for long. Somebody needs to direct traffic."

"I can do that, amigo," Jason said. He walked away from the truck first in a two-step and then a foxtrot. When Jason got to a point behind both the van and the truck, he moved in a waltz box step, and when car horns honked, he waved them around. His dance steps led him through both lanes of traffic, and after much honking and shouting from angry drivers Laura walked into the street and pulled Jason back to the sidewalk. "Did I tell you that you are an angel? Beautiful."

"No, you didn't mention anything like that. Come tell me about it over here out of traffic."

Bobrick and Wilson worked with tow lines, and when Bobrick said, "I think that's got it," Wilson went to where Laura and Jason stood.

Wilson shook Jason's hand and said, "I can't thank you enough, Mister Jason."

Laura hugged Jason and said, "Please be careful. Stay out of traffic."

"Angel . . . Beautiful."

Bobrick hustled over to Jason and said, "It's good to see you healthy, brother. The kid tells me you ate a magic brownie. Good for you, but you better go home or hang out over there in the park. I wish we could talk more, but we have to get this out of the street. Come see us at the farm. Eleanor will be thrilled to hear you're healthy and looking good."

After the truck and van departed, Jason managed to mumble, "Bye

Bobrick."

Jason stood at the corner of 9th Avenue and Lincoln watching cars pass. He called out the colors as they passed. "Silver. Blue. Green. Yellow. A bad mistake. Silver. Red." When he noticed people at the nearby bus stop watching him, Jason felt a wave of paranoia, and he hurried past the bus stop and turned on 9th into the park. A few hundred yards later he passed through a gate opening to a giant meadow. An enormous Monterey Cypress stood in the meadow, and Jason walked toward it before noticing the other people, feeling another wave of paranoia, and turning left to follow a path through tall trees and other plants.

A wall of green bordered both sides of the walk, and Jason recognized some of the plants, such as bamboo. A smaller rock-lined path branched away from the wider paved path, and he stepped onto the smaller path crossing a brook and winding around a pond. Among a group of evergreen trees, one in particular seized his attention, and he froze for a moment before approaching and touching the tree. "It's so blue ... It's ... It's blue."

Jason stood captivated before the tree until a passing group made him again feel self-conscious. He stepped away in long strides passing by more trees and plants of various sizes with some displaying luminescent blooms. He cast wary glances at the blooms, sure too much attention focused on any one plant would betray some secret he should hide. Another long meadow stretched to his right, and when he entered it he saw another tree that entranced. This one had a flat dark green, almost gray color, and it stretched tall, over fifty feet and curved, tilted at the midway point so its top seemed to point to something to Jason's left. He looked to his left and then back at the tree with its tiny needle leaves. Somehow the tree seemed more of a character than a plant, and Jason resisted the urge to speak to it. He turned away from the tree towards some taller ones in the distance. As he neared the taller trees, they began to look somehow familiar, though Jason could not understand why until once among them he saw a sign that said Redwood Grove.

Inside the grove, shadows gave way to a uniform gray gloom, and Jason stepped along atop a soft bed of needles, some green and some brown. His feeling of gloom and paranoia increased, and he turned one way then another in rapid jerks at every noise real and imagined. Fear and pulse rising, Jason hurried ahead nearly breaking into a run before bursting into the open sunlight in an area with flora that looked more welcoming. He passed cacti and plants with thick green triangular stalks, and he saw a sign with the words Succulent Garden. Rejuvenated and calmed by the cacti and the sun, he found a path away from the Redwoods, and he floated along and smiled until he encountered a plant with giant leaves.

Jason stood before one of the leaves and spread his arms wide judging the leaf at over five feet from side to side. A little sign rose out of the grass at the base of the plant and read Poor Man's Parasol. Somehow the greenery and soft breeze put Jason in mind of his grandparents, and he saw first his grandfather in a soiled straw fedora and then his grandmother in a bonnet working a hoe in a garden furrow. Realization of the impossibility of the vision made it fade, but the feeling of his grandparents' presence remained, and he sat on the grass. "I don't know how things got so. I'm a terrible disappointment to yall, and I'm so sorry about the bottle. Yall taught me better than that. You did. Things are gonna be different now. There won't be no more drinking, and something better will come with this new life." Tears formed and flowed, and he said, "I ought to do something with this new chance, but I don't know what. I keep trying to figure out what to do, but . . . but it's like . . . it's . . . What was I talking about?" Jason looked about, saw the giant leaves and a variety of other plants, and said, "Why am I talking out loud? What's with this crying? Weird. And so hungry . . . ain't never been this hungry."

He stood and walked, and though he got lost more than once trying to find the gate from which he entered, he found another gate and passed through to one of the main park roads and followed it around to 9th Avenue. Jason held a hand to his stomach sure he had never before experienced such hunger. Walking toward Irving Street he passed a few restaurants, but found the decision process halting, confusing, and unconquerable. At Irving and 9th, he turned in slow circles trying to decide where to go for sustenance. Some of the storefronts displayed colorful signs, and he thought perhaps he could taste the colors. Dazed he lurched into a drug store and looked around. He saw a glass-topped freezer containing frozen desserts, and he flung open the lid and seized a Neapolitan ice cream bar. Without even stepping toward the register to pay for the bar, he tore away the wrapper and took a large bite. He held his eyes clinched shut as he felt the cold pass down his throat, but he finished the bar and then grabbed another. While he stood next to the cooler with brown, white, and pink ice cream on his face and dripping down his wrist, he saw a display rack that drew him. Jason bent to look closer and saw disposable cameras.

That throwaway camera turned out to be a lot of fun. It set beside the bed the morning after the poisoned brownie in a pile of food wrappers. A hangover didn't come that morning, but the food that came with all them wrappers should have been enough to give a billy goat a bellyache. Instead of a hangover, a picture of a blue tree stuck in my head, so I went back to that garden and took that throwaway camera.

That tree really was blue, not just something from the doped-up brownie. And nearby others had unexpected beautiful colors, including one that looked like bright green metal. The blue one had a sign that said Colorado Blue Spruce, and the one that looked like it could talk or walk away had the name Algerian Fir. Covering that whole garden again without the dope felt every bit as stupefying as the time with the Kansas reefer. I skipped the Redwood Grove but saw the rest of the garden, some spots twice. And that little camera made it more enjoyable. It's been a long spell since regular picture shootin, so even that little fixed-focus job gave me a couple dozen snaps of play. The film ain't been developed, and it may not, but the camera made for a lot of fun.

That poisoned brownie might have been the best thing for me at the time. In the time before, all the days since the doctor said cancer doesn't do that, I had been getting more and more wound up nervous thinking there had to be some way to find purpose and not waste life like before. Thinking about purpose still causes worry, but the time with them young Kansas hippies and then the time with the strange dope gave a break from the twisting and fretting about what ought to be done with a second chance. To be sure, what ought to be done is still unknown, and it bothers me that it ain't happening fast enough, but that time with the reefer cake gave a little hope that things might turn out all right if I relax some.

Bobrick says them Kansas kids is working out just fine. While talking the other day before he went to the fields, he called them kids hard workers and said they appreciate that estate. That ain't too surprising considering the rough time they had in the city with the broke down van. Bobrick said Eleanor had taking a liking to them kids, especially Laura, and that ain't surprising either. They're both good kids, and I feel lucky to have run into em. Trying to imagine the two there on that estate ain't particularly hard to do. Bobrick and Wilson probably have never-ending things to talk about, seeing how they're both handy with fixing things and both dope farmers. And seeing how that estate is about one of the prettiest places there ever was, and that Laura is about the most beautiful young woman there ever was, it just all goes together the way it should. It feels good, lucky to have been a part of putting all that together. If I'd have died like I was supposed to or just stayed drunk like I aimed to, there never would have been a morning near the park for meeting them kids. Any way of looking at it, it sure beats drinking tequila, stomping a fellow, and pistol whipping him before throwing him in the trunk.

The good weather is still holding out, but any day now the warm times will be over. There ain't no place in the world like San Francisco, and I love it now as much or more than ever, but the combination of the cold and all them lost pounds ain't no kind of good. Dope brownies, ice cream, and giant burritos help some, but the fact is I'm still just a piece of my usual size, and the cold creeps right through my clothes. It might be time to start thinking about a warmer place to spend the winter. San Francisco ain't a place with particularly cold winters, but this body ain't in no kind of shape for even a little bit of cold. I need someplace warm at least until there's a way to get some of them pounds back.

The last thing that doctor was supposed to say had anything to do with me getting well. Finally, the notion of dying had settled, and things got calm and peaceful like they ought to have been all along. For certain that doctor would say the black nothing grew just around the bend and headed toward me fast. Nothing gave me any reason to hope for good news. Hope had cut out a long time past. Then he went and said he couldn't hardly find nothing wrong with me. He said it like it didn't mean much, like all them past months of coughing up blood and hurting in my back and chest had been just a mistake to be forgot, like maybe it didn't happen. It did happen, and I still catch myself hunched over when walking and holding a spot on my back until I remember that it don't hurt no more.

More than once during the whole dying business, the knowing about dying gave a sort of freedom. When the black nothing is coming, that means a fellow ain't got to spend much time planning. And when a fellow knows that everything is soon to be nothing, then there ain't a lot of point to thinking about past mistakes. There just ain't a lot that really matters. So when a fellow knows that black nothing ain't coming, or that it ain't expected anytime soon, what does that mean? That's the question that has me all twisted. If death means you ain't got to plan, then life means that you're supposed to think about tomorrow. And if you're gonna live, then you got to try to figure out how to straighten out past wrongs.

I don't sleep much. Back when death was coming, particularly back at that hospice place, sleep could go on for days. Maybe back then the sick body rested up in trying to dodge the black nothing or maybe it had just give up. Nowadays sleep ain't much more than a quick nap. After closing the eyes for a minute, there's the wake-up and the worrying about what ought to be happening. All my life, or most of it after being grown, got spent building and carrying the big load of shame over what the good people would think of me if they knew what sort of sorry places and messes the bottle brought. Now with this second life, what kind of life can be had so that folks won't be disappointed? The sad truth is that I ain't got no kind of ideas on what's supposed to happen or even what to do. I got much clearer ideas on what better not be happening with my new life. There's long lists of the things to quit and dodge. There ain't gonna be no more drinking. That hooch just don't work no more anyway. Used to be some moments of fun happened before the staggering stupidity, but now drinking goes right straight to the falling down mess. It's probably been that way for a long time, years maybe, but I didn't know till now. Anyway it don't matter cause I've had enough, finally. I'm done.

Another thing that just flat cannot be tolerated is wasted time. Even without the drinking to blame, I got a real talent for wasting time. Looking back on all them years, there's a bunch of em where all there is to do is just scratch my head and wonder what got accomplished. Where did the time go? There can't be no more of that. There can't be one more minute of wasted time. If anything can be learned from dying, it's that there just ain't enough time.

Maybe the main thing there can't be no more of is the feeling that good folks are getting disappointed. One way of avoiding disappointing folks is to keep away from em in the first place, but while giving that a hard try times went straight from dancing with a kid with homemade tap shoes right before he died to smashing up a nice lady's Mercedes to throwing a scrounge in a trunk. For some reason, there don't seem to be no way to keep folks out of my life, so probably the only other choice is to change the way I act. That's hard, and I don't even know where to start.

One thing I'll be for sure doing real soon, right at the end of the month, is to give up this silly expensive Nob Hill place. Anybody would have to be a knob head for paying so much. Maybe cause of learning that the black nothing had gone off to chase somebody else, a yearning for a little celebration or even a real big change caused the idea that wasting money on a better roof and bed could fix things. This is for a fact the swankiest place I've ever had, but it ain't necessary. Most of the time is spent sitting in front of this window at night wishing day would come but also dreading day cause of the scarce ideas about what to do with it once it gets here.

More than a fair amount of time gets spent fretting over how to tell the folks in Texas what happened. And maybe a good part of that is about worrying whether to tell them at all. The subject ain't something that's easy to tell, and it's a fair bet that it's even harder to believe. How exactly would a fellow go about telling such a yarn? Maybe I'd call em up some Sunday morning, and when they asked what's been happening, the answer could be that them rumors yall didn't hear about me breaking my head ain't just idle rumors but mostly all true, and then after that impressive stunt came the wandering down to Monterey and Santa Cruz and getting locked up in a looney bin. After getting back to San Francisco, there was some little attempt at not drinking, but that didn't last long, and then I helped a pal sell a bunch of drugs. And then another little attempt at not drinking happened, and that lasted longer cause a doctor told me coughing and death aimed to ruin the party. Ain't no reason to use a telephone for that cause a lawyer got hired for breaking the news, and then I run off intending to get ate by coyotes but instead stayed at a hospice place and danced some before going to a friend's place and destroying part of a house and a fine car. Turns out, there's some flat little places in California that's a lot like the Panhandle, so I stayed there some before going sightseeing in Buick on my way back to San Francisco to get liquored up. Just for the hell of it, I went to see a doctor who said you're not dying, you just have a little cold, and here's some pills. The pills got took, everything is fine, and now I'm trying to decide whether to change my whole life or just go get a burrito. How are yall doing?

There ain't no way anybody is gonna believe that, so I'm wondering if it's worth trying to tell at all. I'm wondering about a lot of things. Seems like all there is to do is just wonder about the million thoughts and questions, but it just amounts to a lot of spinning and speculating, and no answers ever come. Maybe when some folks get in this kind of situation they go talk to other folks to get answers. But I don't see how answers can come from other folks when the questions ain't even straight in my head. The only thing going on is a confusing buzz of feelings, and the only one clear is the one that says something ain't right. There's something that ain't being done, something that's supposed to be happening. You'd think that after hearing death ain't coming after so long of thinking it was would put me in a fine humor, and that happens sometimes. Just as often, though, there's that feeling that something ain't right cause the right things ain't getting done. It's a confusing mess, and I don't sleep much.

Here after while, the day is gonna start, and I ain't got no plans, no ideas on how to make good use of the day. All there is for sure is the notion that this morning needs a burrito. That might be the one thing this town ain't got, a place to get burritos at all hours. So here after while, I'll get dressed and then spend a few more hours agitated until a burrito can be had. Aside from that, I ain't got no ideas at all.

And if the Wine you drink, the Lip you press,
End in what All begins and ends in—Yes;
  Think then you are TO-DAY what YESTERDAY
You were—TO-MORROW you shall not be less.

Pell-Mell

"What's this thing?" Jason asked.

"It's your helmet," the rental clerk answered. "You're required to wear it."

Jason looked at the plastic slotted contraption, put it on his head, and fastened the straps under his chin. "You say this a mountain bike?"

"It sure is. There's your twenty-one gears right on the handles. You know how to use them?"

"I think so," Jason answered. "This one works the big sprocket, and this one works the little one."

"And I need you to sign this," the clerk said.

Jason took the clipboard and the pen. "What am I signing? I already signed some stuff when I gave you the money."

"This is a liability release. It says that we're not responsible if you hurt yourself."

Jason signed and gave the clipboard back to the clerk. He wheeled the bike off the lot, and as soon as he rounded a corner he took off the helmet and fastened the strap around the handlebars. Leaning the bike toward himself, he stepped over with his right leg and started to climb into the seat but stood looking at the handlebar gear selectors. Jason tried to recall the last time he had ridden a bicycle, but he could not remember one since the 1970s, one with a banana seat and handlebars he had turned backwards and adorned with devil face hand grips. That one had not offered twenty-one gears. That one required forward pedaling to go and backward pedaling to stop. While he questioned his judgment over whether to try riding a modern bicycle, he consoled himself by remembering that he had once ridden a Harley-Davidson Shovelhead all over the

Texas Panhandle. If he could handle that vibrating monster, surely he could control a lightweight toy with pedals. Jason thought about a couple of sightly and diminutive daredevil Comanches in the flatland near Sacramento, and he smiled.

Once in forward motion, the first thing he noticed pertained to the seat, or judging by the sharp pain in his backside the lack of a seat of adequate width. Unwilling to leave the sidewalk, Jason found an alley and steered the bike into the narrow way while the front tire switched right then left and the bike wobbled along at a slow speed. When he pressed harder on the pedals, the bike straightened, stopped wobbling, and glided along without sound. At the end of the alley, he took a foot from the pedals ready to put it to the ground if necessary, and he turned the handlebars. Back and forth he rode the bike along the length of the alley, and he experimented with changing gears. Low gears allowed him to pedal fast without much resistance. High gears defied his effort, and he stood off the seat to let his weight force down the pedals. Satisfied that he had mastered the machine, Jason left the alley and rode into the street.

Automobile traffic soon convinced Jason to find a less traveled street, and the one he found offered his first hill. As the pedaling grew more difficult, he twisted the handle bar grips and switched to lower gears. When he reached the lowest gear, he still had plenty of hill to climb, and just as he contemplated getting off the bike and pushing it the remainder of the way up the grade, the street flattened. The bike whizzed along with less effort, and Jason shifted to higher gears to build speed before the next upward climb. With the next climb, he learned to work the gears in a more efficient manner and down-shifted no sooner than necessary. Before he let the bike get too slow and before he began to feel unendurable fatigue in his legs, Jason stepped out of the seat and let his body weight assist in the downward push on the pedals. He reached the crest of the hill without contemplating getting off to push, but once past the upward incline he coasted to the curb to rest and catch his breath.

Before him the street descended at a steep angle and for a long distance. Even for one accustomed to San Francisco's long steep grades, Jason looked down the street and wondered if he could have found a longer steeper hill short of going to Twin Peaks. Prudence told him to turn around and take a safer route, but some other drive urged him to go forward. He pressed just a little on the pedals and let the bike and gravity carry him along. The bike accelerated at an exhilarating rate, and soon

Jason felt the wind rush into his face the way it used to when he rode motorcycles. A car ahead slowed in preparation for a left turn, and Jason veered to the right and zipped past. At the bottom of the hill, the street ended where it joined a wider, busier avenue. Several blocks before the busy avenue, an intersection contained a stop sign, and Jason made preparations to use the brakes. He coasted along and put his hands on both brake handles trying to remember which one operated the rear brake. And then he saw something at an intersection past the one with the stop sign and before where the street joined the wide avenue.

A person with long dark hair and a fleecy pink sweater crossed the street a few blocks ahead. She walked from left to right, and once across the street she vanished. Jason forgot about the brakes and instead twisted the gear selectors. Even in the highest gear, his speed exceeded any he could match with pedaling. A car ahead stopped at the intersection with the stop sign, but Jason continued on at breakneck speed hoping the car did not make a right turn. In an instant he flashed between the car and the curb, and he had to veer farther right then back left to avoid a car already in the intersection. Once through the crossroad, he could not be sure which street prior to the main avenue the fleecy pink sweater had passed. He flew across one and looked to the right, but in the brief second he saw no pink standout. The same happened at the next intersection, and Jason wondered what to do for a fleeting moment before he entered the wide avenue and remembered the brakes.

An ear-splitting blast sounded, and Jason saw the orange and white Muni bus fill the field of vision to his left, and he pedaled fast yet could not match the existing pace of the meteor bike. Before he could worry about the traffic coming from the right, and before he could remember how to operate the brakes, the front tire of the mountain bike collided with the curb of the avenue median, and Jason flew aloft. No longer in contact with the bike, he seemed to hang in the air a while before thudding to the grass, rolling, and then sliding to a stop on his back. Jason lay in the grass savoring the safety and wondering if he retained all his parts. When he sat up, he saw the bike a few feet away in the grass on its side. He looked around, and the cars and pedestrians of the city continued on without taking notice of the disarray in the avenue median.

Jason picked up the bike and hurried back the way he had come. Once away from the wide avenue, he checked the bike for ruin, and then he checked himself. Except for some turf stuck in one of the pedals, the bike showed no evidence of damage. Jason seemed to have escaped injury with only some grass stains on his shoulders and knees. He wheeled the bike onto the sidewalk, leaned it on the kickstand, and then he sat on the curb and hid his head in his hands while he tried to control the shaking. Once composed, he stood and took the bike by the handlebars and began pushing it back up the long hill. After a few steps, he stopped and took the helmet from the handlebars, put it on his head, and secured the chin strap tight. As he walked alongside the bike, he took a hand from the handlebars every few steps and checked to make sure the helmet stayed snug.

Jason had cleaned the turf from the bike's pedals, but the grass stains on his clothes had probably been what the rental clerk had seen that answered his unasked questions about why Jason brought back the bike several hours early. The clerk had, however, repeated his no refund policy, but by that time Jason had already left the lot in search of the nearest bus stop. Once back at the Nob Hill residence and once he had finished showering, Jason had to reopen a suitcase he had packed in preparation for his upcoming departure from the overpriced unit. He found what he needed in the suitcase and then took a suit from the closet. Most of a day remained, and Jason did not want to waste it. He looked around the room and thought about taking the suitcase and some other packed boxes to his storage unit, and then he saw the disposable camera next to a pile of laundry.

While he let memory guide him along to the photography store, Jason wondered if the place had remained in business after so many years and so many rapid changes in photographic technology. He tried to remember the last time he had been to the store, and though he could not pinpoint an exact date he knew it had to be over eight years past. Jason believed that even if the store remained in business they had likely closed their in-store lab as so many others had done in recent years. After he rounded a corner, the storefront let him know the place remained in business, and Jason tried to control a grin as he approached. As soon as he passed through the door, the smell let Jason know the lab remained in operation. Unable to control his widening smile, he stood and breathed the familiar scent.

"What can I do you for, Mr. Handsome?" a thin blond man asked.

"I have some film I need processed," Jason answered. He placed the disposable camera on the counter, and the blond man leaned over the camera, much father over the counter than necessary, and Jason took a short step back.

"Well I hope it's something good," the blond man said. "Anything scandalous?"

"Yeah. It's got some lewd trees and some downright shameless flowers. I bought that thing on a whim. I didn't even know folks still made pictures with film, and then after I shot the roll I figured nobody had a lab anymore."

The blond man looked from the disposable camera directly at Jason and said, "Ding! Ding, ding, ding! You win! You win the prize. That's the stupidest thing anyone has said all day. It's still early, but you definitely win. That's the dumbest thing I'll hear all day."

Jason chuckled, tried to say something in reply but just laughed.

The blond man took a pen from a cup on the counter and a paper from a stack, and said, "Okay, handsome, I need a name and a number." He passed the pen and paper to Jason, and while Jason wrote on the form, the blond man said, "My name is Dan. You want my number too, Jason?"

"Sure, or I could just come back and see you after you process this film. When will it be ready?"

"Give me about three hours. We're running behind today."

"All right. See you then, Dan. Ding, ding, ding."

Outside the store, Jason looked one way on the street then another. He thought about how long it had been since he had visited that neighborhood, and he thought about what to do for the next three hours. After walking to the end of the block, he turned right and smiled when he saw the little nondescript Chinese restaurant. He remembered how in years past a visit to the photo store almost always included a visit to the hole-in-the-wall lunch joint. He sat at the counter, glanced at the menu for only a moment, and then ordered what he always had. When the soup arrived, Jason first marveled at the size of the bowl. He thought perhaps cauldron would be an apt description of the steaming dish. He took the short-handled porcelain spoon and went directly for a floating dumpling.

As soon as Jason entered the photo store, Dan reached below the counter for an envelope. Jason stood at the counter and pulled the prints from the envelope. He looked at a few and said, "Not too bad for a little fixed-lens throwaway job."

"Your composition is outstanding," Dan said. "I wouldn't guess you took those with a disposable camera."

"Thanks. I just bought that thing on a whim. I used to shoot pictures, but nobody uses film anymore, and I got behind in learning the new stuff."

"Nobody uses film anymore . . ." Dan's voice rose in pitch. "You're just full of stupid statements today. Do you work at that, or does it just come naturally?"

Jason laughed while he continued looking at the photographs. He started to put them back into the envelope and then stopped. From the envelope he pulled a disk and asked, "What's this thing?"

"My, my . . . it really is natural for you. Did you just crawl out from under a rock or something? That's your image disk. It has your image files."

"You mean for like computers?"

Dan's feigned stupid look melted away, and he looked sincerely surprised. "Well, yes, for computers. Where have you been? You get film processed, and you get prints, negatives, and the image disk."

"Can yall do this for all kinds of film?"

"Sure. Of course."

"Okay then, Dan. I got one more stupid question for you. Do you have any 120 film in stock today?"

XII. Depth of Field

Ah Love! could you and I with Him conspire
To grasp this sorry Scheme of Things entire,
    Would not we shatter it to bits—and then
Re-mold it nearer to the Heart's Desire!

Ah, make the most of what we yet may spend,
Before we too into the dust descend;
   Dust into Dust, and under Dust to lie,
Sans Wine, sans Song, sans Singer, and—sans End!

Circle of Confusion

Whether due to courtesy or shame, he did not know. But he said nothing to her, and he bore the pain tempered by the feeling that he had done the right thing. The holiday music had long since grown tiresome, and his third cup of coffee at the shop in Outer Richmond made his hands a little too unsteady to continue cleaning lenses. Earlier that day he had set out with gear, far too much gear, intending to take photos at Fort Point. He had been unable to decide whether to take the twin lens reflex or another medium format camera with interchangeable lenses and film backs, so he had taken both. Long before he reached Fort Point, the weight of the gadget bag and the back pain it produced made him annoyed with himself for his amateurish indecision. The light he sought had been right, but the cold and the intense wind stole the desire to make pictures. He walked around the old structure in the howling wind, but he did not remove either camera from the bag. When the intermittent rain fell from the leaden sky, he gave up any attempt at artistry and looked in the bag to discover that he had not brought rain gear or adequate protective equipment for the cameras, but he did find a ball cap. He put on the cap and began walking back to the bridge pavilion and the bus stop.

By the time the bus reached Balboa Street, the rain had stopped, and when he got off the bus he discovered that the intense wind had stayed confined to Fort Point. Seeking relief from the weight of the bag and for lack of anything else to do he had entered the coffee shop. Past the counter and through a hallway a room held several tables and comfortable chairs. He sat at one of the tables and inspected the equipment in the gadget bag. By the time he had started his third cup of coffee, he had given up trying to clean lenses or do anything productive with the equipment, and he sat fiddling with the bag's zipper while he tried to think of another destination. He had heard her voice, but it had taken some time to place it in memory, so he had not looked up from the zipper in time to make eye contact.

"Is anyone using this chair?" she asked.

He shook his head and looked up to see a blonde woman moving the chair to another table. Long flaxen tresses escaped from under her shoulder wrap, and when she sat and removed the shawl her ample blonde mane covered her shoulders and back. From across the room and even in the subdued light, he saw the cobalt eyes. She looked at Jason for an instant, and her quick polite smile confirmed his suspicion that she had not recognized him. Jason pulled down the bill of his ball cap and let his hand linger on the bill while he tried to decide whether to reveal himself and what to say. While he contemplated possible greetings, a man approached her table with two cups of coffee and placed one of them in front of her before he sat. When she looked at the man and smiled, Jason again saw her blue eyes, and he saw how she reached across the table to rest her hand on the man's arm.

Through the hallway and past the counter, he stepped with haste with the brim of the cap pulled low. Without a plan he turned west and walked to the end of the block, and then he walked to the end of the next block, and he had nearly reached the end of a third when he saw the theater. He paid for admission to an afternoon matinée, joined the show after it had already started, and took a seat in the back. She had not recognized him, and Jason wondered if time or the shed pounds had worn away familiarity. He wrestled with feelings at odds. Shame and regret came to mind in recalling their last meeting, but impressions from earlier, happier times remained. Loneliness battled the desire to stay anonymous, untangled.

Jason stared at the movie screen, and he saw subtitles, but he could not identify which Asian language the characters spoke. He sat in a confused melancholy. From one perspective, he had everything he thought he might want. Weeks previous, a doctor had said that the malady in his lungs had subsided, and subsequent visits to that same and other doctors had confirmed that his health had returned and grew stronger every day. No one knew of his current modest but clean residence. No one could contact him and drag him into entanglements. Jason had what he thought he desired most, freedom, freedom from the snares of others and freedom from the filthy pit of his own previous willing enslavement to alcohol. Yet every day, no matter what activity he found or manufactured, seemed somehow the same. Moments of interest flared, like with the discovery that photographic film could still be used as the basis for making pictures. But even that surprising and intense interest sometimes faded or got replaced by drudgery and annoyance, just like his failed trip to Fort Point.

From another perspective, Jason saw his new life as empty, devoid of purpose. Before the illness, he had filled his days with alcohol. After the shocking recovery, there had been a few days of euphoria. Then doubt, confusion, and longing came, and the longing, perhaps the worst part of all, had been and remained mysterious. Longing and loneliness pursued Jason, and they always caught him no matter how many diversions he sought, no matter how many photographic expeditions he pursued, no matter how many times he played tourist in the city he knew and loved so well, and no matter how many times he tried something new—like riding a bicycle because he thought he missed two children he hardly knew. He had the life he thought he wanted, a life free of alcohol and free of human encumbrances, but something lacked, some gaping hole remained.

On-screen characters jumped about and shouted, and Jason refocused for a moment and saw fighting. He recalled an incident, a violent incident, a couple of months past. Usually recollection of the incident filled him with regret, even shame, and fear of consequences. When he thought of it in the dark of the movie theater, he still felt tinges of shame, but in a more powerful and vivid way he felt the missing sense of purpose. In the moments leading to the rash and savage act and in the days following, he had felt a purpose, a clear direction. Perhaps it had been the last time he had experienced any sense of resolve, meaning, or direction. Since that terrible and criminal performance, he had drifted. First in a haze of drunkenness and then in a sober and zen-like acceptance of the death to come. After a moment of elation, he had rushed about in a flurry trying to fill every moment with action, but it all amounted to little more than play acting. None of it had an substantive purpose, and none of it mattered.

Jason stared ahead toward the movie screen and blurted, "Just nothin! A whole lot of nothin."

Light reflected from the white faces that turned in their seats to look at Jason, and after a frozen moment of wondering whether to apologize aloud, he clutched the camera bag to his chest while he took awkward and tentative steps through the row of seats to the aisle and out of the dark theater. Past the concession stand and through the glass doors to the sidewalk, Jason charged avoiding eye contact with theater employees and patrons. He ran a few quick steps to the middle of Balboa, waited for a car to pass, and then continued across the street and farther south along an avenue. The weight of the gadget bag aggravated his back, and the shoulder strap seemed to cut into the area next to his neck. He resolved that once he got the equipment back to the storage unit he would never again remove it except maybe to sell it. The stuff ought to be sold, he thought, for it amounted to a load of junk for which he had no use. Prior feelings of loneliness gave way to a general sense of annoyance, itself a part of a larger atmosphere of gray gloom, much like the leaden sky.

The avenue reached a dead end at Fulton Street, and Jason crossed Fulton. He walked for a while along the sidewalk that ran parallel to Golden Gate Park. Away from the street, and on the park side of the side-walk, a slight rise and a wooded area stretched into the park. After passing the third or fourth fellow pedestrian, Jason's desire to remain unseen made him consider the wooded area. He watched for a break in the bushes, and then at a spot that did not look like a footpath but offered passage through the dense short bushes he left the concrete. The bushes gave way to tall Monterey Cyprus, and some looked like giant toadstools or um-brellas the way branchless trunks rose but nearer the tops of the trees green arms spread to flat-topped lids. Under the cyprus canopy, he passed in a southerly direction, and he grumbled while he switched the heavy bag's shoulder strap from one side of his neck to the other. Jason's forward progress halted at a tall chainlink fence.

He did not remember a fence in that part of the park, and its presence made him angry. He lifted the camera bag's shoulder strap over his head and let the bag fall to the dirt while he rubbed his neck. The fence stretched in both directions, east and west, and Jason wondered about trying to find a route around but decided he would reverse course back to Fulton, catch the number 5 bus, and accept another pointless disappoint-ing day. When he reached down to lift the gadget bag, something large and brown on the other side of the fence moved. Jason stood to take a more direct look, and to the west close to the fence twenty or thirty yards away multiple brown four-legged beasts grazed. Jason hoisted the bag and walked along the fence in the direction of the beasts, and they grew ever larger as he approached.

When he reached the point along the fence closest to the animals, he stood and looked a mere twenty feet ahead at a buffalo, American bison, creature of history, legend, and myth. The one closest to Jason presented a profile, and Jason admired the stoic power. The beautiful brute seemed clothed in the way black woolly fur covered its face and head where two curved horns jutted out and upward. A lighter brown scraggly coat draped over the first two thirds of the animal's enormous thick back before relatively lean and muscular hindquarters emerged. Jason came from a land where buffalo once lived in the millions, but they had been exterminated nearly a hundred years before his birth. He had grown up where names of places and things expressed reverence for the creatures, but most of his visual experiences with the venerated animal had been in effigy or emblem. He had seen live buffalo before, but he had never stood so close to one. After a few more moments of stunned wonder, Jason lowered the camera bag and opened the first zipper. He extracted the twin lens reflex, reconsidered, and replaced it. With the other camera in his grasp, he changed first the film back and then the lens. He stood, changed his mind and the lens again, and then faced the creature. Jason could not control his wide grin, and he did not attempt to do so as he looked through the viewfinder and twisted the rings on the camera lens.

Would but the Desert of the Fountain yield
One glimpse—if dimly, yet indeed, reveal'd,
    To which the fainting Traveler might spring,
As springs the trampled herbage of the field!

Focal Plane

The book he fell asleep with slipped off the bed and crashed into the pile of books on the floor, and the noise prompted him to open one eye a peek. Soft light came through the window next to the little desk, but without a look at a clock he had no way of knowing how far the morning, or the day, had progressed because it had been nearly dawn when he had taken the digital imaging book to bed. He rose on an elbow and leaned over the edge of the bed to sift through the pile of books to find the one that had fallen. When he found it, he tried to find where he had left off reading, and then he looked around for something to use as a bookmark. After giving up the search for a sliver of paper, he grabbed another book on photo editing from the pile and positioned it inside the one he had most recently consulted.

The little desk supported stacks of processed film that came back as photographic negatives and image disks. To cut down on costs, Jason had stopped buying prints and requested only negatives and the image disks. Amid the stacks of envelopes, sat a laptop computer, the same type that Dan at the photo store recommended. Jason rose from the bed and went to the little desk. He looked at the computer screen to get the time of day, and then he turned to walk into the tiny kitchen area, but his foot collided with a stack of refuse. The stack tumbled over, and pizza boxes and food containers from various Indian and Chinese restaurants scattered across the floor. Jason returned the boxes to a more stable heap, and he took two short steps across the breadth of the kitchenette to the coffee maker. He reached into the cupboard for coffee but then noticed that the carafe still held plenty. He took a cold cup to the little desk, and he sipped while he looked at the computer screen. After shivering several times, he stood and grabbed an old and worn field jacket from the closet and draped it around his shoulders like a cape. While he held the jacket under his chin, he felt several days beard growth, and he knew he needed to get started cleaning the small apartment and himself, but he wanted to look again at something on the computer, something that after days of not leaving the apartment still held his interest and often sent him to the stack of books.

Showered, shaved, and dressed he carried the stack of pizza boxes and food containers down the stairs toward the outside door. After dumping the load in the lidded trash receptacle, Jason noticed two police cars across the street. One police officer stood on the sidewalk talking to a woman and writing on a clipboard. Seeing police officers in the Mission District could be a normal everyday occurrence, but this sighting made Jason pause. He thought about the contents of his apartment. Many times over the past couple of weeks he had gone to his storage unit and removed items, usually cameras and other photographic equipment. Yet not once in any of his trips had he returned any items. He thought about the safety of the valuable items in the little apartment as compared to the storage unit, and he headed back up the stairs.

Two camera bags burdened his steps, and Jason grinned a little while he thought that his weight combined with the bags might equal his poundage prior to his illness. He felt good, glad to be out and moving after so many days inside studying, but he had a busy day planned so he decided not to walk the entire distance to the storage unit. After reversing course, he turned on a street going east and made his way with the heavy padded bags to the 16th Street BART Station. Getting the bags through the turnstile seemed tricky at first, but then he remembered how he used to negotiate the gates with camera bags, and he passed through for a short ride of only one stop. In the storage unit, he placed the bags near the door for easy access rather than putting them in the back with the other photographic equipment. He began to leave, but as he shut the door and started to fix the lock, he felt somehow incomplete. Back inside the unit, he opened one of the gadget bags and removed a twin lens reflex camera and several rolls of film. Again he started to leave, stopped, and then stepped to the back of the storage unit and looked in more boxes until he found two 35mm cameras. They looked nearly identical, and Jason tried to choose between the two but instead put them both back in the boxes and returned to the bags near the door. He removed a camera strap from a bag, attached it to the twin lens reflex, threw the strap over his neck, and locked the unit.

Conscious of the time of day, Jason hurried toward the camera store, but somehow he still had an incomplete feeling. He stopped and reached in his pockets for the film he had taken from the storage unit. While he looked at the film, one of black and white and two different types of color film, he also looked up and around and then shrugged and selected a roll. Jason leaned against a building while he opened the camera and loaded the film. The feeling that he missed something subsided, and he resumed his course.

Dan spoke with another customer at the counter when Jason entered the store, so Jason looked at cameras on display. When the other customer departed, Dan looked at Jason and said, "Well sailor, do you have more film for me today?"

"Not today. Today can I ask you some more stupid questions?"

"Ding, ding, ding! Even that question is pretty stupid, cowboy. Of course you can ask questions. That's what I'm here for."

"I appreciate it, amigo," Jason said. "I got that computer you recommended and that book and some other books too, and now I'm thinking about how maybe I ought to look into . . . maybe getting one of them digital cameras. I'm still partial to my medium format and probably always will be, but as you know there's twelve shots, sometimes just eight depending on the camera. Back in the old days, I'd shoot 35mm until real sure what to aim the big film at, and I'm wondering if one of them digital cameras . . ."

"Let me take it from here, handsome. But first, let me ask if you still have 35mm lenses and if they're of the same make."

"Yep and yeah," Jason answered.

"Okay. We could look at some brand new models, but those are more for amateurs. I have some used professional models. Let me step in the back for a second. Don't go anywhere, sweetie."

Dan returned with several cameras, and after much discussion Jason left the store and carried a bag. He also had a second camera hanging from his neck next to the twin lens reflex. Every few steps Jason stopped and hefted the digital camera. Despite its size, it lacked the weight Jason expected. He thought perhaps he would come to appreciate the light weight, but as he looked at the abundance of buttons on the exterior of the camera, buttons for functions he did not understand, he wondered about the wisdom of his purchase. Once again aware of dwindling time, he let the camera hang from the strap while he hurried on.

He reached the coffee shop ahead of his planned meeting, so he bought a cup and sat at a table. Immediately he took the manual for the just-purchased digital camera from the bag, and he turned the pages covering both familiar material and some so foreign he wondered if it had anything to do with photography. After giving up rereading and trying to understand one such unfamiliar topic, he set the manual aside and reached for the coffee. As soon as the cup touched his lips, he noticed that it had gone cold, but he drank anyway, and with his free hand he reopened the manual.

"So you found something safer than dancing in traffic?"

Jason looked ahead and up, and then he looked up some more. An amazonian angel stood before him, and sandy golden ringlets sprouted from under a knit cap. Her azure eyes captivated Jason, and his smile spread before her outstretched arms signaled him to stand and accept a hug.

"My, my you're a sight to behold. An angel." Released from her strong grasp, Jason looked around and said, "Where's the tall green-headed fellow?"

"He's getting me some hot chocolate."

"Now that's a good man. How yall liking things up in Sonoma? Bobrick keeping you pretty busy?"

Laura sat, and Jason returned to his seat and moved the cameras and manual from the table. She said, "We've been busy. That's for sure. But most of the trimming is done, and now we're down here for some Christmas shopping. What do you have planned for Christmas?"

"I hadn't really thought about it. Usually I find a bar, but this year I'll do something different, I guess. Don't know what. Depends on the weather."

"You ought to come up and see us," a male voice said.

Jason turned from Laura and saw Wilson. While Jason stood, Wilson placed Laura's hot chocolate on the table and then shook Jason's hand. Jason said, "I see you got her something and didn't get none for yourself. I'm due for a refill. I'll get some for you too, hombre."

When Jason returned to the table with two cups of coffee, he asked, "How's the van running?"

"Better than it has in years. Better than it has since before I was old enough to drive it," Wilson answered. "You were right. Patrick can fix anything. And it wasn't just the manifold that caused the problem.

Apparently the timing needed adjustment too."

"That ole Bobrick, he's a good fellow. Don't let him talk you into trading the van for some of his kind bud."

Laura laughed and said, "We have more of that than we can ever use. That's not something we're short on at all. Eleanor paid us some cash for some work we did, and that's how we're down here for Christmas shopping."

"That Eleanor, she's a sweet lady," Jason said.

"She thinks a lot of you too," Wilson said. "You ought to come up and see us. She talks about you all the time. She likes to make Patrick tell the story about how you two met in San Francisco."

"Did that really happen?" Laura asked. "Did you dance around in the street and sell all his pot?"

"Well, of course not. Can you see me doing a thing like that?"

After more conversation and after additional rounds of hot chocolate, coffee, and a few pastries, Jason followed the young couple outside. When he saw them approach a Cadillac, he asked, "Where's the van? I want to get some pictures."

"If you want some pictures of the van, you'll have to come see us at Patrick's place," Wilson said.

"Who's car is this . . . wait, let me guess. Eleanor's?"

"It rides like a dream," Laura said. "But he hasn't let me drive it yet."

"That's because we owe it to Eleanor to get her car back in one piece. Laura is a closet NASCAR fan. She thinks she has to draft when a car is ahead."

"That's a shame," Jason said. "One thing I can't abide is a tailgater, even one as beautiful as you. Oh well, let me get a picture of yall with Eleanor's new car."

Laura started to move toward Wilson, but he said, "Nope. Stop right there. If you want pictures of us, you have to come see us at Patrick's. Part of the deal Eleanor made in letting us use her car was to convince you to come visit. We'll expect you by Christmas."

"And if you don't come," Laura said. "We won't get any Christmas photos. Won't that be sad?"

"I can't make no promises. Yall take care, and have a safe trip back. No tailgating, you hear?"

Jason watched the Cadillac drive away, and he felt a somber moment before regaining awareness of the time of day. He had hoped to revisit the storage unit before his next appointment, but that opportunity had passed, so he set off for the BART station toting the cameras and the extra bag.

As the train departed Embarcadero Station, Jason remembered the last time he had passed that way. He had passed in the opposite direction, and he had fled a grim situation. That experience had transpired over two months ago, yet it seemed longer in some ways. Still, as the memory came back in detail, Jason looked down and avoided looking at any of his fellow passengers. When the train arrived at the Richmond Station, Jason disembarked and rode the escalator to the exit. He found the expansive lot with cars, and he looked at one after another that all seemed brand new and shiny despite advertisements on the windshields displaying year models and proclaiming great deals and low mileage.

Jason stopped walking amid the cars and just stared at row after row. A man younger and taller than Jason approached and asked, "Can I help you find one in particular?"

"I hope so," Jason answered. "Do you have any Buick coupes?"

Paying for parking in this town can empty a bank account, and finding free parking can eat up every last bit of spare time. That Buick coupe sure is a lot of fun to drive, but when it's in a good free parking spot, especially one close to the apartment, then it tends to get left there while me and the camera bags burn up shoe leather. It would be nice to head on down around Big Sur while listening to that fancy stereo, but there ain't been time. There was time a few days ago for heading down the Great Highway to Pacifica and then on to Half Moon Bay before turning and going over them hills and blazing back up 280. That whole route is a sight, both the ocean part and the trip back up through the hills and the trees. If finding a place to park wasn't such a headache, I'd take that Buick out every day and drive that Half Moon Bay route at every chance.

One of the best parts of that car is the heater. Another best part is the seat warmer. There just don't seem to be enough big burritos and Chinese food in this town to put the fat back on these bones, and they feel cold all the time. It don't never get real cold around here, but then it don't hardly get warm neither. About the only time it could be considered warm, sometimes even hot, is during the months folks in the rest of the country call fall. That's a long time off, and the little apartment in the Mission District ain't got no heater. The Buick is fun to drive, but from experience with another one just like it I know they ain't fun to sleep in. Something is gonna have to be done to get the chill out of these bones.

Seeing them young Kansas hippies and hearing about my friends Bobrick and Eleanor made me feel good. Meeting them kids in the first place had to be one of them San Francisco happy accidents, and then seeing them again without it being an accident helps give a feeling of purpose, and there ain't been nearly enough of that lately. There ain't no doubt that the invite for Christmas was genuine, and there ain't no doubt that it started with Eleanor. She's still a sweet lady. Part of me wants to take that invitation, but another part wants to keep to myself, and that's the part most often listened to. This time, though, it might be right not to listen to the part that's so worried about tangles. Ain't no decision been made yet. Like the answer to them kids before they drove away, I can't make no promises. But while watching them drive away, for just a second there I might have made any promise to get them to turn around and come back.

And that's the strangest thing about the loneliness. It's always in a fight with that part that wants to avoid the tangles. Life without getting tangled in other folk's business sure is a lot easier, but it seems like it might be the other folks that gives life some purpose. Without other folks around, a fellow has to run long and hard to fill a day with enough things to do and dodge wasting time. Wasted time has to be the worst thing there is. After months of thinking that dying and black nothing came right up around the bend, it ain't possible to abide wasted time. Which is worse, wasted time or loneliness, ain't known, but both are bad enough to make a life miserable. It's complicated in ways that's hard to understand, but it seems like the cure for loneliness and the cure for wasted time might sometimes be the same. But the problem with that cure is that it usually brings a whole load of tangles with it.

That bike ride down that long hill made for a good lesson. A fellow looking for a purpose can't fill a day with any old stuff just to be doing something. In the case of that bike ride, any old stuff could have meant going from hearing I wasn't going to cough myself to death to getting run over by a bus. A purpose, a real one anyway, seems harder to find. After so many months of knowing about the black nothing and after so many months of regret over a wasted life, a fellow might think that news from a doctor saying he ain't gonna die means that everything will be perfect, that he can immediately go on to having the life he should have had all along. But it don't mean that at all. It just means he ain't gonna die that particular day, and as for all the other days . . . On them other days, he gets to take on all the doubts and frets that everybody else has to wrestle with. Hearing from a doctor that a fellow ain't sick no more ain't no special present that means everything is gonna be perfect. It's just a message that the fellow ain't sick, and he ought to get back to work like everybody else. Nothing more.

Getting permission to stop coughing and head back to work ain't all bad news, though. There's all that time in the days for making pictures. Most days the last thing before going to sleep and the first thing after waking is thinking about pictures. It's been a long spell since any thought

Kevin K. Casey

produced such happiness day after day. Making pictures is about the best
thing there is, or maybe the second best thing there is right after thinking
about how to make pictures. The time spent finding an idea for a picture
and then figuring out how to use the tools to make the picture is when
things feel like they're supposed to. All that matters is that picture. The
tools for making the pictures is wonderful fun too. Those cameras that
stayed so long locked in storage ain't useless antiques. The new stuff that
has come along since them old cameras don't make the old ones useless.
The new stuff just means that pictures can be made in a whole lot of new
ways. The new stuff gives more choices.

I may never again be the photographer of years ago. But that might not
be such a bad thing. These days some of the technical parts of the old tools
don't come as quick to mind as they once did, and the new tools is so
complicated they make me feel sometimes like a steer trying to figure out
how to drive a Cadillac. But that's just all technical stuff. What really
matters is the pictures, and that's where not being the photographer of
years ago might be better. These days I see things different, better. So
while the technical parts don't come to mind as fast, the ideas for good
pictures are better. Maybe nearly dying makes seeing beauty easier.

Sometimes it's hard to believe that a few months ago I was dying.

It's easier to believe that a few months ago I did die. Maybe in some
ways that fellow did die.

Booze ain't got no part in this new life. There ain't no urges now, and
as a matter of fact there's plenty of feelings the opposite way, but if the
adventure with the other Buick and then the time right after first getting
back to San Francisco taught anything, it's that after so many years with
a bad habit the old ways can sneak up on a fellow. So there can't be no
taking chances with that hooch ever again. If notions creep into mind, it's
better to find something else to do right quick.

Time is a hard thing to comprehend. Just a little less than a year past,
that backward shortcut down some stairs in North Beach broke my head.
It might as well have happened twenty years ago because that's what it
feels like. Stuff from twenty years ago is sure easier to remember in a clear
way, but that might have as much to do with the consumption of hooch as
it does the passing of time. All that time gone by and not a word to the
folks in Texas. That's shameful. There ain't no other way to look at it.
Knowing that, though, don't mean all the answers and ways to set things
right come clear and easy now. For a fact, I still ain't got no idea how to go

290

about explaining the last year to anybody. And that might be all right. It might be that the last year ain't got to be explained because while nothing has been for sure decided yet, there might be a way to set things right with the folks in Texas. Ain't nothing been decided yet, but it's something to study on. Before that, there's things nearer that got to be settled.

I keep going back in mind to the day that poisoned brownie helped recollect my grandparents. In the past, most of the recollection of them dear folks caused a big pit of disgrace at thinking about how they'd feel about the wasted life and opportunities. But these past few days the feelings is different. Their lives, their history, made the grandparents practical folks. Despite some downright silly beliefs in religion and the book that goes with it, they had down to earth ways of looking at things. Maybe being farmers and going through the Great Depression gave them that outlook, or maybe they started smarter than most folks to begin with. They wouldn't have give a lot of time and thought to what happened yesterday. They'd be a whole lot more interested in today and plans for tomorrow. They stayed real forgiving like that. They'd forgive the booze once it got quit, and there might even be a few things they'd be a little proud of. Grandma would be proud of me picking up the cameras again, and they'd both like that Buick coupe. Granddad was always partial to Oldsmobile, but he'd like that Buick as much as he could like any car made today. He could run it through the back of his garage just as good as he did his last Oldsmobile after that stroke and losing his license.

My mind goes to them folks a lot. Maybe I been practicing apologies and squaring things with them before moving on to the still-around living folks.

It hurt a bunch, but seeing that pretty Irish barmaid with her date done some good. For the longest time, a haunting notion that an apology needed to be made to set things right dawdled about. Seeing her with that other fellow showed that time don't stop just cause I ain't around. Folks don't freeze up and stay stuck caring about me and my shortcomings. Most folks move on with life and have better things to do than freeze up or wallow in some thoughts of my nonsense. Maybe sometimes saying sorry ain't the best thing. Maybe sometimes the best thing is to move on with life and stop doing whatever caused the need for an apology. That don't mean I ain't to blame for some scroungy behavior, but it does mean that sometimes the best way to say sorry is to knock off the ugliness and get back to work.

There's big burritos and Chinese food to be had, and there's always a better parking place. Ain't no picture ever made that couldn't be improved on with another try, and that sure is true in my now rusty state. Maybe figuring out how not to waste time ain't such a mystery after all. Maybe it's about doing the best with today and keeping tomorrow in mind too. Ideas for pictures can be started today, made tomorrow, and improved on the day after that. Along the way there's burritos and Chinese food and empty parking places for those that are quick and lucky. Maybe that's all there is, and maybe that's all right.

A Book of Verses underneath the Bough,
A Jug of Wine, a Loaf of Bread—and Thou
    Beside me singing in the Wilderness—
Oh, Wilderness were Paradise enow!

Miles Where Arroyos Crack

Jason drove along the narrow paved road while she slept in the backseat. He watched for road signs, but he could not recall seeing any for a long time. For much of the easterly drive, after dawn permitted sight of distance, flat land had extended from the highway to far-off hills. With the change to southeasterly, the road had narrowed and the hills seemed to close in, and the area adjacent to the road held vineyards. Beyond the vineyards, golden grassy treeless hills presented occasional rock outcroppings. Though not yet willing to classify his condition as lost, Jason planned to ask for directions at the first opportunity, but he did not remember seeing any indications of habitation—other than vineyards—since some little place called Shandon. Perhaps it had been there, Jason thought, that he had taken the wrong route.

They had spent the night at a motel in Paso Robles. The original plan had been to stay someplace farther south and east, perhaps in the Palm Springs area, and if weather permitted Jason had hoped to find a place to pitch the tent and camp for the night. But efforts at outsmarting traffic failed, and their progress slowed in the East Bay. After San Jose, they rejoined Highway 101, and night overtook them in Paso Robles. During the night at the motel, Jason had decided to abandon the plan to continue south along 101 and instead to turn east so they could pass through Bakersfield in homage of some of his favorite childhood country music artists before returning to a southerly route in search of Interstate Highway 10. Somehow Jason had lost the way along the morning's easterly route. He thought that perhaps he had gone south at Shandon when he should have gone north.

She had expressed no dissatisfaction at rising well before dawn at the

293

motel, and she had been eager to join Jason in the car. Since then, she had slept in the backseat. From time to time, Jason looked in the rearview mirror, and each time he saw her he smiled. Sometimes she opened one or both eyes to catch Jason stealing glances, and then she returned to peaceful sleep. Many times Jason had wanted to turn on the radio, but he chose instead to let her rest undisturbed. The seatbelt adapter that Bobrick had made worked well, and she changed position when comfort demanded.

First on the left side of the road and then the right, the vineyards stopped, and the terrain grew rockier. The hills closed in, and the route seemed more like a path through a canyon than a valley. The car's heater had been off since before dawn, but the temperature inside climbed, and Jason opened his window a bit. The fresh warm air felt drier than any Jason had experienced in a long time. She stirred in the backseat, and Jason looked in the rearview mirror to discover her awake.

"How's my baby psychedelic appaloosa? Did you have a good sleep?"

She stood, wagged her tail, and strained against the seatbelt attached to her harness. Jason reached behind the seat and pat her head. "Sit back down, baby girl. We'll stop up ahead in a little bit."

When he found an area with enough space, Jason slowed and steered the car off the road. He walked around to the passenger side to let the little dog out, and he said, "Now you stay close and off the road." She zipped around investigating and sniffing while Jason searched the interior of the car. "Did you happen to see what become of that map, little darlin?" He moved to the trunk of the car and began removing suitcases and camera bags. After pushing the stowed tent and sleeping bags to one side of the trunk, he sifted through smaller items, like a shocking pink zippered pouch and a peace sign medallion, but he could not find a map. Jason repacked all the items in the trunk and called for the dog. She did not come right away, and Jason saw her twenty yards ahead sniffing a flower at the edge of the road. He walked to her and pat her back.

"That sure is a pretty one. If I didn't know better, I'd think it was a bluebonnet. What's it doing out so late in the year?"

They resumed their course, and when Jason looked in the rearview mirror, he saw her awake and resting her head between outstretched paws. "Baby girl, on top of losing our map, this amounts to some pretty poor planning. New Year's Eve ain't the best time for traveling. We might have trouble finding a motel that ain't too rowdy, and it might be too cold for camping in most places. We sure don't want to be out on the roads tonight. Well, this empty one might be fine, but it probably won't get us all the way to Texas. Ain't no telling where this one is taking us."

The car passed over a small bridge and dry creek. Trees grew along the bank of the creek, and Jason took notice of their wildly curved trunks and branches. They stood too far away for him to see the bark, but he did notice a few remaining golden leaves, and he had a strange feeling. The tress resembled cottonwoods, and he knew those trees from his childhood in Texas. Surely, he thought, they had to be some other kind. After the bridge, the canyon walls closed in on the road, and some of the immense rocks that stretched from the canyon floor to the sky had a red hue. Jason thought that he must be impatient to arrive in Texas, and the feeling caused him to see things that should not be occurring for hundreds, thousands of miles farther east. "It's a good thing the folks back home don't know we're coming, little darlin. At that rate we're going, they'd be worried."

He turned on the radio, twisted the knobs, and pressed buttons, but no music came. The height of the canyon walls kept much of their route in shade. Jason looked ahead in the road, and said, "Uh oh, baby dog, looks like we've run plumb out of pavement." The car's tires crunched dirt and gravel once the blacktop ended, and Jason slowed and then stopped. He tried to remember how long he had been on the narrow paved road since the last town, and he tried to calculate how much time would be lost in backtracking. While he thought, he noticed that up ahead the road forked, and the branch to the left seemed to go straight into the rock itself. He drove closer to the divergence and saw that one arm of the road branched into a natural break in the rock leaving little or no room on either side. After a moment of contemplation over whether to get out and take a photo, Jason turned the steering wheel and drove into the break. Since they would have to backtrack to the main road and perhaps even stay in Paso Robles again, Jason thought they might as well see a little more of the area first.

Sheer rock rose from the side of the road higher than Jason could see from inside the car. "I sure would hate to be here after dark," Jason said. After a few hundred yards, space on either side of the road widened, and after a half mile or so the sheer rock gave way to steep but grassy hills. Jason noticed the well-kept condition of the road, and he wondered why the road stayed so well-graded when he had yet to encounter another vehicle. First he thought perhaps the lack of other vehicles could be due to the approaching holiday. Then he recalled other dirt roads from his youth. Parts of the Texas Panhandle, particularly areas near the Canadian River, had a network of well-maintained dirt roads that did not have signs and usually did not appear on maps. Those roads existed because of the oil and gas industry, but Jason had not seen any evidence of oil or gas production along the sign-less California road. The only evidence of enterprise he had seen at all had been the vineyards. Nevertheless, the dirt road beneath the Buick permitted smooth travel.

At a wide spot in the road, Jason slowed and reversed course. "Well, that was worth seeing, baby dog. We're gonna have to head back now. I guess we might be staying in Paso Robles again if we can find a place that ain't too rowdy tonight. We probably ought to buy another map too. This time you look after it so it don't get lost."

They traveled the smooth dirt road through the golden hills and watched for the immense rocks and the path back to the paved road. Ahead Jason saw a fork on the road, and he stopped the car. "I don't recall any other roads on our way in, do you baby girl?" Both branches appeared identical. One continued straight ahead, southwest, while the other extended in the direction Jason guessed as being due south. He thought perhaps he might have missed another road joining to their left on the way in, so he chose the south route. Golden grassy hills extended on either side of the road, but they did not close in, and no giant walls of rock appeared. After several miles the road curved, first to the east and then to the northeast, but still no colossal red stone closed in to flank the road. "Guess I chose wrong," Jason said. "We're gonna have to turn around again."

Before he could turn around, the road ended. It widened at the end and then just stopped. Beyond the edge of the road, golden grass slopped down into a dell before rising to another hill. Large oak trees climbed the slope. Jason stopped the car at the end of the road. "I surely did choose wrong."

The dog whined, and Jason asked, "You need to get out for a little bit, baby girl?"

He got out of the car and walked around to the passenger side to let her out. Free of the car she trotted beyond the end of the road into the yellow grass. She stopped abruptly, whirled three times, and then emitted an urgent high pitched cry. Jason looked first at her, saw the direction she looked, and then scanned the area ahead until he saw something move. A few dozen yards ahead a cottontail rabbit hopped through the grass. "Don't you do it. Stay. There's plenty of rabbits where we're headed. Of course, there's rattlers, water moccasins, and copperheads too, but we'll discuss that when the time comes. Come back over here, darlin."

The little dog joined Jason back at the car, but her attention stayed out in the field. "That sure is a pretty sight. Wish we we're seeing it under different circumstances. Remember how I was saying I'd hate to be caught out here after dark? We better be getting on back to the paved road."

The dog stayed focused on the field, and Jason too enjoyed the view of the oaks rising from the golden grass. He reached in the car for a camera and then closed the door. "Well, we're here. We might as well check it out some before we turn back." As Jason stepped away from the car, the dog sprang off the end of the road, and Jason called after her, "You stay close. I don't know what the snake situation is out here." He noticed that she stood on what seemed to be a path, and he followed her. She bounded ahead, waited for Jason to catch up, and then darted ahead again. He followed her along the path that twisted through the oaks and then down into a shallow valley.

It came faint at first and then more distinct, and Jason looked at the little dog to see if she noticed the noise. He tried to concentrate, tried to identify the sound, but the closest sensation he could compare it to seemed absurd in the current environment. Jason thought he heard a Telecaster guitar on an AM radio. The oaks grew denser, and the noise ceased before being replaced by the distinct sound of wind chimes. Jason followed the dog around an old oak with considerable girth, and he saw a stone building with a flat roof. The little dog stayed closer to Jason as they rounded the building, but when they came to an open door, she zipped inside.

"Elly! Elly May, come back here."

Jason heard a high-pitched female voice, and he entered the building to see a tall silver-haired woman with glasses leaning over and petting the little dog. The place seemed to be a sort of store with a few racks of items and a long wooden counter in the back.

"Aren't you the sweetest thing," the woman said to the dog. When the woman stopped petting the little dog and stood straight, the dog turned and trotted to Jason's side.

"Well, you made it," the woman said. "We didn't think we'd have much of a crowd this year. It's been getting smaller and smaller every year. No one comes in the back way anymore. Is that your car up on the dirt road?"

"We left the car up on a road," Jason answered. "I guess we kind of got here by accident."

"Then welcome to Comfort Springs," the woman said. "I'm Eileen, and you haven't lived until you've had Clayton's New Year's barbecue. Clayton is my husband. He's working on the barbecue now. It'll probably be ready in a couple of hours."

Jason stood before an old metal soda pop vending machine. He ran his hand along the door on one side and asked, "Does this thing still work?"

"It sure does. It doesn't take money anymore, but it keeps the pop cold. Have one."

Jason opened the door and pulled a glass bottle from the rack. He twisted the top, but it resisted. Jason smiled and said, "This is the real thing. It's been awhile." He looked at the front of the machine, found the bottle opener, inserted the top of the bottle, and pulled down.

"We can have someone bring your car down if you'll leave the keys. You can go have a rest or go soak in the springs."

Jason looked at the little dog and then reached in his pocket for the car key. He placed it on the counter, and Eileen gave Jason a piece of wood with a chain attached to a key. "Your cabin is number four. It's on the other side of the springs. Just follow the path up and over the hill and over the bridge, and you can't miss it."

Jason followed the little dog along the path in the evening's amber light.